# A FUTURE SPY

ANDREW WATTS

DALE M. NELSON

SEVERN RIVER
PUBLISHING

A FUTURE SPY

Severn River Publishing
www.SevernRiverBooks.com

ISBN: 978-1-64875-372-5 (Paperback)

# ALSO BY THE AUTHORS

**The Firewall Spies**

Firewall

Agent of Influence

A Future Spy

Tournament of Shadows

All Secrets Die

## BY ANDREW WATTS

**The War Planners Series**

The War Planners

The War Stage

Pawns of the Pacific

The Elephant Game

Overwhelming Force

Global Strike

**Max Fend Series**

Glidepath

The Oshkosh Connection

Air Race

## BY DALE M. NELSON

**The Gentleman Jack Burdette Series**

A Legitimate Businessman

The School of Turin

Once a Thief

Proper Villains

The Bad Shepherd

**To join the reader list and find out more, visit**

**severnriverbooks.com**

# 1

Lieutenant Glen Denney paced.

He'd lost track of how many times he'd walked this circuit in his suite atop the Four Seasons Hong Kong. Bright sunlight spilled through the gap in the curtains, tracing a white-hot line across the tortured geometry of his upset room.

Glen was scared.

He didn't know how much longer he could stay here. He'd already maxed out his credit card on the honeymoon. This suite was supposed to be the capstone. Two glorious nights with his new wife in a room they couldn't actually afford.

But he couldn't leave. Glen didn't have a phone. His wife only had the room number. If he left, if they kicked him out because he couldn't satisfy the mounting tab, how would Mia reach him?

Mia.

Jesus God.

Glen ran a hand over his closely cropped hair. If there was enough to grip, he would have pulled it out. He had no idea how he'd explain this to his commanding officer when he got back to Hawaii. Right now, he didn't care. Getting Mia out was the only thing that mattered.

They honeymooned for ten days at an exclusive resort in Melati Beach, Thailand, which Mia had gotten thanks to her connections in the hotel industry. They finished in Hong Kong because Mia wanted to show Glen her home. They planned the last three days here, where she'd grown up. Glen wanted to take her home in style, so he overextended himself and got the suite at the Four Seasons. He didn't worry about it. There was a deployment coming and, with that, extra cash.

Then came Macao.

Like Hong Kong, Macao was a "Special Administrative Region," technically part of the People's Republic of China but with a separate government and looser restrictions that encouraged foreign tourism and gambling.

Glen knew she played cards. In fact, he'd introduced Mia to his buddies in the squadron via their monthly poker game. After a couple of demure hands, she'd wiped the floor with the lot of them. He tried to talk her out of spending time in the casino. Glen played, but the speed with which he lost three hundred dollars at a blackjack table suggested he'd be better off watching Cirque de Solei. But Mia insisted and Glen would deny her nothing. He loved that girl like nothing else. She was the sunrise, and Glen would give her the world if it was in his hands.

Hands.

Just a couple of hands.

That's what she'd asked for.

A few hours, tops.

The casino staff told him next to nothing. The Macao police told him less.

They said she was counting cards, trying to bilk the casino. Glen did his best to give the casino manager every bit of the ugly American, threatening heaven, earth, and the full might of the US Consulate. Casino security escorted him from the building. They said the matter was up to the police when they dropped him on the pavement.

Glen didn't know where Mia was, whether she was being held in some gamblers' jail in the casino (if such a thing existed, but Glen suspected it did) or if she was in police custody. He found a cab driver who spoke English and found the police station. Demands to see his wife went unacknowledged. Hours later, midday perhaps, he'd been awake so long he couldn't tell time—jails and casinos had a lot in common. When a policeman roughly guided Glen to see her, there was his beautiful wife behind a pane of dirty glass. The only way he could talk to her was through a greasy phone.

Mia told him to call her cousin, Sze Wai, who went by "Wayne" with Westerners. He was a prominent businessman in Hong Kong who had political connections and could at least explain the government to Glen. He could help Glen free her. Even in his exhausted, agitated, and racing mind, Glen knew what she meant. Who would he have to bribe or threaten?

He gave Mia the number to the Four Seasons, the only number he had, and told her he loved her. He would not leave until she was free.

That was yesterday.

Glen was a Navy P-3 Orion pilot based in Hawaii and met Mia one wild night out with his buddies in Honolulu. They fell in love fast and were married within the year. That was when America had been fighting in Afghanistan for two years and just entered Iraq. No one knew how long they'd be home. There was a frenetic energy in the off-duty time. They packed in all the excitement they could, because they didn't know how long they had until someone shipped out again.

It was the same with Mia. The world being what it was, they ran at their relationship at full speed.

Mia was the daughter of an American hotel manager and a Hong Kong native. Her family had a happy and modest life in Hong Kong when it was still under British rule. But it didn't last. Her father got ill in 1993 and returned to the United States for treatment, where they found an aggressive, fast-moving cancer. He died within the year. Mia's mother was not a naturalized citizen and had trouble finding work. Her father was not close with his extended family and they found no help in America. With no other options, they returned to Hong Kong. After university, Mia followed her father's footsteps in the hotel trade. It was a way to honor him, she'd told Glen once. She was a manager at the Mandarin Oriental when they met in 2002. Mia arranged it so they could have their wedding reception there. Glen could never afford that on his own.

He met her older relative, Wai, some months before the wedding. Mia called Wai her "uncle," but in her culture, that was as much an honorific title as it was a familial one. Wai ran an import/export concern in Hong Kong and jetted between there and Honolulu. They'd had dinner with him once on a business trip a few months ago and shared several drunken toasts during the reception.

They were to have been Wai's guests for dinner at his home tonight.

Glen called him in a panic and explained what had happened. Wai told him not to worry, to be calm, he would handle it.

Glen looked at the phone and willed it to ring.

When it didn't, he wanted to throw the damned thing against the wall.

Glen *thought* of calling the consulate. In fact, that was long overdue, and he knew he'd have to explain his delay when he finally did. Mia was a dual citizen and therefore under the protective umbrella of the US Consular General here in Hong Kong, which also serviced Macao. But involving the State Department would trigger other events, things that would spin out of his control. The consulate would notify his chain of command. Disciplinary action would follow. He'd already had to get his marriage "cleared" because Mia was a dual citizen. Imagine what they'd do when they found out Macao's police arrested her for card counting. Glen's frantic mind already raced down the blind alleys of consequence. They'd strip his top-secret clearance and, with that, his flying status.

A hard knock on the door ripped Glen out of his mental whirlpool. He stalked over to it, furious and needing to vent his frustration at whoever had the temerity to bother him right now. Glen ripped the door open and there was Wai, wearing a light gray tropical-weight suit, white shirt, and navy tie. He was of average height, shorter than Glen, and still in amazing shape. Wai had played club soccer since he was a teenager and was on a semi-pro team during his university years. He still played in a local club and was a devil on the pitch.

"I have news," he said.

"What is it?"

"Perhaps it's better if we speak inside?"

"Right." Glen moved aside to let Wai enter.

Wai walked past him to the large window that dominated one wall. "I have good news and troubling news. We'll start with the latter. You should have a seat." Wai pointed to a chair, then walked over to the bar, selected a tall glass, and filled it with water before giving it to Glen. "Mia is in much trouble. The casino intends to press charges."

"They can't do that," Glen stammered.

"Of course they can," Wai said, as though explaining to a child. "She was counting cards." He held up a hand. "Please don't argue with me. We have little time. Macao is modernizing quickly, though it still has a way to go. There is a certain criminal element that directs things there. One such element owns the casino where Mia was caught cheating. Macao is a place where much is overlooked and the owner wants this to go away—meaning he wants Mia tried and jailed quickly so as not to attract attention—therefore, he's made certain financial assurances with the Macao police."

"I don't understand. Just tell me who I have to pay and I'll do it."

"It's not that simple, Glen. The Macao police are going to try her, and with the casino owner's donation, the magistrate will certainly find her guilty. There will be a prison sentence, perhaps five years. They don't want Westerners thinking they can cheat and get away with it."

"Jesus Christ, she's from *here!*"

"I am aware," Wai said flatly. "But she's also half-American, and that's how they view her in this case."

"You said something about good news?"

"I have a friend in the Chinese government. He works on the mainland, in Shenzhen. I contacted him and explained our situation. He came this morning to meet with the authorities, see if anything can be done." Wai walked over to Glen's closet, opened it, and perused the contents. "Wear this," he said, and handed Glen a pair of lightweight khaki pants and a blue linen shirt. "I don't suppose you brought a jacket or proper shoes?"

"What?"

Wai closed his eyes and sighed. "Please, just get dressed. Liu Che is waiting for us."

Settled during the Qin Dynasty, Macao became a Portuguese colony in the sixteenth century and still bore many of the Western hallmarks. Portugal relinquished Macau as an official province following the so-called Carnation Rebellion by a military coup in Lisbon in 1974. For the next twenty-five years, Macao would continue to be administered by the Portuguese government but was officially part of China, similar to Hong Kong's relationship with the British. In 1999, the Portuguese transferred control to China, though the small island would remain a self-governing Special Administrative Region until 2050.

Glen dressed as properly as his honeymoon wardrobe allowed and followed Wai to a train, where they made a forty-minute journey to Macao. Wai had a car waiting for them at the terminal. From there, the black car with dark windows took them across another bridge to the northern island and the Public Security Police Force building on the Avenida do Dr. Rodrigo Rodrigues.

"When do I get to see Mia?" Glen asked as they exited the car.

Buttoning his jacket mid-stride, Wai looked at him and said, "My friend, that depends on you."

Wai led him inside and exchanged words in Chinese with the desk sergeant. There was a nod, and another officer escorted them upstairs. They walked down a peach-colored hall to a room with smoked glass. They entered and sat. Glen couldn't read the writing on the door. He didn't know if this was an interrogation room or a police captain's office, or if Mia was on the other side. Two men were in the room. One was a police officer, and if Macao's law enforcement followed the same uniform traditions that Glen was used to, he was a high-ranking one. The other wore a simple but well-tailored black suit and tie and glasses with rounded frames.

There was a fast conversation in Chinese.

The man in the suit spoke in perfect English with a British accent.

"Good afternoon, Lieutenant Denney. My name is Liu Che and I work for the Chinese government. I am here to help you." Liu said a few quick words in Chinese. The police officer stood and moved to the door. Wai followed. "The inspector has graciously allowed us the use of his office for our conversation. Please, have a seat."

"I want to see my wife."

"All in due time, Lieutenant. May I call you Glen?"

"How did you know I'm in the Navy?"

Liu smiled. "Apart from the haircut? Wai informed me, as did the police. You made quite the scene outside the casino yesterday morning. Many of their patrons are also aware you're a naval officer, it seems." Liu lifted his shoulders in a nonchalant gesture.

If he'd slept over four hours in the last two days, Glen might've had the energy to feel some kind of shame.

"I'll be direct, Glen. Your wife is in a lot of trouble."

"Wai told me."

"This is an embarrassment for the casino owner and the government. Americans come here and believe laws don't apply to them. The government wishes to make an example of Mia."

"We don't believe that. Look, Mr. Liu." Mia taught him in Chinese culture, surnames appeared first in the name. "I just want to get my wife back. I'll do whatever I have to." *Here comes the price tag*, Glen thought. He ran down the mental tally of his accounts. Glen had a few thousand left in savings. He'd burned most of it on the wedding and honeymoon. He might have to ask his parents for a loan. Western Union it here by tomorrow.

*That'll make an awkward Christmas*, Glen thought.

"I'll do whatever I have to," he repeated.

"That's good," Liu said. "First, have you contacted your consulate, or your superiors in the Navy?"

"No," Glen said. "I haven't spoken with anyone."

"That's good," Liu said. "Please refrain from doing so. I think it's best that we handle this... *locally*. Your government can be a little heavy-handed. Mia's actions embarrassed important people here and the last thing she needs is for the Consular General to throw his weight around, making demands."

"I understand."

"You must remember, Glen, that Macao is its own government. They are technically part of the People's Republic, yes, but they manage their own affairs. I, too, am in a precarious position, even intervening on your behalf, as I have no legal authority here." Liu placed heavy emphasis on the latter part of the sentence.

Waves of tiredness crashed over Glen. He was weary, but it was the rip current of exhaustion that threatened to pull him under. It was so hard to focus. "So, what are you saying, exactly?"

"I need a show of good faith from you, a willingness to show contrition. My counterparts here must see how truly sorry you are for this insult."

"I understand," Glen said at length. "How much is it going to cost?"

Liu smiled. "Oh, I assure you, Glen. It's nothing like that. You are a pilot, yes? I believe that's what Mia said you did for a living."

"That's right."

"The P-3 Orion, if I'm not mistaken."

"I can't talk about that, as I'm sure you know," Glen said, finding some steel for his voice.

Liu looked around the room. "This is...not a nice place. I fear for Mia's safety here. I have no influence over what happens within these walls." Liu paused and let Glen imagine the implications. "I think if, perhaps, you would answer some questions, I might affect a release. Nothing of serious importance, just enough to show your willingness to be cooperative."

Glen fought to keep his hands from shaking by balling them into fists, and his tongue felt like it had been left in the sun to dry.

He looked up at Liu's dark eyes.

# 2

---

*Macao, S.A.R*

Glen's pulse exploded in his veins, accelerating from a sluggish atrophy to hyperawareness as the adrenaline coursed through him. The room was hot and stuffy. Repressive tropical air stomped in from the open windows like a press gang, threatening to drag him somewhere terrible. He could hear mosquitos buzzing in the room, homing in on his scent, and sweat dripped from his forehead. His ears registered a churning ceiling fan, its soft mechanical whir reminding him of distant helicopter blades. The halogen lights above his head buzzed, hot and loud.

Liu began, "Your wife is in a dangerous position. But she is lucky that she has you. You can help her. I have a wife, and I care for her very much. I can see you are worried. You don't need to be, because everything you need to do to secure Mia's release is within your control. We, men like you and me, are *good husbands*. We don't need our governments to interfere. I would like to have a very simple conversation with you, Glen. Just ask you some questions. At the end of that conversation, we will let you and Mia go home."

Liu smiled, a soft, knowing curl of the lips. On anyone else's face, it might even look friendly. No one spoke for a long time. Finally, Glen broke the silence. "What do you want to know?"

Liu gave Glen a notepad and pen and asked him to write some information based on his prompts. Glen wrote his name, his naval rank, and the name of his unit, Special Projects Patrol Unit 2 (VPU-2), Marine Corps Base, Kaneohe Bay, Hawaii. Liu asked if this was true, a Navy squadron at a Marine base. Glen said that was accurate. The Navy transferred control of the site to the Marines in the nineties. Liu asked general questions about his airframe, the P-3 Orion, the Navy's sub hunter and maritime patrol aircraft.

Liu wanted to know the aircraft's range, whether that differed from Lockheed-Martin's stated range. Glen answered, and Liu nodded, as if Glen had just gotten a test question right and Liu already had the answer key. He asked about the various configurations of the aircraft and current deployments. Glen wrote these down on the notepad. Liu wasn't even asking about anything highly classified. Sure, this was "confidential," but that hardly counted. He knew from those god-awful OPSEC briefings he had to sit through that the Chinese were already so thick in the US aerospace industry they almost certainly knew most of what Glen was telling him.

If confirming a bunch of shit the Chinese already knew meant Mia wouldn't spend another night in jail, what was the harm?

After each answer, Liu nodded, saying, "good" or "yes" and encouraging Glen along.

About an hour and several pages of notes later, Liu took the notepad and said he'd return. He was gone a long time; exactly how long Glen couldn't tell. He seemed to lose his sense of time. While he was alone, Glen felt a strange sensation of distance to the room. He was apart from it. He was somewhere else.

Liu returned and said he had verified that the information Glen provided was correct. "This is good. It creates a foundation of trust. Partnerships are built on trust. Trust and openness will keep Mia safe." Glen heard Liu say these words, though they were distant, like they were shouted into a cave and he only heard the echoes. Liu helped Glen to stand, guiding him with a gentle hand beneath the elbow.

"We're going to move our conversation away from the street," he said, then led Glen down a hallway to a windowless room with beige walls. Glen became aware now. Maybe it was the soundproofing panels on the walls or the scratched wooden table, grooved and dented during the countless interrogations whose psychic echoes were etched into the walls. He could smell desperation and panic sweating out of the tiles. Or perhaps it was the black half-dome drooping down from the corner of the ceiling, a dark cyclopean eye boring into his soul, peeling through the layers of secrecy the Navy taught him to erect.

Glen knew what this was now.

And he didn't care.

Or rather, he cared *less*. He needed to save Mia.

Glen Denney never thought he'd test his marriage vows in the interrogation room of a Macao police station. Doubtless, this was the surest definition of "or worse." But he would do what was required. That was love, that was honor.

Liu asked harder questions. Ones that made Glen squirm in his seat.

He wanted to know about the frequency range of the sonobuoys the Orions deployed to track submarines. Liu then asked about the different patrol squadrons and what their unique missions were. He was interested in knowing about the operational portfolios that were not disclosed. "I already know they hunt submarines," Liu scolded in response to Glen's original answer. "Tell me more about the special projects unit. What makes it unique?"

Glen shifted in his seat. "I would rather not answer that."

Liu nodded and waved the question away, as though swatting a fly. "Of course. I understand. I am only trying to help. The better your answers, the more likely my superiors can intervene on Mia's behalf."

Glen felt a bead of sweat roll down his face.

"Perhaps you could instead tell me about the missions of the various maritime patrol squadrons."

Glen described how the aircraft's mission evolved from maritime patrol and sub hunting to providing airborne command and control and limited attack. He glossed over some of the reconnaissance missions but answered the rest with Liu gobbling up every word, inhaling the knowledge.

"We can carry weapons in the internal bomb bay and on wing pylons to engage maritime and land targets."

"What weapons?" Liu asked. "What are their designations?"

"The traditional load outs are Mark 46, 50, and 54 torpedoes, mines, and

AGM-84 Harpoon antiship missiles. We added the AGM-84K SLAM-ER two years ago." Glen pronounced it "slammer." "We can also carry AGM-65 Maverick antitank missiles. Now that we're engaged in Iraq, we're using the P-3s to attack land targets from a safe distance. That's what the Slammers and Mavericks are for."

Their conversation on electronic systems went well into the afternoon.

Glen hadn't eaten since Mia's arrest, had hardly slept, and was at his physical limit.

His head slumped into his hands. At least he caught himself before his forehead smacked the table. "Are we done?" he asked in the weary voice of a desert traveler days without water. "When do I see my wife?"

"All in due time," Liu purred. "You have been very cooperative, Glen. This shows me how much you love your wife. I appreciate the humility with which you have answered my questions. You are allowing the people of Macao to save face."

There was a knock at the door and one of the Macao police officers handed Liu a bottle of water, which he gave to Glen. The next moments were a blur. They escorted Glen from the room and brought him back to the inspector's office. The inspector was waiting for him. There was a portable television on the officer's desk with a built-in VHS unit. Liu entered a moment later with a tape in hand. He inserted the tape and played the first few minutes of their several-hours-long "conversation."

Glen asked, "What are you going to do with that?"

"I will keep this, just for assurances. Please consider this just a helpful reminder of our agreement not to involve your government. I'm sure they would have a different view of your pragmatism." Liu shrugged, a casual gesture.

"I just want my wife."

"Of course."

Liu nodded and the Macao cop ushered him out in a move that was just south of a full frog march. He dragged Glen downstairs and brought him to the main entrance, pointed at a bench, and said "Sit" in English. The room was packed and stifling, a holding cell at the end of the world. Still, people on both sides of the law had loud, animated exchanges. Glen was there an hour before he heard his name called by a scared, tired voice.

He turned and saw Mia pushed through a pair of smoked glass doors. He had to restrain himself from decking the cop for being rough with her. Glen ran to her, took her in his arms, and said, "You're safe now." Mia buried her head in the crook of his neck and said she was sorry. He told her she had nothing to be sorry for.

Glen took her from the police station. He had just enough money in his pocket for cab fare to the train station and two tickets back to Hong Kong.

Glen ignored the hotel manager when they returned to the Four Seasons but knew he couldn't put it off for long. He was two days extended on the reservation and his credit card was maxed out. He also didn't know how they were going to get home. They'd missed their flight back to Honolulu yesterday. He'd deal with the airline after he settled things with the hotel, but for now, he needed to get Mia food and sleep.

When he'd showered, eaten, and slept, Glen went down to the hotel manager to sort out the situation. When he arrived at the desk, the manager informed him that the matter was resolved. Glen asked what he meant.

"Your bill is satisfied, sir. Also, your guest wished me to tell you he has arrived and was waiting for you in the hotel bar."

"My guest?"

"Yes, sir."

Confused, Glen walked into the hotel bar, a contrast of inky darkness from the night outside and dim lights except for the backlit bar. There was Liu Che, wearing a dark suit and glasses, sitting with a whiskey in a lounge chair. He motioned for Glen to sit in the other chair. A server appeared and set a glass down, amber liquid and crushed ice.

"It's Johnnie Walker Black. I took the liberty." Liu lifted his glass. "To our continued collaboration. Gānbēi."

Glen left his drink on its napkin. "Continued collaboration? Mr. Liu, I think you are confused. I did what I had to do to get my wife out of jail. That's as far as this goes."

"You and I are partners now, Glen. Together, we worked to free your wife from her circumstances. This is worth celebrating, no?"

Glen relaxed a little. His mind was tired and jumping into shadows. He thought Liu was talking about something else.

"I know that you're eager to return home, but I wanted to see you before you left. I wanted to reiterate that it's important that you keep our brief chat today between us, between... friends."

"What do you mean?"

"Your country differs from mine, Glen. I've seen what happens when Americans like yourself do things to steer their way out of problems like this. Ones they've caused for themselves." Liu waved his hand and smiled. "I know what you're about to say. Mia *was* cheating. Anyway, in these situations, sometimes people feel compelled to go to their government or their employer—in your case, I suppose that's the same—to explain what happened. I hope you do not do this, for your and Mia's sake, Glen. They would jail you. Your promising Navy career would be over. Your face would be on the television. They would make up salacious lies about you, invent fictions because that's what sells newspapers in your country. Am I right? Like you, I am a patriot. We have similar beliefs about duty. Duty to your wife and your nation. I don't want to see you get into trouble. Especially when you did nothing wrong. Perhaps we can meet again in time. I'm sure we would laugh over all this." Liu smiled again.

"No." Glen shook his head. "I did what I had to, but it was just this once. I appreciate your help, I do, but I cannot meet you again."

"Just the same, I'll monitor you to ensure that you won't get into trouble. We have access to some information that may warn us if you're being investigated." Liu set his glass down. "Perhaps time and some distance will offer you perspective. I wouldn't mention this arrangement to Mia. I am certain she feels terrible guilt and shame already. We shouldn't make it worse, yes?" Liu stood. "You are a good husband, Glen. Something tells me your wife will need your... support in the years to come."

Liu buttoned his jacket and left.

# 3

---

*London, England*
*Present Day*

Sir Archibald Chalcroft leaned over the long granite island separating the open kitchen from the dining room to grab his gin. He held it for a moment before taking a slight sip. Then, drink in hand, he turned to face the dining room, picturing the man he'd be speaking to in the morning, and continued his rehearsal.

Chalcroft lived in Southwark, London, with his wife and their two younger children. Their eldest daughter, Brooke, was in her first year at Cambridge. They lived in a contemporary townhouse of white and gray, black doors and warm wood. It was a wonderful home, a reward—for his wife, Vanessa—for a life of dedicated service to his nation and the Crown. Archie spent twenty-five years as an officer in the Secret Intelligence Service. All but his last years at River House were operational assignments abroad. Upon retirement from a legendary career in MI6, the Queen named Archie a Knight Commander of the Order of Michael and St. George (KCMG). Sir Archie returned to public service after a short stint in private industry, running for and winning a seat in the House of Commons representing Southwark.

Tomorrow, he would meet with the Prime Minister.

Hence, the practice. And the gin.

The Foreign Secretary was about to appoint Archie to be the next chief of MI6. Tomorrow's meeting with the PM was a formality, a discussion on the nation's priorities, the dangerous new world they found themselves in, token words on "bold new direction," and the customary speech on the relation-ship of scandals and aging to bad wine. Most chiefs of the intelligence service served a four- or a five-year term, but the incumbent had fallen ill—cancer was the word—and was stepping down a year early. Bad luck, that. Archie knew the man and liked him.

Archie wasn't nervous. Perhaps edgy was the better term. An interesting sensation for one accustomed to enticing members of the KGB and later SVR into selling out their countries on his behalf. Archie once recruited a Saudi prince on a vice-ridden bender in Bahrain, where the saying was "Allah had an eyepatch" that prevented him from seeing what went on there. Allah might not see, but MI6 did. Archie ran guns to Yemeni freedom fighters, narrowly avoiding being killed himself, but he was still on edge about meeting with the PM about a job he was profoundly qualified for. British humility, he supposed.

Still, it was time. His service in Parliament was useful, but that had run its course. He needed to get back to River House, back into the service. It wasn't a back alley in Khartoum, but it would suffice.

One of the chief lessons he'd learned during his twenty-five years in the service was that he often found himself, simultaneously, as the first and last line of defense. That would not be any truer now. Archie made a note to use that line in his acceptance tomorrow. The PM would love that sort of cloak-and-dagger phrasing, even if he'd miss the deeper meaning of it.

"You'll do fine," Vanessa said, and he paused his delivery at her approach. She rested her gentle hands on his shoulders, kneading the tense muscles.

Archie turned to face his wife.

"I was more worried about you," he said with a smile.

"I'd rather you were a spy than a politician anyway," Vanessa countered.

Archie studied his wife a moment. Her blonde hair was still golden, blue eyes dark and piercing. But she was pale and looked tired. Archie's eyebrow lifted. "Feeling all right, dear?"

"Not really. A little run down. The boys brought something back from school, I think."

"Sorry, darling. I'd been so focused on tomorrow that I hadn't noticed." Jack, fourteen, and Thomas, sixteen, both had their father's constitution and were rarely ill.

"Both of them said they were tired and wanted to sleep."

Archie checked his watch. It was only nine.

"God, I hope it's not another strain. Think we've about had enough of that, yeah?"

Vanessa rested her hand on the long marble island.

"Why don't you go lie down?" Archie said. "I'll check on the boys."

Archie set his drink down and walked over to the faucet for some water. His throat was dry.

A form appeared in the hallway.

"What is it, Tommy?" Vanessa asked.

Archie took a step forward before his son even finished speaking. The boy didn't look steady on his feet.

"Jack fell, Mom," Tommy said in a hurried voice.

"What?" she asked, a mother's protective instinct rising.

"He was splashing some water on his face and just..." The boy paused to catch his breath. He shook his head, like he was trying to clear it. "Just, sort of..."

Archie and his wife both rushed toward their son. Archie reached Tommy first, grabbed him by the arms to steady him. "Sorry, Dad. I just felt a little faint. It's Jack." Tommy stopped again to get his breath. "Jack fell." His breathing was heavy and labored. "He didn't hit his head or anything, but I wanted to come down and tell you."

Archie's first thought was it was strange that his son didn't just yell down. But as he looked at him, Archie didn't think Tommy had the wind to. He could tell something was wrong. The boys were definitely coming down with something. Archie recalled a virus Jack brought home when he was in primary school that went through the family like a brushfire.

Vanessa was already climbing the stairs, taking them two at a time and calling after her youngest boy.

"Tommy, why don't you go lie down? I'm going to check something and

I'll be right in." Archie went into the hallway to the combination fire alarm and carbon monoxide detector. Loss of breath, confusion, and a quick onset were the hallmarks of silent poisoning. There was no alert on the device, which gave him minor relief. A flu he could manage. Bollocks on the timing, though. He needed to hold out long enough to meet with the PM tomorrow, then his body could collapse for days for all he cared.

"Archie!" His wife sounded shrill and terrified. She screamed.

Archie turned and made fast steps to the stairs, rounding them and calling to his wife. Nothing. He bounded up the stairs. Halfway up, he struggled to get full lungs. He hadn't been this winded since that time in the Hindu Kush. Archie's hand went to the banister when he was about four steps from the top and he gripped it hard, the edges of his vision darkening. A lance of bright pain shot down his left arm and Archie gasped once, a rush of strained air forced out of his mouth. He felt a brief sensation of weightlessness and the confusion of suddenly seeing his ceiling.

Blackness enveloped Sir Archibald Chalcroft before he crashed to the stairs.

# 4

*Langley, Virginia*

"What a bunch of kangaroo court bullshit," Colt shouted at the wall-sized monitor in the National Technical Counterintelligence Unit operations floor. Colt, who was standing on watch duty, focused on the TV feed showing the CIA's head of the National Clandestine Service and Colt's former boss, friend, and mentor, Jason Wilcox, get excoriated on national television during a Senate Select Committee on Intelligence hearing. According to the committee's ranking member, Senator Preston Hawkinson of Wyoming, the proceeding's intent was to understand how the Russian Federation could launch a space-based weapon at an unclaimed atoll in the Atlantic, obliterating it, when neither the Defense Department nor the Central Intelligence Agency had any knowledge of its existence.

Calling this a circus was charitable.

The camera feed cut to Senator Hawkinson, who opened this next segment with his tight, nasal invective. "What I'm hearing, Deputy Director, is that the CIA just didn't know that Russia had a space weapon. One that I'll remind you was as powerful as a nuclear bomb and could have targeted the US homeland." The tinny sound drilling out of that man's mouth could burrow through a bank vault. Colt watched, amazed at Deputy Director

Wilcox's patience, as the senator asked questions without giving his subject the opportunity to respond and then got every technical detail wrong. "Questions" was a generous term. They were more long-winded assaults on Wilcox, the Central Intelligence Agency, and their whole profession. When the senator broke off long enough for Wilcox to answer a question, Hawkinson accused him of incompetence, evasion, willful ignorance, or all three. There was even a charge of insubordination.

Colt knew that for a fact.

He'd been there.

He also knew it was nowhere near as powerful as the nuclear detonation Senator Hawkinson claimed, but why let facts get in the way of a good soundbite.

On that day, Colt, his partner Fred Ford, two Mossad officers, and their CIA aircrew evacuated on US Air Force Special Operations Command CV-22 Ospreys moments before the island erupted in a fireball. The island was the property of Guy Hawkinson, the raving senator's nephew, and it contained some of the world's most advanced research in artificial intelligence and quantum computing. Colt's organization, the National Technical Counterintelligence Unit (NTCU), mounted an operation, codenamed STONE-BRIDGE, attempting to insert an intelligence officer into Guy Hawkinson's organization. CIA believed Hawkinson stole years of research from an American inventor and businessman named Jeff Kim. CIA also believed Hawkinson was colluding with the Russian government. If the Russians got their hands on that technology, it would advance their own efforts by decades, putting them at dangerous parity with the United States. The Russians were effective at cyberattack, deception, and influence operations, but lagged far behind in terms of pure research and development. Hawkinson and the Russians had some type of agreement.

Then Hawkinson, it seemed, altered the terms of their arrangement and the Russian president did not take it well.

Instead, he launched eighteen projectiles from space and sank an island.

Russia justified the strike by accusing Guy Hawkinson of launching cyberattacks into their country, targeting their infrastructure and economic centers. It was a classic Russian ploy. They invented a fictitious justification to commit an atrocity and then, when they acted, told the world, "We warned

you we had no choice." The Russians blamed Hawkinson for an electronically delivered total blackout of the city of St. Petersburg, which CIA assessed
the Russian president had done himself to buttress his justification. Dozens
died in the chaos in St. Petersburg. The Russians were, in their own words,
simply retaliating with the most expeditious tool at their disposal. There was
a sort of grim logic to it. Deploying naval and air assets to attack the island
would have been impossible given its proximity to the US.

And, as the world had learned in Ukraine, Russia's military was a cruel
and clumsy beast, not the hyper-modern war-fighting power they attempted
to project.

Senator Hawkinson took to the airwaves after the event, excoriating the
Administration, the heads of CIA, and the Defense Department for not
knowing the Russians had such a weapon. Then, he turned his ire on the
Secretary of State for failing to find a diplomatic solution that would have
prevented the attack. He demanded accountability, and it appeared this
would be it. Rumors were already circulating the beltway about "reform."

So Colt watched the proceedings and fumed.

Senator Hawkinson, who for all Colt knew was complicit in his nephew's
crimes, was attempting to dismantle their agency and make one of the finest
public servants Colt had ever known a scapegoat.

Jason Wilcox was the youngest Director of the National Clandestine
Service (DNCS) since Alan Dulles and a regarded operations officer. More
than that, he'd been Colt's handler during his nearly decade-long undercover
assignment and hand-picked him for NTCU. Wilcox was a legend in the
service, a friend and mentor to many. He was a good man who excelled in an
incredibly difficult job without compromising his integrity. Watching him get
dragged over a fire pit to score political points was as obscene as it was
unjust.

Senator Hawkinson demanded an open, unclassified hearing so that it
could be televised.

Without the benefit of a classified session where they could discuss
actual intelligence, Wilcox couldn't defend himself, CIA's analysis of the
threat, or their response to it. Wilcox couldn't explain what actually
happened. He couldn't tell the senator that yes, they knew about Arkhangel-2
and that the assessment shared by CIA, the Defense Intelligence Agency

(DIA), and the Air Force Research Lab (AFRL), where the plans had been stolen from, gave it a thirty-percent chance of success. He couldn't tell the senator that yes, they believed an American businessman, Guy Hawkinson, the senator's nephew, had stolen research and was trading it to the Russians, and that this appeared to be a retaliation by the Russians. Or at least a kinetic method of covering that collusion up. Wilcox could only dissemble and evade, and each time he said that his appropriate response was classified, Hawkinson accused him of "hiding the truth."

Wilcox got in one good shot, however.

When pressed why the Russians would attack an island both close to US territorial waters and owned by an American company, Wilcox answered, "I don't know, Senator. Perhaps you should ask your nephew."

Colt mashed the remote's "off" button in disgust. He already knew what was coming. Wilcox, he suspected, did too. Colt tried to refocus his mind on his actual job. Since returning from the island last fall, Colt's primary case was monitoring the continued deployment of China's Belt and Road Initiative. In 2013, the People's Republic announced a sweeping campaign to invest nine hundred billion dollars in infrastructure across the world, following the path of the original Silk Road across Central Asia into Europe, continuing to the Middle East and West Africa. NTCU's concern was the Chinese deploying 5G cellular and internet technology as a chief component of their infrastructure investment.

The unit believed that once deployed, the Chinese could monitor every packet of data, every text message, video chat, and phone call that transited its networks. Italy, a NATO member, was a partner, as were Singapore and South Korea, two of America's staunchest Pacific allies. Colt was speaking with members of South Korea's National Intelligence Service to see if they would allow NTCU to plant some digital eavesdropping exploits into the hardware, but so far they'd balked and NTCU's proposed op, PINSTRIPE, was on hold.

Colt's intuition about his former boss was prescient. Wilcox's resignation came at the end of the week.

Jason Wilcox would know that Senator Hawkinson could not let CIA escape without exacting his pound of flesh over the perceived "intelligence failures." Another man would shift the blame. He'd fire those closest to the problem in the time-honored show of bureaucratic efficacy. He'd start with NTCU's chief, FBI Special Agent Will Thorpe, and then take out the two officers responsible for the operation, Colt and Ford. That was how risk aversion slithered into the Clandestine Service and convinced officers in the field not to take chances.

But Wilcox did not.

Instead, he sacrificed himself and resigned from the Agency he'd dedicated his life to. By offering himself up on the altar of bureaucratic bloodletting, Wilcox spared those below him, knowing that Senator Hawkinson wouldn't have the political capital to demand further purges. Wilcox's deeper purpose was clear if one knew where to look—keep fighting, keep looking, bring Guy Hawkinson down. Wilcox served himself up so that Colt and Ford could continue their work.

On his last day at Langley, as Jason Wilcox was leaving the building, many in the NCS packed into the hallway to see him off. Wilcox walked down the line, shaking hands and giving wan smiles, words of encouragement to his many, many old friends. As he was about to exit, he admonished the assembled officers to give no quarter.

Jason Wilcox said to the assembly the NCS's time-honored phrase, which dated back to the days of the OSS, "Good hunting." His eyes found Colt in the crowd. Then he left.

---

The director appointed Dwight Carswell Hoskins to replace Wilcox.

Hoskins was a headquarters mainstay and hadn't been in the field in fifteen years. He'd aligned himself with the now-director years ago, when the director had been on the senior staff at the Office of the Director of National Intelligence. Hoskins, then a liaison officer to ODNI, recognized the man was rising within the political circles. Hoskins checked the right boxes for the head of the Clandestine Service. He'd been Chief of Station twice, first in the Argentine capital of Buenos Aires and then in Bogota, Colombia. A run of headquarters staff tours and a liaison assignment at ODNI showed a facility for maneuvering within bureaucracy. His last assignment was as Director of the National Counterproliferation Center. His appointment as DNCS was a signal that in the wake of the Arkhangel-2 attack, the intelligence community needed to resurrect its Cold War focus on identifying and curtailing the spread of weapons of mass destruction.

Hoskins' reputation was that he'd been a competent operations officer, but he was a political climber and none of the stalwarts in NCS trusted him.

Hoskins demanded a briefing on STONEBRIDGE his second week on the job. The message was obvious. His predecessor was just fired over this thing and Hoskins wanted to know if it was going to gut him too.

Colt and Ford had two days to prepare their briefing.

Ford was a street-savvy operator with a personality as large as his frame and one of the most cunning and daring case officers in the game. But he hid that talent beneath a gregarious, sometimes bloviating exterior that made him seem as much Bluto Blutarski from *Animal House* as it did James Bond. Over the year they'd worked side by side, Colt believed this was as much an act as a defense mechanism, Ford's way of hiding in plain sight. Ford liked that the suits rarely took him seriously and felt that gave him the freedom to maneuver.

Colt, Ford, and Thorpe stood outside the small conference room that connected with the DNCS's office. Colt stood in the middle. Ford and Thorpe had five years of sour blood running between them, and it was only through that special brand of bureaucratic kismet that they again worked together. It was worse for Ford, because Thorpe was the boss.

After twenty minutes of awkward queuing outside the conference room, Ford said, "Looks like punctuality is out this year."

Thorpe sighed but said nothing. Colt admitted to himself that he allowed Ford's caustic assessment of Will Thorpe to color his opinion of the man, and their early interactions were difficult. But Thorpe backed them on STONE-BRIDGE. His support was grudging at first and required, on one occasion, DNCS Wilcox's intervention, but he'd done it. Thorpe approved the operation on the island and agreed with their assessment on the threat Guy Hawkinson presented. He also backed them when the shit hit the fan afterward, and in Colt's book, that counted for a lot.

The door opened, and an aide appeared. "Gentlemen, the director will see you now." He escorted them into the small wood-paneled conference room and told them where to sit at the long table. Hoskins sat at one end, immersed in a conversation that hung over from the previous meeting.

They waited for another few minutes until Hoskins turned his attention to them. Two of his aides sat on the other side of the table, next to Hoskins.

"Good afternoon, gents. Thanks for coming by today. Let's get started."

"Thank you, sir. My name is Special Agent Will Thorpe. I'm head of the National Technical Counterintelligence Unit."

"FBI? Fox in the henhouse, eh?" Hoskins said, with the obligatory and tired interagency dig. His staff chuckled because they had to.

"Yes, sir. As you know, the FBI has the statutory lead for domestic counterintelligence, but we staff our organization with officers from across the intelligence community. We have a squad of special agents charged with conducting the investigations, as well as officers from CIA's Intelligence and Science and Technology divisions. We have NSA hackers, primarily for defense, threat analysis, and damage assessment. And two case officers." Thorpe motioned to Colt and Ford. "We originally ran the unit out of FBI headquarters under a different name, but we moved it here three years ago after that version of the group's name leaked. We're here today to brief you on STONEBRIDGE. Colt McShane and Fred Ford were the operational leads for STONEBRIDGE. Colt?"

They agreed Colt would deliver the briefing. Ford was very popular and well known among the operational rank and file, but he left a debris field among the senior staff that could be seen from space.

Colt nodded to the aide manning the slide deck to begin the presentation.

"Good afternoon, sir. Two years ago, Guy Hawkinson stole sensitive intellectual property from a company called Pax AI, Jeff Kim's company. Hawkinson contracted to provide private security to Kim's research lab and used that access to steal Kim's IP."

"So, why is this our problem? That sounds like something for you boys at Justice," Hoskins said, looking at Thorpe.

"A year ago, Hawkinson contacted an SVR officer, Colonel Sergei Petrov, and attempted to sell that AI research to the Russian government."

"Colt, this still sounds like an FBI problem to me. Now, I want to know why CIA is involved in this thing. I want to know why we're targeting an American businessman, and I want to know everything we *didn't* say at the Senate hearing."

"Sir, artificial intelligence is the next battlefield, the next arms race, and the next strategic threat—all rolled into one. And it's happening now. Our unit's mission is twofold—first, we are the operational defense against foreign actors stealing technology from our government and from industry. Second, we are here to leverage our most advanced technical capabilities against those adversaries."

"Isn't that NSA's job?"

"The NSA doesn't work in the field, sir. That is why NTCU was created. We have to operate in the digital space as much as in the real world. Guy Hawkinson stealing AI research and attempting to sell that to the Russians is incredibly dangerous. Russia, and their clients, are our most persistent cyber threat with influence operations, cybercrime, and overt hacking. A partnership with the Russians would give them an opportunity to play catch-up."

"I don't understand. You just said they're the number one cyber threat, but they also need to play catch-up?"

"Yes, sir. The Russians excel at influence operations—they always have, going back as far as the NKVD. They've expanded this in the digital age. In recent years, they've executed massive disinformation campaigns, using AI-controlled bots to spread tailored messages on social media—what we call 'fake news.' The Russians churned up British nationalistic paranoia during the BREXIT campaign and ran a sustained, in-depth active measures campaign to influence our presidential elections in 2016 and 2020. They have penetrated our critical infrastructure, hydroelectric dams, electric grids, and oil distribution. We think these were test runs for accessing municipal computer networks before the aforementioned elections. They are also quite good at cybercrime, particularly digital extortion. What they *aren't* good at is innovation. We believe that active cooperation with Hawkinson started sometime last year. They both attempted to infiltrate Jeff Kim's research facility the year before. The Hawkinsons were successful; the Russians were not. We believe the arrangement was for Hawkinson to give the Russians more advanced AI and quantum computing technology in exchange for financial backing."

"So the Russians were bankrolling Hawkinson, and he was going to give them technology in return, is that it?"

"That's correct, sir."

"So why'd they try to nuke him?"

Colt clenched his teeth to keep from frowning. Using terms like that only confused matters. "The purpose for STONEBRIDGE, sir, was to get someone inside Hawkinson's organization. We knew he was working with the Russians, we just didn't know how or why. Hawkinson used the money they'd given him, plus he liquidated many of the family businesses to establish a research facility on an unclaimed atoll in the US Virgin Islands."

"An island is pretty remote. Logistical challenges," Hoskins said.

"Yes, sir. But a quantum computing array generates massive amounts of heat and electromagnetic activity. Submerging it gives them water cooling and shields the EM interference."

"I've heard of quantum computing and I know we're doing it, but I'm afraid I don't know what it is. I'm an operator, Colt. You gotta dumb it down for me."

*An operator.* Hoskins hadn't been in the field in over fifteen years.

"In the simplest terms, a quantum computer stores data and performs operations using subatomic particles rather than physical hard drives like your desktop. This gives it unlimited memory and unrivaled computational power. A quantum computer can solve problems of such complexity that it might take a conventional machine years or more to solve. Coupled with artificial intelligence, which is the ability for a machine to learn and train itself in a limited fashion without human input, quantum computing is becoming the biggest advance in technology since, well, fire." Colt saw the words form on Hoskins' mouth, saw the cloud of confusion in his eyes, and knew the DNCS was about to ask, again, why this was CIA's problem.

"To paint a picture of the threat, our friends at NSA think quantum computing could render all current encryption algorithms useless. It could also hack conventional computer systems, even secured ones, without human input and in ways that humans haven't conceived of. Which means there aren't defenses for it today. We also believe quantum-enabled AI could lead to terrifying advances in bio-warfare and genetic engineering."

Ford broke in, "And we were worried that Hawkinson was giving this shit to the Russians."

"Okay," he said, holding up his hands. "I get it. So we've got an officer in Hawkinson's organization?"

Colt continued. "Yes, sir. YELLOWCARD confirmed Hawkinson had built a quantum computing array on his island using the technology he stole from Jeff Kim."

"But if he's partnered up with the Russians"—Hoskins rolled his hand—"why did he launch cyberattacks at them? I read the briefing and I've seen the transcripts between POTUS and KOESCHI." KOESCHI was the IC cryptonym for the Russian president, named after a kind of un-killable boogeyman in Russian folklore. When the Russians launched Arkhangel-2, they justified it by saying that Hawkinson was using his island to stage cyber-attacks against the Russian Federation and blamed Hawkinson for blacking out St. Petersburg.

"No, sir. We don't believe Hawkinson was launching cyberattacks. Hawkinson tried to change the deal and KOESCHI feared that would expose Russian involvement. When it became clear to the Russians they couldn't control Hawkinson anymore, they blew up the island. That's what Director Wilcox wasn't able to say in that farce of a hearing."

Colt caught Thorpe's eye. *Easy*, he cautioned.

Hoskins nodded, and for once he had no rejoinder. He made several notes in his folio with swooping strokes. Without looking up, he asked, "So if he decided not to sell this stuff to the Russians, what's Hawkinson's end game?" Hoskins leveled Colt with hard eyes. "And, I'll ask again, why is this CIA's problem? Guys, I'm not asking just to be a hard-ass. I need to prepare for tough questions. I also want to make sure we're the right people to handle this."

Colt took a deep breath, knowing this was where they would lose Hoskins.

"Sir," Thorpe broke in. "This isn't just CIA's problem, and remember, NTCU is an IC-wide unit. We're not on the level of a fusion center, like the one you used to run, because the community felt it best that our organization remained out of the public eye. But this threat is something that should concern leaders at every level of government. NTCU has an operational mandate and we have broad authorization under FISA."

Hoskins nodded, appearing satisfied.

In their briefing rehearsals, this was the part where Colt told him about Trinity, a group formed in the Manhattan Project to safeguard technological development and to make sure no one like Nazi Germany ever developed an atomic bomb. How that group morphed over time to safeguard mankind's pathway to developing artificial general intelligence. He was to tell Hoskins about Archon, the group that broke from Trinity because they felt that the only way to keep mankind safe from world-shaking technologies was to control both of them. Guy Hawkinson and his sister Sheryl were part of it.

Instead, Colt said, "Sir, the chief concern with Guy Hawkinson is that he's not a nation and, as we've already seen, there are a multitude of bad actors willing to bankroll him. Russia looks to be heading for a collapse, but what's saying that it's not Iran or the Chinese that come knocking? If his quantum computing technology proceeds as expected, we estimate he's two years away from rendering all current forms of encryption irrelevant. It can crack the public key infrastructure in seconds."

"Okay." Hoskins slapped a hand on the table. "That's the information I need. That's tangible stuff. So, what's involved in STONEBRIDGE?"

Thorpe jumped in again. Colt didn't make eye contact with him. "Sir, we have one officer in place. The cryptonym is YELLOWCARD. This intel is restricted handling, limited to yourself, the director, the Deputy Director for Intelligence, and NTCU. We understand and appreciate the political sensitivities involved. We also understand the position this placed your predecessor, and now you, in. However, we believe the technology Hawkinson is developing, in the wrong hands, presents an existential threat."

"All right, this is what I'm willing to do. You may continue STONE-BRIDGE for now, but I want regular updates and finished intel. I want you to put the same rigor into those as you would the PDB."

"Yes, sir."

"I'm not done. No activity outside the original CONOP goes forward without my direct authorization. We'll take it month by month."

···········

"Well, at least he didn't shut us down," Ford offered when they got back to the unit.

"You went off script a little, Colt," Thorpe said.

"I was reading the room. We were treading water in high seas as it was. I wasn't about to tell him about Archon. He'd have closed this up and sent us all packing."

"I'm not saying I disagree with your assessment, but what happens when we need to loop him in? Plus, Nadia's intel is going to have references to it. He's going to demand answers, and then we're going to have to explain why we didn't tell him today."

Thorpe left Colt and Ford in the common area.

"There's one big problem with leaving Archon out of the brief. Other than what Thorpe just said." Ford spoke in strained tones.

"What's that?"

"I know they have this whole Illuminati vibe, but we have to lay the groundwork now. Let's say we take this thing all the way. Send a direct action team out of Ground Branch and they put a bullet in old Hawk's head from a thousand meters. What then? Archon isn't done. I know you want some get back for what he did, but don't let it cloud your judgment."

Colt had a lot of sleepless nights since the island, and for several weeks after he returned, he felt uncomfortable under the open sky. He'd had two panic attacks he'd told no one about. For all the talk about "seeking help," Colt knew it was a career ender. You go for a psych eval and the next moment, your clearance is getting pulled or, best-case scenario, you're restricted to running a desk at headquarters supporting people in the field.

Colt might be at Langley now, but at least NTCU got him into the world.

Though the contradiction was clear.

The field. That was the place where Russians could drop rods from space...

Colt, at least, learned to recognize the black thoughts when they surfaced. He closed his eyes, focused on his breath until his pulse slowed. When the wave subsided, he got back to work.

"Excellent report this morning," Thorpe said, catching Colt as he returned to his cubicle.

The new reporting cadence frustrated Colt. Instead of taking the field with a new playbook, he was writing analyses of the game they weren't playing.

"I guess," Colt said. "But thanks."

"Hey—we can't control what he thinks, only what we put in front of him to shape the thoughts, right? Any YELLOWCARD traffic?" Thorpe asked.

"Nothing today. I wanted to talk about getting her a new COVCOM."

"Why is that?" Thorpe asked.

"The rig she's got now is the one we gave her before she first went to the island. I think we need something with better encryption. And I'm just concerned about the level of security and scrutiny Hawkinson has now."

Thorpe nodded. Running covert agents wasn't his wheelhouse. Thorpe was a cop, and he deferred to Colt on most operational matters. If he asked a question, it was out of genuine curiosity or so he could advocate the move up the chain. "Hand it off to Ford," Thorpe said. "The word just came down from DNCS. You're going to China."

# 5

*Geneva, Switzerland*

Nadia Blackmon felt the street.

This was the part of her job that she loved the best, getting black, becoming invisible. Each time she stepped onto the pavement in Geneva, she remembered last year's hard lessons in Washington, D.C. First, evading Colt and Ford, her CIA handlers and mentors. Later, it was the FBI surveillance teams. She learned how to pick up a tail, how to know if she was being followed and, if so, whether that person was alone or part of a team. Nadia learned every street had its own cadence, its own rhythm. She learned that whatever else one did as an intelligence officer, whatever secrets they stole, whatever targets they cultivated as assets, intelligence work happened on the street.

And she loved it.

But she also recognized that she had a lot to learn.

Geneva was a global city and one of the best places in the world for an undercover American. She didn't stand out. Most times, she didn't rate a second glance. Nadia breathed in the city, inhaled the street. It was late March and spring was dawning after an ugly winter. The streets and trees were dry; snow still capped the surrounding mountains. The late-afternoon air was warm, but the breeze still carried the lingering, pervasive chill.

Hawk Technologies' new headquarters was a small, manmade island in the Rhône just as it met Lake Geneva, between the city center and Old Town Geneva. The offices on Quad De L'lile had been a bank that folded last year, and the building owner was happy to meet all of Guy Hawkinson's demands on the property. Particularly, the massive construction Hawkinson insisted on in the basement levels that would afford them water cooling for the quantum array. Nadia learned that even before the incident on the island, Guy purchased this building and planned to move his operation here. The corporate headquarters for most of the Hawkinson family of businesses would move to Geneva over a period of years. Nadia believed the intent was to be out of US jurisdiction, though Guy told his employees at every opportunity that this gave them the chance to work with some of the world's leading scientific organizations. After the Russians leveled his island, Guy sped up the timetable.

Amazingly, after that event, the world seemed to forget the person Guy Hawkinson was. Nothing like near annihilation by one of humanity's worst criminals to facilitate some reputation laundering. Whatever people suspected Hawkinson of before, they quickly forgot. Geneva welcomed Hawk Technologies like decamped refugees. Nadia's first reports back to Langley focused on the many international organizations that reached out to Hawkinson to explore research partnerships. UN High Commission for Refugees was already working with Hawk Technologies to develop technology to help resettle displaced people. The idea was to algorithmically determine what communities it could place them in to achieve the highest probability of positive assimilation, rapid employment, capacity to absorb them, and a minimal amount of social friction. Guy was in discussions with CERN, Europe's advanced particle physics research institute, to pair his quantum computing array with their supercollider.

Nadia hopped on the light rail on the bridge that connected the quay with either side of Geneva and took it north into the city center. She exited the tram several stops before it reached Geneva's central train station, where she headed on foot, stair-stepping through the city blocks and periodically checking her six the way Colt taught her. Nadia reached the sprawling train station and weaved through the throngs of commuters and travelers, then made her way to the mall and found a coffee shop. She bought a cappuccino and a magazine.

Once at her table, she sipped coffee and looked over the top of the French magazine, scanning the crowd for patterns and anomalies. Were there faces or outfits she recognized from the street? Was anyone paying attention to her? Lingering a little too long in the corridor across the hall? She nursed her coffee for twenty minutes and then moved. About fifty feet from the coffee shop, Nadia patted her pockets like she was looking for a phone and turned back toward her table, scanning the crowd to see if anyone moved or was watching her. Satisfied, she turned and headed out the north exit. Nadia hailed a cab and told him in functional French to take her to an address in Geneva's Frontenex neighborhood, southeast of the lake.

Dense trees packed Frontenex, and despite the lack of foliage, they broke up the sight lines and also made it hard to fly a drone low overhead. She followed the winding road through the woods to the palatial Hotel Parc des Eaux-Vives, originally a mansion constructed in the eighteenth century. Nadia entered, slightly underdressed, and walked out to the terrace. The temperature was about fifty degrees and a gas heater stood beside each small cluster of chairs. Nadia spotted her companion and walked over. He was sitting on a dark brown outdoor sofa with red cushions beneath a heater, a beer in a pilsner glass in front of him on the glass-top table.

Nadia checked her watch as she walked. Forty-eight minutes total. As surveillance detection routes (SDRs) went, that was short enough to be considered lazy, possibly careless. During her training, Ford shared stories about SDRs in denied areas—places like Tehran, Beijing, or Tripoli—that ran twelve, fourteen hours. This was nothing. But then, this was Geneva. It wasn't like she was trying to outflank the Russian SVR.

Chuck Harmon was her handler at Bern Station. Though Nadia had a COVCOM device, Langley preferred her reports to go through the cable from Bern. The COVCOM they'd issued her before leaving for the island—a small, encrypted satellite transmitter made to look like a penlight and a portable cellphone battery—was to be reserved for emergency use. Hawkinson, as they'd expected, had tightened his operational and technical security to a level that would be tantamount to paranoia almost anywhere else. Hawk

Technologies employees stored personal electronics in a secured Faraday cage in the office lobby. Thanks to her position as a department head, Nadia learned Hawkinson installed interrogation devices to scan phones inside the individual lockers—ostensibly for malware, but truly for indications of an insider threat.

Colt asked the Sci Tech wizards if they could design a recording device and embed it inside an analog watch. They were still working on that. They'd explored creating a web-based, secure communications protocol, but Hawkinson's new security procedures eliminated that option, at least while she was onsite. Hawk Tech security blocked access to the internet, with exceptions granted only for research, such as looking at an open source code repository. Even when they granted access, security actively monitored traffic and logged every keystroke.

Nadia thought her face-to-face meetings with Chuck were unnecessary Agency paranoia. She had an encrypted messaging system that broke data up and bounced it over half of the internet. Secure comms with headquarters wasn't the problem in her eyes, but they insisted on the in-person thing. Chuck was a nice enough guy. He was in his mid-thirties, married, and occasionally brought his wife to their meetings to bolster his cover. The first time he brought her, Chuck said that Agency spouses were themselves given training before an overseas assignment and sometimes supported operations if they were willing.

Nadia maneuvered through the chairs. "Hi, Matt," she said, using the name he traveled under.

"Hey, Claire." He stood to give her a friendly hug.

Chuck signaled for a beer for Nadia, then set his phone on the table. He recorded their conversation using an app the Agency developed so that he could transcribe it accurately for the cable later. They had a few minutes of small talk, then Chuck steered the conversation to her report.

"Hawkinson's charm offensive is working," she said. "They've just started a project using AI to predict when a famine might occur using a combination of meteorological data and historical pattern analysis. The UN would use that to pre-position food, water, and medical supplies to areas of predicted need."

"That doesn't sound so bad," Chuck said.

"No, it's not. It's exactly what the world needs. The problem is the guy doing it. He's covering himself in good works. Also, I've seen the code. It's based directly on Jeff Kim's original weather predictor."

"Where is the data coming from?"

"It's all open source. I've said this in almost every report. I really need people to pay attention. The sheer amount of raw data that's available is mind-blowing, and it expands exponentially *every day*. Open source information isn't the next threat. It's already here and we're behind."

"So, what, we should be like China? Control everything?"

"Do you *read* my reports, Chuck?"

"I read them. I don't pretend to understand them all."

"There is so much raw data in the world, the biggest problem up to now was that there was just too much of it. It's everything in the newspapers and on TV, the weather, not just that it's raining but macro trends about climate. It's financial and market data, user names, speeches, and literally everything posted on the internet. It's government budgets and congressional testimony. It's the satellite photos private firms now take of everything—including military forces—ours, theirs, everyone's. No human, no group of humans, could sort and assemble it all. It's impossible. But not for an AI that doesn't sleep. Pair that with Hawkinson's quantum array, you've got a machine that can think in any direction with the raw data to do it." Nadia shook her head and reached for her beer, noticing Chuck's perplexed look.

"Dumb version, no offense, is that Hawkinson will soon be able to draw on any publicly or commercially available data source. An AI could scan every soundbite a public figure has ever made, break up the individual words, phrases, hell, even the pregnant pauses, and re-string them into an entirely different message. Plus, the audio technology is so good, it would sound real. You wouldn't even need video, but an AI could generate that too. Someone could make an outright lie sound like a policy statement, like having the president say America would be oil free by 2025. The White House would disavow it as fake, but given where we are today, half of the country would believe it. You could tank the petroleum industry overnight and the shock waves would last for months, years maybe.

"This is called deepfaking. What's worse? That same open source dataset allows you to troll public opinion before you launch the attack. You could actually sample everything they've ever reported, ever written in an op-ed, anytime the topic has trended on Twitter, what it's polling data might be. Everything. Aggregate all of that and launch the attack at exactly the worst moment." Nadia shook her head and grabbed her beer. "Now imagine that capability in the hands of someone like Guy Hawkinson or whomever he sells it to."

"Jesus."

Nadia said nothing for a time. Then, "This is a big deal, Chuck."

Chuck patted the air between them in the "I got it" gesture, and Nadia regretted being so aggressive. Like many techies, she got frustrated when nontechnical people didn't pick up on the gravity of what she was saying.

"What is Hawkinson up to?" Chuck asked, redirecting the conversation.

Nadia wasn't quite "inner circle," but she'd gained Hawkinson's trust on the island when she'd beaten his lie detector. His device, unlike the standard government polygraph, assessed every known biological indicator of deception, from pulse to pupil dilation, eye movement, twitching, to posture and body temperature, and rendered a confidence rating. She'd beaten that by convincing him that the machine was wrong, by giving him a technologically sound reason for it. Guy believed her. She knew he was looking for a mole in the organization, but he'd zeroed in on Ava Klein. Fair point. After all, she *was* a Mossad officer. Guy offered to evacuate Nadia on his yacht with the rest of his senior staff. They sailed to South America and returned to the US on a chartered jet to settle affairs. Once she'd arrived in Geneva, they made Nadia a department head and had several project leads reporting to her. She met with Hawkinson on a semi-regular basis.

"I hacked into some of the protected files. Don't ask how, it'll bore you. There's a lot of imagery for Greenland and Argentina. He's also spinning up a carve-out for a climatological study group in Greenland. We'll have a small quantum computing facility here in Geneva, but I think his next big thing is going to be Greenland. Guy is traveling a lot, probably two weeks a month."

Greenland had millions of square miles of completely untouched land, more every day now that glaciers were melting at the rate they were. Argentina was a different story. The country vacillated between open and closeted hostility toward the United States. It also had one of the most educated and technologically savvy populations in the world, thanks to a high-quality state-funded higher education system. Ironically, they also enjoyed a legacy of staggeringly corrupt governments. Perfect for a wealthy industrialist unofficially on the run from the US government.

Chuck looked around, making sure that no one was moving within earshot. He leaned over to pick up his beer and quietly said, "Here's the unit's current information requests. First, anything on Archon. Langley thinks they've gone completely dark since the island." Though this wasn't Chuck's case, Colt read him in on the operation so that he could be an effective intermediary between Langley and Nadia. If he thought Archon was crackpot stuff—and Nadia wouldn't blame him if he did—Chuck didn't say.

Nadia moved to sit next to Chuck on his couch and vamped showing him something on her phone. "It's radio silence on my end. I have heard nothing since I got to Switzerland. I have seen Samantha Klein at the office twice, however." Klein was Ava's aunt and original Mossad handler. Mossad forced her to retire after the disaster with Jeff Kim's research facility and Mossad's involvement became public knowledge. Samantha was on Guy's Caribbean island acting as a "security consultant," and Nadia originally believed she was part of the organization they eventually came to know as Archon. But after Samantha covertly saved Ava's life and helped her escape, proving her loyalty to Israel, they reevaluated that assessment. Ava knew Nadia was CIA but had not shared that information with anyone—so far as they knew.

"Has she tried to contact you?"

"No," Nadia said. "Not yet."

"Okay, I'll run this up the pole, but sit tight on it for now. Don't make any overtures until Langley okays it."

That was the answer Nadia expected. As her handler, Chuck was conservative. She couldn't blame him. This wasn't his case, and he wasn't part of the unit.

"Any signs of Sheryl Hawkinson?"

"No. Word is she's back in California running her VC." Nadia took a small sip of beer. "What's the latest on my new COVCOM?"

"Nothing yet. At least nothing they've told me. They are working on the watch, though."

Nadia shook her head but said nothing. She didn't think a passive recording device would do much for them, but perhaps it was better than nothing. What they really needed was to get inside the secure servers, but that was almost impossible. Nadia didn't even have access to those. Langley, so far, ruled out trying to inject code. She knew Hawkinson's AI was actively scrubbing their network for intrusion detection and estimated that it would be good enough to find any software exploit they attempted to use.

Ford told her once this case was the most analog high-tech operation he'd ever run.

The inherent contradiction was that Hawk Technologies was so locked down, they'd have to rely on old-school, low-tech spycraft to learn anything.

Chuck said, "Keep up the good work. I'll send this out tonight, and if there's anything pressing, I'll get it to you right away." He stood, and Nadia joined him.

They said their goodbyes and departed through different exits. Nadia walked toward Lake Geneva and the boat terminal at Port Noir. She'd take the water taxi across the lake rather than walk.

The challenge with an SDR in a city this small was that travel options were limited. Geneva, with a population of about two hundred thousand, was a contained city, huddled around the edges of the lake as though it were grasping it for sustenance. Nadia didn't own a car and Langley's bean counters determined that since her apartment was within walking distance from the job site, she could walk or take public transportation. She'd grown accustomed to similar logic in the Air Force. God help the person who tried to fight against the travel regs. But Nadia did anyway, hissing at the woman behind the Global Services counter and telling her she would be undercover and what if she needed to exfil. A car was a tool. Give her the tool.

Her supervisor—Colt—got an angry phone call from Global Services to remind his subordinate about Agency travel policy.

She could've rented a car, but that thought hadn't occurred to her after she'd planned the SDR. Driving around the lake would have been effective in spotting a tail but impractical, as it would've taken two hours or more to go around the long way. As Nadia made the expeditious choice to use the water taxi and cross the southern tip of the lake, she could practically hear Fred Ford's voice in her head admonishing her to take her time, to use caution, and to remind her that a fifteen-hour SDR for a five-minute meeting might seem inefficient as all hell, but it certainly beat the twenty years in jail.

*Dude, I'm in Switzerland*, she could almost hear herself saying.

The sky was ablaze with early-evening light and the air was wet and heavy. Clouds ringed the mountains to the north.

Nadia was reviewing the mental map of her SDR home when she saw him.

Navy topcoat, collar up, and gray wool ballcap to hide his eyes, standing just off the dock at Quai du Mont Blanc. He was white, blond, likely early forties, and average height and build. There were only ten other people in her water taxi and the dock was mostly empty. It wasn't tourist season, and the locals stuck to the light rail or walked. She didn't know exactly how she *knew* he was waiting for her, but she remembered Colt telling her about the strange alchemy of the street. It was a vibe, a feeling, a sixth sense. People just seemed to know when they were being watched.

Quai du Mont Blanc ran along the banks of Lake Geneva. Trees lined the broad sidewalk at precise intervals along the lakeside, but there was no other cover. Traffic was heavy and slow along the road, so Nadia stepped out into the street, acting like an impatient tourist weaving through the crawling cars. She dashed across the four-lane boulevard and hopped onto the far sidewalk, casting a glance over her right shoulder, ostensibly to get one last look at oncoming traffic but really to see if Ballcap was still following her.

He stepped into traffic to cross the street.

The man hadn't ridden the boat across the lake with her, which either meant there was a surveillance team she'd completely missed or he had other means of keeping tabs on her. Her mobile was Agency-issued and heavily modified and hid her location from the local cell towers. If he'd been using technical surveillance, it wasn't from her phone.

During Nadia's training, Colt and Ford attempted to pull a fast one on her by slipping a tracking tag into her backpack. She'd found it, hacked it, and deactivated it. Nadia stepped across the street to the Fairmont Grand Hotel. There was a restaurant on the street level, Le Café, and Nadia slipped inside and found the ladies' room. Once inside a stall, she opened all of her pockets, felt the lining of her coat for tears, and checked the buttons. Then, she did the same number on her handbag. She carried very little, except for a spartan wallet and phone. This, she knew, was one of the more tangible limitations of her rushed training—Nadia simply didn't know the spectrum of surveillance threats. Switzerland was a neutral country; there was no opposition service in the classic sense. Did the Russians operate here? The Chinese? The Iranians? She just didn't know. Yes, the Swiss had an intelligence service, but they wouldn't be looking at her. They didn't follow Americans for the hell of it the way the Russians or the Chinese did. It also wouldn't be security from Hawk Technologies.

So who was it?

Not only that, how did they find her?

Nadia wasn't familiar with drone technology, but knew the Agency operated handheld models. If they did, it was a good bet that an opposition service would too, and one that small would be hard to see at altitude. She made a note to ask about that in her comm back to Langley. Nadia forced herself to remain calm, to remember her training, but holy hell was it hard in practice.

In typical European fashion, the Fairmont Grand Hotel occupied every inch of a city block. Nadia used the interior exit from the restaurant to the lobby and wended her way through the hotel. She took the hotel's north exit and found herself on a busy street. A quick glance up and down the sidewalk didn't reveal Ballcap, so Nadia again took advantage of the chugging traffic and crossed the street. She spotted her pursuer rounding the hotel's northwest corner and quickly disappeared down the street, finding a small plaza, the Place de la Navigation, bare trees surrounding a fountain. She counted fifteen or so people, mostly school age, either on benches or standing around the fountain. Nadia stepped quickly across the plaza, putting the fountain between her and the direction she'd come from. As she neared the city center, she saw more mixed-use buildings, and on the far side of the plaza, she spotted a row of sidewalk cafés. Nadia took the distance in long strides, the tables already filling with dinner crowds despite the cool temperatures. She ducked inside a falafel shop and shouldered her way through the mostly younger crowd to order. Nadia was sure that if she was being tracked, it most likely wasn't a bug planted on her, which meant it was a surveillance team or technical assistance. Or both.

Nadia slowly ate her falafel wrap, trying to burn as much time as she could. Ballcap never entered the place. When she'd finished, she worked her way to the back of the café to the restrooms and instead opened the third door, a service entrance leading to a courtyard. Typical of a European city block, five- and six-story buildings wrapped around an open area in the center. There were three exits from the courtyard, all of them large enough for a vehicle to pass through. No sign of Ballcap in the courtyard. Nadia looked up, but the darkening sky made it impossible to see anything. She took the southern exit to the courtyard and thought about where to go next.

She didn't see Ballcap here either.

Nadia hailed a cab to the airport, where she changed cabs again and exited at a restaurant she knew several blocks from her apartment in old town. Nadia walked up, pretended to look at the menu for a moment, and then walked back to her place. She needed to get her COVCOM device and make a satellite shot back to Langley. This couldn't wait until her next in-person meeting with Chuck, likely more than a week away. She also needed to warn *him* that she was followed.

Nadia entered her apartment and immediately checked for signs that it had been tossed.

The problem with rookie mistakes was that you were usually too inexperienced to know you were committing them in the moment. Nadia knew now her SDR was hastily planned and insufficient. She didn't truly believe she was under threat because this was Geneva.

She knew better now.

But how many times had Nadia been surveilled over the last six months and missed it?

And who was watching her now?

# 6

*Hong Kong, S.A.R.*

Colt knew he couldn't write in a cable, *"This is a total shitshow,"* but that was exactly what this operation was.

The new DNCS wanted a bold action to take the focus away from the lashing the Agency was receiving in the press and on the Hill. Though Wilcox originally authorized BRUSHFIRE, Hoskins advanced the timeline to coincide with a DoD op and to show that he was doing something. Colt wasn't alone in worrying that Hoskins was forcing this operation in order to get the Agency a win.

Operation BRUSHFIRE's primary objective was to capitalize on instability in China. It was an aggressive, old-school active measures campaign. The Agency hadn't attempted something like this in years, and never in China. BRUSHFIRE's secondary aim was supporting the defense of Taiwan. Ever since Russia invaded Ukraine, political leaders in the West were increasingly worried that China would see their lack of direct involvement as a signal of America's waning commitment to the defense of Taiwan. CIA's China analysts argued they did not share that conclusion and that when China invaded, it would be on a timeline entirely of their choosing.

When Colt arrived, the military component of the operation was already underway. The Defense Department wanted an operational test of an AI-piloted aircraft called "VIPER 2.0." The project resurrected mothballed F-16 tactical fighters from the boneyard at Davis-Monthan Air Force Base in Arizona. They replaced the human controls with a robotic guidance system to control the avionics, navigation, and weapon systems. The Air Force had long used decommissioned aircraft as target drones; this simply took it to the next step in evolution, replacing the human, ground-controlled guidance with an onboard AI developed by the Defense Advanced Research Projects Agency (DARPA). VIPER 2.0's AI went undefeated against human pilots in simulated dogfights for three years before its operational test phase. The Air Force VIPER 2.0 aircraft were flying a continual Combat Air Patrol (CAP) around Taiwan, refueled by Navy Stingray midair refueling drones. The Navy augmented the operation with a test of its own Orca autonomous submersibles patrolling the Strait of Taiwan.

The heads of both US Indo-Pacific Command and US Strategic Command warned that China would attempt to take Taiwan by force by 2027. TRITON SHIELD was as much a test of bleeding-edge military capability as it was a direct showing of America's commitment to defend the island. The goals of Operation BRUSHFIRE were more nuanced. The Chinese Communist Party had been dealing with a growing level of unrest for some time. The populace still believed they were technologically behind the West. Though the US intelligence community believed China was actually ahead of America in the AI race, their tech sector writ large wasn't innovating as fast. Further, the global supply chain in many sectors began moving away from China following the pandemic and subsequent shipping delays. Diversification of suppliers meant reduced risk for global customers and negative economic impacts for China. This opened or re-opened economic sectors in Asia and other parts of the world hungry for the lucrative Western business.

"Some eggheads think China is heading toward an economic collapse driven by intense cooperation with the West, similar to what brought down the Soviet Union," Hong Kong's Chief of Station, Gina Rankin, told Colt when he arrived. "I think that's ivory tower bullshit, and it's overly optimistic. But their economy is in trouble."

"What's the direct threat?" Colt asked. He liked Rankin immediately. She had a reputation for being a bit of a cowboy, had bucked Agency brass and kept her job as COS. The rumor was she carried a boot knife in an ankle holster. The other rumor was that both had seen action. She was five feet even, thin but square-shouldered, and had a jaw that looked like it could crack stone. Rankin's eyes were dark and lively. She was a woman from another time, a warrior-scholar.

"The most direct challenge to China's regional stature is the Indo-Pacific Economic Framework." This was a technological development and defense pact between the United States and Japan. The pact comprised mutual defense commitments similar to the NATO alliance, coupled with collaborative research and development for both military and civilian uses. "Agency analysis is that communist party leaders in China are not just fearful of the pact, it humiliated them. Respect is everything in China, Colt. They believe they are the preeminent power in Asia and need to be seen as such. It offends them that the dollar is the base currency in the world economy. They see this pact as a loss of stature. BRUSHFIRE's intent is to capitalize on that by fomenting civil unrest here in Hong Kong. HK has long been a bellwether for the rest of China. That said, I think the timing is stupid, and I told Hoskins that."

"How'd that go over?" Colt asked.

"Well, we're doing the op now, so that should answer your question," she said in a way that meant the answer was obvious. "Now, to you, Mr. McShane. I kind of know what NTCU does and I kind of know why *you're* here, so why don't you tell me what they told you, so you and I can get on the same sheet of music about what we're going to ignore. First up, how much do you know about Hong Kong?"

"Crash course from the China desk," Colt said. "British gave up control in 1997 and it reverted to the PRC, but the Chinese government kept it a semi-autonomous, self-governing state."

"That's pretty close," Rankin said. "One country, two systems is the phrase they like to use. Unlike the mainland, HK is governed by a Chief Executive and Legislative Council. That's kind of a combination of city council and House of Representatives. Within the Legislative Council, they're largely divided between pro-democracy, localists who want to preserve HK's independence, and pro-Beijing communists. We covertly support the former two; the fervency depends on the prevailing winds from Washington. The

People's Liberation Army handles Hong Kong's defense and they staff it entirely with troops from the mainland. No indigenous defenders, if you will. Helps keep them 'objective,' in Beijing's eyes. Increasingly, Hong Kong is indistinguishable from the mainland."

"What's the opposition like?"

"That's an interesting question. Until 2020, they couldn't operate here officially. Doesn't mean they weren't. But Beijing passed a new national security law that brought Hong Kong and Macao under the mainland's purview. The State Security division is staffed with local talent, unlike PLA. And I'll tell you, they are inscrutable. They fervently want to protect Hong Kong from foreign interlocutors, namely us and the Brits and Taiwan. They generally follow the lead of their parent service on the mainland, but they do occasionally thumb their noses at Beijing. Information-sharing and coordination between here and the mainland is poor. They know who we all are, but as near as we can tell, your cover is still good."

That was Colt's primary concern before taking the TDY, but Hong Kong Station reassured him that even though MSS in Beijing knew he was a CIA officer, the HK bureau most likely didn't. Colt's cover was a State Department economic analyst there to assess recent changes in US import/export policy toward Hong Kong.

"So, back to my original question. Why are you really here?"

"NTCU's mission is to disrupt foreign attempts to access US Intelligence and our industrial base by technical means," Colt said, and Rankin gave him a grim, cut-the-shit stare. "We use cool gadgets and computer nerds to spy on the guys trying to spy on us," he deadpanned. "We try to stop governments from stealing US technology and are mostly concerned with technical penetration..."

Rankin lifted her right eyebrow.

"And I genuinely don't know why I'm here," Colt finished.

Rankin nodded and pointed her index finger at him.

Colt continued, "I understand BRUSHFIRE is to amplify existing unrest over CCP policy and recent crackdowns. There have been vehement protests here for the last seven or eight months. What I can help do is deploy some tech that will make it harder for the opposition to find our involvement.

Protect your assets. Stuff like that. Basically, I can give you some technical top cover to pull off your op."

"That's great. Our primary asset is a blogger and dissident journalist. That already has him on their radar, but unofficially, the guy is a total subversive. He does it all—organizes protests, writes articles under a host of pseudonyms in a dozen Asian newspapers, makes and distributes leaflets, shitposts anonymously on state-run media, he'll even graffiti." Rankin laughed.

"What kind of surveillance are you running into here?"

"It's pervasive," Rankin said. "About as bad as the humidity and just as sticky. Don't kid yourself, China is the world's preeminent police state. The mainland has three cameras for every citizen. Those are all tied into facial recognition tech that is crazy good and accurate. They have these electronic billboards at crosswalks and they scan the faces of everyone there, right? That's linked into a national database. If someone has unpaid parking tickets or is late on a phone bill, they flash that up on the screen." Rankin snapped her fingers. "They can even identify the ethnic minorities based on subtle physical characteristics. They're using that to single out ethnic minorities, specifically Uyghurs. It's scary. Now, HK isn't there, but they are catching up quickly. There are multiple cameras on every street corner, in parks, and on almost every building. They can track your every movement, triangulate position between cameras and cell phone towers. Makes getting black hard, especially since they already know who all of us are." Rankin's voice trailed off. "I want to give the DoD thing in Taiwan a little time to simmer before we really start BRUSHFIRE. As it is, I feel like Langley is pushing too hard and too fast. This needs time to build. I told them that, but the powers want action now. We're going to start ten separate protests around Hong Kong, coupled with targeted online posting written in advance under various names in different styles. Our guy also has articles queued up in Chinese and English web editions for Hong Kong's major newspapers, particularly the ones with large foreign readership. The intent is to look like ten, twenty times the number of people involved initially and then flood it with positive coverage. Give the appearance of a concerted, widespread effort. The goal is for it to spread to the mainland. Phase two will kick off in about six months with similar actions in Shenzhen, Guangzhou, and Shanghai to coincide with DoD's follow-on, TRITON SENTINEL."

"I can help there, as well. We know the CCP controls and monitors internet traffic," Colt said.

"And all the providers are state-owned, as are the device manufacturers," Rankin interjected, sounding tired.

"Right. But we've got some ways of creating virtual private networks that the CHICOMMs can't shut off. That should give you and the Beijing Station team all the coverage you need to launch these follow-ups."

The concept of operations was designed to play on the Chinese people's fear that they still lagged behind the West, despite their staggering leaps forward. DoD would execute a show of force highlighting specific military advancements designed to show just how wide that gulf was. Then, CIA would foment a wave of protests, fueled by dissident journalists that would stoke already smoldering fires and give Beijing something serious to worry about. Many in the Agency saw this as payback for a string of intelligence losses to the Chinese over the last twenty years, but mainly for former operations officer turned Chinese spy Jerry Chun Shing Lee.

Colt was excited. He was glad to be back in the field after six months in headquarters and the second-guessing and institutionalized scab-picking better known as "after action reports." This was an important mission. The HK Station had excellent operators and a solid leader.

It would be good to be on the street again.

Then it all went to hell.

# 7

*Three weeks later*

Tsang, the head of Hong Kong's MSS bureau, loomed over a map of the city. Several of his adjutants and representatives from the Hong Kong Police Department stood nearby, but at a respectful distance. There were six red circles on the peninsula. Three in the central neighborhoods of Prince Edward and Mong Kok, another in West Kowloon. Across Kowloon Bay, there were three more circles in Wan Chai, near the convention center; Happy Valley, near the sports complex; and North Point along Java Road. Four more circles were drawn on both sides of the bay, yellow to indicate a lower confidence level. Each of the circles identified the location where they learned the riots would begin, illegal protests against the government fomented by dissident criminals. Cowards, really, who had no appreciation the lengths true patriots like Tsang went to in order to provide safety and security. These people were little better than the rats scratching behind the walls.

"We've been tracking the spotter's phone and traced him to these spots. Then we used the cameras to confirm it was him. There were multiple trips to these locations." Tsang's deputy pointed to the rings. "We've been following him for some time because of his involvement in the July 2021 riot."

Tsang nodded, recalling the file.

His man continued. "Pattern analysis revealed several trips to each of these locations on subsequent days, two visits per day."

"What was the timing?"

"A midday and early evening route."

"When they would be the most busy."

"That was our assessment as well, sir. Then we followed him to a meeting with the journalist Fung Li. Phone records show multiple calls and texts to Fung, particularly during the scouting runs. We also tracked the spotter's usage of websites used by previous riot organizers. We have an officer posing as a collaborator. He has access to the website and is familiar with the codes they use."

"Very well done, team. I am pleased." This operation was three years in the making. Tsang appreciated the irony that this so-called "pro-democracy" movement had given them the very tools he needed to smash them. The massive rioting in 2019 and 2020 began after the establishment of the new Fugitive Offenders Bill, which allowed the Hong Kong government to extradite political dissidents to the mainland for trial. Following those riots, Beijing passed the new National Security Law, which finally brought Hong Kong under the umbrella of the Ministry of State Security and gave Tsang the capabilities he needed to ensure peace on the peninsula.

Fung was a central part of the 2019 and 2020 riots, and he published libelous falsehoods about the government in any newspaper that would print his filth. Hong Kong police were watching him since 2019 and also knew each of the spotters he used, the people who would scout locations to spark the riots. Once the MSS established the Hong Kong Division, Tsang relied heavily on their existing operations and local intelligence network. The Ministry did not need the police. They could execute the arrests themselves, but Tsang wanted to send a message. They would cast a wide net, show these dissidents the superiority of their numbers. A true show of force.

"What is our plan for the arrests?" he asked.

"We have two hundred targets," the senior inspector from the Hong Kong police said. "This is the entire network, we believe."

"Tracking them was easy," Tsang's deputy said. "Once we had the spotter's phone, we could trace his location to the various meetings, and that uncovered much of the rest of the network. It took months of diligent work." The dissidents used an end-to-end encrypted private messaging app called X-Chat to communicate. Gaō Bai, a Chinese privacy advocate, dissident, and software developer, designed the app. But Gaō was actually a cutout, a persona created by the MSS for this exact purpose. MSS designed and fielded the app using the Gaō persona and pretended to take it offline every so often until the shadowy Gaō could relaunch it on another server, having evaded the MSS once again. Meanwhile, all of X-Chat's users were communicating with each other on the app, believing it to be completely secure. MSS could track the dissidents by monitoring the phone's location covertly via the app. They then used Hong Kong's omnipresent camera network to observe the meetings so they had visual verification for the courts.

Tsang smiled. He was pleased. This was indeed first-rate detective work. Of course, their patrons in Beijing showed them where to look. Such information-sharing was uncommon and would certainly mean that Tsang now owed a favor, but he deemed that worth it.

Tsang said, "We make the arrests tomorrow."

---

"This is from my guy in HKPF, Chief," Duane Barrett said. He was the station's head of operations and had the stick for BRUSHFIRE.

"Shit," Rankin said. Rankin, her Deputy Chief of Station, Barrett, and Colt sat inside the sealed Lucite container that they lovingly referred to as the "trash can." It was the only truly secure place in the US Consulate, free from electronic eavesdropping. This was where they held all the BRUSH-FIRE planning meetings. Barrett just learned from a source in the Hong Kong police that the MSS identified Fung Li as the person responsible for planning and coordinating the upcoming protests. Both the police and the MSS had sweeping arrests planned. From the sound of it, these would be the largest crackdowns since the 2020 riots. Barrett's source didn't know about BRUSHFIRE or that Fung was also a CIA asset. He was just doing his job as a source in giving his handler the hot info he'd just uncovered.

Colt didn't understand. They'd deployed an Agency-developed secure messaging app for everyone in the dissident network and given them VPNs. The government still pulled this apart.

"What's the exfil plan for Fung?" Rankin asked. Every CIA asset had an emergency exfiltration plan to get them to safety if the opposition found them out. China's geography made this a uniquely complicated problem.

A dour look washed over Barrett's face. "Plan A was to smuggle him onboard a commercial vessel. We've got a gentlemen's agreement with MI6 to put any of our people on a container ship. The Brits rigged up a comfort pallet inside a container; it's got a bed, TV, MREs, and a chemical toilet. Once they're outside of Chinese territorial waters, the captain gets them out and gives them a stateroom until they get to wherever they're going."

"I can tell by your tone that's not an option," Rankin said dryly.

"The *Brunswick* isn't due back into port until tomorrow. Typhoon in the South China Sea delayed it by a few days. Plan B is to have one of the Agency's boat service subs pick him up." CIA had a small, specialized air and boat service used primarily for infiltration and exfiltration of covert action teams, but could occasionally deploy for an exfil of an important asset. They had a few coffin-sized robot mini-subs that were launched from US Navy vessels and would appear at a precise time at a specific location on a beach. The case officer would put their asset in the sub, push it into the water, and it would automatically return to the Navy ship. And after that, a new life in the United States.

"We're sixteen hours in the air from the East Coast," Rankin said. "Even if Langley green-lights it, they'd never get it here in time. And it's not like Fung is a PLA general."

Barret shook his head. "He can cause them a hell of a lot of trouble."

"We can waste time bitching about how we want the world to be or we can come up with another option."

"Could you sneak him into the consulate and sneak him out later, when the sub is ready?" Colt asked. This wasn't his show, and he was careful about overstepping his bounds. The consulate was US sovereign territory, and the Chinese couldn't arrest Fung as long as he was inside it.

Rankin's face broke into a not-quite smile. "We've got so many local nationals working here. Unless we somehow got him inside the station— which, for the record, I'm not willing to do—there's no way we can keep his presence here truly secret. Then he gets outed as an Agency asset and that causes a lot of problems for us down the road."

"I got it," Barrett said. "We can have a new passport made in a few hours. Disguise kit to change his appearance and fly him out of Hong Kong International to Taipei. He can ditch the disguise and fly to the US as a private citizen from there. I can go with him under my dip creds."

Rankin thought it over. She leveled a finger at Barrett. "Make it happen."

---

The US Consulate General was on the island of Hong Kong, and Fung Li's apartment was in Kowloon City on the peninsula. It was a little over five and a half miles using the Cross-Harbour Tunnel. At this time of night, just after three in the morning, it should take him about fifteen minutes. Counting time for surveillance detection, Barrett planned two hours. That was cutting it, but time was in short supply. He'd use a combination of walking and cabs to get to the vehicle his support asset left on the peninsula, and they would use that to drive to the airport. Barrett would also need another forty-five minutes to apply the various prostheses to make Fung look like the passport photo that they'd worked up overnight. A support asset would meet them at HKIA and do the brush pass exchange before Fung got to the counter. They had an agent in Hong Kong's Immigration Department who'd stolen twenty blank Hong Kong passports last year. The team was working on that while Barrett picked up Fung. He had a noon flight to Taiwan.

Barrett loved Hong Kong at night. It was a brilliant, electric, hyper-modern city of enormous, glowing skyscrapers and lush, vertical mountains that looked like fingers pushing up from the ground. The city reminded him of the science fiction novels he read as a kid. Hong Kong was what the future looked like. The sidewalks were mostly empty, but Barrett knew he was being watched. That feeling was inescapable here. It was a prickly feeling on the back of his neck that he never quite shook.

You never got used to the cameras. The moment you did, it was time to go home.

Barrett stair-stepped several blocks and doubled back to check his six. Finally, once he'd reached the bay, he hailed a cab and gave the driver an address on the other side. It was an after-hours club, popular with expats, and asking to go there wouldn't raise any suspicion. Barrett watched the skyline on the far side of the harbor as the cab approached the tunnel, but his mind was on the mental map of the peninsula's streets and routes he would take to get his agent to safety. Barrett tuned out when they entered the tunnel and focused entirely on getting through the next three hours.

They got him on the far side of the tunnel.

The cab emerged from the muted green glow of the tunnel to the stretch of road that gradually ascended to street level. The toll plaza was a concrete canyon with twenty-five-foot walls. Hong Kong Police Force cruisers, lights flashing, blocked the road. If they were anywhere else, Barrett would have attempted a moving jump from the car and taken his chances on foot, but there was nowhere to go. He couldn't very well scale the retaining wall, and the far side of the tunnel would be blocked off now, even if he could make that on foot.

Barrett swore to himself in the backseat.

He got a text off before the HKPF officers swarmed the car, guns leveled at him and the now panicked cabbie. The number was an old-school trick. He texted a three-digit sequence, 3-0-9, then closed his burner phone.

---

"Goddamn it," Rankin shouted from her office. "McShane, get in here now."

Colt was there in seconds. They'd all stayed on hand that night working ops support for Barrett's exfil.

"What's up, Chief?"

"Barrett just messaged the duress code to our deadline. HK police just arrested him."

"Was it one of the LNs downstairs?" Colt asked, remembering Rankin's earlier comment about the local nationals tipping off the authorities. Though Colt had been in CIA about twelve years, he was one of the rare ops officers who hadn't had an overseas posting. Instead, Colt's first decade was what the Agency called "non-official cover." As a NOC, he'd lived every day under a fabricated identity in a commercial company gathering critical economic intelligence in the US and abroad. Though he had more true undercover time than eighty percent of the clandestine service, he was still a rookie in many ways.

"I don't think so," Rankin said. "Duane didn't leave from here. He went home a little later than normal, showered and changed, then went to a bar for an hour to burn time. Idea was to make the consulate watchers think it was a regular night. He bar-hopped a bit and then started his SDR, so I don't know exactly where they got him. He just texted his duress code. They must have been on him since he left the consulate and followed him everywhere he went. We can't seem to hide from the bastards."

"Do you think MSS suspects Fung of being an asset?"

Rankin shrugged. "I don't think so, but I can't be certain. Not that it really matters at this point."

"I can get Fung out," Colt said.

Rankin shook her head. "No-go. You're a TDY officer. Besides, if you get caught, they'll try you for espionage. Most likely, you'll be sent to a prison on the mainland and we will never see you again. I'm willing to take that chance with one of my people because I know them. No offense, but I know nothing about you."

"Let me try."

Colt could see this was eating Rankin up. The Agency went to extraordinary lengths to protect its assets. Case officers knew they weren't protecting saints, but whatever the individual circumstances were that made someone spy on their country were irrelevant when it was time to get them out. If people were going to risk their lives to get secrets to the Agency, the Agency would move heaven and earth to get them out safely if they could. A case officer's relationship with their agent was one of the most intimate there was, and case officers were extremely protective of them. Many officers knew things about an agent that even their spouses, lovers, parents, or priests would never get.

"I lost one once," Colt said. He knew there wasn't much time. "I was running an SVR major that I'd recruited out of the Houston *Rezident.* We learned that an FBI agent was playing for the other side and I was meeting with my asset to cover the exfil plan. I watched her get gunned down in broad daylight in a San Francisco park."

"That was you?" Rankin said with a distanced professionalism. "I read about that. I'm sorry."

"So I know what Barrett is probably going through right now. The CHICOMMs aren't following me. As far as they know, I'm an econ geek. Please let me help." CHICOMM was analyst shorthand for "Chinese Communists," used throughout the operational community as a derogatory term for the regime that ran the People's Republic.

"You don't know these streets."

"You have a map? Besides"—Colt flashed her a knowing grin—"I bought a few toys to test out in the field. They won't even know I'm here."

"They better not, Colt. If you get caught exfiltrating an asset, it's life in prison." Colt could see in her eyes she knew there wasn't another choice. "You have until I get this cleared by your people at Langley to get ready."

---

## 8

*Los Angeles, California*

Jeff Kim flew on a chartered Gulfstream to Burbank's Bob Hope Airport where a black Audi e-tron sedan took him south to a restaurant in downtown LA. Crawling through the sludgy sluice of traffic on the 5, Jeff made a note to invest in one of the emerging air taxi companies. Jeff's time was his most valuable resource, and he despised wasting it. This meeting could easily have been a phone call.

Still, he understood the other party's reluctance and their insistence on meeting at a neutral location. Though, meeting in San Francisco would have required that Jeff only sacrifice a few hours of his day rather than half of it. People didn't understand how disruptive it was to take him out of his flow. If Jeff had forty-five minutes in a car, he might as well use it.

Forty-five minutes to drive twelve miles...

If ever there was a problem for artificial intelligence to solve.

Jeff's eyes tracked to the mottled green and tan mountains rising above the car. California dreaded another historic drought year and already the forests were scourged with ugly brown stains where things just weren't growing back. Jeff typed a note on his phone that he should again reach out to the State of California, the Department of Natural Resources, and CalFire to offer his wildfire predictive mapping tech. Saturn, his virtual assistant, research assistant, and next-gen AI experiment all rolled into one, would take the request from his phone and schedule the meetings. A human on the phone couldn't tell the difference between the two. He might not be able to prevent the damned things, but it could certainly give evacuation efforts critical lead time and help firefighters better focus their efforts.

That done, Jeff focused on the meeting.

This would be an act of contrition.

And, again, he understood the other party's feelings on the matter. After all, Jeff had gone through some tremendous lengths to free himself from their previous "arrangement." Necessary steps given the partnership and the other party's recalcitrance at letting go. Which he felt fully justified for. Though Jeff Kim rarely felt the need to justify his actions to anyone.

But this time would be different.

Fifteen years ago, he was a Stanford-educated son of Korean immigrants that no one in Silicon Valley wanted to take a gamble on. He talked of a bold new future ushered in by artificial intelligence. Jeff's pedigree and his tech got him in the door, but no one would take him seriously. He was a little *too* visionary to be considered actionable by the investor class. By no one but a small arm of the Chinese government called the Ministry of Technical Cooperation. They told him at the time they existed to bridge cultures, to invest in promising new ventures. So he took their money when his own government practically laughed him out of the room. Jeff built one of the most successful AI R&D companies in America and spun off many related product lines, from robotics to virtual reality. By then, Jeff suspected that the Ministry's aims weren't as altruistic as they made them out to be. By then, Jeff also did not care. He had what he needed. And when the time came to cut the cord, and free himself from the interlopers who got their tentacles into his business, he did so.

Now Jeff would propose a new partnership. But this time he wasn't an untested grad student. He was a captain of industry and they would agree.

The terms were simple.

All he needed them to do? Destroy Guy Hawkinson.

Liu Che dressed in a five-thousand-dollar Savile Row suit, black with a crisp white shirt and emerald tie. A sliver of silk peeked above the fold of his breast pocket. Liu sat in a deep booth of maroon leather in a Chinese restaurant three blocks from the Consulate General of the People's Republic of China. Besides cooking authentic Sichuan cuisine, the owners were naturalized American citizens but maintained a strong loyalty to their true home. They afforded a safe place to talk. Liu had flown here two days ago to meet with his counterparts at the consulate regarding a case that overlapped their respective operational jurisdictions. Liu added a day onto that trip to meet with Jeff Kim.

He'd given the entrepreneur and erstwhile asset two weeks to dangle before returning his call and another two before Liu actually agreed to meet with him. Liu was angry that Kim seemed to have forgotten their agreement when it was no longer convenient for him. That was disrespectful. The people of China had invested significant amounts of money and helped cultivate Kim's early successes. Intelligence officers could go years without hearing from their assets. Sometimes they couldn't learn anything of value to give to their handler, other times they couldn't safely communicate. But this was different. Kim attempted to distance himself from his benefactors. He believed the ridiculous stunt of burning his company to the ground would somehow make the Chinese government forget about their long relationship. However, as a student of deception, Liu had to appreciate the boldness with which Kim acted. And it was only two years. A short time for a nation that measured its heritage in millennia, but Liu's government paid well to plant seeds for Jeff Kim and it was time to harvest that bounty.

Or Liu would pave it over.

Kim initially balked at having to fly down to Los Angeles. He said that would cost him a day of productivity. Wouldn't it be simpler if Liu just flew to San Francisco on his way back to Washington? Liu calmly said, "Simpler for whom?"

Liu sipped his tea and looked at the paper lights hanging from the ceiling with disdain. This was what Americans thought China was. They would learn soon enough.

Jeff Kim arrived late.

This Liu would forgive. He wasn't sure that even Kim's technology could solve traffic in this city. Kim wore light gray pants, a white T-shirt, and an unzipped black hoodie that was about as thick as paper. Liu did not stand when the hostess guided Kim to his table with a lithe twist of her hand. Kim offered a wan smile and sat, assuming that he was welcome to. Liu's long, dark eyebrow lifted over his right eye, but he made no other sign. When Kim had slid into the booth, Liu said, "Please have a seat, Jeff." If Kim detected the sarcastic polish on the words, he said nothing. "Thank you for coming." And with that, Liu established that this was *his* meeting.

Liu pointed with two fingers, subtly, at Kim's side of the table. A server appeared with a teacup and a small pot. Liu lifted his own cup, sipped one time, and set it down.

"It's been some time," Liu said. "What would you like to discuss?"

"We're not talking here," Kim said.

"Then what are we doing?"

"This is a public place." Kim's eyes narrowed. The man's anxiety was palpable.

"Jeff, ours is the only English conversation taking place in this building." *And it's being recorded.*

Jeff Kim was silent and stared at the table. Liu could almost read the other man's mind. He'd seen this so many times with an agent, the asset considering their options.

Jeff tapped something on his phone and set it on the table.

"Why am I here, Jeff?"

"I would like to resume our partnership," he said.

"I'm not sure that's possible," Liu said. "You embarrassed my government. You embarrassed *me*. I know you appreciate the gravity of that in my culture. Besides, we gained very little for our end of the partnership. I'm not sure I could convince my superiors, even if I were interested in trying."

"I understand your embarrassment and I'm sorry if it caused you any difficulties, but it was necessary to hide our cooperation. I don't think you appreciate, Che, that three intelligence services *and* Guy Hawkinson penetrated my company."

"Three? It seems, perhaps, you should focus on security for a time."

"I was too trusting. I won't make that mistake again."

"Why do you need help from the People's Republic?" Liu asked, spreading his upturned hands across the table. "You have rebounded admirably from your recent... difficulties. Your company has regained much of its market share. You even had cash on hand to make an impressive acquisition last year." Liu's superiors were particularly interested in the VR company Jeff acquired. China invested heavily in virtual reality, led the world in many respects, but Kim's coupling of EverPresence's novel approach with his own tech would be years ahead of anyone else. If the reports Liu had seen were accurate, they could authentically render a virtual scene and make it almost convincing to the human eye. By comparison, every other VR looked like a cheap cartoon.

"You're familiar with Guy Hawkinson," Kim said.

"Of course."

"That day, at my facility, Hawkinson stole some of my most advanced research. That's what his entire operation was about."

"Seems like something you should take up with your Justice Department," Liu said, offering a grim smile. It was the first emotion he'd displayed in the meeting. "A noted downside to capitalism, I'm afraid. There is no control over who steals what."

"There is a new arms race and it has already started. I don't think you want to be on the downside of it."

Liu sighed. "What are you proposing, and what are you offering?"

"I need help with Hawkinson. The United States government obviously isn't doing anything about him. His uncle is a US senator. He's also moved his company out of US jurisdiction."

"But he's still an American. Your laws apply to him no matter where he is in the world." Liu understood Kim didn't believe in governments or their sovereignty, but that was a tiresome and unnecessary philosophy.

"Even if my government were interested in doing their jobs, they wouldn't do it in time. Hawkinson is going to use my research to build his own general intelligence. He's also taken my quantum computing designs and, based on what I've seen him do, applied them. He's close, Che, and that makes him dangerous."

Liu's eyebrow lifted again, but he remained silent.

Kim placed his hands on the table and leaned forward, closing the distance between them. When he spoke, his voice was a low growl. "By my estimation, Guy Hawkinson is about two years away from making encryption irrelevant. That's what my technology is capable of. Who will protect your secrets then, Che? Help me and I can not only protect you from whatever he's developing, but I can make sure you maintain parity with the West."

"What help do you require?" Liu asked.

"Take Hawkinson off the board."

"We're not killing people for you, Jeff."

"I'm not asking you to," Kim hissed, and then lowered his voice, looking around. After a second to compose himself, he continued, "I'm not asking you to kill him. I just want you to help me defeat him. My company doesn't have offensive cyber capabilities. But that's not exactly the only tool in your toolbox, is it?"

"Arrow in the quiver is more historically accurate, but yes," Liu said, though he noted the irony that his Ministry's shield still displayed the crossed hammer and sickle of communism. "I'm quite certain there are things that the people of China could do to prevent Guy Hawkinson from gaining AI supremacy. I suppose that the key question is whether they should care."

"I understand China had a particularly harsh winter, and you lost most of the winter wheat crop. Two years in a row, isn't it? Perhaps with more accurate forecasting of global weather patterns you could—"

Liu waved his hand dismissively. "I want nothing Guy Hawkinson has already stolen from you. I can get that on my own. But virtual reality is very interesting to my government."

Kim shook his head. "Out of the question. If that IP leaked, it would be obvious who did it."

"You can't come here, beg for my help, and then attempt to dictate the terms." Liu shrugged and slid an inch to the right toward the end of the booth.

"Che, wait."

"If you expect my government to listen to another proposal, Jeff, you need to show that you are serious. I already told you I want nothing that Guy Hawkinson has already stolen from you. I want something new. Something useful to the Chinese people. We are linking the developing world with an umbrella of beneficial technologies that will uplift and enhance lives.

Consider how you might partner with that. Your approach to VR would be a valuable addition to our Belt and Road Initiative."

"If I do this, you will remove Guy Hawkinson?"

"He will not threaten you again." Liu stood from the table.

"Thank you for your time, Che," Jeff said with a slight smile. He picked up his phone and waved it at Liu. "Oh, if anyone was eavesdropping on this conversation, I think they might find the recording a little... garbled."

There was just enough time to catch the 1:30 flight from LAX to Dulles. Liu arrived just after nine that evening and an embassy car took him to his home in D.C.'s Woodley Park neighborhood, perhaps a mile from the embassy grounds. Liu greeted his wife, who'd stayed up to meet him, warmly. Their children, both teenagers, were likely awake but in their rooms. He told his wife that his trip was successful, but shared no other details—she also worked for the Ministry. They restricted their conversations at home to trivial matters. Carelessness was how the FBI uncovered Chi Mak and his network in California.

Liu told his wife he would be up to bed in a few moments. She poured him a glass of Bordeaux she'd opened for dinner, kissed him on the forehead, and went up to their bedroom. Liu sipped the wine and went into his study. The Chinese had an insatiable appetite for French wine and were its largest consumers outside of France. One of the perks of living in Washington, Liu found, was that the selection was much better than what he could get in Beijing.

Liu pulled his laptop from his bag and set it on the desk in his study. He had two windows facing the tree-lined street and another facing the side of the house, though the thick wooden blinds were closed. Liu turned on his desk lamp and navigated to an app, where he entered a brief command. He leaned back in his chair, enjoying the wine and the silence for a moment.

The app he used would send a covert message to his agent, informing him it was time to meet. The signal would appear as a notification on an app on the agent's phone, conveniently manufactured in the People's Republic. One benefit of the government controlling China's largest technology companies was the Service could direct them to build whatever they wanted. In this case, enhancements. Not only could they monitor any conversation or message sent from the device, but they could also communicate securely with their assets without fear of being discovered. Not unless one of the opposition agencies cracked the phone open and probed the chip itself. Unfortunately, his agent was required to have a government-issued phone for his official communication, and that was too locked down for them to penetrate. The signal Liu just sent would appear as an alert on a weather app with a benign message about a warm front moving through the area, code for him to open an additional app—one of those odious crowd-sourced business and event rating tools. The location that appeared in that application would be their meeting site.

On the far side of the Potomac River, Vice Admiral Glen Denney, a noted night owl, would be reading that message at this moment.

Liu looked forward to the meeting. They had much to discuss.

# 9

---

*Hong Kong, S.A.R.*

Dawn broke over the skies of Hong Kong, illuminating the towering glass buildings in a pinkish fire. Colt took a cab from Hong Kong Island to Kowloon. By the time he'd left, Colt learned Hong Kong police apprehended Barrett just as his cab exited the eastern harbor tunnel. No word yet on where he was being detained or on what charge, but Rankin woke the Consul General up with the news.

Colt left the consulate hidden under a blanket in the backseat of another case officer's car. The driver took him away from the consulate shortly before dawn and navigated west on their predetermined route. Jenny Sūn was a second-generation American of a Chinese family, had relatives here in Hong Kong, and spoke like a native. She was on her second operational tour after the Farm and had been through the Agency's Denied Area Operations course. "We've got a chaperone," she said as they left the consulate.

"Copy," Colt said from beneath the blanket, crouched behind the passenger seat.

"I'm going to drop you near the zoo. There's a winding road leading up to it they won't be able to take at speed. I can slow down just enough for you to make the trees." They'd chosen that spot because the HK team believed it was one of the few stretches of road without camera coverage.

"Sounds good," Colt said.

Jenny drove as fast as she could without breaking the law, hoping to lose their pursuers at a light. Colt guessed from the casual cursing coming from the front seat that her plan wasn't working. The car made a series of left turns and Colt could feel the vehicle's plane change as it started moving uphill. Jenny sped up unexpectedly, pulling into one of several bootleg turns that snaked up the tall hill, and Colt had to brace his arm against the door.

"Get ready," she said. "They haven't made the turn yet."

"I'm ready," Colt said, throwing off the blanket but staying in a crouch.

Jenny accelerated again, rocketing the car down the straightaway, and then pressed hard on the brakes. "Go, now!" She slowed just enough. Colt jumped out the back door. He landed on the street, folding himself into a ball and clutching a backpack against his chest. Colt rolled several feet, stood, and sprinted for the trees. He must have looked like a drunkard after a field sobriety test, his equilibrium upended from the roll. He took one fast look to get his bearings. It was a one-lane road, and he'd exited the right side of the car, putting him on the downhill. There was a thin sidewalk and then a metal barrier, waist-high. Colt jumped over the barrier after two long strides and landed in the dense undergrowth, hearing the crunch of several ferns beneath him as he slid on his backside down the steep slope. Above him, he heard a car passing without stopping.

It worked.

If he made it through the day, he was buying Jenny Sūn a beer.

He navigated the slope and climbed a black iron fence that dropped him on Lower Albert Road. Colt jumped the fence and landed in a crouch before checking the empty street. While kneeling, Colt opened his backpack and put on the black ballcap and glasses. The lenses had a photo reflective coating that bounced light back at the source, effectively shielding them from cameras and rendering image recognition software useless. The large, aviator-style lenses obscured most of his face on camera. His cap had infrared LEDs that fired beams back at cameras. He wouldn't be able to blind them all, but he'd get a lot.

Colt opened his phone and thumbed an app that activated an Agency-designed signal baffler. His phone would now be invisible on the local cellular grid. He then walked his planned SDR, looping several blocks, backtracking to see if he'd picked up any tails—he had not. Satisfied, Colt hailed a cab on Bonham Strand West and asked the driver to take him to the Shek Kip Mei district, home to several of Hong Kong's universities. An odd-hours drop-off wouldn't look out of place.

Fung's home was about a mile and a half away in Kowloon City. Colt stair-stepped the blocks and cut across the sprawling, lush Kowloon Tsai Park to block any vehicular tails he may have picked up, though he was confident that he was black. The city was waking around him. Car traffic increased and delivery vehicles made their rounds.

Their support asset stashed the car at Kowloon City Plaza, but unfortunately, Barrett had the keys. Luckily, the support asset, a local on the Agency payroll, had a second pair. He'd be waiting at the bus stop across the street at 7:35 to execute the brush pass. Per the plan, if Colt wasn't there at exactly the right time, the asset would disappear and Colt would need to find a different way to get Fung to the airport. That gave him a little over half an hour to apply the disguise.

The other problem was Fung himself.

They had no way to warn the journalist that the Chinese arrested Barrett. Colt had to convince Fung that his life was in danger, that Colt was on his side, and that he needed to leave with a man he'd just met.

Colt worked his way across Kowloon Tsai Park. A low level of mist clung to the grass. He moved quickly, veering between the park's swimming pool and a soccer pitch, both illuminated by huge overhead lights. There was no cover here, but Colt was so far from the road that spotting him would be nearly impossible unless they were airborne. A quick glance over his shoulder confirmed no one was following on foot. Colt reached the thick line of trees that marked the park's eastern boundary. Beyond that was another steep, wooded slope that eventually dropped to a street below. Colt hopped off the path and half-ran, half-slid to a line of trees that he used to break his descent. Then he hopped the metal rail and landed on the sidewalk, finding himself on a silent side street.

Colt slid out his phone, verified that the baffler was still hiding his location, and pulled up his map function. He hadn't had time to familiarize himself with this sprawling city, didn't know its rhythms. He didn't know the *street*. Colt spent a little time orienting himself to Hong Kong during his time here and notionally knew his way around. It was a complicated, alien city. Unsure of exactly where he'd exited the park, Colt found he was just around the corner from Fung's home, less than half a mile. He made fast steps through the waking city. The pink sky had a brief flash of orange before turning blue. The air was cool and cloying.

He found Carpenter Street and the block-long Kowloon City Plaza, where the drop car was. He checked his watch. It was already six-thirty, and he swore to himself. He was running out of time. Colt moved down the block to Fung's street and rounded the corner. A wave of relief hit him when he didn't see HKPF cars lined up outside the building. Fung's apartment building, like many in the city, was a five-story box of one flat stacked on another. He found the building and stepped beneath a blue awning. There was a pet shop on one side and a bodega on the other. Colt tried the handle; it was unlocked. Fung lived on the third floor. The walls were white with peeling paint, hard tile floor, and no decoration other than the metal banister that followed the staircase. Light came from a street facing a smoked glass window at the end of the hall, opened outward.

Colt bounded up the zigzagging staircase two steps at a time. When he hit the third floor, he was sucking wind. Anxious, he prepared to pound on the door but quickly caught himself. That would sound like the cops' hammer-fist knock. Colt took a breath and rapped quickly but lightly with his knuckles.

No answer.

He knocked a second time.

A voice responded from the other side of the door, speaking Chinese. It lifted just slightly at the end of the sentence, which Colt hoped meant he was asking a question. Hopefully, "Who is it?"

Fung's apartment was the only one on this level. There was a small landing, the stretch of hallway with the apartment door before the stairs wrapped around to the next level. The hall was otherwise open air. Anyone above or below could easily hear anything Colt said.

He leaned close to the door. "Mr. Fung?"

"Who are you?" the voice replied, this time in British-accented English.

"My name is Craig Archer," Colt said, using the alias he traveled under. He knew that Fung and Barrett were close and had worked together for four years. "I'm a friend of Duane Barrett's," he said. Case officers didn't normally share their true names with assets, no matter how tight they were, but he knew from the short time he'd spent with Barrett's case file that after Duane pitched Fung on working together, Fung agreed on the condition that Barrett tell him his real name. It was a matter of trust and respect, Fung said. He needed to know the young CIA officer had skin in the game. With Rankin's approval, Barrett agreed.

"Where is Duane?"

Colt knew Barrett gave Fung a disposable phone for emergencies so he could make a one-time phone call and then smash the SIM chip and throw it away. Given how quickly the opposition rolled Barrett up today, they didn't want to trust Fung's phone. Barrett and Fung also used an end-to-end encrypted messaging app the Agency developed to send coded communications using innocuous phrases. The emergency bug-out code was "are you free for dinner thursday?" A message sent in all lowercase signaled an emergency. "Dinner" meant that they would leave at six the following morning. "Thursday" was code for "Exfiltration Plan B." The app was secure, but they couldn't be sure about the phone it was loaded on. Until they knew how MSS unraveled this operation so quickly, Hong Kong Station had to assume their other communication tools were compromised. However, Colt was counting on the code phrase.

"Duane wanted me to ask if you were free for dinner Thursday," Colt said, his voice just above a harsh whisper. His pulse was creeping up. Time was running out. He heard several locks disengage, and the door opened. Colt wasn't sure what to expect, but it wasn't this. Fung looked to be in his upper fifties or early sixties and thin. He had a thick gray mustache and black hair flecked with so much gray it would be white within a year. Fung's mouth pursed in a lemon-suck expression and Colt could see from the cracks around his mouth that it was likely always in that position.

Colt's mind immediately went back to what Barrett had said about him earlier. *This guy will even graffiti.* Colt couldn't picture this grandfather as the scourge of Hong Kong's government, a radical and riot starter. Maybe that was the point.

The small apartment beyond Fung smelled of smoke, and the shades were drawn. A single table lamp was turned on in the living room and Colt smelled old, burnt coffee on top of old, burnt cigarette butts. Colt closed the door behind him.

"Mr. Fung," he said in a low voice, holding a finger to his lips. Colt pulled a silver pen out of his backpack, clicked the button, and waved it over all the surfaces in the apartment to scan for electronic surveillance devices. Once that was done, he opened his phone and scrolled through his music app. Eavesdropping was still possible, even without a bug. A well-placed infrared laser aimed at a window could pick up the subtle vibrations in the air caused by speech. The MSS would need line-of-sight to Fung's window to know Colt was there, or else be monitoring Fung continually. Neither seemed likely. As a precaution, Colt put his phone next to the window, selected the Beastie Boys' *Licensed to Ill,* and pressed play. He found the fast-paced lyrical handoff between the three Brooklyn rappers would confound any attempt at listening through the windows.

"The Ministry of State Security arrested Duane this morning. We don't know what happened, exactly, but we know they are aware of your plan to stage riots across the city. A source tipped Duane off and he was coming to get you when they arrested him."

"Is he okay?" Fung asked, and Colt could see genuine concern in his eyes.

"We don't know yet," Colt said. "I'm taking over and we're going to get you out. Right now."

"I can't leave," Fung said, defiant. The small man even straightened, seeming taller somehow. How Fung was such a problem for the Chinese government was no longer a mystery. Colt could hear the spirit in his voice. "We're going forward with these protests, Mr. Archer."

"No, you're not," Colt said. "The MSS knows all about them. They know who your spotters are. They know everyone who's helping you and they're all getting arrested today."

"That's exactly why I can't leave. I need to stay and fight."

"From a prison cell? Because that's exactly where this ends up. My government can't protect you once you're inside the system."

Fung shook his head. "I'm sorry. I appreciate everything you've done. Please tell your government that I appreciate everything *they've* done and certainly Duane. But I need to fight for my people, fight for Duane. They can't just hold an innocent man without charge."

Colt wanted to correct him, but didn't. Of course the Chinese government could. They could do whatever they goddamn wanted, and that was the point. Men like Fung were their conscience, acting out, causing trouble, shining lights in the dark, and making an absolutely impossible stand against a tyranny they couldn't hope to overthrow.

Colt's mind immediately went back to a meeting with Svetlana, his Russian SVR agent. Based at the Russian Consulate in Houston, Colt met her at a barbeque shack in China Grove, just outside San Antonio. Over ribs, brisket, and long necks of Shiner Bock she'd told him everything about the SVR's operations in the southern United States and Mexico, how they were funneling weapons to one of the Mexican cartels for no reason other than to facilitate instability in that tortured country and to increase drugs moving into America to cause problems there. He remembered those Baltic blue eyes, sharp. And he remembered watching that light drain out of them after her own service gunned her down in San Francisco. She'd wanted to be her country's conscience, too. She loved Russia, but not what it had become. They were a fierce people who had never known true freedom in the modern age. She didn't love America, but she didn't hate it and thought the renewed Cold War that the Russian president was so keen on fostering would only end one way—with Russia's destruction.

And she'd died for it.

"Mr. Fung," Colt said in a cold but soft voice. "You have important work to do and it shouldn't die here. If you stay, they *will* arrest you. I don't know Duane well. I just met him, but I think he's a good man and he's doing God's work. He risked his life to get you to safety, and it's going to cost him. He is in their custody now. Whatever happens next, we—you and I—cannot let that be in vain."

Fung stared at him for a long time in the smoky silence.

"I wouldn't like to play cards with you, Mr. Archer."

"No, you would not," Colt said with a wry smile.

They moved into Fung's living room, where Colt explained the exfil plan as he started working the disguise kit. The kit had step-by-step instructions, tailored to match the doctored passport photo. Colt did his best to narrate what he was doing. It not only helped him internalize the instructions, but he also found that helped the subject understand what was being done to them. Colt worked in the details of the exfil plan, because he couldn't be sure how much Barrett had time to brief him on.

"We're going to the airport by car, which we'll pick up at the mall parking lot up the street. We created a new passport for you last night to match the disguise we're applying now. Someone is going to hand you a new passport when we get to the airport. Duane taught you how to do a brush pass, right?"

"Yes, he did," Fung said. Then he added, "This music is really terrible."

Colt smirked. "My parents hated this record when I was growing up. Once you've got the passport, you'll get your ticket at the counter."

"Where am I going?"

"Taiwan. Someone from our team there will meet you. You'll be able to remove your disguise. We will have a Taiwanese passport waiting for you with your regular photo, but there will be a fake name. You'll board a flight to San Francisco and resettle in the US under a new identity."

Colt finished up with the disguise kit, closed it, and put it back in his pack. Fung looked fifteen pounds heavier and ten years younger. There were appliances in his mouth to lift the cheekbones and change the contours of his chin. His hair was blackened. Fung wore a girdle that expanded his midsection and Colt brought a jacket that had curved pads on the shoulders, back, and arms to give him a bulkier silhouette. Fung would be okay as long as he wasn't frisked, though if it came to that, it was probably over already. Finally, Colt gave Fung a pair of contact lenses. They wouldn't change the color of Fung's eyes, but they acted like Colt's glasses and would spoil optical identification by rendering the images unreadable.

Colt checked his watch.

"You have three minutes to pack up anything you'll need."

"I am packed," Fung said, and Colt could hear the sadness in the old man's voice. He was giving up his entire life and his home, fleeing with his life and little else for a new, anonymous one in America. Colt didn't know if Fung had a family. He only knew there wasn't a wife they needed to evacuate now. Deciding it was best not to ask, Colt used a secure messaging app to signal Rankin that they were on the move.

"Leave your phone here. You'll get a new one in the States. They're probably tracking that one." Fung nodded and left it on the counter.

They left the apartment, and Fung stopped to lock the door behind him. He looked sheepish as he pulled the key out of the lock. "Force of habit," he said.

"It's okay. Let's go."

Colt led Fung out of the building. They turned right on the street toward the mall when Colt saw them. He looked behind them to confirm what he already knew.

Hong Kong police vehicles tearing up the street in both directions and coming straight for them.

"Oh, shit."

# 10

_Hong Kong, S.A.R._

"We've got about ten seconds," Colt said. "Let the kit do its work. They won't recognize you on sight, but you need to hurry to the end of the street before they get a cordon up and start questioning people. Meet me at the end of this street." Colt pointed south.

"I thought we were going to the mall."

"We assume that's burned," Colt said. "Just put your head down and go. Don't pay any attention to the police." Colt disappeared down the adjoining alley with seconds to spare. They were going through backup plans like knives through butter. Fung wasn't his asset, and he didn't know, couldn't know, what kind of prep work Barrett had done with him during their work together. Colt didn't know Barrett either, but he was a fast judge of character —that was a case officer's indispensable skill. It was the thin line between knowing whether the meeting you were about to have was a potential recruitment or a trap. Colt's assessment of Barrett was that he was a solid c/o and trusted that the man prepared his agent.

If he hadn't, Colt and Fung would be in a Chinese prison.

Colt stepped into the alley. Maybe ten feet separated the buildings, and there were piles of construction debris, plastic jugs, bags, and other random detritus. Colt stepped over the junk and moved into a covered, lit hallway that ran the length of the block. He took off at a dead run, pressing against the side of the hallway as he blasted past a local, a cigarette dangling from his lips, no doubt wondering what the Yankee was doing in his alley.

As he ran, Colt watched the end of the tunnel for lights or other signs the HK police had picked up on the switch. But by the time he reached the end of the hall, no police cars blocked his path, no scores of cops in riot gear rushed down the tunnel after him. Colt stepped out onto the cross street, busy with morning traffic and the ever-present sound of impatient horns and idling engines. He chanced a look back the way he'd come. No signs of pursuit. But Fung hadn't rounded the corner yet. He'd be walking normally, so it would take him a few seconds longer. Colt waited, and the seconds ticked off his watch like the force of gravity itself was pulling them backward. Looking around the corner was too risky, so Colt had to assume the authorities were looking for additional Americans after they nailed Barrett. Though Colt's legend was safe, that wouldn't help him if the Chinese found him with Fung Li.

Fung stepped around the corner, and Colt exhaled a huge breath.

"They were questioning everyone. But I slipped away in the confusion." Fung didn't have any ID that would back up his new alias.

"Let's go." They crossed the busy street and made their way south to Prince Edward Road, beneath the elevated Boundary Street. There, they hopped on a city bus. Fung sat in the front, Colt moved farther back and stood. They rode several blocks to Saint Theresa's Hospital. Colt walked to the front, "accidentally" bumping Fung as he exited. That was the signal to get off the bus. Once outside, Colt dropped to a few paces behind Fung. "Just keep walking," he said in a stage whisper. "Walk into the hospital and wait for me. Scratch your head if you understand."

Fung flicked at his ear and Colt realized that the hair dye might not have dried. Out of the corner of his eye, Colt watched Fung enter the hospital, then waited a few moments to see if the police swarmed it. The riskiest part was next. Colt decided they shouldn't ride to the airport together. Hong Kong was a massive, multicultural city of millions. A native and a white man could walk the streets and not draw attention. Colt had Chinese photo surveillance beat and the MSS couldn't follow his phone. The problem was arriving at the airport. HKIA was on an island, accessible by only one road and one rail line from Hong Kong proper. If the MSS and HKPF were already covering the airport—he assumed they were—they would look for Chinese citizens traveling with Americans. Colt could've found a better way if he knew the city at all, but three weeks just wasn't enough time to learn it. He hoped that in his desire to help, he hadn't doomed Fung Li.

Colt studied his map a moment longer and then went inside.

He found Fung drinking a coffee from a Styrofoam cup, doing his best not to look like a CIA asset on an emergency exfiltration.

"How's the coffee?" Colt said. Fung closed his eyes and shook his head. Colt spoke in a low voice. "Go outside and get a cab. Go to the Lai King MTR station. I will ride in a separate cab. We'll take the train straight into the airport. Blending into the crowd is our best chance." He paused and waited for that to sink in. "Listen, this is the most important part. No matter what happens to me, you keep going. You're looking for a man wearing a Hong Kong Football Association jacket. He's a local who works with us, and we trust him. He's going to walk past you in the ticketing hall at Row N and give you the passport. It'll be tucked inside a magazine. Do you have any questions?"

Fung shook his head. He knew what was at stake. Barrett had prepared him well.

Colt watched him leave through the front doors and go to the cab stand. When Fung was in a cab, Colt went to the next one in line. He asked the cabbie to drop him at the Lai King train station, which sat on a plateau in central Hong Kong, overlooking the lower city. While he was riding, Colt tried to find the train schedule. His phone was already down to a third of its power. The jammer worked wonders, but it was a power hog. He connected it to a backup battery from his backpack and rode the rest of the way to the train station in sheer wonder at the impossible geometry of Hong Kong.

Approaching the enormous metro station, Colt couldn't count the number of different elevated rail tracks that curved above the lush treetops in a strange contrast of concrete and iron over vegetation. Colt paid the cab driver and got out. He spotted Fung in the crowd and followed him into the packed station. After purchasing a ticket on the airport line, he trailed Fung about thirty feet as he made his way down an escalator to the track.

There was a police presence at the station. Colt couldn't tell if this was normal or part of the dissident sweep. Two officers got on the escalator. He guessed four people separated them. Colt stepped onto the platform, moved past Fung, and found a place to stand in the crowd, then joined the tidal flow of people pouring into the car. The police, he noted, stayed on the platform. Colt was in the car behind Fung. As the train started moving, he pushed his way through the crush to a spot near the door between their cars. He couldn't transit the cars, but he could at least keep watch on his charge.

As the train left the station on an elevated track and curved south, the broad expanse of Hong Kong unfolded before his eyes. The impossibly tall buildings stretched into the sky, glowing in the reflected morning sunlight. The train crossed a bridge spanning the blue-green waters of Kowloon Bay and then onto Hong Kong Island, where his day's journey began. They rode to the northern side of the island, then along the coast to the west, and then back out over the water. Colt saw signs for Hong Kong Disneyland. The train arced around a line of emerald skyscrapers and continued on to the airport. The trip only took about twenty-five minutes.

Colt exited the train and had a few nervous moments before he caught Fung in the crowd. He followed his charge up to the departure level. HKIA, like the city it represented, was sprawling, almost too large to take in. Once they reached the escalator, though, the crowd thinned, and it was easier to spot his man. Fung followed his instructions well, walking, but not too fast. Just another guy with some place to be.

They designed the exfil plan to run without signaling from Agency personnel. That was a precaution in case the MSS arrested anyone else.

A pair of bodies broke up Colt's line of sight—dark blue uniforms, black tactical belts, and dark blue berets. Both had pistols in holsters strapped to their legs; one also had a submachine gun in a tactical sling. A hand came up and pressed into Colt's chest as one of the men rattled questions at him in Chinese.

Colt flashed a dumb smile. "I'm sorry, I don't understand. Do you speak English?" He made eye contact with the cop questioning him, the one without the SMG, but kept Fung in his distant vision.

"What's your business?" the cop asked, this time in English. The tone was the same.

"I'm here to pick up a colleague flying in from the United States today."

"This is the departures level," the cop said.

"I know. I've only been here a few weeks myself. I'm still trying to figure this place out. It's pretty big."

"Do you have identification?"

"Of course." Colt produced his diplomatic passport with his alias. "I work for the US State Department," he said. "I'm an economist."

In his distant vision, Colt saw the distinctive red and black jacket of the Hong Kong Football Association. He passed out of view, blocked by a cop. When Colt saw him again a few steps further, he noted the man's hands were free. The cop was still asking him questions, now about the colleague he was meeting. The man in the jacket made eye contact with Colt, his attention drawn by the HK airport cops accosting an American. He gave an almost imperceptible nod and disappeared from Colt's view.

Colt returned to Langley two days later.

The two airport unit officers detained Colt for about thirty minutes to question him, but let him go. Since Colt wasn't a permanent party and the Hong Kong government didn't know he was there on an alias, he wasn't on their list of suspected Agency personnel. Taipei Station confirmed they met Fung in the airport, got him changed, cleaned up, and on a flight to San Francisco with his new passport. Fung and Barrett were both back by the time Colt arrived at Langley. The Hong Kong government had nothing to charge Barrett with and wouldn't risk extraditing him to the mainland. The current thinking was the HKPF jumped the gun and arrested him too soon. If they'd have just followed him to his pickup, they would have gotten them both. Instead, they gave Barrett persona non grata status out of spite. He could never return to Hong Kong. Barrett would ride a desk in the China Division until the Agency brass could figure out a new field assignment for him, but this wouldn't tarnish his record. He thanked Colt for getting his guy out.

Things weren't any better in the unit.

Hoskins was furious BRUSHFIRE folded and was looking for a head to put on a spike. It wasn't until then, chased by cautions from Thorpe and Ford, that Colt understood how isolated he was at Langley. He spent eight years undercover, answering only to Wilcox, then Chief of Station in Vancouver. Wilcox was his sole lifeline back to the Agency. Colt didn't have the successive overseas tours where he could build his network with fellow case officers, or build a reputation with influential Chiefs of Station or Division Chiefs. He didn't even know many of the staff operations officers who made things happen in the background at headquarters. He never got to make those connections, never got to grow his network or had a patron who rose through the organization and looked out for him.

Instead, he was largely unknown and unsponsored.

"You did good, kid," Ford said. "Rankin sent a cable back while you were still in the air. You acted fast and were selfless. None of them would've blamed you if you hadn't volunteered to go out. Rankin said you had to talk her into it."

"Fung is a good man, and he's doing good work," Colt said over his third coffee that morning in the NTCU common area. "I wasn't going to let him twist in the wind, get picked up." He took a sip of the acrid, burned brew. They used to have a guy from the NSA in the unit who roasted his own beans, ground them, and made some of the best coffee Colt ever tasted. Unfortunately, he'd returned to Ft. Meade, and they were back to drinking whatever nondescript bagged shit they pulled at the coffee fund. "Thing I don't understand is how the MSS figured it out so fast. I mean, Rankin even said she thought they were moving too fast, but that op was her baby. The HK guys planned it well. We figured MSS was probably up on some phones, and Fred, you wouldn't believe the camera coverage they've got in that place. You are always being watched. It's eerie. Still, there's no way BRUSHFIRE should collapse like that."

"I agree," Ford said. "That's why we have an eleven o'clock with Pete Pritchard."

"Who's that?" Colt asked.

"He runs China Division. And we've got just enough time to swing by the food court and get better coffee."

Ford filled him in before they left, since they couldn't talk about the meeting until they were in the China Division's SCIF. Ford explained Colt earned a lot of goodwill with the division team by his exfiltration of their asset. Without Colt, the MSS would've arrested Fung, or worse. Ford reached out to Pritchard while Colt was in the air to see if he could learn anything else about the failed op. Pritchard was an old colleague and friend from Ford's Far East Division days. Pritchard, after much of Ford's signature cajoling, admitted there was "some late-breaking shit," but also said that Ford wasn't cleared to step in it. Still, Pritchard knew that a favor was owed and was going to see if he could get them read in.

Fresh coffees in hand, Ford and Colt arrived in Ford's old operational stomping grounds, China Division. Though his twenty-five-plus years in the Agency spanned the globe, the balance of Ford's career was spent in the Far East, with operational tours in Singapore, Hong Kong, and Beijing. It was the Beijing assignment where he'd first met FBI Special Agent Will Thorpe, their now boss, and lost an agent. The fallout of that operation got his tour curtailed and Ford sent back to headquarters. If not for Wilcox's intervention and subsequent reassignment to NTCU, Ford's agency career would've been over.

Like Ford, Pete Pritchard was a big man, and Colt had a hard time picturing him in the field. He had white hair and a mostly white beard that gave him a disarming look. But his eyes were hunter's eyes. This was a man with street time and a lot of it. Handshakes and introductions went around; Barrett was there and again thanked Colt in front of the superior officers for his quick and brave action. Pritchard then led Colt and Ford into his office, where he closed the door.

"As I'm sure you guys know, we have been mostly blind, deaf, and dumb inside PRC for the better part of a decade," Pritchard said. In 2011, the Ministry of State Security rolled up nearly every Agency asset in China in the span of a few days. They displayed an eerily coherent competence they hadn't before shown, and the Agency was able to get perilously few of its assets to safety. The Agency knew now that the Chinese compromised the allegedly secure messaging site the Agency used to covertly communicate with their Chinese assets. They got out who they could. For too many, case officers handed agents backpacks of money and sadly told them, "Good luck." It was all they could do. Almost every agent in the People's Republic was lost, and over a decade later, the Agency still wasn't back to where they'd been.

"So," Pritchard continued, "we've got very little early warning for this sort of thing. But we have a source inside 2PLA—that's the intelligence division of the People's Liberation Army. I'm not going to say anything more than that. Because of where our asset is, all of the intel is restricted handling. His c/o, station chief, and me are the only ones who see the raw intel outside of DNCS, DDI, and the director. I just got clearance to tell you two. And that took some doing."

"Tell us what," Ford said, quickly getting impatient.

"The Chinese have a mole in the US government," Pritchard said. "We don't think inside the IC, but they're definitely getting high-level information. They knew about BRUSHFIRE."

"That was to coincide with a DoD operation," Colt said.

Pritchard nodded. "That's right, and we had to brief our DoD counterparts beforehand. Our team talked to the J2 at Pacific Command. I briefed the Pentagon's liaison officer, God only knows who *he* told." It was a fact within Agency culture that they believed no one kept secrets as well as they did. The Agency had an Associate Director for Military Affairs, which was a three-star flag officer who was the liaison with the Pentagon for all Agency support. They had a support staff called the Office of Military Affairs, manned by Agency personnel.

"Do you think this was just a lucky break or did the MSS know where to look?" Ford asked.

"I've been at this long enough, Fred, to know that luck only comes when you know way more than the other guy. I think the MSS knew that BRUSH-FIRE was going down. Now, we didn't share any operational details with the Pentagon, just broad strokes, but they would know that it was coinciding with TRITON SHIELD. I don't know, man. We had to tell the PACOM guys that our op was happening on HK, just in case it tipped off something bigger."

"So you're saying they had high-level operational info but not tactical details," Colt said, running the traps in his mind.

"That's right. OMA looped in the PACOM J2, Joint Staff J2, and both ops were authorized by the president. So the National Security Council knows, presumably SECDEF's direct staff too."

"Well, that narrows it down," Colt said dryly.

"There's more, and this is why I'm cleared to read you in," Pritchard said. "They know about STONEBRIDGE."

# 11

---

*Arlington, Virginia*

Vice Admiral Glen Denney elected not to live on base with most of D.C.'s flag officers. Instead, he'd purchased a fully renovated five-bedroom mid-century home in Arlington's secluded Woodmont neighborhood a few miles north of the Pentagon. The rear half of the house had floor-to-ceiling picture windows, and they could almost see the Potomac through the forest. Having lived in the microscopic lens of base housing throughout his Navy career, Glen decided it was time for a little privacy.

Certainly, this made it easier for Mia to attend her Gamblers Anonymous meetings without raising suspicion, like it had at Pearl. The Denneys had been in the D.C. area for several years, but prior to that, he'd been on the J3 staff at US Indo-Pacific Command at Pearl Harbor. They were very happy to be back in Hawaii. Maybe the island wasn't far enough away for Mia to escape her demons. Or maybe it was returning to the place she first got a taste for cards. Whatever the reason, they weren't on the island six months before she was in some quasi-legal "casinos" in the darker parts of Honolulu. Glen quietly paid her debts, as he always had, and convinced her to resume the GA meetings. Mia tried to be discreet, but her departures at odd hours didn't escape the notice of the other admirals' wives on their cul-de-sac.

Glen learned during a security clearance refresh investigation that several people noted Mia's absences, and the investigator calmly told the admiral that he'd need to look into it.

Then, something strange happened. The investigator said everything was in order and the case would be closed. Glen found out later that Liu intervened on his behalf. He didn't know what Liu did or even how he knew, but the problem evaporated.

Lesson learned. When they moved to D.C., both Glen and Mia had enough of base housing. Living off base made certain other activities easier. Getting Mia out of trouble didn't come without cost.

The crash of plates brought Glen back to the present. He turned from watching the darkening sky out the wall-length windows to the kitchen, where his oldest daughter, Miranda, was doing her best to direct her younger two siblings to clean the dinner dishes. Miranda, sixteen, was tall for her age, lithe, and, like him, a natural leader. Though they chaffed under the yoke of their older sister, in the time-honored custom of younger siblings, Juliet and Michael always fell in line behind her. Juliet, thirteen, was like her mother, a creative free spirit who was hard to pigeonhole. Michael, eleven, may have been the most talented of the three. He was a natural athlete and a gifted student.

Glen felt Mia's arm slide around his waist. "They really do work well together when they aren't fighting," she said.

"They just need to do what I say and everything is fine," Miranda quipped, overhearing her mother, which started a revolt from the younger two.

Knowing they had about ten additional minutes before the dishes were done, Mia asked Glen if he wanted more wine.

"No thanks, hon. I need to step out."

"What for," she asked.

"We have another round of testimony coming up with the Armed Services Committee, and the legislative liaison guys are trying to prep the battlespace. I was on the ops floor all day and didn't get to return any phone calls, so I'm meeting one of the LL guys tonight to trade notes."

Glen learned over time that the most effective lies were just a few degrees from the truth. The Chairman of the Joint Chiefs of Staff was indeed preparing for upcoming Senate hearings, and Denney, as the head of the Joint Staff Operations Directorate, J3, would prep his boss on current ops across the armed services and the continuing fallout from the Russian attack on the Virgin Islands the previous fall.

But that's not what he was doing tonight.

Glen kissed his wife, gave the usual admonishments to his children to do their homework, soon to be ignored, and went to the hall closet. He grabbed a black North Face jacket instead of his usual leather A2 and headed to the garage, then climbed into his black Tesla Model X and backed out. Finding even a few minutes alone these days was nearly impossible, and as the director of operations for the Joint Staff, Glen was in one of the military's most visible positions. He was rarely without minders. Glen had an Air Force colonel as his chief of staff, plus *his* support staff and a Navy lieutenant commander as his aide, whose primary function was to manage Glen's email and calendar—triaging and delegating the things he didn't need to deal with. It felt like a school of remora was flitting about him at all times.

It was a minor miracle that he was even home for dinner while the sun was still up. Glen gave his junior aide the typical mentor's speech. You might love the Navy, but the Navy won't love you back, so invest in your family. And that was all true, but it was a plausible way to make sure they blocked off his calendar one night a week so he could be home with Mia and the kids instead of attending to the multitude of official demands on his time. It also provided Glen a convenient excuse to shake his staff when he needed privacy.

*A few degrees off the truth*, he thought.

Glen drove south on Spot Run to pick up the George Washington Memorial Parkway along the Potomac. He got off the GW at the cloverleaf at Key Bridge exit, reversed direction, and headed back north along the parkway. Glen pulled the Tesla off the road at a scenic overlook that afforded a view of the river and D.C.'s Clara Barton Parkway on the other side. Ignoring the "Park Closes at Dusk" signs, Glen parked and noted three other cars in the lot. He'd been here often enough to know that photographers often stayed to catch the last rays of sunlight. It was early spring yet nothing was in bloom. Glen thought that the trees looked like desiccated hands. He walked up the path from the parking lot, hearing the familiar footfalls approaching from behind.

"Good evening, my friend," Liu Che purred as he matched Glen's stride. "How are you today?"

"Well enough," he said. "It's a busy week."

"I can imagine," Liu said. "I know your time is precious, so perhaps we should cut to it? Here, I brought you a coffee." Liu handed Glen a cup with a plastic lid, which he gratefully accepted, if for no other reason than to warm his hands.

Liu didn't engage in small talk, which Glen appreciated.

"When we spoke last month, you were preparing for the upcoming Armed Services Committee hearings," Liu said.

"The chairman will testify next week," Denney confirmed. "I'll be preparing him on all of our current operations, with a focus on Operation TRITON SHIELD." As the Joint Staff J3, Denney had visibility of all US military missions activity across the globe, save the few Joint Special Operations Command (JSOC) activities restricted to presidential eyes only. Each four-star combatant commander directed the operations within their respective areas of responsibility, and that activity filtered up to the Joint Staff J3 for monitoring, situational awareness, and communications. Denney's directorate also managed the National Military Command Center (NMCC), which kept eyes on every critical activity around the world and managed the emergency action messaging to commanders, command-and-control centers, and special purpose aircraft all over the world.

There was little the US military did that Glen Denney did not have eyes on.

Which meant there was little the Ministry of State Security didn't also have eyes on.

"The big focus of this hearing is the Russians. SASC is angry that neither we, nor the intelligence community, knew about the project." The Russians were holding to their story that Arkhangel-2 was a weather satellite, consistent with their doctrine of spreading falsehoods long enough that people believed them to be true. The head of the DIA would be fired. This was a costly mistake for the intelligence community. It already cost CIA the head of their clandestine service and now SECDEF was going to offer the three-star commander of DIA to placate the policymakers.

"My government continues to be interested in the STONEBRIDGE operation," Liu said.

Denney sipped his coffee to mask his frustration. He'd told Liu what he knew about that last month and was annoyed Liu was asking again. Denney learned of the operation because US Air Force CV-22 Osprey helicopters evacuated CIA officers from Guy Hawkinson's island just before the Russians obliterated it. NMCC tracked that operation and issued the emergency action messages to warn of the Arkhangel strike. A naval blockade around the island followed. But since then, there had been inadvertent disclosures about the mission as the blast radius expanded to encompass the broader intelligence community, the Defense Department, and the National Security Council. Everyone was desperate to avoid the wrath of Senator Preston Hawkinson, who sat on both the Senate Intelligence and Armed Services committees.

Denney knew little remained secret in D.C. for long, and STONE-BRIDGE was no exception.

Hoping to avoid the dreaded calls for "reform" and subsequent loss of budget, authority, and power, DoD and CIA collaborated on what each was going to testify to knowing or not knowing in advance. It was a rare and surprising show of solidarity among the insular, secretive cultures in a town where information was often more valuable than money. There was also the fundamental law of information inertia to consider: leaking, that time-honored Washington institution to control a message or influence it in the press. Reporters knew to talk to him on deep background, journalism-speak for a non-attributed source.

From where he sat, Denney could learn a lot. CIA's military liaison officer talked to him to get the proper story on what the Joint Chiefs were going to say to Congress. Denney had valuable information to trade, which CIA wanted to prepare their own testimony, and he used that to learn valuable details about STONEBRIDGE that CIA wouldn't ever have disclosed. Plus, the Air Force general who served as CIA's military affairs officer wanted to play nice with DoD, knowing he'd be coming home soon. Between the scrambling to save themselves before the Senate hearings and what he could learn from reporters trying to verify what *they* were learning, Glen knew quite a lot.

If only it had been enough.

"I've told you what I know," he said matter-of-factly.

"I understand; however, we'd like to have the name of the CIA's asset inside Hawk Technologies."

Glen looked over at Liu. He was pushing it.

Glen didn't believe China was the strategic threat America should worry about. Russia destroyed an island with a space weapon and was now at war in Ukraine. Though the conventional Russian military was utter garbage, their information warfare capabilities were second only to America's. They trained, equipped, and employed non-state hackers to harass Western governments, civilians, and corporations. And Russia was still a nuclear power, run by an unstable man. North Korea was a nuclear power run by an equally dangerous and equally unstable leader, and an unpredictable one at that. Iran's own nuclear weapons program was back in production, and it was their stated policy to wipe America and Israel off the map. Africa was in chaos. With all this happening, they were also expected to worry about China?

There were too many spinning plates. Glen knew, because he was the one person with eyes on each of them. If he could safely stop just *one* of those plates from spinning, it was worth it.

Glen viewed his work with Liu over the years as providing strategic stability and fostering healthy competition in a region that needed no more conflict. America spent twenty years in Afghanistan and almost that much in Iraq. Military readiness was as low now as it had been since Vietnam, but many in the Defense Department wanted to point America's guns at China. How stupidly devastating would a war with China be? Glen viewed himself as an unofficial line of defense.

But by that same token, why weren't Liu's interests limited to the Pacific region? Denney couldn't fathom China's interest in Hawkinson and would again remind his old friend that he was not privy to CIA source material or operational data.

"We've been over this, Che. I don't have access to that. No one in the DoD does. I also don't need to know, so I can't ask questions about it without raising suspicion. I have gotten a lot of details from our military affairs officer, but he's not cleared for it and I can't ask again."

"But you found out about BRUSHFIRE," Liu said.

"That was different. The NSC directed DoD and the Agency to coordinate those two." They feared triggering a war, Denney knew, but left it unsaid.

"Would your National Security Council know about STONEBRIDGE?"

Denney shrugged. "I assume so, but that's speculation. Again, they don't share sources, but certain kinds of operations require NSC approval first. I imagine they know about it."

"I see," was all Liu said. Then, "Well, on behalf of my government, thank you for the information on BRUSHFIRE. We appreciate your continued commitment to peace and stability between our two peoples."

Denney lobbied the chairman against TRITON SHIELD, calling it an unnecessary provocation. There was no operational reason to test that technology in Taiwan. He believed America's commitment to the defense of Taiwan, enshrined in US law in the 1950s and reaffirmed later, was foolish and outdated. The country would go to war over an island the rest of the world recognized as Chinese?

Denney tipped Liu on TRITON SHIELD, so the Chinese government knew this wasn't the precursor to an actual military operation. He'd learned of the CIA operation to foment unrest in Hong Kong because the NSC insisted that DoD and the Agency share information on their respective activities so that one didn't inadvertently reveal the other. SECDEF wanted assurances the Agency wasn't trying any of its usual bullshit that might ruin the AI weapons test and show of force. Glen wasn't privy to much, just that the CIA was planning something on Hong Kong, that their chief spook moved up the timeline to coincide with TRITON SHEILD.

"Anyway, we are quite grateful," Liu said. "We've made a deposit in the usual place for fifty thousand dollars."

"I appreciate that," Denney said.

"Well, I'm sure you need to get back to your family. I look forward to our meeting next month. Again, the People's Republic would be grateful for anything you learn about STONEBRIDGE."

Liu left Denney, disappearing into the darkness.

# 12

---

*Geneva, Switzerland*

"It's a complete and utter fuck-up, is what it is," Sheryl Hawkinson shouted loud enough that Guy was worried it was going to shake the windows.

Guy had his back to his sister. He was looking out over Lake Geneva and admiring the unobstructed view of the dark blue waters with the light of a setting sun dancing across them. The mountain lake's far side blazed red, like coals in a forge. Guy was happy with his choice of relocating to Geneva and wished he could spend more time in the city. True, "hiding" in a town this small was hard, but that wasn't the goal. Rather, the term was now called "reputation laundering."

Following the Russians' attack on his island, he'd experienced an unexpected surge of goodwill from the global community. Though his own government remained hostile, Europe embraced him with open arms, welcomed them as refugees. After all, Russian aggression was something they well understood. The Russian president, leering and diabolical, oozing deceit and deception, overplayed his hand and found himself outside the greater European community that he so desperately wanted not just to be part of but to lead. However, a series of catastrophic overreaches—attacking Hawkinson with a space-launched kinetic weapon and a disastrous invasion of Ukraine—isolated Russia from Europe. Perhaps forever solidifying them as "not" European.

And Guy Hawkinson was never one to waste a crisis.

In the six short months since his relocation to Switzerland, Guy pressed the goodwill with the United Nations and many other international organizations based here. He announced new research initiatives to combat climate change and famine, vowing to use his research apparatus for the good of humankind. The European Union gobbled it up. Multiple projects were in development, with some already underway.

But the US Justice Department was still a lurking specter. Cozying up to the British, the Swiss, the UN, and the Germans may provide some level of insulation, but it wasn't a shield. Thanks to contacts he still had in government, amplified by some covert digital surveillance tools he'd deployed on Justice Department networks, he knew they were looking at him. Guy had done business with many federal agencies as a security contractor and a software provider, and he had his hooks in all of them, giving him an extensive early warning net. The FBI knew of his association with the Russians. Jeff Kim would continue being a thorn in his side. Maybe now *wasn't* the right time for an assassination campaign.

"Are you even listening to me, Guy?"

"Unless you lower your voice, Sheryl, they're going to be listening to you in New York."

"You need to explain to me—"

Guy wheeled on his sister and closed the distance between them in two long strides. "I don't *need* to explain *anything* to you. I told you we needed another two years before I would be comfortable using this in the field. But you are incapable of listening."

Red lines flushed across Sheryl's already clifflike cheeks and her eyes narrowed to angry slits.

"They asked for a surgical removal, not a massacre," she said.

Guy shook his head slowly. "We created the world's first biological sniper rifle. It did the job. But I cautioned you, and them, that if we used this before we operationalized it, there could be consequences."

"You didn't tell me you killed an entire family."

"Since when have you cared about collateral damage?"

The weapon was, without question, miraculous. It just needed more time.

The original MIT research team called them "xenobots." They were AI-designed, programmable biological robots developed from frog DNA first attempted in 2018. The bots were self-replicating, meaning a few could create more, imprinting them with the original programming. One of the project's first uses was helping patients who experienced difficulty with blood clotting. Guy's team pivoted on that and designed the xenobots to swarm a target's heart and simply start replicating. Once activated, they would cut off the blood supply to the heart and the target would experience a fatal heart attack. The xenobots then died with the host, rendering them undetectable in an autopsy.

The real secret was the targeting.

The bots used the subject's DNA imprint to start their replication cycle. In theory, someone could deploy the bots in a large population and be harmless to everyone but intended targets. That, again, was the theory. Unfortunately, for Sir Archibald Chalcroft, M.P., the xenobots couldn't distinguish between Archibald's and his children's DNA. Guy had a research team of Archon loyalists scrambling to understand why the targeting hadn't worked. These engineers weren't the ones who'd developed the bots, though, which made the investigation much more difficult. But Guy couldn't exactly loop his bioengineering team in on the bot's true purpose.

"Chalcroft was a Trinity member. He knew the stakes. He's a combatant," Guy said dismissively. He walked over to the wet bar to pour himself a drink.

"His children weren't," Sheryl spat.

Guy poured a scotch, tilted his head, and said, "You're only concerned about the potential for exposure. Please don't do the 'but the children' bit."

Guy hated that his actions took innocent lives. He'd trained every day as a soldier to prevent civilian casualties. Chalcroft's children weren't in this fight. Of course, Guy understood collateral damage was often an unavoidable part of war. That was one thing he hoped his technology could one day prevent. Yes, Chalcroft put them at risk by continuing his association with that absurd, antiquated band, but his sins should not translate to his family. In fact, one of the primary goals was to prevent secondary effects like this.

Guy felt genuine guilt and remorse, but he refused to allow Sheryl or their seniors within Archon to hold his nose in it. Guy told them the tech wasn't ready and that it was too soon after the Caribbean disaster to poke their heads out of the foxhole. But he couldn't sway these idiots. They spent so long immersing themselves in grand strategy that they were completely blind to tactical realities.

His drink prepared, Guy turned to face his sister. He didn't offer her one. "Sheryl, I'll say this only once more. I warned you not to do this. I told you the weapon wasn't ready yet. You acted anyway. You told the rest of the organization we could do it. Or you didn't tell them we couldn't. Ultimately, it's the same thing. I won't be blamed for it." Guy took a healthy drink from his tumbler. "Now, there is *no* risk of exposure. The bots died when the host did. Even if they didn't, it would just look like a massive blood clot."

"You can't be sure," Sheryl half-shouted in a tremulous voice. "You can't be sure of anything."

"Like hell I can't. We tested that. The only part that wasn't ready was the DNA targeting. I was very specific on that point."

"I'm not worried about the British police, Guy. If Trinity finds out, we have this—"

"They. Won't," Guy said.

"They'd better not," Sheryl said. "I'm leaving."

"It's not the train station, dear sister. You don't need to announce your departure."

Guy tried to summon empathy for her, but she made it so damned hard. Sheryl had returned to the US after the island to run her business but enrolled her two children in boarding schools here in Switzerland. Likely, the experience was the same for them, just with the improved scenery of the Swiss Alps over New Hampshire. Instead of being a pragmatist, she was burning jet fuel flying between Geneva and Palo Alto to balance managing the businesses, maintaining a public face in the States, and liaising with Archon here in Europe. Again, Guy tried to feel for her. They were new to Archon and not yet fully proven or accepted. This Chalcroft debacle wasn't helping. Neither Guy nor Sheryl were full members of the leadership.

That would have to change.

Already, one of his AIs continually and secretly scrubbed the world's open networks for vulnerabilities and tested them. The system logged all new vulnerabilities for later exploitation, doing the work of an army of human hackers. The zero-day exploits that system uncovered gave Hawkinson's team unhindered access into many of the world's computer systems, networking equipment, and smartphones. Already, he could eavesdrop on the conversations of certain world leaders.

And that was just the beginning.

One of their chief targets was the command-and-control systems of the world's nuclear arsenals. Yes, those were air-gapped and fully isolated systems. But so was the Iranian nuclear reactor at Natanz, and the chain of exploits eventually called "stuxnet" still infected it, setting Iran's nuclear program back a decade. One of Guy's top priorities was to gain access to the nuclear kill chain of the world's nuclear powers so that he could render them inert. It was a lofty goal, to be sure, taking years to achieve. But it was a worthy effort. After all, one could not conduct diplomacy with a gun to one's head. Level the playing field and, well, things became possible. Archon's goal was still to win AI supremacy, but what good was ruling over a destroyed world?

Guy's door opened, and his lieutenant, Matthew Kirby, entered. Kirby was still recovering from his torture and maiming at the hands of the Russians and their barely leashed monsters in the mercenary outfit known as the Vavakin Group. Guy got Kirby the best medical care money could buy, the most advanced rehabilitation, and he still walked with a limp. Likely, he would for life. Guy offered to let Kirby retire on the island paradise of his choice. Hell, Guy offered to buy Matt his own island in the Exumas, but Kirby declined. He worked like a man possessed, focused and dedicated. Kirby was one of the few on Guy's staff who knew about Archon and its mission. He wanted a world where people like Colonel Sergei Petrov and his devilish superiors in the Russian government could never act with impunity. Or at all. The Russians captured and tortured Matt on American soil. The US government did nothing about it and then rolled over to let the Russians bomb Guy from orbit.

"Hey, Matt," Guy said.

"I saw Sheryl storm out of here. She looked pretty pissed." He smirked. "More than usual, anyway."

Guy shrugged. "Grab a drink. I was just about to call you."

Kirby walked over to the bar, poured a glass, and then met his boss at the pair of oversized leather chairs offset from the main office.

"Samantha Klein phoned," Guy said. "She's coming in tomorrow."

Klein was his lifeline into Archon, instrumental in the Hawkinsons' introduction into that society.

"Is this another mole hunt?"

"'Periodic security review,'" Guy said, and swirled his glass with a sarcastic flourish. "Look, she's not wrong. We have to stay vigilant. CIA and Mossad have both tried to get in here. Now we need to be on guard for MI6, too."

"Ease up, boss. You're making me feel claustrophobic."

Guy smiled.

"All the same, I agree with her. We need to keep eyes out. I wish she'd knock the mole shit off. We had leaks on the island, but we plugged them."

"Think this is just covering for her niece?" Kirby ventured.

"Partially, yeah." Samantha's niece, Ava, was a Mossad officer who had worked her way into Hawkinson's company under the cover of being a top-tier management consultant in D.C. Samantha outed her on the island. Guy attempted to have Ava executed, but she'd escaped. *Say this about Mossad, they don't go down easily.* But ever since the island, Samantha believed there was still a leak. She had a particular ire for anyone Hawk Technologies hired in the three to four months leading up to the incident, arguing, "That's when the wheels came off the bus."

Guy said, "Give her whatever she asks for. She can interview anyone she wishes with supervision, but I want a report on everything she does."

"You got it."

Guy didn't know exactly why, but he didn't fully trust Klein. Yet another reason that he should call the shots.

# 13

Langley, Virginia

*Hollywood ruined us for command centers,* Colt mused as Thorpe opened the meeting.

NTCU was home to some of America's most sensitive technical intelligence and most advanced equipment devised for espionage. Together, the sleuths, analysts, hackers, scientists, cops, and the two spooks in the unit scoured the physical and digital world for technical intelligence threats against the United States. But take their offices out of this building and drop them in any government building in the world, most people wouldn't bat an eye.

Amazing what you can do from a cubicle farm, Colt noted wryly.

The senior staff sat in a dark conference room with one glass wall that looked into the unit's common area. There were Venetian blinds on the glass that they closed for eyes-only briefings. The common area was a ring of safes and cabinets, a couch they'd gotten from "somewhere," a refrigerator, microwave, and coffee pot. A fifty-four-inch television hung over the coffee counter that pulled from the Agency's cable TV feed and was normally tuned to a news channel, switching between domestic and international sources. A short hallway connected the common area and the offices for those fortunate enough to rate them and high-walled cubicles for those who didn't. Next to the cubicles was the so-called "Radio Shack," a small lab for the sorcerous minds on loan from CIA's Sci-Tech Division to cook up new gear or reverse-engineer any opposition gadgets they found in the field. Current Ops floor was the one high-tech-looking room that matched Colt's imagined mental picture of the National Technical Counterintelligence Center.

Current Ops was a windowless black room behind another cipher-locked door (the NTCU itself was already a SCIF) with rows of UHD monitors covering an entire wall. The ubiquitous row of digital clocks showing time zones across the world sat atop the monitors. Two rows of workstations were manned by CIA staff operations officers and NSA code monkeys. Thorpe, or his deputy, had a station at the back when he needed to be there. From Current Ops, the unit could observe the global information threats with feeds from throughout the intelligence community and monitor any operations in the field in real time.

"Team, Chinese intelligence has a mole in the US government," Thorpe said. "We learned about this from a restricted-access source. Based on what's leaked, we know their spy is highly placed. They have access to military operational data and finished intelligence products. FBI's foreign counterintelligence team is convening a task force with CIA CI, and us supporting. Colt and Ford—and this comes from DNCS." Thorpe pronounced the office symbol "dinkus," which made it sound like a schoolyard slight. "You two run point for us and liaise with the task force."

"What about YELLOWCARD?" Colt asked, not hiding his anger. "We're running an operation."

"I understand," Thorpe said, "but we know DNCS's feelings on that. I am continuing to remind him of it and leveraging my chain at the Bureau."

The early tremors of a counterargument began shaking deep within him, but Colt forced them down. He rode out the rest of the meeting as Thorpe gave instructions to the team, telling them which of their current activities could pause or cease entirely to free up personnel for the mole hunt. Colt asked for a word after the meeting.

When the last person out closed the door behind them, Colt said, "We can't ignore Nadia's last cable." In her last meeting with her handler from Bern Station, Nadia described a massive effort underway for Hawkinson to use artificial intelligence to source, parse, and assess the incalculable sums of data available in the public domain. Many in the IC believed that this information, collectively referred to as "open source intelligence," was perhaps more dangerous than the secrets nations kept.

Further, with the propagation of commercial satellite and imagery companies, whose outputs were all in the public domain, it created surveillance opportunities that hadn't previously existed. Governments used them to amplify existing surveillance, providing around-the-clock coverage of a target. But what if every picture taken by every private satellite could be collected and analyzed in real time? Militaries would have a much harder time hiding operational activity, for example. Terrorists rarely had the resources or the knowledge to buy satellite time or make sense of it, but what if an unscrupulous actor sold that finished intelligence to them?

The implications of OSI being weaponized on a larger scale were terrifying. Before now, they considered OSI a "horizon threat." There was simply too much data for it to be actionable. The challenge of finding actionable information was insurmountable with current technology. The problem was sorting through the sum of all available data to make any sense of it, to find exploitable patterns or insights. It was far too difficult for even a legion of intelligence analysts.

But an AI could do it.

Whatever else Guy Hawkinson might do, this was potentially the most destructive and wide-ranging. Of anyone in the world, he had the resources and technology to do it. On the micro level, OSI was the vulnerable system, the unsecured passwords and the stolen data hidden and sold on the dark web. It was the crowd-sourced reports, it was the transcripts of every meeting ever posted online and nearly every public thing governments did. On the macro level, properly machine aggregated and analyzed, OSI could give someone predictive insight into the trends that moved entire economies. Theoretically, someone could know what markets to short, and what to invest in and when with godlike levels of confidence.

"We're not ignoring it," Thorpe said. "And you've taken the measures we discussed, right?" Irritation flooded his voice. Thorpe was in a difficult position. NTCU was a joint unit, and he didn't technically answer to anyone at CIA, but he had to maintain a close relationship with the Agency's counterintelligence team and those in his home service. Thorpe struck a delicate balance of supporting the bureaucratic whims of the senior CIA officers he notionally reported to here. He didn't have the political power to buck Agency leadership because he wanted to.

Or because it was the right thing to do.

That would shatter the tenuous alliance that allowed NTCU to exist.

"We have taken the measures, yes," Ford said, jumping in before it got too heated. "I reminded her not to cut corners on her SDRs, but I agree with Colt's earlier assessment that she needs a new COVCOM."

"I understand and I have asked. For now, we continue as usual. She should only use the sat shot for emergencies. Bern Station runs everything else."

"Jesus Christ, Will. Bern is two hours away," Colt said. "We have an agent in the field who spotted enemy surveillance *three weeks ago*, and we haven't done shit about it. The knuckle draggers in CI don't even seem that concerned."

"We don't even know who—"

"Like hell we don't," Colt said.

Colt could see the fault lines of stress cutting deep grooves on Thorpe's face. He knew this was the further consequence of not telling Hoskins about Archon. They needed help with Nadia and they weren't likely to get it.

After a few breaths, Thorpe continued, "You're not going to like this, but I owe you both the unvarnished truth. We already know that Hoskins will not rock the boat with Senator Hawkinson, so it's not surprising he doesn't take this seriously. I don't know if it counts for much, guys, but he's wrong and I told him so."

"You did?" Colt said.

"I did." Thorpe nodded. "I told him that if the Russians would risk a war with us to take out Guy Hawkinson, that ought to be a pretty big wake-up call that he's dangerous. Hoskins actually said, 'the enemy of my enemy.'" Thorpe shook his head in obvious disgust. "He directed me to shift that operation over to Bern Station for handling and said we're out. He reiterated he doesn't understand why this is CIA's problem."

"We're not just—" Colt started to say, then stopped. The other two men understood and agreed with him already. Rhetoric didn't help.

"Hoskins thinks that as long as NTCU is under his roof, it's an Agency tool. Look, he's wrong about Hawkinson. But I can only push this so far and so hard."

"So what do we do, Will?" Ford asked.

"Like I said, we need to transfer Nadia's handling over to Bern Station. They will monitor current intelligence for a few weeks, maybe longer. However"—his voice took on a sardonic lilt—"unless there's an assassination in the offing, they need to plan for her extraction." Thorpe could read the expression on Colt's face and countered it with one of knowing concern. "Guys, for what it's worth, I believe everything Mossad told us about Archon. I understand bank robbers, I understand Branch Davidians and Oath Keepers and goddamned ISIS. I know how to handle shit like that. What keeps me up at night is the thought that there's this doomsday techno-cult that some of our world leaders just might be part of. For the record, I don't trust this Trinity either, but they at least seem to be on our side."

"So you understand why we can't stop," Colt said. "You understand what's at stake, even if they don't."

Thorpe let out a long sigh. "I do. Listen, our top priority has to be uncovering this mole."

"Will, you and I both know CI investigations take *years*," Ford said.

"That's true. I said it's our *top* priority. I didn't say it was our only one."

And that was when Colt understood.

Thorpe continued, "I've done what the Director of the National Clandestine Service, your boss, asked me to do, which is to shut down *our* operation against Guy Hawkinson and transfer YELLOWCARD's handling over to Bern Station. But I'm a busy man and I can't be everywhere at once." He smirked. "Besides, I'm an FBI guy. When I need something from you two, I can only ask nicely. I can't give you orders. So I'm asking you nicely to please shut down your clandestine operation against Guy Hawkinson."

Colt exchanged a fast glance with Ford.

"Listen to me, both of you. Please. Archon is serious. Russia shooting things at us from space is serious. Guy Hawkinson cornering the market on open source intelligence is serious. If this breaks badly and you get caught, the worst thing that happens to me is I get sent back to the Hoover Building with a shitty new job. You two will be done. You may even face criminal charges. And if that happens, the *best* outcome we can hope for with Nadia is that she's arrested."

No one spoke.

Ford broke the silence by pushing his chair back. "Thank you, Will." He stood and extended his hand.

"Good hunting," Thorpe said, shaking it.

# 14

---

*Washington, D.C.*

Jeff had never heard of the National Arboretum, so it was ironic he learned of it from a Chinese intelligence officer. He navigated his car into the enormous rolling park in Washington's northeast quadrant, peering over the steering wheel at the undulating expanse of green and brown. It had been a long time since Jeff had to drive himself. Irritated that he was even *here* in Washington, let alone at a park conveniently on the far side of the earth, Jeff didn't understand why Liu insisted on meeting at a location so far away from everything. He thought the man's obsession with security was antiquated and inefficient. Jeff had a dozen ways to communicate electronically that no one could detect. Hell, he probably could've invented a new one with the time it took him to travel here from California. What a waste of his time. Though, given how densely populated D.C.'s western suburbs were with technology companies, the odds of Jeff being spotted there were sufficient to draw attention. He had largely withdrawn from public life following the attack on his company. This was the first time he'd left California since then.

*All the more reason*, Jeff told himself, *to not be here.*

He'd implored Liu to consider meeting him in San Francisco, practically pleaded with the man. Liu simply didn't understand how disruptive it was to rip Jeff out of the flow to fly across the country for a fifteen-minute conversation.

Or Liu did, and was doing this because he could.

Jeff pulled off the main road to park, then walked up to the picnic table next to a towering coniferous tree where a man was reading a magazine. Spring had come to the nation's capital, and the trees were showing fresh buds, flowers were blooming. Jeff approached the wooden table. He wore a light jacket, sunglasses, and a black ballcap.

Liu Che sat at the table pretending to read. Seeing Jeff approach, he set the magazine down and slid it into his shoulder bag. Liu stood, slung the bag over one shoulder, and walked to meet Jeff.

"It's a pleasant afternoon, let's walk," he said, padding across the soft grass to an asphalt footpath that snaked its way through the park. It was a weekday, and the place was nearly empty. "We have discussed your proposal," Liu continued. Jeff knew that he'd be speaking in vague terms since they were outside. "We believe there is still much we can accomplish together. However, this time there must be certain considerations."

"Like what?"

"Well, we need a token of your sincerity that you intend to take this partnership seriously."

"I do, otherwise I wouldn't have contacted you." Jeff did not hide his annoyance.

Liu stopped walking and turned his head slightly. "You caused my government and me considerable embarrassment, Jeff. If I'm going to trust you again, you need to give me something worthwhile to start. We'll open with the source code for the eVR platform."

The objection was on Jeff's lips, but he held it.

People laughed at Steve Jobs when he said people wanted a soundtrack for their everyday life at their fingertips. Those scoffers objected again when he made a phone whose secondary function was making phone calls. And then the iPhone didn't just dominate the device market but became indispensable to life, to commerce, to connection. Jeff knew that true virtual reality would not just shake the world, it would reframe it. It wasn't just the virtual shopping malls—yes, that would get the masses in the doors, but what about the impact on science and exploration? What could they learn about the universe when they saw exactly what their telescopes and space probes saw? When, instead of peering through a microscope, a scientist was standing inside a cell and examining it or walking through the brain to examine exactly how neurons communicated and moved? How much more effective would surgical procedures be when doctors could see inside the body in all dimensions?

VR would enable realistic, immersive tele-health and distributed education. People in the poorest, most underserved communities would have access to real-time "in-person" education at the best schools. Governments and NGOs would readily subsidize the cost of those VR sets. An immersive VR experience would connect the world like never before, smashing through so many of the barriers that existed today. This technology, appropriately applied, could well be the unifying catalyst for the world.

Jeff would make augmented reality, the layering of computer-generated images over the real world, ubiquitous in five years. With Pax AI's eVR platform integrated into eyewear, they could layer user-relevant, contextualized data onto a person's field of vision. Jeff was an angel investor in a startup designing contact lenses with micro LEDs to render images directly on the wearer's eyes. If they fully realized that tech, Jeff would just buy the company. He saw a much safer world. His glasses would identify whether anyone within proximity to the wearer had a criminal record and if they were a violent or sexual offender by accessing data already available to the public. He would create functionality that would help children readily identify the grown-ups they could trust based on parental configurations and give them clear warnings when they were at risk. Further, it could signal authorities if the child became endangered.

They would similarly change "work" by virtualizing the work environment. People could collaborate from anywhere and finally democratize the hiring process, allowing companies to bring the best minds together. It was so much more than remote work. Virtual reality would put people in the same "room," regardless of where they were in the world.

And these were simply the ideas on the near horizon, the stepping stones that would give them the investment capital they needed for the epochal changes.

Virtual reality paired with artificial general intelligence changed *everything*.

Jeff kept his eyes off Liu and instead focused on the path ahead.

Jeff analyzed the risks and the attendant threats. He imagined someone stole EverPresence's source code, the software's DNA. Jeff believed it nearly impossible in practice, but decided to test the hypothesis as a mental exercise. Perhaps a disgruntled employee downloaded it onto their machine and sold it to a competitor? If said competitor built their own version, Pax AI might lose their lock on the market, but they would still be first. And the competitor wouldn't have Jeff, wouldn't have Saturn, and the advancements they were developing together.

Other companies made phones that played music, Jeff reasoned, but they were barely ubiquitous.

And honestly, what advancements had the Chinese made in recent decades that shaped the world? They were practically making innovation a crime, except in their government-directed tech companies. If the Chinese somehow gained the eVR source code, what, truly, could they do with it? All the advances Jeff envisioned, the way he would reframe the world, Saturn held these, or they were still concepts in his own mind, not yet articulated anywhere. Sure, he'd needed to tease his vision with the EverPresence team in order to make the sale attractive to them. He offered glimpses of this golden future to investors, but the true secrets of potential were safe with him.

The Chinese government installed an oversight board in most of their technology companies. These government minders directed what those companies did, what they developed. They only built things that were relevant to the government's goals. Entrepreneurs, innovators, inventors didn't exist in China the way they did in the West. Yes, the Chinese currently led the world in AI research and quantum computing, but Jeff knew they could only take it so far before their practices stymied the very advances they sought. Their policy of walling their citizens off from the global internet, controlling what they saw, what they learned, would only set them further away.

The US government would never allow a Chinese-developed VR platform to be sold in America for the same reasons they now restricted modems, phones, and computers made by Chinese firms.

So if the Chinese got his VR tech, what could they do with it? They couldn't beat him.

Jeff thought, however, of the EverPresence team as he considered his actions. This was their work, though their vision fell far short of his own. Without question, Jeff had taken a novel concept with promise and put it on the pathway to be the next iPhone, the next automobile, the next internet. Without him, the cash-strapped startup would have sold to a gaming company, relegated to rendering realistic dragons and race cars and alien soldiers. Still, as a victim of theft himself, Jeff knew how it felt to have someone stand upon one's shoulders and claim as their own that which they had not earned.

It would sting, yes.

Better to endure some pain now than live in a world where Guy Hawkinson had a back door into the world's data. Guy was a traitor and a thief who built an empire on the backs of better men. He could already rival the world's leading technology companies with what he'd stolen from Jeff. And Hawkinson was what he'd always been, a mercenary. A man like him could sell AGI to the worst of humanity. The only thing Jeff truly feared was someone developing a machine that could think and reason like humans and then weaponizing it. Theoretically, AGI could self-learn on a quantum scale, making the kinds of intellectual advancements in weeks that took humans a thousand years. Technologies the human mind hadn't yet imagined would be born, harnessed, and deployed in relative eye-blinks. In his darker moments, Jeff envisioned swarms of AI-controlled drones that could target anyone Guy Hawkinson considered a threat. There would be no defense.

Any technology could be dangerous. Man couldn't survive the winter without fire. But uncontrolled, fire creates untold devastation. AGI was no different. Unless its creator designed ethics into the learning model, it would be calamitous for humankind.

Today's thought leaders couldn't agree on whether Artificial General Intelligence, a computer that could think and reason on a human level, was even possible. AI, distilled to a somewhat reductive concept, was essentially calculation and supervised learning of a single task. AGI required application of judgment and common sense. It was the missing link that eluded the top scientific minds in the field.

But if it was possible, the fate of the world may well depend on Jeff Kim getting there first.

AGI wasn't the only threat Guy Hawkinson posed to society. It wasn't even the proximate one. Guy might not cajole, bribe, or coerce the scientific minds necessary to follow his crooked path to AGI. He was already a grave threat to the world with what he'd stolen, now having the capability to troll the world's computer networks autonomously, looking for vulnerabilities. These exploits gave Hawkinson, or the malefactors that paid him, access to a staggering number of public and private networks, machines, and systems. He could conceivably access the private communications of citizens and public figures alike, sneaking into their decision loops.

Using the predictive tools Hawkinson stole from Jeff, he could anticipate macro trends in global financial and commodities markets and subtly manipulate them. Or he could use that information to crash entire economies. Who needed nukes when you could bankrupt a nation?

"I'm waiting, Jeff. We'll take the EverPresence source code, but that doesn't end your obligation to us."

"Fine," Jeff said. "But we need to make it look like a theft."

"Out of the question."

"No one on earth has this technology. If eVR clones start popping up in Beijing, people are going to know where it came from. This is unlike anything your companies are developing now. I've seen them and they're not anywhere near mine. I locked our source code in a vault that five people in the world can access."

"If you think I'm going to let you publicly accuse my government, you're sorely mistaken."

"I'm not going to just give you the source code. It would be too easily traced back to me. We need a convenient fiction."

Jeff fought to keep his anger in check. Used to dealing with lesser minds. he chose seclusion, in part, because too many people brought their problems to him. The technical mountains they couldn't climb were sand hills to Jeff. Asking the master was far easier than walking the challenging path to enlightenment. Liu was no different. He wanted Jeff's technology the easy way and had no appreciation for the lengths Jeff would have to go through to get it.

"Please try to understand," Jeff said, without hiding the condescension in his voice. "Our security system monitors vault access continually. It's impossible to access without creating a record. Even if I just gave you the current version of our operating system, your engineers couldn't figure out how it works at the root level. It doesn't need to be elaborate and I don't need to mention your government. We won't even make a public disclosure for some time. Once competing systems appear, I need to claim theft or it will trace back to me. I'm not willing to sacrifice someone for this."

"I will agree with this," Liu said, "on the condition that you never accuse my government. If you do, our retribution will be severe." He paused his stride. "And we won't stop at simply telling your government where it came from."

Jeff considered Liu's words. This would be his last chance to back out. If he agreed, he was in this partnership. At least until he engineered a way out. "I understand," Jeff said. "I just need a few weeks so that I can access the data, securely transfer it, and eliminate any trace of access. Now what are you going to do for me?"

"Guy Hawkinson will no longer be a problem for you," Liu said.

"What are you going to do? That's what I want to know," Jeff said sternly.

"Jeff, I think there are things better left unsaid, no? You only need to know that Hawkinson is no longer a threat to you."

"No," Jeff said. "I need to know. I need to know how you are going to handle Hawkinson or there is no deal."

"My country has many tools at its disposal," Liu said.

*He's being elusive on purpose*, Jeff concluded.

"I expect more detail before this continues," he finally said. "If I am not convinced that you can do this, I'm not giving you anything."

Liu Che smiled. "I would expect nothing less, Jeff."

Liu gave Jeff a "secure" means of contacting him via the internet when the transfer was ready. Jeff, who didn't tell him that Saturn could rip it apart in seconds, smiled as he walked back to his car.

It felt good to be playing offense for a change.

# 15

*Langley, Virginia*

Colt stared at the message without comprehending it, hoping it would go away or that he'd read it wrong. They'd received a cable from Bern Station overnight. Colt hadn't told them yet they were taking over operational control. There was no way they could justify shuttering this op after they read the cable. It was a short message, but it contained a trove of serious information.

Nadia was inside the communication loop between Hawkinson and Archon.

1. No evidence of oppo surveillance on 4/6 meet w/ YELLOWCARD. Emphasized increased caution/diligence. Believe technical surveillance highly likely.

2. YELLOWCARD reported Hawk Tech (HT) AI aggregating massive amounts open source & secured data. Believe hacked commercial genetics labs in US, EUR & Asia, stolen DNA info. HAWKINSON stated

the hack was "test" of proposed security tool offering / demonstration. YELLOWCARD found raw lab data on an encrypted server.

3. YELLOWCARD decrypted traffic between HAWKINSON and ARCHON. YELLOWCARD helped create quantum encryption algorithm used for HAWK/ARCHON comms. HAWK stated the tool was new proprietary commercial offering to hide development of ARCHON comms tool.

4. YELLOWCARD cannot access most secure HT servers. Again requests technical means.

⸺

"I was just about to ask if you read that," Ford said, standing at Colt's cubical opening. "I bet Chuck Harmon has *no idea* what he's talking about." He shook his head. "There is an actual shitload of bad news in those four paragraphs."

Colt had to agree. "Hawkinson is hacking genetics labs. Think he's after biometric data?"

"So what, eight years ago, the Chinese hacked OPM and got the personal information of nearly everyone with a government clearance, right?"

"Yeah," Colt agreed. In 2015, the People's Liberation Army cyber division hacked the Office of Personnel Management databases where they stored confidential information on government personnel to adjudicate security clearances. This included names, dates, and places of birth, social security numbers, addresses going back twenty years, financial information, and close associates who vouched for their character. Essentially, anything a hacker would need to impersonate someone online and have an excellent head start on cracking their personal security. Or worse, using that information against them. For example, the Chinese knew whether someone was a financial risk or if they maintained questionable personal associations. Everything a security investigator dug up while determining whether someone was a security risk was in those files.

It made for a trove of potential blackmail material. The things an intelligence service used to turn a citizen into a source.

But that paled in comparison to the potential havoc of maliciously using a person's genetic record.

That data could spoof biometric security, considered by many to be un-hackable because of its unique and indelible link to the individual's biology. A password could be cracked but a retina could not.

"Apart from the facial recognition on your phone, biometric security isn't in widespread use yet. They may be trying to get a head start on being able to hack in ten years."

"I guess." Ford lifted his thick shoulders in a shrug that looked like it was more effort than the gesture was worth. "Seems like a lot of effort for an uncertain payoff, though."

Colt held up an index finger and said he had an idea. He opened a file on his computer and unlocked it. Anything they learned about Archon was stored locally and kept off the main Agency network. Colt reviewed what Mossad told them about Archon in that revelatory meeting last year. They were trying to create a global oligarchy with them at the top, the ruling class. It was master race stuff.

"Maybe I'm paranoid, but considering what we heard about Archon's actual goals... what if aggregating genetic data was the first step toward culling the herd? What if Hawkinson and Archon developed the ability to determine who among the global populace was likely to develop cancer, or Alzheimer's, or Parkinson's disease?"

"Can they do that?"

"I mean, genetic engineering is nascent, but I invested in some of these kinds of companies when I was undercover. A lot of the human genome project is understanding the factors that lead to disease and seeing if they could identify those factors early to prevent them. The malicious side is companies getting to this stuff and using it for things like credit determi-nations."

"Like, 'Sorry, Mr. McShane, you're eighty percent likely to develop colon cancer so you can't get insurance.'"

"Exactly like that. Taking it a step further, what if they could determine intellectual and physical aptitude? I know it's a stretch, but what if Hawkinson is trying to pick the winners and losers in society?" Colt said.

He actually shivered.

"That matches what little we know about Archon," Ford said. "You know who uses these labs?"

"Everyone?" Colt said.

"Everyone. I don't know the tech stuff as well as you, but we had a few cases when I was in the Asia Division. Chinese hackers trying to get into genetics labs and shit like that. They take a vacuum approach to collection, take whatever they can get and see what's useful later. We assumed they were taking it to get a lead on genetic engineering." Ford whistled. "Shit, man, governments use these labs. They outsource genetic testing because it's such a specialized skill."

"And Hawkinson just got a bunch of them. Nadia's COVCOM shot last month said Hawkinson deployed an AI that was just trolling networks, looking for vulnerabilities."

"I remember reading that," Ford said. "I tried to ask one of the NSA nerds what that meant, but he just went 'company IT guy' on me. You were in the Kong so I've meant to ask since you've been back. Is that how he's getting into these genetics labs?"

"That would be my guess. Remember, the people he's hired at Hawk Tech all think they're working for a cool tech company. They're not trying to break into systems."

"But you're saying an AI could?"

"When a hacker is trying to access a computer system, they're looking for a vulnerability—an unpatched hole in the code. Software is so complex these days, it's almost impossible to deploy it without there being *some* kind of hole. Once they think they've found one, they research it to see if it's legit or someone else found it first. There are sites on the dark web that are just repositories of this stuff. The goal is to find what's known as a 'zero day.' It's a vulnerability that the owner hasn't patched because they don't know about it yet. Meaning if the system is hacked, the owner of the software has zero days to respond."

"That's what we did with stuxnet, right?"

"Exactly. That was multiple zero days chained together to target the command-and-control systems for centrifuges Iran used to enrich uranium. Hawkinson's AI looks to be scouring the internet and continually testing systems for vulnerabilities. Nadia says that when it finds them, it autonomously validates their effectiveness and then logs them for use."

"Stockpiling," Ford said.

"Exactly. He's doing the work of an army of hackers. Coupled with the quantum computing technology that he stole from Kim, this AI will learn and replicate at rates the human mind can't even comprehend. Imagine being able to go from the Dark Ages to the Apollo Program every twelve hours." Colt stared at his screen, searching for the words to express the fear he felt, like the distant rumble of a summer storm on the horizon. "I don't know, Fred. He's got something else in mind here. Even the 'culling the herd' thing we talked about, that's not something that he can do overnight. It feels like there's a closer threat. I just can't see it yet."

"I agree," Ford said. "We haven't talked about this much. I guess what happened on the island is still pretty raw. It is for me. I didn't take him seriously. When we were *on* the island, I thought Hawkinson was just another jumped-up, rich asshole who could afford to push back. But, like you told Thorpe, if the Russians are going to risk a war with us to nuke his operation, he's got something scary in mind. And it's not hacking biometric security."

Neither man spoke for a long time. There were no words that could quite fill the space.

"Job one is figuring out what he's up to and how it connects to Archon. We need proof if the suits are going to take this shit seriously." Ford raised his other hand from behind the cubical wall. He was holding an iPhone box. "S&T just delivered this. They wanted you to field test this on your trip to the Kong, but it wasn't ready."

"What is it?"

"You're going to love this. Meet LONGBOW. The nerds wanted to call it HAWKEYE, but the lawyers wouldn't let them in case the Marvel Comics people ever found out."

"Lawyers won't let us codename a top-secret gadget for fear of getting sued by a company that will never learn of its existence." Colt shook his head. "That fits. What's it do?"

"They replaced one of the camera lenses with an RF interrogator. They can hack another phone via RF signal. The camera just needs to be pointed at the phone you're trying to hack and the device will automatically target it. You just take a picture with the app our cyber guys designed, looks like any camera app on a phone, and LONGBOW does the rest. We'll get access to anything on that phone and anything the phone touches. You'll have to explain how this works —I'm an operator, Colt," Ford said, mimicking DNCS Hoskins from their first meeting. "They tell me they can access the firmware, or some shit like that."

Colt whistled. "That's the crown jewels of hacking. Phones are especially hard to get firmware access to because of the limited number of manufacturers. They must have gotten into a chip factory somehow. Firmware exploits are hard to detect and harder to counter." He was about to say more, but even in a CIA vault... some things were better left unsaid. "This will get us nearly unfettered access to anything on the phone. This is great, but Nadia still needs a line of sight on Hawkinson's phone."

"I know," Ford said. "But that's the kind of spy shit we trained her for."

Ford explained the strategy. This was their way in, their digital burglar to sneak through Hawkinson's physical security. If they got on Hawkinson's phone, they could tunnel into anything he connected to, including his company's restricted files. This was their way to circumvent the prohibition on bringing devices into the building. They built LONGBOW on the assumption that Hawkinson wasn't following his own security protocols.

"How are we getting this to her? We're not putting this in a dip pouch, are we?" The Agency often used the State Department's secure diplomatic bags to move equipment and other assets into or out of a country covertly.

"Well, that'll get it in-country without a problem," Ford said. "But one of us needs to give it to her and train her on it. Besides, we can't tell Bern Station DNCS wants to hand over the keys and shut down the operation. They'll freeze us out. I think one of us goes, trains her on the device, and gets the no-shit download on what's going on in Geneva. We'll be in a better position to plan our next move."

"I agree. But if we get caught, it's our ass."

"Not necessarily," Ford said. "If someone says anything, we just tell them we needed to brief our c/o on the exfil plan and get her some new COVCOM equipment—which is technically true. We just tell the Bern guys on the way out rather than the way in."

"You should go," Colt said. "I'm already the pretty face on this CI task force and after Hong Kong, DNCS is watching for me."

Despite Colt having saved their asset from arrest and exfiltrated him, which also saved the life of a fellow CIA officer, Hoskins was blaming everyone involved in BRUSHFIRE for its failure.

"Not a radar you want to be on, but I agree with you. Besides." Ford hefted his girth in a comic motion. "I kind of blend into the background, so no one is going to notice I'm gone."

Ford showed Colt how the LONGBOW worked so that he could retrieve the feeds Nadia transmitted. Rather than a satellite shot like they were doing now, LONGBOW would break up the messages, encrypt the data packets, and send them back to Langley via different routes through anonymized cloud-based servers. Even if someone intercepted a transmission, they couldn't decipher the message unless they had all of them. One could only decrypt the data at Langley using a cipher randomly generated every few seconds. Its one limitation was its inability to handle large amounts of data—text files, compressed photos, things like that.

Ford would leave in two days. Colt prepared a cable for Bern Station informing them he was coming and to notify Nadia, telling them it was a routine check-in with their officer. The Bern team were excellent partners and Colt didn't enjoy deceiving them, even if that was the nature of the business. And DNCS left them with few good options. They weren't giving up on the Hawkinson case just because he had a powerful, highly placed relative. DNCS was putting everyone in jeopardy by *not* pursuing this, by not exposing the Hawkinsons for what they were. He just couldn't see it yet.

Headquarters disease, Colt had heard a few people call it.

Spend enough time away from the street and forget what real intelligence work was.

Colt closed up his workstation and headed out to his car. Once he was in the parking lot, he retrieved his phone from the glove box and powered it on. When the device connected to the local cell network, it vibrated to life with incoming notifications of missed calls, texts, emails, and alerts from a dozen apps. No one realized how much information they were barraged with every day until they received it in batches.

Colt quickly triaged the notifications, determining what he'd ignore until later. There were several on Wormhole, an encrypted messaging app that deleted read messages and didn't store copies on any company-owned server. It wasn't as secure as something the Agency might develop, but it was a reasonably safe way to send unclassified messages. Wormhole also had a secure calling function.

He tapped the message from Dieta Becker, Ava Klein's pseudonym on the app that she only used when communicating with Colt. His pulse sped up instantly. They had spoken only two, three times since escaping the island. Beyond the pure security of it, and the fact that they worked for different intelligence agencies, Colt believed neither of them wanted to revisit the horror of seeing those fiery white streaks rain down from the night sky to atomize the island. He wondered if Ava had trouble sleeping or didn't feel safe outside, like him.

Colt desperately wanted to know that she was safe these long months, but he couldn't ask. Their relationship was hard to discern. They first met twelve years ago. Colt was a Navy surface warfare officer assigned to a destroyer, and Ava was, allegedly, a piano prodigy about to enter graduate school for business at her father's behest. He and Ava were like wildfire. Colt would have left the Navy for her, was ready to, when fate pulled them apart. A Palestinian terrorist detonated a suicide bomb that killed her parents—at the Haifa restaurant where she was supposed to introduce him. Colt didn't learn that Ava survived for weeks. She cut off their relationship, told him it was too painful for her. Really, what she'd done was join Mossad at her aunt's urging so that she could become an angel of vengeance against the people who took her family from her.

Colt and Ava met again ten years later with fate still playing a hand. Now, both of them were intelligence officers for their country's respective services.

Then came Jeff Kim. And Guy Hawkinson. And, eventually, hellfire from the sky.

Colt opened the message.

**CALL ME IMMEDIATELY. URGENT.**

Colt checked his watch and hastily calculated the time zone differential. It would be about four in the morning in Tel Aviv, assuming they still posted Ava at home.

Colt thumbed Wormhole's "call" function, waiting to connect to a phone on the other side of the world. His pulse, already elevated, quickened still.

"I'm glad you got this," she said abruptly. Whenever they spoke, Colt had to remind himself anew with how direct Israelis were. "I got a call from someone claiming to be part of Trinity."

"This isn't a secure line," Colt said, though it was as secure as they were likely to get. Ava worked for another service. There was an entire series of authorizations required for them to even communicate over an official line, and since they weren't working on a joint effort, they had no reason to.

"We don't have time for that. They said I had to meet him immediately, that he had urgent information about Archon. They also said I had to bring you."

# 16

*Langley, Virginia*

As soon as he disconnected their call, Colt ran back into the building and through the labyrinthine security to the NTCU SCIF. Thankfully, Ford was still there.

Colt made sure no one was in earshot.

"I just got a message from Ava."

"Ava, the stripper you just met and fell in love with, Ava? Because that's the only Ava I want to hear you talking about. Do you—"

Colt didn't need the lecture. If anyone learned Colt had unauthorized communication with a Mossad officer, he'd get launched out of the clandestine service like they shot him out of a cannon.

"It's not like we're 'in touch,'" Colt said. "We just have ways of communicating. It's like a hotline." He gave Ford a crooked smirk.

"Colt," Ford said in a warning voice.

"Don't tell me you don't maintain sources off the books."

"Listen to me, kid, and let this burn into that pea-sized lizard brain of yours. I bend rules all the time, when the mission requires it. But I never break them and I sure as shit wouldn't have a liaison with an officer in a foreign fucking service without reporting it. This is what can wreck us."

Ford's entire agency career was in the field, running and gunning in the dirtiest and darkest parts of the world. He'd once given a duffle bag of money and American whiskey to a Senegalese foreign minister in the African bush. They narrowly avoided their lives getting cut short when an Egyptian cobra climbed into the back of their Land Rover. The minister had information about neighboring Mali that helped the US nudge that country toward a more stable government. Ford served in post-invasion Iraq, because he had to, but argued there was little reason in collecting intelligence if "we were just going to level the damn place anyway" and transferred to the Agency's Asia Division. He recruited assets, he ran cases, he squared off against the Ministry of State Security and the People's Liberation Army Intelligence Directorate in China. And the bureaucrats at Langley, who blamed him when an asset got killed, almost ended his career.

When Wilcox put them together, two vagabonds of the covert world, Ford laid out his ethos in plain language. Colt could get on board or he could find another partner—*it's us against the Seventh Floor Suits*. Not that they were actively looking for ways to subvert authority; rather Ford believed the further away you were from a problem, the less value you had in trying to solve it. The bureaucrats were as far away from the field as one could get, in Ford's view.

Ford's career was peppered with official and unofficial warnings for skirting protocol, but never once for acting unethically. He was an ends over means devotee, as long as both sides of the equation balanced out within the legal frameworks established for the Agency's mission. Ford might twist a regulation, even ignore one, but he'd never break the law. Colt knew Ford believed he didn't understand the distinction.

"Would you have done it if Ava was a man?" he asked, turning to face Colt.

"What?"

"Would you have gone if Ava were a man?"

"Of course I would have."

"Just remember that every time you meet with an officer in another service, it's Day One. No matter how many times you've met them before."

"This is different," Colt said.

"No, it isn't. The problem is that you think it's different. The rules apply to you."

"Funny advice coming from you."

"I only bend the regs that I know better than anyone else, and it's *always* a calculated risk. When I can predict the outcome and I know that it's ethically justified. I never break a rule because it's easier or faster, or because I feel like it, or because she's pretty."

"I got it. I'll be more careful."

"You're still not getting it. If Hoskins hears about this, he'll shut the operation down, possibly even the entire unit. Is that what you're after, cuz that's the train you're putting us on?"

Colt said nothing but felt his cheeks flush with humiliation. He knew Ford was right.

"Now, if you're going to break the law thinking with your dick, we better get something for it. Why'd she contact you?"

"She said Trinity wants to meet. With both of us."

---

Colt retracted the cable he sent to Bern Station and sent a new one, saying he would meet YELLOWCARD in Vienna instead. There was no way to mask his travel from the all-seeing eyes of CIA global services. They could insert an officer in many covert ways, but each of them required authorization from the Agency's bureaucracy. None of those options were open, so Colt bought a commercial ticket and charged it to the NTCU fund site. Colt just had to hope that DNCS had better things to do than tracking the movements of a single case officer. Ford would take his place on the Chinese mole hunt task force and they would pray.

They agreed Thorpe shouldn't know about Ava.

Unauthorized communication with a member of a foreign intelligence service would get him in water so hot it might never cool down. But what could he do? If he told Thorpe and Thorpe said no, he'd lose the contact with Trinity and whatever else he might learn.

Ford said, "I don't need to know what you're doing as long as *you* know what you're doing." And left it at that.

Colt notified Vienna Station he would be in the city, but that the op was compartmented and Vienna wouldn't be read in. Colt expected minimal support.

He arrived in Vienna and checked into his hotel in the city center. It was clear but chilly, the temperature hovering in the upper forties. The sky was light blue, a sharp contrast to the mostly gray and yellow architecture of the city. Colt found Vienna to be one of the most labyrinthine cities in Europe. The buildings, so close together, formed walls that seemed to lord and loom over their inhabitants, trapping them in a beautiful, baroque maze.

Colt purchased a coffee from a café and walked around the city. He wanted to reconnoiter their meeting site, but according to Ava, their alleged Trinity contact would not say exactly where they would meet. For security, he'd told her. That was the second indicator of potential trouble. The first was the meeting itself. Trinity wasn't a government. There was no way to know who its members were. Instead, Colt and Ava had to trust this source was on the level and it wasn't a trap. What limited information they had on Trinity had largely come from Ava's service, and Mossad wasn't exactly sharing the details on how or where they got it. Colt's jury was still out on Trinity. He hadn't decided if he trusted them yet, but as long as Trinity opposed Guy Hawkinson, that made them allies. Of a sort.

The growing specter of concern didn't leave him as he walked through Vienna's baroque corridors. It clawed at him, scraped at the confidence Colt had in his decision to come here. Would he have even done it if not for Ava?

By the time he'd hit his third hour walking through the city, Colt contacted Vienna Station for support. He needed to check in with them anyway, to let them know he was in the country. He also wanted someone he could trust to watch his back. In his curt response to Colt's pre-departure cable, the Deputy Chief of Station gave him the contact information for one of his ops officers, both his direct line at the station and his mobile. Now lunchtime on a weekday, Colt expected him to be at the station, so he called that number first and identified himself by the legend he told them he was traveling under. "This is Craig Archer. I'm here on travel from Foggy Bottom for an economics forum."

"That sounds fascinating," the voice on the phone said.

"I have a few hours before my first session. Any chance you're free to show me around?"

"Yeah. I've got time. You hungry? There's a döner kebab shop on the corner of Museumplatz and Burgasse. I'll see you there in about thirty."

"Sounds good."

---

Colt unwrapped his döner, the Turkish version of a gyro, and bit into the steaming spit-shaved stuffed pita as Nick Conte gave him the abbreviated and unclassified version of the station's ops tempo. "This place is a colder version of Casablanca. You've got every international agency working out of here, plus OPEC, so you have the usual Middle East lawlessness with intelligence. We're right on Russia's doorstep, and those jokers are always up to something. Even now, despite everything. Speaking of, word on the street is you were involved in that island thing."

Word traveled fast, even in an intelligence agency.

Colt looked up and pulled his gaze back down.

"Well, if I was..." he said, forcing a smile as his mind immediately went to the same question. If Arkhangel was the weapon the Russians used... what were they holding in reserve? What secret terror had that regime yet to unleash on the world?

"I know, I know. So, how can Team Weiner Sausage help you?"

Colt snorted at the poor joke.

"I'm meeting a potential source for the first time, and I know nothing about him. I was hoping for some backup. Counter-surveillance."

"Is this a walk-in?"

"Not really," Colt said. "Another asset set this up." A cold sensation passed through his body when he referenced Ava as an "asset." Any mention of her would be risky. Conte would already report his and Colt's interaction in a cable to the Euro Division chief, which might raise suspicion. But if Colt admitted he was meeting with an Israeli intelligence officer, it certainly would. That would trigger an additional cable to the Agency's counterintelligence section and the Israel desk to verify that they knew about the meeting. Colt's best chance of preserving the secrecy of this operation was to keep it quiet, even if that meant being evasive, if not outright deceptive, to one of his own.

Colt hated the feeling.

Finally, he said, "Any chance I can check out a pistol from the station armory? I don't know exactly what I'm walking into here."

Conte sucked air through his teeth. "That's going to be a tall order," he said. "Look, man, I want to help you out. I'm more than willing to carve a couple hours out and do overwatch for you. We let you get armed up, my chief is responsible if something goes down. We'd need to get read in on your op if that's going to happen, and since it's not one of ours—whatever it is— we'd probably need some kind of clearance from headquarters."

Colt read between the lines and appreciated the out he was being given.

Colt could hardly blame them for being cautious. It wasn't as though he'd been showering them with information about his op. He remembered, too, a lesson that Wilcox taught him early on: the Agency's cultural pendulum was ever swinging toward risk aversion, or away from it, usually as a reaction to the Agency getting raked over the coals for something that looked bad in public. Good case officers would take whatever risks they could get away with in the hard job of collecting intelligence. When the headquarters staff stopped backing them up for fear of repercussions from the Seventh Floor, or from Congress, case officers took fewer chances. This bred risk aversion into the service and could take a generation to fix. When the pendulum swung too far, blame masked as "accountability" got visited on the rank and file.

People stopped taking chances.

Wilcox's resignation sent a shock wave through the Agency and sent the message to the field that Congress was coming for them.

"I understand," he said. "Not a big deal. I just don't know this contact."

Conte dropped the matter. Colt shared what little he knew about the surveillance detection they'd run and said he'd contact Conte as soon as he had a suitable location.

An hour later, Ava notified him through the secure messenger that she'd arrived in Vienna. Colt gave her a location to meet, a heavily wooded park on the western bank of the Donau, close to the soccer stadium. When he saw her approach, all the old feelings came surging back. This was a woman he'd have shelved his Navy career to be with who'd been ripped out of his hands by a terrorist's bomb. Fate and circumstance brought them back together nearly a decade later, but this time duty and obligation to their services and their respective nations had pulled them apart. The next time, it would be Guy Hawkinson and the Russian orbital weapons program.

Not one normally given to superstition, Colt wondered, not for the first time, if their relationship was cursed.

"I, ah, don't know what we do here, exactly," he said. Colt gave her a smirking half-smile that felt foolish on his face.

"Nothing," she said curtly. "We don't know who's watching."

"Right," Colt said sheepishly.

Ava fell in step beside him. She declined his hand and quietly said, "It's good to see you. How are you doing?"

"I don't know how to answer that question, actually."

"I was sorry to hear about Wilcox. He's a good man. He didn't deserve what happened to him."

"Thank you. Hawkinson." Colt shook his head. "Son of a bitch is covering his tracks."

"Well, let's hope we learn something we can use."

"Have you heard from your contact?"

"I have. We will meet him in about three hours."

Colt stopped walking and turned to face her. "Ava, what do you really know about this guy? Did he provide *any* proof that he was actually a representative of Trinity?"

"It's not like they have badges or business cards, Colt. But, yes, I believe he's on the level."

"Why?"

"Because he said he had information about my father."

# 17

*Geneva, Switzerland*

Samantha arrived at Hawk Technologies like a desert wind, subtle but blazing. This operation appeared to be slipping out of Hawkinson's control, and she needed to get this back on track. Samantha knew there was a leak in Guy's organization and that their hasty retreat from the island only gave that mole an easy way to burrow deeper into Hawkinson's company. Guy thought like a soldier. Once he trusted, it was absolute. He needed to think like an intelligence officer—everyone was a source, a potential source, or the opposition.

Though Mossad excommunicated her after the debacle with Jeff Kim, Guy, and the Russians, Samantha knew that was for show. They needed to give up *someone* to the Americans as a good faith gesture. She was nearing retirement anyway. However, Samantha still had plenty of allies within the service and knew that Mossad was not running any active operations against Guy Hawkinson. That meant it was CIA.

Samantha needed to expose that little worm before they found out about the strike against Sir Archibald Chalcroft. Unfortunately, Guy remained adamant that his people were trustworthy, each of them vetted. Samantha hadn't achieved this position in life by stopping when men said "enough."

She came armed with a curated list of suspects, but was narrowing her focus to the most likely candidates.

Nadia Blackmon remained at the top of the last list.

Samantha monitored Blackmon's apartment without Guy's knowledge. Archon's decentralized nature meant few people knew where all the pieces on the board were. Or what the board was. Samantha had operatives in many of the world's major cities, and most of them did not know who they actually served. One such agent bugged Nadia's apartment (along with twelve other employees). To date, their surveillance operation unearthed little beyond what would amount to water cooler gossip and fodder for rudimentary blackmail.

Samantha's driver turned the black Audi A8L left onto Quai du Cheval-Blanc, a leafy thoroughfare that ran along the river. He made another immediate left turn and pulled into a parking space in a small, triangular-shaped park nestled between three roads. Samantha grabbed her small red leather shoulder bag and exited the car. Beyond the road, even over the low hum of traffic, she heard the river as it pushed itself under a nearby bridge, lapping the pylons. Samantha saw two men, one seated and one standing, at a bench underneath a tree. One was Bastian Stager, an officer in Switzerland's small but quite capable Federal Intelligence Service. He was quiet, efficient, and effective. He answered to Samantha and Samantha alone. Best, Hawkinson knew nothing about him. The other man was Gerhard Schroeder.

Schroeder was tall and thin, in his early fifties, and had severe, angular features that looked designed rather than grown. He was tan, had close-cropped brown hair that was now sprinkled with gray. Schroeder worked for the International Telecommunication Union, a UN agency that promoted cooperation and information sharing in IT and communication spaces, and established global standards for all forms of communication from radio and TV, wireless and internet, even satellites. Schroeder led the Study Group on Machine Learning.

He was also a member of Trinity.

Samantha stopped several feet from him. "Guten tag, Herr Schroeder," she said in an amiable tone before switching to English. "That's the last of the pleasantries."

Schroeder said nothing, and Samantha admired his discipline. A coward would stammer, "What do you want?" Samantha despised people who wasted her time with obvious questions. She wouldn't compel someone into her presence if she didn't *want* something.

"I don't believe in torturing people to get what I want, Herr Schroeder. I think we're all better served if you just tell me what I want to know now, without me having to stoop to barbarism." Stager shifted his stance, as if reminding Schroeder he was there, orbiting just off the seated man's shoulder.

"Are you going to get on with it, or just keep talking about how beneficent you are?" Schroeder said.

Samantha allowed herself a slight smile. This would be fun.

"Your work in the machine learning group is quite interesting. Being able to recommend the ontologies and the machine learning standards the global research community will adopt is something, is it not?"

"Yes, it is," Schroeder said. He did not know why he was here.

"Work of great value to the world. And to Trinity." Samantha waved a dismissive hand. "Don't deny it. We already know. We've been reading your mail for months." Schroeder was an incredible find. Thanks to Stager's position in the Swiss FIS, he had access to their all-source communications intelligence gathering network, codenamed ONYX. ONYX was based on the American ECHELON system and worked similarly, intercepting telephonic, radio, internet, and satellite traffic, then filtering raw data by keyword for aggregation and analysis. ONYX intercepted Schroeder's communications with another Trinity cell eight months ago, though the FIS dismissed it because Trinity's encryption and transmission tech just made it look like digital noise. The system was quite ingenious, hiding the signal in the noise. But Stager knew better and downloaded the intercepted transmission. He brought it to Samantha, and she had one of Guy's senior engineers decrypt it with their quantum array. Hawkinson trusted the engineer to keep his mouth shut, not that he'd know what he was looking at, anyway.

Archon was now inside Trinity's communication loop, at least within one of their cells. But what a get! Schroeder's work informed the frameworks that many of the world's research institutions would base their own machine learning frameworks on. Trinity desperately wanted to control that. And now Samantha did. Or would by the end of this conversation.

"We've intercepted and decrypted every transmission you've made since last September." Samantha reached into her bag and pulled out a tablet, opening it to the document reader she'd left onscreen. She handed Schroeder the tablet and let him read it, watching the grim knowledge that they hacked him wash over him in a dark wave. It crashed down his face and pulled his expression down with it. Schroeder stiffened, sat back on the bench, and dropped the tablet on it. Samantha admired his spirit, still defiant. Schroeder said nothing. "The Central Intelligence Agency is running a mole in Hawk Technologies. We want to know who it is."

"I don't know what you're talking about."

"Hand me the tablet."

"Go to hell," Schroeder said.

Stager dropped a heavy hand on Schroeder's shoulder, then bent over and picked up the tablet. He handed it over to Samantha, who opened a different app. This showed several live feeds of Schroeder's home, both inside and out. Samantha turned the tablet around, a bemused and annoyed expression on her face. She understood there was always some amount of theater involved in these matters, but she was growing tired of it.

"One of these feeds is from your home security system, which we are inside. The other is a camera we've set up. Since your children are at school and your wife is at work, there's little to see here right now." Samantha checked her watch. "However, at 12:15, one of my men is going to enter your home and go through your things. You're going to watch him." She looked at her watch again for effect. "Right on time," she said, smiling, and turned the tablet back around to face Schroeder.

She could almost narrate the event by reading Schroeder's expression as he watched the operative enter his home and move room by room, inspecting various things. She watched the horror on his face as their man went through his children's rooms, went into his bedroom—the one place on Earth where Schroeder should feel completely safe—and watched as the stranger went through his wife's belongings.

Gerhard Schroeder would never feel safe again.

The best threats were the ones left unsaid.

"Let's begin again, shall we?" she said, keeping the tablet open. "We know the CIA has an operative inside Hawk Technologies. We would like to know who it is."

"I don't know," Schroeder said in a small voice. "I don't know." He looked up at her, his eyes heavy with anguish. "I only know that there is one."

*Well, that's something, at least,* she reasoned. Samantha knew when someone was lying to her. Mossad taught her well. Schroeder was telling the truth.

Not knowing the spy's identity was troubling and would require arduous work to uncover, all the while masking the search. Still, knowing that there *was* a spy was valuable enough. That should convince Guy he was being shortsighted and obtuse. That he should take her warnings seriously.

Samantha folded up the tablet and returned it to her bag.

"We can read your most guarded communications. We can send an agent into your home on some random weekday. Imagine what we can do if provoked." Samantha paused for effect. "Gerhard, you work for me now. I will be in touch."

Then she turned on her heel and left.

Samantha had an apartment in Geneva that served as her base of operations in Europe. She returned there to consider her options and plan out the next few moves on the board. She now had a Trinity agent under her control, a thief in the temple, so to speak. More than that, she could now influence *their* attempts to guide the way many organizations approached machine learning.

Samantha opened a bottle of Alsatian Riesling, poured a glass, and took it over to the massive window that looked out over Lake Geneva. Two glasses and two hours later, Stager called.

"Blackmon just bought a rail ticket for Vienna," he said.

"Can you follow?"

"I'm already on it. The train departs in an hour."

# 18

---

*Vienna, Austria*

The sun dropped below the horizon, filling the low sky with a last blazing slash of red beneath the heavy indigo. Colt and Ava walked an asphalt trail along a canal offshoot from the Donau, a lush and dark tree canopy overhead. The path ran through a heavily wooded city park, partially obscuring them from above and across the canal.

A jogger blasted past them without a word. They could feel the vespers of sweat-heavy air trailing him. Both Colt and Ava jolted at the sudden movement, their instincts honed to react to such a thing. Watching the jogger fade into the distance, Colt was reminded that while they were more concealed on this path, they had fewer escape options. They were blocks away from any transportation and weren't likely to dive into the canal.

Was that the plan all along?

Their instructions were vague. Walk along this path between a pair of bridges, the Kleine Ungarbrücke and the Boerl. Street lamps, pale green from exposure, winked on, casting a dim yellow-orange light on the path. Neither of them spoke as they walked, keeping their attention focused on spotting someone looking for them.

"Another runner, eleven o'clock," Colt said as a shape appeared fifty yards in front of them, stepping off a concrete stair that led into the park.

"I've got him," Ava said.

The man looked to be about six feet tall and wore running gear. He had a dark hat pulled low over his head and wore athletic glasses with clear lenses. The man used the stairs to begin his warm-up stretching.

They were on their third pass between the two bridges. The longer they spent out here, the more Colt felt they were here just to be watched. The more it felt like a trap. What other reason than to get them both in the same place?

"Excuse me," a voice said from behind them. Colt and Ava turned. "Act like you're giving me directions," the runner said in a low voice, accented English. Colt nodded and pointed to the far end of the Stadtpark. "Hotel InterContinental, room 1225," the man said. He stepped forward, pressing a key card into Colt's hand. "The hotel is at the southern end of the park." He took off down the path at a run.

Colt looked at Ava and flashed the key card.

"Let's go," she said. They turned around and walked back in the direction they'd come, cutting through the park, which ran the length of several city blocks. Colt hadn't seen Conte while they were in the Stadtpark, which was the sign of a good counter-surveillance. Colt also didn't have a way to tell him that the plan changed, so he hoped the Vienna Station team was watching and picked up on it from Colt's movements. They exited the park at the southern end and saw the Hotel InterContinental across a four-lane street, dominating the entire block. They crossed the street and entered the brightly lit, elegant lobby, grateful to be out of the cold. Ava spotted the elevator bank, and they took that to the twelfth floor.

"Are you sure about this?" Colt asked. He decided not to tell Ava that he had backup. He wasn't sure how she'd react, and since she had said nothing to him about whether Mossad was watching them, he elected not to say anything at all.

"What choice do we have?"

"We still don't know they're on the level."

"This is our only lead. And he mentioned my father."

Colt knew the void her father's death left in her life and could only guess the pain she felt at having him ripped away from her so suddenly. But his death wasn't a secret. He was a prominent businessman. Someone could easily use that as a way to get her to trust them. Colt couldn't signal Conte without raising suspicion. He wasn't letting Ava go alone, so there wasn't a decision to make, really.

Ava reached across the space between them and took his hand.

"I told Katz about the meeting," she said.

"What did he say?"

"I'm here, aren't I?" Ava flashed that crooked smirk that had wrapped Colt up the night he met her.

"Okay," he said. The elevator door opened, and they hurried to the room.

Colt tapped the key card on the pad. He pushed the door open when the light winked green. It was a large corner suite with heavy gold curtains drawn across the windows. Two doors on the left led to other rooms. He saw two couches aligned to the corner of the room, a coffee table in front of them. A grandmotherly woman sat on the couch. She wore a brown and gold shawl draped over her shoulders and sipped whiskey from a tumbler. The woman smiled at them and said, "Good evening, Ms. Klein, Mr. McShane. Please, do come in and have a seat."

She stood and favored them both with a kind and soft smile.

"Before we begin, are either of you armed?"

"I'm not," Colt said.

"Neither am I," said Ava.

"Good." The woman motioned to the bar. "Please have some refreshment. There is beer for Mr. McShane, and Ms. Klein, I ordered you a bottle of the Chateau Margaux. I know I should've decanted first, but I figured you would want to open the bottle yourself, for security."

Colt opened the bottle of Bordeaux with the corkscrew on the table and poured a glass for Ava. He selected a local Viennese lager for himself from the ice bucket and poured it into a glass.

"What do we call you?" Ava asked.

"For now, you may call me Ann," the woman said. Now that he could focus on it, her accent was British. London, if he had to guess. Colt brought his and Ava's drinks over to the couch and sat next to Ava.

"How did you know to contact us?" Ava asked. "And how did you do it?"

Ann refilled her scotch from a crystal decanter on the coffee table. "As to the latter, can we just agree that I can reach you however and whenever I want? We have a lot to discuss and not much time. I'd like to not waste that on technical mumbo-jumbo." She said the latter phrase with a sarcastic lilt. "My organization has been watching you both." Ann picked up her tumbler, sipped, and then held the glass on her knee. "Yes, we've got people in your respective organizations and they've been looking out for both of you. A helping hand, so to speak, putting you both in the best possible positions to succeed."

"Succeed for you, you mean," Colt said.

"Is there such a difference? And anyway, how is it you two keep ending up on assignments together? Coincidence? Chance is far too fickle for that."

"I'm sorry, I don't buy it. That's too convenient," Colt said.

"Ever the cynic, Mr. McShane. Nevertheless, four years ago, during your stint as a NOC working for Mr. Wilcox, you went TDY to Taiwan and inspected the factory of a chip manufacturer that your cover company was to invest in. Did you not?"

An eerie feeling swept over Colt, crawling down his back.

"Oh, let's not lie to each other, Colt. We're all spies here. On this tour, you planted some naughty code in the firmware of those chips, didn't you? CIA can get complete control of any device those chips went into and no one would know. You got an Intelligence Commendation Medal for that."

It took every ounce of will to force his body not to shake. The op was called ARCTURUS and was as black as they came. It was the thing he didn't tell Ford about when he gave Colt the LONGBOW. While most of Colt's work during those years involved gathering economic and technical intelligence on the global IT industry, Wilcox occasionally deployed him on covert operations like ARCTURUS. During his tour of this chip factory, Colt deployed an exploit designed by the Agency's hackers that put them inside the firmware of every chip built at that facility. Thanks to his work, the CIA could remotely access almost any smartphone made in the last four years. The then-CIA director presented Colt with his commendation medal and instructed him to take a good mental picture because they would never declassify it.

"That job could've gone to someone else. We also made sure they assigned you to NTCU. Yes, Wilcox made the final selection, but our man interceded on your behalf. Is that sufficient, or shall I keep going?" Ann's voice again took on that grandmotherly lilt.

Colt took a healthy drink from his beer.

"Good. Now, Ms. Klein, can I assume I've convinced you or shall I run down your résumé as well? No? Good. The Americans wouldn't let you back in without our help." There was a gentlemen's agreement that allowed the global intelligence community to operate. Every country acknowledged that they would have operatives under a variety of covers, usually posing as diplomats working within other countries. The rule was don't get caught. The State Department expelled Ava following the operation in Jeff Kim's mountain facility and her exposure as a Mossad officer.

Ann exhaled, took another sip of scotch, and set her drink on the table. "Good. Well, I'm glad we're all friends. I don't actually have a strike team skulking about in the bedroom waiting to kill you if you don't agree. Don't have the resources for that kind of thing anymore. Trinity isn't what it used to be, I'm afraid."

"I don't understand," Colt said.

"Katz told you about our split in the nineties, yes? Some of our members concluded it wasn't enough that we were safeguarding the world from potentially dangerous technologies. They wanted to play an active role in picking the winners and the losers. Felt we should have a hand in global affairs. It came from the same place as our founders, just a horrific twist on the logic. Their argument is mankind can't be trusted with technology or governance. Don't agree with them, think they're fit for jackets. Though, considering how the twenty-first century has played out, I can't fault their logic." Ann studied their reactions. "That's a joke."

"Archon is dangerous, I agree. But how is Trinity any different?" Colt asked. "Trinity is still in the game of picking winners and losers, right?"

"Not exactly. Technology is a double-edged sword, always has been. Remember, we were born out of the project that created the atomic bomb. We believe artificial intelligence will change the world for the better, but only if done ethically."

"An easy argument when you set the ethics."

Ann huffed.

"We founded Trinity on the belief that we would one day create intelligent machines. But those scientists knew from their experience on the Manhattan Project how dangerous technology, *any* technology, could be in the wrong hands. They wanted to guide the scientific development of computers, of machine learning and artificial intelligence. The goal was always to ensure that AGI, if achieved, would be created by a democratic people. You mentioned picking favorites, Colt. We did, to a degree. Did we ensure the United States created the internet rather than the Soviet Union? Of course we did. We worked with our partners in the intelligence community through the years to sabotage certain efforts, but generally speaking, we are bad at playing offense. Most of our members are scientists, academics, and businessmen. Very few of us are 'operational.' They didn't even want to let *me* in until I showed them a PhD in Mathematics from Cambridge."

Ann smiled wistfully. "It's not always cloak and dagger. Use our powers for good, and all that. Sputnik was a wake-up call. Didn't require a lot of engineering to put it in orbit, and what they had, they got from the Germans, anyway. The space program was a wonderful cover for our efforts. Same with the Cold War. Gave us a plausible reason to push the envelope, so to speak."

She paused and took a drink. "Eventually, we understood that altruism alone wouldn't win the day. Some of us, anyway. But when data itself could be a weapon, the danger now isn't *just* thinking machines, it's information. The Russians proved they can manipulate public opinion with social engineering, bots, and precisely applied disinformation. They influenced one of your elections and got us to quit the EU. Now, imagine what superiority in this space looks like. Guiding what people think isn't hard when you control all the news sources. We started debating this amongst ourselves as far back as the nineties. That's when we became concerned about *information* as much as hardware."

"Output versus computational ability," Colt said.

"Yes, exactly that. Some of our number theorized there would come a time when the two would become indistinguishable. One of the leading theories on realizing AGI is that it will come from leveraging the incalculable amount of computational power available on distributed virtual networks today."

"Self-replicating and self-learning," Colt said. He was familiar with the theory. The idea was to connect the multitude of individual AIs, each capable of learning and mastering its own function. Those AIs then connect with each other, combining to form a collaborative intelligence. There were many problems with this approach, mainly because commercial concerns drove narrow AI development—systems to solve specific problems or address market needs. To thoughtfully and purposefully combine so many narrow AIs, the parties involved would need to make profit a secondary, even tertiary goal. They would also need to develop a common language to link them. It was a moonshot idea, but it *was* an idea.

"Precisely," Ann said.

"Katz told us about a split. A schism, I think he called it," Ava said.

Ann nodded. "That's right. We came to a point where the original goal of shepherding AI wasn't enough for some of our members. Thought we should control it. Thought that we'd moved past the point where governments were relevant. Why pay taxes to an inefficient, possibly corrupt bureaucracy when a computer could already make the trains run on time? So they left, forked off to form their own organization. A lot of the early cybersecurity firms came out of that split. They were quiet for a long time, amassing resources and getting themselves into useful positions."

"Such as?" Colt asked.

"Running venture capital firms? One of them sold his security firm for half a billion dollars, became the darling of Silicon Valley for a while, and advised three US presidents. Weren't any consequences *there*," Ann quipped. "Meanwhile, Trinity has been in a state of decline, I'm afraid." She leaned over and refilled her scotch.

"Why is that?" Ava asked. "It seems like a noble goal."

"Sales pitch is a bit tough. Come join our secret society founded at the start of the Cold War to build smart computers," Ann deadpanned. She shrugged and drank. "Archon has been running a rather devious influence campaign of their own, which doesn't help. Painting us as computer-worshipping techno-zealots. That 'AI is God' rubbish. Then, they arm the *other* side. Done a rather good job of that, I'm afraid. The anti-tech crowd, Luddites who blow up Apple stores. Try to convince them that computers will take their jobs, that they need to take the power back. Now, they're putting pipe bombs in computer factories and Molotov cocktails through storefronts. Riots from London to Singapore." Ann shook her head.

"What's the endgame?" Colt asked.

"Chaos and instability. If you have enough sustained chaos, problems that governments can't solve, people are quite ready to accept an alternative. They want to upend the world order so that they can remake it."

For the first time, Colt could see the true picture. Archon wanted to upend the global order so that world leaders would turn to them for solutions. But instead of offering them, they'd subtly take control. On the one hand, they fomented this movement where people believed technology itself was the enemy; on the other, they had people questioning the value of government in the new modern era.

"What do you want with us?" Colt said.

"We need eyes and ears in the field, dear boy. Lots of fields. Too damned many of them. We are mostly academics and none of us are young. We need agents in the field, people who can act as our eyes and ears. Hands if necessary. And the next obvious question, what's in it for you? I'll confirm that the Chinese government has a highly placed spy in the US government."

Colt winced at the mention of this in front of Ava. Regardless of his feelings about her or trust in her, she still worked for another nation's intelligence service, and this information was a valuable commodity. Particularly for a country whose official policy was that the side they took was based entirely on the pragmatism of the moment.

"No, I don't know who it is. But the nugget I'll offer you is based on what they're getting. We believe they are in the National Security Council or have access to that intelligence. Correlation of data points, my boy. No, you can't ask me where I got it from. You should know better than that. We know about YELLOWCARD, and we know they are in danger. Archon is aware of them too and the wolf hounds are out."

"How do you know about YELLOWCARD?" Colt demanded. "You need to tell me that immediately, or this meeting is over and I tell my agency and the FBI everything I know."

"Easy, love. We're on the same side."

"Are we?"

"We know about YELLOWCARD the same way we know about the Chinese spy. Because *we* have someone in your NSC. I wasn't going to share this, but to prove bonafides, I will. Sir Archibald Chalcroft was one of ours and we believe Archon murdered him. We don't know YELLOWCARD's identity, so you can be sure the Chinese don't." Then she added, "Yet. This is a 'when,' not 'if' thing, Colt."

"Sir Chalcroft was about to be appointed the next head of MI6, wasn't he?" Ava said.

"That's right. Archie was a good man and a patriot. And he was my friend. His death is a substantial loss, for Trinity and for Britain. Inquest said he died of a heart attack, but both of his boys did too? That's entirely too convenient. And we can't figure out how they did it. If they can get *him*, none of us are safe. We think that was the start of their campaign to wipe us out."

The tumblers started falling into place in Colt's mind. Nadia's last report talked about Hawkinson hacking into private DNA collection companies. NTCU believed AI could one day create bio-weapons; tracking that kind of proliferation was one of the unit's primary missions. Using DNA to target such a weapon would be the difference between having a sniper rifle or a cluster bomb. Archon could release it into a wide area but it could only be lethal for one person.

And there was no way to detect it, no way to guard against it.

Colt opened his mouth to speak, and Ann looked to him.

He grabbed his beer and took a long sip, immediately reconsidering.

There was still no way to prove that Ann was who she said she was. Ava was a member of a foreign intelligence service. Sharing information with either of them without prior authorization was highly illegal.

He knew he couldn't stand up in front of Thorpe or Ford and share that raw intel on the strength of what he'd learned here today.

Ann studied them both. Her eyes narrowed just slightly.

"Ava, what did the Israeli government tell you about your father's death?"

Ava was silent for a long string of shallow breaths.

"Basically, what you'd read in the papers," she said, her lively voice suddenly small and soft. "Hizballah claimed responsibility for the bombing. They did it in response to an Israeli action in Lebanon."

"They're half right," Ann said. Then, dismissively, she added, "As usual. Hizballah hired the suicide bomber who walked into the café that day. But Archon money paid for it and Archon told them to be there. Didn't know it, of course, but when someone showed up quadrupling the fee, they weren't about to ask questions."

Colt looked over at Ava and saw the tears welling in her eyes. A surreal feeling washed over him as Ann spoke. It was like watching a movie, but the picture was off, too bright in some parts, too dark in others, a picture that was both out of focus and yet completely knowable. Had the skipper not recalled Colt to the ship, he would have been there at that café to meet her parents.

And killed alongside them.

Ava survived only because she was late trying to reach him.

"Your father was one of us, dear," Ann whispered. "He was a good man, and I admired him. But he was a hawk. He knew what Archon was, how dangerous they were. He was going to go on the offensive. They found out and killed him for it. I'm offering this information hoping it will motivate you to work with us."

"What do you want me to do?" Ava said. She closed her eyes to hold back the tears.

"Well, ideally it'd be both of you." Ann shifted her gaze to Colt. "Frankly, for what we have in mind, we don't think this works without Mr. McShane."

"What is it," Colt said. He was struggling to control his patience. He'd flown to Europe against his best professional instincts, and for what? Confirmation of something he already knew? Learning Archon was looking for Nadia was important, and perhaps that changed the calculus on whether to keep her in play, but so far he wasn't seeing any real reason he should keep this up.

"Hawkinson learned a few lessons from his little sojourn in the Caribbean and tightened up his security rather well. We don't have any view of what he's doing now. I'd like you to get a little program we've developed into his network in Geneva. Once inside, it will beacon out to the internet without alerting his security protocols, open up his totally closed-off network. It will give Trinity the ability to listen in, but we can also kick down his door if and when we need to."

"We thought of that and ruled it out," Colt said. "He's got a quantum-powered AI actively trolling for insider threats. He'll sniff you out in no time. I'm not risking my case officer for that."

"Ah, well, if the Central Intelligence Agency thought of that and ruled it out, we should just close up shop, eh?" Ann leaned back in her seat and considered the drink in her hand.

Colt stood. His patience was fraying, and he needed a way to mask it.

"Okay then. How will you make it work?"

"It's called 'information sharing' for a reason, Colt. When you share, I share. You were about to say something when we were talking about Chalcroft and you thought better of it, masked it with your beer."

"You know exactly why I can't. You also know there's no way I can help you. It's beyond illegal. They can kick me out just for sitting here."

"Ever the Boy Scout, Mr. McShane. Intelligence is rarely collected in the light of day, son. This is not a war you're going to win following the rules." Ann stood and smoothed out her skirt. "We paid for the room through the night. Take as long as you both need to discuss it. You're welcome to the wine. It was a four-hundred-euro bottle, so it'd be a shame for it to go to waste." Ann walked toward the door. "Should you decide to help us, there is a memory stick on the counter. YELLOWCARD needs to implant that in Hawkinson's network. The software will do the rest."

"Why should we take that risk?"

"What choice do you have, Colt? If you *do*, we keep looking for the Chinese spy. I suspect we'll be faster than your... task force. As I said, most of our organization are scientists and academics. They don't want to get involved. It took *a lot* to get me here and give you that. Our help doesn't come often." She pointed at the memory stick on the side table. "If you pick up that stick, then it's in our interest to keep YELLOWCARD safe, isn't it? Do the right thing, McShane. Protect your asset and help score a much-needed match point for the good guys." Ann looked over at Ava. "I'm very sorry about your father, Ava. I was quite fond of him. Your mother as well. We were... close."

"How do we get in touch with you?" Ava asked.

"There's a card underneath the memory stick. I hope you will help us. We need your help. And you'll need ours, I suspect, before this is all over."

Ann gave them both a wan smile, turned, and left.

Colt watched Ann walk from the room, leaving him with an impossible choice.

He could risk Nadia's safety to inject an unknown exploit that CIA didn't control into Hawkinson's network, putting her in mortal danger. Even if she succeeded, Nadia was still a rookie, and she'd likely get caught. On the other side, there was the Chinese spy, and Colt knew it was only a matter of time before Nadia was exposed at the NSC. Senator Hawkinson's witch hunt had too much momentum. The Chinese could sell that information to Guy and the senator. That was the best outcome. The worst was that Archon also had access to the NSC, and *that* was how Nadia got burned.

"We need to talk about this, Colt," Ava said.

"I'm thinking," was his only reply.

"What are you going to do?"

# 19

*Arlington, Virginia*

Glen drove home, or rather, the car did. He had a hundred things on his mind, and focusing on the road was not high enough on the target list. It started with the panicked phone call from Mia. She knew, she goddamned *knew*, that he was briefing the Joint Chiefs today and called him ten minutes ago in a panic. Glen got through the meeting. He knew how to work under pressure. Claiming a family emergency, he cleared the rest of his events for the day, much to his aide's chagrin, and raced home.

Glen had a sour prescience that he knew what was coming.

He'd gotten that phone call before.

He arrived home shortly after lunch. The kids wouldn't be home for hours, so he and Mia had plenty of time to get to the bottom of it.

Glen found her in the kitchen. Long, dark streaks hung beneath her eyes like black wings where the mascara ran. Glen saw her there, clearly in agony, and the anger abated somewhat. He was furious, yes, but as the sight of her anguish injected some reason into his mind, he forced himself to remember that she was also sick. She was an addict, and "control" was measured in degrees rather than absolutes.

Glen's phone buzzed in his hand. He silenced the call. Texts to respond followed immediately.

For God's sake, he was *the* J3, the Director of Operations for the Joint Staff. She had to appreciate that he couldn't just go home in the middle of the damned day. Anger returned and bile rose in his throat with it.

"What happened?" Glen snapped.

"I'm sorry," Mia warbled.

"That's not an answer."

Mia looked at him, trembling.

"I... I went to a game."

"Goddamn it, Mia," Glen thundered, slamming his free hand down on the counter. "Do you have any idea what you pulled me out of?"

"No." Her voice was small, meek.

"I was meeting with the Joint Chiefs of Staff!"

"I'm sorry, Glen, I—"

"Don't." He held up his hand and pressed his eyes shut against the mounting throb in his temples. "I don't want to hear it." Glen took several breaths, but did not find calm. "Now, what happened this time?"

"It was a card game in Chinatown. Supposed to be low stakes. But I started winning. And then other players came in and I kept winning. Then... then, I didn't."

"How much?" Mia didn't answer. "How much did you lose?"

"A hundred and twenty thousand."

"How in holy Christ did you lose a hundred and twenty thousand dollars playing cards?" Glen ran his fingers through his hair. "We don't have... Mia, we can't cover that. We—"

"I know that, Glen!" she shouted, fists clenched as she practically vibrated with fury.

"Mia, do you understand what this means? I've hidden your... problem our entire marriage, but if this gets out, I *will* lose my security clearance. God only knows what happens if they decide to look into all the times I've covered for you."

"I know, and I'm sorry, but this isn't my fault. I was on a run and—"

"Don't give me that bullshit excuse anymore. You know what they're grooming me for and you're trying to end my career." When his tour as the J3 was done, the Chief of Naval Operations intended to appoint Glen as the Commander of Naval Air Forces Pacific. It would be the culmination of his entire career, the role he'd dreamed of since his first days as a gold bar ensign. Glen didn't care whether he was promoted beyond that, AIRPAC was the driving goal all these long years. It made the sacrifices, the compromises, the... favors for Liu Che palatable. Now, he was on the verge of losing it all because Mia's gambling was again out of control.

Mia wailed and exploded into tears. Seeing his wife break down, Glen felt washed in guilt. He put his arms around her in an awkward embrace, feeling her racking sobs. Eventually, Mia calmed and wrapped her arms around him as he told her, soothingly, that they would find a way out. They always did.

Mia took a sedative that her doctor prescribed for anxiety (the reasons for which she was a little vague about in their sessions) and went to lie down. She could never truly appreciate the lengths Glen went to in order to protect her. Ever since that horrible morning on their honeymoon when he walked her out of a Macao police station, Glen swore he would go to the ends of the earth for her. Mia was right. It wasn't entirely her fault. Glen studied compulsive gambling over the years of their marriage and knew that the risk, the thrill of winning, drew her in. She felt an inescapable pull to up the ante every time she bet. Mia couldn't just *play*. Worse, when she lost badly, she would often disappear for days to wage a pyrrhic battle to get the money back. Usually, she failed and would shift between despondence and fury for the next several days, sometimes even weeks. Their children knew something was wrong with their mom, but Glen and Mia shielded them from the whole truth.

Every time Mia did this, Glen was reminded of the hard choice he made those many years ago, his own disastrous bet that he doubled down on when his wife again slipped into trouble. He made no excuses for life being unfair. Glen also admitted that he'd benefited from this. Liu helped him, steered him, put him in positions that were to their own mutual benefit. Glen didn't much care that the Chinese government benefited from his experience. In his mind, he was doing what he could to prevent two superpowers from coming to blows. Wasn't it a GRU colonel who proved the Soviet's build-up during the Cuban Missile Crisis was a bluff? Glen saw himself in the same light. He loved his country deeply, and that meant making certain sacrifices that few had the dedication, or the foresight, to see through.

Glen had the same obligation to his wife. He would do the unpleasant, necessary things to keep his family safe.

He had a phone call to make.

―――――――

Liu enjoyed walking the wooded paths of Theodore Roosevelt Island. It was a small, kidney-shaped island in the middle of the Potomac River between Rosslyn and Foggy Bottom. The only negative was there was one way in and one way off, unless one intended to swim. Liu navigated through the park until he found the elevated wooden walkway through the swamp and the little offshoot into a marsh.

Admiral Denney arrived precisely on time, dressed in running gear, a windbreaker, cap, and sunglasses. "We shouldn't meet so close to where I work during the day," he said in a low voice. "We're practically in the Pentagon's shadow."

"You called me in a bit of a panic," Liu said. "And I believe your country has a saying about the relationship between begging and choosing. Now, why did you need to see me?"

"I need money."

Liu's eyebrow lifted. "I hope Mia hasn't been dabbling in the cards again."

"This isn't funny."

"How much?"

"One hundred and twenty-five thousand."

Liu whistled softly. "That's quite a sum, my friend. I imagine your superiors would not look favorably on Mia's problem. Were such a thing to come to light."

"You think?"

"Of course I can help you, Glen. Haven't I always been there for you? It is also in my country's interest to continue our partnership. But this is a lot of money. I need to justify such an expense to the people of China."

"I'll do anything you ask."

"I know you will, because you're a devoted husband. You already know what I require."

"Liu, we've been over this. I can't get that. I'm not cleared for it."

"Glen," Liu said in a tone that was equal amounts patronizing and matter-of-fact. "You are the Director of Operations for the Joint Staff. I should think there are few doors closed to you."

"I've *tried*, but I don't have access to that kind of information. The Agency doesn't disclose sources, and even if they did, that's a restricted-access project. Our Agency LNO couldn't get it, so how could I?"

"Because you're the Joint Staff J3," Liu repeated in a tired voice.

"Look, I already tried. I talked to our congressional liaison office and the Agency's Military Affairs chief. I told them that info on STONEBRIDGE would help us prep for the Senate hearings. Offered to trade favors. No one bit. CIA's military affairs officer said he couldn't share, that I wasn't cleared, wasn't ever going to be cleared, *and* that I should stop asking."

Liu sighed inwardly. How typically *military*. No appreciation for subtlety.

"So who *would* have that level of access?"

"Everything is being run by the NSC. They, ah, they just convened this new strategic working group to focus the government's response to technological challenges."

"Interesting," Liu said.

"I was up for consideration, but the CNO is grooming me for the Commander of Naval Air Forces in the Pacific."

"Glen," Liu said with a short laugh and a long smile. "We know so much about the Pacific Air Forces. That would hardly be a role worthy of our collaboration and your talents as a strategist. Now, if you were on the National Security Council, I think we could do some truly meaningful work together. You would be in a unique position to ensure that our nations didn't come into a shortsighted and destructive conflict."

"Our partnership is much more meaningful with my heading all the Navy's air operations in the Pacific. I've also been working for this my entire career. I've earned it."

Liu had to admire the conviction with which Denney spoke. It was a pity that Americans had such a poor conception of grand strategy.

"Do you know the name of the frontrunner?"

"Lieutenant General Darius Rubio. He's currently the commanding general of Army Cyber Command."

Liu considered this for a time. The strategic advantage of the identity of CIA's spy in Guy Hawkinson's company was immeasurable. Considering the advances Hawkinson made with the technology he'd already stolen from Jeff Kim, coupled with what China was now receiving from Kim directly, they would make a next great leap, possibly even bringing them into parity with the West.

That should quiet the detractors at home. And for a fraction of the cost and time of what that development would have been. This would be one of the greatest coups in the history of espionage.

"Thank you. You'll hear from me soon." Liu walked to the end of the platform and turned back.

"I'm glad we understand each other," Denney said.

"I'll make sure that the funds are in your Jameson account." They'd furnished Denney with several identities that he could use to open bank accounts where they transferred funds from a host of shell corporations the Ministry maintained for just such a purpose. As far as the American IRS was concerned, Todd Jameson was an international real estate broker, so it was completely normal for him to receive cash payments from Panama and Macao and Vanuatu. "Glen, speaking as your friend, you need to get your wife's gambling under control."

# 20

*Vienna, Austria*

Colt decided Trinity was on their own.

He had an officer to save.

"Ann" may have told Ava the truth about her father's murder, but she hadn't given Colt any reason to trust her. She confirmed the Chinese had a spy in the government, something CIA already knew. Without telling Colt something new, like where the spy was, the "information" was of no use to him.

He flew all this way, risked exposure, and broke some rather important rules for nothing.

Colt left the InterContinental and stepped into the chilly night. He looked across the street and saw Conte standing there. The two locked eyes for a moment and Colt gave him a slight nod, their all-clear signal. He nodded and vanished into the night.

"Colt," Ava said, matching his long strides. "Colt?" she repeated when he didn't answer. "We *need* to talk about this."

"What I *need* to do is make sure my c/o is safe." Because of Hawkinson's presumed capabilities, they'd agreed to a comms blackout, but Colt could still send emergency messages through an Agency-built app similar to the one he used to communicate with Ava. He pulled out his phone and opened the app, then tapped out a message and hit send.

**there are no dinner reservations**

The coded text let Nadia know she was probably being followed. Leaving the first letter uncapitalized signaled that the transmission was genuine and hadn't been sent under duress.

Nadia didn't immediately write back.

The train ride from Geneva to Vienna was ten hours, so they wouldn't see Nadia until morning. If Archon really was following her, she would be at risk that entire time.

"Colt." Ava grabbed his arm and made him stop walking. "This can't wait."

"There is nothing to talk about."

"This." Ava held up a fountain pen. Apparently, she'd palmed it when Colt was watching Ann leave the room. It was a helpful reminder that he wasn't the only operative here. Ava unscrewed the pen's case, revealing a USB-C port.

"I'm not touching that."

"Don't be naïve," she snapped.

"*I'm* not. We don't know what that is, who wrote it, or what it'll do. We know nothing about her, other than her name isn't 'Ann' and we don't—"

"She told me about my father."

"Ava, she told us *just enough* to set the hook. Think about it. A Chinese spy, which I already knew about, but not exactly where. Just vague notions of quid pro quo. If Archon was trying to rope us in, this would be a pretty good way to convince us they were Trinity. Even the bit about Sir Chalcroft is information Archon would have."

"They wouldn't tell us they were developing a bio-weapon, Colt."

"Maybe, maybe not. We didn't exactly hide the fact that we were developing the hydrogen bomb. That's part of the gamesmanship. You let the other side see just enough of your cards so they only push the bluff so far. You want them to know what you can do. That's how deterrence works."

"Archon wouldn't tell me they murdered my father."

"They would if they thought it was disposable information." He immediately regretted the words, regardless of how true they were. Ava's expression darkened. "Ava, I'm sorry. That came out wrong, but objectively speaking, that's exactly how Archon would pretend to be Trinity. If I was trying to recruit a source, it's what I'd do."

"So you think we're being played?"

"I honestly don't know. Ann just didn't give me enough information to trust her."

"If she was Archon, why would she give us a software exploit to put in Hawkinson's computer?"

"That's a hell of a way to identify a spy." Colt shifted his gaze from Ava to the street and then in the other direction. A couple having a heated conversation in English wouldn't draw attention, but that wasn't an excuse to throw tradecraft to the wind. His eyes scanned for anyone watching them or looking away. "Let's walk," he mumbled. They dashed across the street and through the now dark Stadtpark. If someone was tailing them, they'd need infrared.

As they were walking, Colt said, "Ava, please give me that pen."

"Why should I?"

"Because I want my team to scan it first. If it does what she says it will, I can have it to Nadia in two days by dip pouch." Of course, that would mean admitting where it came from, but Colt would deal with that in the proper time. For now, what mattered was that it was under his control.

Ava paused a moment and then handed it over.

------

When Nadia got Colt's message, she felt like someone dipped her spine in ice water. Once she read it, she grabbed her backpack and walked to the dining car for a coffee. She wanted to see if anyone followed her, but she also just needed to *move*. They could train her for almost anything, but not the feeling she got when she realized she was utterly on her own and hours away from support. She ordered a coffee and found a booth. She wouldn't be sleeping now, anyway.

Halfway through the cup, Nadia realized she hadn't written Colt back. She opened the app to acknowledge the message but paused for a few moments to remember the correct reply. Nadia could wave off, but where would she go? Hopping off the train and jumping onto one heading right back to Geneva would sure confuse the hell out of any potential pursuer.

Nadia thought about the man who'd followed her when she'd gotten off the boat. She tried to recall his face, but couldn't. She remembered he was average height, blond, but then so were half of the police line-ups in Geneva.

*Shit.*

Nadia returned the message, confirming she would still meet him. She'd learned something that Langley absolutely had to know about. Even if she got burned here, it'd be worth it.

They had to know what Archon was capable of.

---

"I need your help," Colt said.

"You have a funny way of instilling trust lately." He could hear Ava's sardonic wit behind the jab, though, so at least he knew she was open to it.

"Whatever side Ann was on, I'm certain someone is following Nadia. Can you help me run counter-surveillance?"

Colt could hear Ford's voice exploding in his head, a geyser of curses blasting into the air in brilliant and flaming light at the prospect of using another service's officer on an unsanctioned op. But what choice did he have? Someone needed to run interference so he could actually meet with Nadia. If he called Vienna Station for support now, they would have to report it. Colt couldn't pull the "meeting with a sketchy contact" bit twice in one night. They'd cable this to EUR Division at Langley, who'd immediately go to Thorpe. But they might also just escalate the question of "what in the hell is NTCU doing" all the way to DNCS Hoskins.

"Are you going to help Trinity?"

"I'm not convinced yet that we were even talking to them. You realize the shit I will get in if I do that without authorization."

"I didn't know CIA was so risk-averse. You heard what she said, Colt. This isn't a war we can win playing by the rules."

"Well, I don't intend my sideline time to involve federal prison. Look, Ava, I need your help to make sure that I can meet with Nadia in the clear." They rounded a corner on another brightly lit street, moving through the labyrinth that was central Vienna. They'd taken two cabs and a U-Bahn so far. Colt could not be certain they were black, but right now he'd settle for a dark gray.

"I'll help you with Nadia," she said. Ava looped her arm around his and pulled herself in close. "It's cold."

---

Nadia snapped herself awake and only then realized she'd dozed off. Her hands immediately went to her jacket pocket for her phone. Feeling that, she opened her backpack, a travel ruck that held a change of clothes, laptop, and some small gear. Everything looked to be in place. The train's speakers crackled to life, announcing they would be pulling into the Vienna Hauptbahnhof soon. Stewards moved through the cars offering coffee and a light breakfast, which Nadia declined. Her stomach couldn't handle food right now. She turned to look out the window and watched the high-speed train race past the verdant Austrian countryside and then slide into the city.

When the train stopped, Nadia shouldered her backpack and moved to the exit, stepping off the train into a bright, cold morning. Early light streamed down through a large, angled skylight in the Bahnhof's silver roof. Nadia made fast glances to her left and right but could not make out any faces in the pressing throng exiting the train. The tracks were outside the main building, so she'd need to take an escalator down a level to cross under them in order to exit the Bahnhof. Nadia pushed through the crowd to the escalator. She stepped off that and hooked around to her right, finding herself on a U-Bahn loading platform. She looped behind the escalator to give herself an eye on anyone following her, then waited ten minutes, enough time for one U-Bahn train to cycle through, before walking to an elevator.

---

Ava and Colt got a late dinner and found a hotel near the city center so they could grab a few hours of sleep. Colt didn't think it was smart for them to split up, and Ava agreed. He could be a stubborn, overly pragmatic son of a bitch, but Ava always trusted his instincts. Colt believed he was right playing this cautiously. She wouldn't fault him; he had his own council to keep. The *only* thing that bothered Ava was that Ann never once mentioned her aunt. Samantha revealed she was a member of Trinity when she'd saved Ava's life on Hawkinson's island.

Why wasn't Samantha the one who'd contacted them? Ava thought that would've gone a lot further in convincing Colt to help them.

It occurred to her, though, in the early hours of the morning when the wheels turning in her mind kept her from sleep, that Samantha might not meet them. Trinity was likely a highly compartmented organization. If they feared Archon could assassinate their members with the biological weapon, Samantha might not be willing or able to expose herself.

Ava said a silent prayer to her aunt and benefactor. Samantha sacrificed her career to shield Ava from the fallout at Jeff Kim's facility and then risked her life on Hawkinson's island to save her again. She was also the only family Ava had left.

Ava and Colt started moving early. They found a coffee shop two blocks from their hotel and had a fast breakfast. Neither was hungry, but both knew they needed to eat for the energy. Colt's words of caution about using Trinity-provided exploits to tunnel into Hawkinson's networks were wise, though she hadn't vocalized that to him yet. Ava was still on an unsteady footing with her service. While the CIA considered the operation on Hawkinson's island a success, Mossad did not. They burned a critical officer's cover in the extraction, her bodyguard Moshe, and got nothing for it in exchange. Mossad had no one in place, no one to gather intelligence on Hawkinson and Archon. More than that, there was no formal acknowledgment of cooperation between CIA and Mossad. CIA would not be sharing any Hawkinson-related intel.

Not officially, at any rate.

Katz was still in Washington and Ava couldn't contact him without raising suspicion. He was the only one in Mossad besides her and Moshe who even knew of Archon's existence. Meanwhile, here she was in Vienna with a CIA officer, both of them so far off their respective reservations it was laughable.

"What's the plan?" Ava asked as they stepped off the municipal light rail at Laurenzgasse, a few blocks from the Hauptbahnhof.

"We fan out and look for the opposition," Colt said.

---

They entered the train station through different doors, communicating through the Wormhole app. Colt wore the same camera fuzzing glasses and ballcap he had in Hong Kong. Nadia's train was due in five minutes. This was a large station, difficult to cover with just the two of them. They agreed that Ava would post in the main station and Colt would go to the platform. He hoped that if Nadia spotted him, she'd remember her training and move right past him. They were supposed to meet in the Schweizergarten a few blocks from the Bahnhof, and Colt needed to make certain no one followed them.

Colt worked through the Bahnhof, descending to the U-Bahn tracks and then taking an escalator up to the platform to meet Nadia's train. He found a silver pillar beneath a glowing blue and white sign indicating the platform, and waited there in a small cluster of people. Nadia's train pulled in exactly on time and the flow of travelers washed onto the platform. Nadia told Colt what car she was in and he spotted her easily. He watched her looking around, trying to spot the tail, and he thought she did a good job hiding that. Nadia hit the escalator and Colt moved to follow, stepping on when Nadia was three quarters of the way down.

Nadia stepped off the escalator and doubled back behind it.

Then Colt spotted the tail.

# 21

*Vienna, Austria*

Colt saw the man on the escalator. He was blond, wore a dark blue jacket, and was watching Nadia with a subtle shift of his head. On any other morning, Colt might have thought this was a guy watching a pretty girl get off a train, thinking about asking her to grab a coffee. But it wasn't, and Colt knew a predator when he saw one. The man stepped off the escalator and, instead of following Nadia, went right toward the opposite U-Bahn platform, where he could watch her. Colt followed him and moved to stand a few feet behind him.

He had a clear line of sight to Nadia, about fifty feet away. She'd tapped the elevator button and was standing with her back to the wall, scanning the crowd. Morning commuters clogged the U-Bahn platform. Already, Colt's direct line to her was broken. When she turned toward the elevator, her watcher lurched forward with a quickness that took Colt off guard. He put his hand into his jacket.

Nadia stepped out of the elevator and made her way into the Bahnhof's main area, checking her phone for a message from Colt. Finding nothing, she moved through the swelling crowd to the long shopping mall in the station's main hall. Since there was no word from Colt, she had to assume they were proceeding according to plan. Their meeting spot at the Schweizergarten was across the street from the train station, unless she received the wave-off signal before then.

Nadia veered through the crowd toward a café for a quick bite and a coffee. The shock of having fallen asleep had worn off. She felt like she was letting her guard down. She bought a pastry and a coffee, remembering a lesson Ford taught her about always stopping to eat whenever you had the chance. She returned to the hallway, aiming for the exit.

That was when she noticed someone matching her stride in her peripheral vision.

Colt surged forward, attempting to catch up with Nadia's watcher. He faked a trip and forward fall, crashing into the man and knocking him off balance. Colt stammered an apology in pidgin German. The man's head whipped around, eyes blazing.

The man's jacket was open and Colt could see a pistol holstered beneath his left armpit.

Nadia studied the person next to her but couldn't tell if it was a man or woman without looking. Nadia declined her head to take a bite of the pastry so she could sneak a look at them when they tried cutting across her path and bumped into her.

"Ah, Entschuldigung," the person said. It was a woman. She wore a hat and sunglasses, but something about her face was familiar. "There is a bathroom just before the exit. Meet me there now," she said in English, then added, "I'm here with Colt."

As soon as she spoke, Nadia placed the voice.

Ava Klein.

Ava Klein of the Israeli Mossad.

She'd also infiltrated Guy Hawkinson's company. They met the previous summer just after Nadia got in place. Nadia knew she'd escaped the island with Colt. She also knew that Colt assigned Klein a cryptonym that was named for an Israeli songbird.

Whatever that meant.

Now, she wanted to meet in a bathroom.

What the actual hell was going on, and where was Colt? Why had he sent a Mossad officer to meet her instead of coming himself?

The real question was, did Nadia believe this woman enough to follow her into a bathroom?

Nadia watched Ava lithely move through the crowd, weaving between the bidirectional foot traffic.

*Jesus Christ*, she thought, and followed.

Nadia stepped into the bathroom. Ava Klein stood at the sink, freshening herself up. Another woman left a stall, washed her hands, and exited. As soon as she was gone, Ava said, "I'm here with Colt. He found your tail, someone who tracked you from Geneva. He wanted to stay with them, so he sent me to meet you. I'm going to help you get clear."

"Who is it? What service?"

"We don't know, but we think it's Archon. We don't have much time." Ava handed Nadia her jacket, hat, and sunglasses. Nadia went into a stall and mimicked a contortionist's act as she changed into her spare set of clothes, then put on Ava's jacket and hat. She handed Ava her jacket.

Ava stepped forward and gave her a quick hug. "Take this," she said into Nadia's ear, then stepped back and handed Nadia a fountain pen.

"What's this?"

"Memory stick. Open it at the center to find the USB connector."

"What's it for?"

"You're supposed to put this in one of Guy's secure computers. I'm giving it to you just in case either you or Colt can't get clear."

"I thought..."

"Plans change in your service as quickly as they do in mine, I suppose. Don't worry about the people following us, I'll try to draw them off so you can get clear." Ava slid into Nadia's jacket, gave her a fast squeeze on the shoulder, and slipped out the door.

Nadia went back into a stall and waited five minutes before leaving. She walked back through the Bahnhof mall, looking for a different exit.

*Well, it's probably not a Mossad setup if she's letting me leave.*

Something caught Nadia's attention, a blur of motion in the corner of her eye. There was some kind of commotion, but it wasn't her concern. She turned and pushed out into the morning sun.

---

Their eyes locked and the watcher did the split-second combat math telling him Colt's "trip" was anything but an accident. His hand shot into his jacket for the holster. Colt snapped a fast knuckle strike at the man's throat. He hit the windpipe and his opponent staggered back, choking. Colt leaped forward, closing the distance. He thrust his right elbow up in a strike at the man's jaw and pushed forward, driving him back against the wall.

The man punched Colt with a hard, arcing strike to the temple. Colt's vision exploded into a galaxy of stars as the other hand grappled with Colt's for the gun. Colt felt a wave of hot pain and nausea and then doubled over. His opponent kneed Colt in the groin, then snap-kicked him in the jaw while he was bent over, sending him flying. He landed on his back and slid against the metal column that housed the escalators.

The watcher's hand went into his jacket.

Colt pushed himself into a squat and propelled his body forward as his opponent drew the pistol. The momentum crashed them both back into the wall. Colt shouted, "Pistole! Pistole!" The German word for gun. Shouts erupted around them. With their bodies pressed together, the other man couldn't get his pistol free to fire, but it was out of the holster, pushed against his body, and Colt knew he was just one elbow jerk away from a gut shot.

He stepped back to allow for a few inches of space. The gun came out. Colt thrust both of his hands in and down, pushing the gun away from him and taking advantage of his stronger downward pressure. The blond man's face twisted with ugly fury.

Colt shouted, "Polezei!"

The man's eyes flared with anger. "Fotze," he spat. Colt didn't know what it meant, but his ire transcended language, telling him everything he needed to know about his opponent. Colt had diplomatic cover, though that didn't protect him if he broke any laws, like assault. Based on how quickly his opponent's demeanor changed, Colt guessed he didn't have any legal cover here.

This wasn't an Austrian cop, this was an Archon agent, likely based in Geneva. If he was legal, he'd pull his gun on Colt and wait for backup.

All around them, people scrambled, shouting.

The Archon agent whipped his pistol out in a wide arc, catching Colt in the face. Lances of fiery pain shot across his cheek and mouth, and as Colt slumped to the ground, the Archon agent took off at a dead run down the platform.

Nadia left the Bahnhof through the southern side of the building, found a cab, and took it into the city. She had the confused cabbie drop her off ten minutes later and started walking back in the other direction for a while to check whether she was tailed. Then she picked up a different cab and had him take her to the Schweizergarten.

The Schweizergarten was a large, wooded park spanning several city blocks. Nadia found Colt beneath an enormous willow tree, next to a pond with a spouting fountain in the center. When she got closer, Nadia saw a large, ugly welt forming on his left cheek.

"Either I was followed or you're terrible with women."

"I'm glad you made it," he said, shifting his gaze to look past her, ignoring the jibe. "I wish we had more time, but I think it's best that we keep this as quick as we can." Colt scanned the park and said nothing else.

"What happened?"

"Archon followed you. I'm pretty sure he got away. I slipped out in the commotion."

"I saw Ava," she said. The look on his face said it was best not to ask any more questions.

"For now, keep this just between you and me. Don't put this into cables and don't discuss it with Bern Station." Colt paused, and Nadia realized he was waiting for some kind of reaction. She nodded, and he continued. Keeping something off the books didn't seem right, but she assumed he'd have good reasons for it and would eventually share them. Nadia thought the compartmentalization just created more inefficiency, the same as in the military. You never seemed to have the authority to talk to the right person about the right thing without a bunch of approvals first.

Colt continued. "We met with someone claiming to be from Trinity. She said Archon knows there's a mole in Hawk Tech and they are looking for you."

"Does that mean you're pulling me out?"

"Not right now," Colt said. "We need you right where you are. They said that Archon just assassinated the guy named to take over MI6. Allegedly, he was a member of Trinity."

"Assassinated? I heard on the news he had a heart attack."

"According to this source, they've developed some kind of biological weapon. Now, I didn't tell them this, but I put that together with one of your recent cables. Hawkinson hacking into the databases of private genetics companies, lifting DNA records." Colt's breathing was heavy, labored, and he spoke in halting fragments, like he was still trying to catch his breath.

"Shit, that's how he's targeting," Nadia said, and Colt nodded.

"Obviously he'll never get the records of everyone on earth, but the more governments and companies move to biometric security, the more people use these off-the-shelf DNA kits, the bigger targeting repo he has. This is just one use case for that data."

Nadia exhaled audibly. "Well, that kind of takes the air out of my balloon."

"What do you mean?"

"The thing I had for you today, which I didn't put in my last report through Bern, is that I recruited a source in the company. He's a genetics engineer specializing in biorobotics. He said Hawkinson recruited him out of MIT, gave him a nearly unlimited R&D budget and access to the quantum array."

"How'd you do it?"

"He asked me out, and I got him just drunk enough to talk. Anyway, he admitted they aren't supposed to talk about what they're doing, but I got the sense he wanted to impress me. He said they're building something called 'xenobots,' genetically engineered biological robots. He called it the future of medicine. Said they're supposed to go into a human body and do repairs on blood vessels, clear arteries, stuff like that."

"Or block one. I know *nothing* about genetic engineering," Colt said, "but I have to imagine that Hawkinson could develop a tech like that and then give it over to some less scrupulous Archon engineers to weaponize it."

"Jesus Christ," Nadia said at length.

Colt looked down at his watch, then scanned around them in all directions. She knew that look.

"Nadia, I have to tell you, this is top-shelf stuff. Really, Ford and I are both incredibly impressed with the work you've done." Nadia felt her cheeks flush. "We need you to stay in place a little longer. I'm going to take this back to Langley and we're going to figure out how to stop it."

"Okay," Nadia said. Whatever they needed her to do, she was in.

This was what she missed from her time in the Air Force, from her life. This was the *mission*.

"Two more things, and these are both critically important." Colt paused and looked her straight in the eyes to make sure she was paying absolute attention. "First, the Chinese government has a spy in the US government."

"I kinda assumed that," Nadia said.

"This is serious. We've got two sources that confirm it now. One of them tells us they have access to intel that passes through the National Security Council." Nadia could see why that was a problem but didn't understand how it applied to her. "Senator Preston Hawkinson is excoriating the Agency right now over STONEBRIDGE. CIA and DoD are both testifying in front of bullshit show trials."

"I've seen them," she said, and the pieces connected in her mind. "Shit, Colt, are they going to find out about *me?*"

"That's why I'm telling you. It's entirely possible, unless we get them first. We don't know yet exactly what happens if the Chinese uncover your identity, but we think it's possible they might use that as some kind of leverage with the Hawkinsons. If that happens, we're going to pull you out immediately. Your existing exfil plans are still in play. Now, you should know that Ford and I are both on a CI task force. The only thing we're doing is trying to find this asshole." Colt waited for her to ask questions, but she didn't have any. This was a lot to process. Colt reached into the depths of his jacket and pulled out a small box, handing it to Nadia. She opened it to find an iPhone.

"A new phone?"

"Meet LONGBOW," Colt said. "There's an infrared emitter in place of one of the cameras. Aim this at any current smartphone and activate the photo app we created called Snappr. It's already loaded. The app will inject an exploit via the IR signal and we'll be able to access it from Langley, even if it's turned off."

"How is that possible?"

Colt smirked. "By the time this gets declassified, we'll all have telepathy." His smile dropped. "You've got to get that onto Guy's phone. The top priority is finding out who they plan to use this weapon on next. Hand me your old phone." Nadia reached into her pocket and gave it to him, watching as he turned it off.

"I'm taking this home. We want to see if they're using it to track you. Good hunting," Colt said, and stepped away. Nadia watched him fade into the park.

She looked at her watch. A ten-hour train ride for a five-minute meeting. If that didn't summarize government logic, she didn't know what would. Nadia, at least, got to take a flight back. She dropped the phone box in her backpack, along with the pen Ava had given her. Funny that Colt didn't mention that, given what they wanted her to do with LONGBOW. Which one took precedence if she could only do one? They had little time, though, and Nadia imagined Colt would not waste any of it covering something Ava had already briefed her on.

*Ours is not to reason why*, she said to herself, and walked out of the park.

---

Colt left the park.

Ava was already on her way back to Israel. They agreed it was best to split up in hopes of drawing off a tail. Colt's own flight was in a few hours. He desperately wished he could go to the US embassy and transcribe everything he just learned in a cable, but he wasn't about to commit this to official traffic until he talked to Ford and Thorpe first. He also wanted to get this memory stick in front of NTCU's tech team so they could figure out exactly what Trinity...or Archon's...code really did. At least he'd have the long flight back to Dulles to think about how he was going to bring this up. Colt patted his pocket where he'd dropped the pen. *That's odd*, he thought, not feeling anything. Anxiety rising, Colt checked all of his jacket pockets and then went to his pants. The pen was nowhere to be found.

Ava.

Colt remembered her slipping her arm in his earlier that morning and saying she was cold. His mind only registered it as a sign of affection. It never occurred to him it could be anything else.

He had forgotten entirely that she, like him, was an intelligence officer and had objectives that weren't necessarily the same as his.

"Oh shit," he said aloud. Colt had Nadia's phone. She wouldn't have LONGBOW set up yet. He didn't have any other way to reach her until he got back to Langley, which meant he couldn't tell her not to use it because that would reveal that he'd met with Trinity. Allegedly. Colt knew she was flying back to Switzerland, but he had to tell Conte what happened at the Hauptbahnhof so they could keep it quiet.

*Shit.*

This was not good.

# 22

---

"They are looking for love in all the wrong places," Ford said. The task force was not going well. After hearing Ford's description of it, Colt couldn't imagine why they would have expected anything else. Multiple government agencies involved, each one believing they should be in charge. While the law was clear that domestic counterintelligence was the FBI's show, CIA was reluctant to relinquish control because the lead came from one of their foreign sources. The rationale for NTCU's involvement was murky. On the surface, it appeared to be a traditional counterintelligence case. An opposition service recruited a source within the US government and was exploiting it. The government created NTCU because the Chinese, the Russians, the North Koreans, and the Iranians, to name just a few, recognized that cyber provided an asymmetric advantage and allowed them to strike at the United States in ways they simply could not with conventional forces. After a decade of her adversaries probing America's networks, stealing technology and intellectual property, manipulating elections and laying the groundwork for strikes on critical infrastructure, the intelligence community wised up and created NTCU to go on the offense.

This was not their show.

Colt believed the only reason for it was to give them a shiny object to chase so Hoskins could look Senator Hawkinson in the face and not fear losing his job.

"Have we deployed CERBERUS yet?" Colt asked, and reached for his beer can. He'd just returned from Austria yesterday, but because Ford was tied up on the mole hunt, they had to debrief after-hours. Colt, Ford, and Thorpe sat around the table in the common area with containers of food from Pasa-Thai, just down the road from the Agency.

Ford scooped another hefty portion of pad thai from the container in front of him and dropped it on his plate. He cracked a fresh beer and took a few bites from his plate. "Not yet. Tech is still calibrating it, but they hope to have it up at the end of the week." CERBERUS, named for the mythical guardian of the underworld, was a tool NTCU developed with a software development firm named Element14. Element14, which was the atomic number for silicon, built a software solution deployed with the Agency, FBI, DEA, Treasury, the military, and even some of the nation's major police forces. The system connected massively distributed data points to identify logical connections between them and then make intelligent predictions based on suspected patterns of behavior. A terrorist's cellphone traffic connected him to a bomb maker, linked to a funding source in the Middle East, connected to a bank that was used by the Iranian Revolutionary Guard Corps, and those funds paid to a Palestinian family identified a suicide bomber before he could step onto a bus in Jerusalem.

NTCU worked with the company to take that technology a step further and created CERBERUS. This system started with a dataset—for example, the group of people who had access to the leaked NSC intelligence—and worked backward using nearly every data point available to government databases, social media, public records, and even bank data to identify the most probable candidates for espionage. The FBI's spy hunters would take it from there. CERBERUS was still in the beta stage, software speak for an operational trial.

CERBERUS did not need NTCU's only two CIA case officers to run. The tech team would do that supported by the contractor. Ford—and soon Colt—would be "supervising."

"I've read your after-action report," Thorpe said in a flat tone. "Now why don't you tell us everything you left out of it?"

Colt took a long pull of beer and thought through his words carefully. Ford and Thorpe had been with him when the Mossad's D.C. Station Chief Katz told them about Trinity and Archon. Both of them recalled Wilcox's warning echoing Katz that Mossad took Archon seriously and the Americans needed to as well. However, as he looked at the only two people who *might* believe what just happened, Colt couldn't bring himself to say it.

First, there was the initial deception. Colt said nothing to Thorpe about Ava's phone call that prompted him to switch places with Ford on the trip. Then, Colt conducted an unauthorized operation with a member of another nation's intelligence service, using her to run counter-surveillance and ultimately meet with his own agent. All of that off the books. Thorpe was a cop to his core. Counterintelligence was just the thing he applied that training to. He lived in the black-and-white rules of law enforcement, not the perpetual charcoal of intelligence work. Thorpe wouldn't understand Colt's decision, would certainly not go along with it. Whatever good will Colt earned so far would dry up like water in the desert when he found out.

Since they already knew about his tussle with the Archon operative, the Vienna Station cable just reported it as a "member of unknown opposition service." There was little Colt could hide.

"Colt," Thorpe prompted.

Colt came clean. Mostly.

He told Thorpe about Nadia's first message to him, which he couched as "maintaining a source," and he recounted the meeting with "Ann." He walked them through Nadia's tail and their three-dimensional SDR inside the Vienna Hauptbahnhof, then his fight.

Colt said nothing about the pen and the Trinity-developed exploit. And he sure as hell said nothing about Ava palming it and then slipping it to *his* c/o without his knowledge.

"So, this 'Ann' told us she's a Trinity agent. She said Archon assassinated Archie Chalcroft. Apparently, he was one of theirs. We put this together with Nadia's reporting on Hawkinson's bio-weapon efforts and his DNA collection. Now, we can paint a picture about how Hawkinson did it. I met with Nadia after Ann, so I didn't have all these data points until later. Nadia is working on a source inside Hawk Tech. He's a biorobotics engineer, genetic-scientist type."

"I know what all of those words mean individually, but not when you use them together," Ford said. Thorpe leveled a silencing side eye but said nothing.

"She said Hawkinson hired this guy out of MIT. He designs biological robots called 'xenobots.' Chalcroft died of a heart attack, right? But so did his kids. That tells me they figured out how to inject him with it, but the DNA targeting doesn't work yet because the bots couldn't distinguish between him and his two sons."

"But the wife survived," Thorpe said.

"Exactly. Different DNA. They are close, but they don't have it yet. Ann confirmed Chalcroft was one of theirs. She also said that Ava's father was too, and that Archon murdered him."

"Jesus Christ, if that doesn't set a hook," Ford mumbled.

"I know it was wrong of me to meet with them without telling you."

"And to not report your contact with Klein."

"Will, I won't justify that, but I won't apologize for it either. This business is based on sources. I guarantee you a dozen phone calls a day happen between clandestine service officers and 'friendly' foreign services, and I'll bet half of them get reported. If that. It's how shit gets done here."

"It's pretty clear to me and it should be to both of you," Ford said, "that it's time we wrap this up."

"What are you talking about?" Colt said. Thorpe remained silent.

"Once Nadia does the LONGBOW shot and we're inside Hawkinson's phone, we need to exfiltrate her. We can see everyone Hawkinson talks to and listen in on those conversations. Even if he made some kind of super-secret messaging app to talk with his Archon cronies, we should be able to jailbreak it. We're not any closer to finding this mole, and if Nadia's name leaks to the senator, you can bet his first call is to his nephew. Guy will kill her without blinking an eye."

"It pains me to say this, but I'm with Ford," Thorpe said. "LONGBOW means we don't need to risk having an asset physically in place."

It was a gut punch. Everything they'd sacrificed to get Nadia into position, to include Colt and Ford almost getting killed, and now they were just going to yank her out?

"We don't know that Hawkinson's phone ever enters the building or connects with the network," Colt argued. "We don't know what his research is without that."

"With what Nadia has already uncovered, we can conclude that Hawkinson is pursuing massive open source intelligence collection, AI-enabled hacking, and courtesy of her most recent report, DNA-targeted biological weapons," Thorpe said. "This is a compelling justification for a larger effort."

"But—"

Thorpe held up a hand, breaking off Colt's protest midstream.

"I have also reached the conclusion that this operation falls outside of the unit's charter. A clandestine intelligence collection effort is something best managed by CIA directly. That's not our job, Colt."

"Look," Ford said. "Nadia's got a natural aptitude for this, but she's not really trained. If half of what Mossad told us about Archon last year is true, they might be as capable as any tier-one opposition service. And they can recruit operatives from any demographic, any nationality. Very hard to see coming. It could be a cop, a soldier, a bank teller. Hell—it could be someone's grandmother for all we know."

An image of Ann flashed through his mind. *You're more right than you know.*

Ford continued, "We have to pull Nadia out as soon as she does the LONGBOW shot. Then we can figure out how to transition the case to someone else. Archon almost got to her in Vienna. If your report is accurate, she didn't pick up the tail. They're probably watching her with more than just eyeballs."

Ford's "if" stung Colt more than anything else.

He felt anger boiling up inside him, threatening to spill over.

"I think everything I've shared is justification for keeping her in place," Colt said. "I reiterate that just getting into Hawkinson's phone doesn't mean we'll get access to his network."

"Of course it does," Ford barked. "Nadia said the phone lockers are because of the shit that went down in the Caribbean. Hawkinson knows *he's* not a traitor, so he'll just exempt himself from the requirement. It's almost certain that he's going to link that phone and any device he has to Hawk Tech's internal server."

*If that's true, why did they need the Trinity hack?* Colt wondered. Trinity couldn't know that CIA developed LONGBOW and intended to deploy it here. This was a second way into Hawkinson's network. *Unless it does more than beacon,* he reasoned. Ann flatly told him that trust was a two-way street. He wasn't willing to give, and she responded in kind, refusing to tell him anything more than that the hack would give Trinity an undetectable tunnel through Hawk Tech's firewall. What if they'd engineered something more, like the ability to scorch that son of a bitch's networks to the bare metal? *Or to light up every Archon-connected device on the planet, give us a chance to strike back,* Colt thought.

"It's too risky, Colt," Thorpe said. "This is already more than we're authorized for. We'd still have top cover if Wilcox were here. But Hoskins won't back us."

"We also can't prove that this Ann is really Trinity. It's not like they've got name tags," Ford said.

"Listen to me, both of you," Colt said. "Hawkinson is developing a weapon for Archon that we have no countermeasure for. Maybe he's years away from perfecting it, but it's also just *one* example of what they are capable of. We don't even know what else they have. The point is, we don't really know. If we pull Nadia out, now that she's got a source, we lose our one good eye on that. LONGBOW is a great door kicker, but it's no substitute for a case officer on the ground. If you say that's not the unit's charge, fine, I'll hand it over to the Bern team. You can transfer me to Bern and the Euro Division. I want to see this through. I *need* to see this through. This thing almost got me killed, and if you can't understand that, at least you can agree that this weapon is too dangerous to be in their hands."

Thorpe, to his credit, held his fury until the end.

"Give me tonight to think about it," he said. "No further contact with Klein. If we continue sharing intel with Mossad, it will be done through the proper channels and we're going to follow the process. Am I perfectly clear on this, Colt?"

"Yes."

Thorpe would have suspended Colt if they could have spared the manpower from the mole hunt. At least that's what Thorpe told him. Colt suspected that the real reason was that if Thorpe removed him from the task force, it would raise too many questions that none of them wanted to answer. The next morning, Thorpe told Colt that he still believed Archon was real, that the Hawkinsons were deeply involved, and that it was a grave threat to the country. If Colt told them about the contact with Ava in advance and the meeting, they could have deployed surveillance and possibly verified if this Ann was who she said she was.

"How?" Colt challenged.

"You said it yourself, Colt. I'm a cop. Finding people is what I do. I have more years hunting spies than you do being one," Thorpe said in measured tones. "Our chief problem is that the rest of the government isn't ready to believe Archon exists, let alone is a threat. They understand nation-state actors, they understand terrorism, but this is something wholly different and our leaders don't know how to rationalize it yet. When that happens, they'll discount it. I've seen this too many times. Frankly, it's how we treated terrorism before 9/11." Thorpe exhaled a long breath, then reached for his coffee cup and leveled his eyes at Colt. "I'm going to allow you to continue running YELLOWCARD, with caveats. I see all cable traffic. Ford too. Nothing goes out without approval. You break off all contact with Ms. Klein unless it becomes an operational necessity."

"Ava is our lifeline to Trinity. What do I do if she contacts me?"

"I'm going to speak with Mr. Katz and ensure that doesn't happen. If he has intelligence to share on Trinity or Archon, it'll come through channels."

"What are we doing about the Archon threat?"

"I don't know yet."

"What do you mean you don't know yet?"

"Colt," Thorpe said in an even voice. Colt sensed the rising anger. "I need to figure out how badly you've screwed this up and what our options even are at this point. Now we have a Chinese spy in our government. That person might figure out who Nadia is if we can't find them first, among God knows what other damage they will cause. I just don't trust Hoskins or someone else to not disclose her identity if Senator Hawkinson presses too hard. Once that's out in the open, we lose everything. Focus on the mole. You are on your last ounce of grace. I want to make sure that's clear."

Colt left the unit's SCIF and made his way through the Langley complex to the secure conference rooms set aside for the task force. He couldn't believe they were taking their feet off the gas right now. This was the time to be aggressive. Instead, they were going to what? Wait and see?

He hoped Ava wasn't suffering any blowback. Colt didn't know Mossad's culture or if they were as bureaucratically vindictive as the Agency. He wanted to warn her what was coming, to tell her that his silence was because they ordered him not to talk to her. Not because he was angry with her for slipping his agent a thumb drive. But Thorpe's notice at the end of their meeting was clear. What was the greater duty? Would he let the woman he still loved get burned over this, or would he play the loyal soldier and follow orders?

There was a clear repercussion either way.

# 23

*Palo Alto, California*

Jeff Kim walked through the cool shadows of the towering redwoods, gravel crunching softly under his feet. The dry air held a heavy mixture of blossoming flowers, pine resin, and a trace of salt from the ocean on the other side of the mountain. He moved swiftly. If someone was going to catch up with him, Jeff would make them work for it. He finally convinced Liu to meet him near his home, suggesting Wunderlich Park on the ocean side of the mountains that separated Palo Alto from the Pacific. Liu agreed and Jeff reasoned that meant Liu was finally ready to deal on his terms. Mostly. The Chinese increased the price of cooperation, significantly and painfully in Jeff's mind. Liu said it was the cost of Jeff's silence and the embarrassment it caused the Chinese government.

Fine.

At least he wasn't flying back and forth to Washington in a day.

The trail led him out of the trees and to a hilltop beneath a brilliant blue sky. Coyote bush, blooming white, dotted the hillside. The air was crisp, clarifying. Jeff made a note that he needed to schedule more time for hikes. It cleared the mind and brought focus. It was good to disconnect occasionally.

"It's a perfect morning for a stroll," Liu purred behind him.

He didn't hear the man approach. Liu wore black athletic pants, a light jacket, and sunglasses. Jeff couldn't recall ever seeing him without a suit.

"Do you have the materials we agreed to?"

"I do," Jeff said.

"Excellent. But I don't *see* them," Liu said.

"What, you expected me to walk around with a briefcase that said 'information' on it?"

Liu demanded some of Jeff's personal advancements besides EverPresence's source code. It wasn't enough that the Chinese reaped the benefits of the company Jeff acquired, they wanted something of *his*. That was the punishment, and the message.

The Chinese economy was in trouble. The pandemic forced them to curtail operations at their ports because there weren't enough people to work them. This further compounded the mounting backlog of stuck cargo lingering from the start of the pandemic. They never caught up. The result was a Gordian knot of jammed goods. China was once the world's leading manufacturer of consumer products, but buyers were already sourcing products elsewhere aided by intelligent systems developed in the US to locate underutilized production centers.

A devastating winter harvest caused food shortages at home and eliminated the surplus, which the Chinese typically sold throughout Asia. This further injured an already bleeding economy. To make matters worse, since they hadn't solved the problem at the ports, much of the fertilizer and equipment needed for China's inland farms couldn't ship in time for the spring planting season. China's internal infrastructure—roads and rail transport—hadn't caught up with the country's enormous size and massive population. They relied on shipping to move domestic goods. Much of the farming supplies were stuck, or there were no trucks available to transport them. The near-term outlook was bleak, the longer term even worse, with a critical food shortage not just possible but likely. This, coupled with three years of near-recession due to the Chinese economic policy of command economy and ignoring the sovereignty of debt, bit at their heels like a rabid fox.

The irony was that in many ways, the Chinese tech sector outperformed America's. Their AI and quantum computing advancements equaled if not surpassed many in the US— except Jeff's, of course. The Chinese tech sector used to mirror Silicon Valley, but in 2013 they left. Instead of building analogs to America's successful applications, the Chinese leapfrogged those and created a whole new economy of on-demand services—food and alcohol delivery, single-use scooters, massages and pedicures. Things that were now common in America got their start in China. And they were all paid for on WeChat, China's one app to rule them all. WeChat was an omni-tool, a self-contained social media platform, instant messenger, travel agent, and video chat, conferencing, and gaming platform. WeChat integrated with the user's bank account for seamless electronic payments and was now the primary means of executing financial transactions in China.

WeChat created nearly incalculable sums of data on user preferences, likes, and dislikes. It knew what services were popular and at what price point. It knew where people traveled, when, and by what means. It knew what games they played. The app knew what its users talked about—the businessmen, the teenagers, the students, the government bureaucrats and party officials, the engineers, the journalists, and the entrepreneurs. That data was invaluable to the development of artificial intelligence because it provided a wealth of information for a multitude of systems to learn from and grow smarter. And it gave the Chinese government a crystal-clear picture on the intimate details of the lives of WeChat's 1.2 billion users. The Chinese Communist Party installed an "advisory board" in each of their major corporations that oversaw its operations and ensured it held to party ideals and the president's vision.

"What do you have?" Liu asked.

"I think you know that our virtual reality is better than anything your country has developed. This will be the indispensable communications and media platform of the future. Your technology industry will have a head start of several years on your competitors in the West. But it goes beyond that. Your military and police can use this to create truly realistic training. It will also open up new horizons for you with robots and remotely operated vehicles. You can apply that to safe minerals exploration in Afghanistan or your space program."

"What else?" Liu said, as though ticking off items from a shopping list. "What are you giving me of yours?"

"The VR code is mine. I've already made substantive improvements over EverPresence's original design, and as a platform, it's capable of far more than even when I purchased it. But beyond that, I'm going to fix the problem at your ports," Jeff said. He tried to hide the magnanimous notes in his voice. "I'm going to give you the code and the blueprints for our Cyberport concept. I have pilots running in Long Beach and Seoul, if you'd like to see for yourself. The AI continually analyzes your current traffic flows, your capacity, your wait times, your throughput and your bottle-necks. It simultaneously optimizes each of those attributes, bringing in environmental factors such as weather and actual staffing levels by skill. It will bring precise timing cues to each cargo movement. Then it's paired with robotics to unload ships, transport to line haul, and load trucks. The system precisely times and updates to the second. If a truck doesn't show up on time or a ship is early, the system automatically re-prioritizes the queue.

"We're already seeing a hundred and twenty percent increase in efficiency and reduced human staff by fifty percent. It will predict the exact manning requirements and port capacity based on evolving inbound and outbound traffic."

"The Port of Shanghai is already automated," Liu said dismissively. "It's the most advanced port in the world."

"One terminal is and it still requires human operators. What I'm offering you is a way to automate everything. But it's not just applicable to your ports. You can repurpose the underlying code to air and ground traffic control systems. At its core, the system continually optimizes complex networks in real time to predict surges, lags, and disruptions in those systems. It will adapt in advance of those changes. Think of what you could do with a fully optimized road network in Beijing." When Liu said nothing, Jeff added dully, "It's the greatest advance in logistics since cardboard boxes. The technology is deployable. It will work in any port. That is the beginning of what it can do."

"We can do this already. I assume you've heard of CityBrain? You have yet to impress me today, Jeff."

"Yes, I've heard of that effort. I think we both know I can do better. But how about another example. How far out can you extrapolate complex pattern analysis?"

"How far?" Liu said, irritated. Jeff realized that he would have to describe this slowly and carefully, as he would to a child.

"This capability will allow you to analyze the US military's movements, its operations plans, and its doctrine. Combine all of those factors and run simulations to show you, accurately, what they would do in a given scenario. This type of analysis takes hundreds of specialists today. I'll assume you already have much of the source material you'd need for such analyses," Jeff said sardonically. "My system can predict what your chief opponent will do in almost any conceivable scenario."

Jeff was giving the Chinese an incredible tool, if they had the foresight to realize it. He could sense the wheels turning in Liu's mind and imagined where his thoughts were going. Unprecedented control over who moved where. So typical of how the Chinese government thought. For all their talk of "great leaps," they were still singularly focused on control. Jeff was giving Liu the keys to modernize the Chinese infrastructure by orders of magnitude. The port technology could be worth billions if they deployed it smartly. China could stay the world's manufacturing center if they wished to, but they needed to evolve their operations to do it. The world was moving beyond simply adding more people to more sweat shops.

The United States and others were seeking other sources. They were impatient with the months of delays, which made them realize the inherent risks of a single supplier for so many of the world's goods. China could reverse this trend within a year or two if they were smart and used Jeff's technology wisely. Once the current tensions between China and the West subsided, they would be ready to do business again. Commerce brought short memories, Jeff knew. By making the Chinese shipping infrastructure the most efficient in the world, they would once again be the primary source of commodities, regardless of national politics.

But to accurately war game the American military? That was true power.

It took a while, but Liu saw it.

"I am pleased, Jeff," he finally said. Their walk had taken them on a short loop through the forest and was now angling them back toward the parking lot. "I see that you've taken our conversation to heart."

"Indeed."

"But again, *where* is the code?"

"I'm transmitting it to you. I've developed an advanced file transfer protocol system. The data will be broken up, encrypted, and transmitted across any network. If you were to visualize it, it would look like beads of water moving simultaneously over the largest spiderweb you've ever seen. My technology obfuscates the endpoints; it is completely undetectable. Even if the American *government* intercepted it, which they can't, the data is completely inaccessible in its component parts and cannot be accessed without the download cipher."

"This seems a safer way to communicate," Liu said.

"It is." They emerged into the mostly empty parking lot. Jeff spotted his vehicle immediately, a black Lucid Air, one of the first on the market and nearly a thousand horsepower. He rarely drove himself (frankly, he'd rather delegate it to Saturn anyway), but when he did, it was quite an experience. It also set him apart from the Tesla-obsessed Silicon Valley. Jeff knew Elon and didn't care for him, but also thought the security in his car's operating system was porous. Someone hacked Tesla's operating system and it would happen again. "Now, I think we can agree I've satisfied my end of the bargain?"

"I do," Liu agreed. "I think your contribution to the advancement of the Chinese people is commendable."

"So what are you doing about Hawkinson?"

"Your own country has delivered the tools we need. The American government established the precedent for a nation to sanction an individual in their pursuit of accountability for Russia's president. The European Union followed suit and the world's courts have upheld this. We can sanction Mr. Hawkinson into poverty in a matter of years for any number of crimes, frankly."

"That's not good enough, Liu. I need something *now*. That's what we agreed to."

"We agreed to nothing," Liu hissed. "I said only that we would deal with Hawkinson. That will be done. We are not your assassins, Jeffrey. Our way ensures that Hawkinson cannot come back. Further, it will brand him a global pariah and that will close off his new partners. This is the deal. You may take it or leave it."

"It seems I have no choice."

"Now how do I access the material you've sent?"

Jeff opened his phone and activated the secure messaging protocol Liu used to signal their meets. He sent a web address through it.

"And the download key is there?"

"Nope," Jeff said whimsically. "As soon as I see action with Hawkinson, you'll get the key."

"Don't play games with me," Liu said in a low, dangerous voice.

"Don't play them with me, either. Guy Hawkinson stole from me and I want to see him punished. *That* was our agreement."

Jeff left Liu and walked to his car.

He abhorred giving out something for free, particularly the fruits of his intellect. Though Jeff was ambivalent about giving the Chinese the port technology. There was a global good there. Man should have delegated that work to machines long ago. If he helped people get fed, helped the global economy to modernize, the net result was positive even if the regime doing it was notoriously corrupt. The VR question was another matter. Jeff was giving the Chinese government the ultimate surveillance tool. They could track everything their citizens did while immersed in VR, AR, or Extended Reality. Worse, their ability to influence what the Chinese people saw and thought and discussed would be unparalleled. This would take the world's premiere surveillance state to terrible new heights.

It was also not his problem.

---

The drone, hovering just above the treetops, transmitted a UHD video feed to a pair of monitors inside a van just over a mile away. It stayed behind and above the two individuals, identified as SUBJ1 and SUBJ2, on the feed. The two surveillance techs in the van knew who SUBJ1 was immediately. What computer geek didn't? It was Jeff Kim. SUBJ2 was another matter.

"We get the conversation?" the special agent asked, stoop-walking back to the console. He'd been viewing from a third monitor in a different workstation.

"We did," the drone operator said. They played it back.

"That's a clear ask-and-answer," he said. NSA tipped them to the collaboration courtesy of a signal intercept. Apparently, they were up on a server in mainland China belonging to the government and picked up encrypted traffic between SUBJ2 and Jeff Kim. NSA turned the comms over to the FBI, who opened up a CI case. That was nothing new. The Bureau started a new counterintelligence case against China every twenty-nine minutes. Using that intercept, they followed Kim to a meeting with SUBJ2 at the National Arboretum about four weeks ago, but the audio feed crapped out. All they could do was confirm that these two gentlemen enjoyed a delightful walk in the park.

This was different. Kim offered intellectual property for what looked like intervention by the Chinese government against a business rival.

The Bureau created a file on Kim after that shitshow at his San Francisco headquarters two years ago, though they were actually watching him to make sure that Russian intelligence didn't infiltrate his organization—physically or digitally. The Bureau hadn't considered that Jeff Kim might work with a foreign power himself. Now, as soon as anything substantive came up, it became "restricted handling" and triggered an immediate phone call to the head of the National Technology Counterintelligence Unit.

The special agent grabbed his phone and dialed.

# 24

---

Colt trudged through tense days on the task force. Ford's initial assessment was correct. They were looking in all the wrong places. Colt couldn't share the source of the intelligence telling him to look at the NSC. He couldn't tell them that a representative of a shadowy collection of scientists, businessmen, government officials, and spooks tipped him off. So, Colt did what spies did best. He deceived. The task force lead was the head of CIA's Counterintelligence Division. There was little that passed between these walls he wasn't cleared to know. Instead, Colt used NTCU's new tool as a smokescreen. He told the task force head that CERBERUS triangulated the leak at the NSC. They were so desperate for leads, no one questioned him. They didn't even ask to see the results. Colt knew it was a dangerous play. If CERBERUS fingered the wrong person, the Chinese spy might escape, or worse, stay hidden.

He measured it was worth the risk.

Ford's icy and petulant demeanor made Colt's penance on the task force worse. He made one attempt to mend the relationship, but his partner's verbal whipping suggested that was a bad idea and so Colt decided to just keep his distance. He focused his time on CERBERUS. The system analyzed every member of the National Security Council, the Principle's Committee, and their respective staffs. It parsed millions of data points to identify which of them would be the most susceptible to foreign influence. CERBERUS culled the personnel and financial records, their bank accounts (because of the direct deposit info) of every target, and read every email they sent using a government system.

CERBERUS rooted classified and unclassified databases, public records, court filings and law enforcement files, bank records, and social media posts. For example, had someone taken a vacation in Asia—ever—could that serve as a cover for a clandestine meeting with the Ministry of State Security? That was one data point in a galaxy of information CERBERUS collected, parsed, and assessed. The system read anything the target published in periodicals, trade papers, speeches, and media appearances in order to assess sentiment. Were they ever critical of the US government or seen as favorable to the positions of the Chinese? Had they ever advocated for a position or issue that might benefit the Chinese? Once the system reviewed the individual, it pored over the records of their spouses, their children, their parents, and their relatives. If there was a plausible opportunity for connection, they would find it.

CERBERUS's tentacular reach scoured every digital record the government possessed and any open source material it could publicly access. For now, the task force chief limited CERBERUS to just the direct members of the NSC and their respective staffs. By design, the system could go so much further. By tapping into the distribution records of the documents the NSC produced, the system could trace anyone who might have access to the intelligence reports, the operational directives, or the NSC decision memoranda. The lead's rationale was to focus CERBERUS's efforts, to optimize them, but Colt believed he was afraid of exposure. CERBERUS's existence was so highly classified that, outside of NTCU, only the task force lead, who was the CIA Chief of Counterintelligence, DNCS, the CIA Director, and the NSA Director knew of its existence. Colt understood why. It was a peerless surveillance tool that rendered confidence intervals on potential for foreign influence. Not only was this devastating in the wrong hands, but any citizen would rightly be terrified of the privacy implications. The CI chief believed the more people they looked at, the greater the risk of exposure. Colt attempted to explain once that the technology didn't work that way, but Ford waved him off.

The system eventually identified three primary targets, twelve potential targets, and thirty that it rated "unlikely" but "further analysis suggested." Of the primaries, one was a staffer linked to the National Security Advisor who'd studied abroad in Shanghai in grad school. She lived above her means on maxed-out credit cards and had a condo in D.C.'s Kalorama neighborhood.

The second was an Army Lieutenant Colonel, Foreign Area Officer specializing in China, proficient in Mandarin and ethnically Chinese, with familial ties to the country. He traveled to China thirteen times during his seventeen years in uniform, including trips from his two postings in South Korea and Hawaii. The colonel cleared each of these trips in advance and Army counterintelligence debriefed him after each one.

The last suspect was a political appointee to the newly formed Directorate of Technological Defense. He was a Silicon Valley serial entrepreneur with several highly successful companies under his belt. An electrical engineer by training, his second company developed a novel facial recognition algorithm, partnered with a special camera lens that more accurately rendered facial features on screen. That required outsourcing to manufacturing centers in China. That company sold to Apple, and he moved on to the next venture.

Colt thought each of them was a viable candidate for espionage. They each had an opportunity, and one, the staffer, appeared to have financial pressures that was a definite warning signal. Still, Colt didn't like any of them for it. CERBERUS could not identify any obvious patterns of deception, indications that any of their respective stories did not add up. However, since the governments at all levels hadn't digitized all of their records, the system could only look back so far. Still, there were millions of potential data points to identify, sort, connect, and decide on. The NTCU techs and the contractor reps had to monitor the application constantly and continually refine the search algorithms to validate that it was learning within set parameters. Colt reviewed the systems analyses and redirected the search based on his intelligence officer's insights.

The task force lead announced the Army officer was their prime target.

Colt suggested he was the least likely candidate. The colonel documented his travel well and never missed the subsequent CI interviews. He also had regular polygraph exams because of his clearance level and passed each one. The task force lead all but pushed their proverbial chips in front of the colonel. Colt could read between the lines. It was the safest shot to fire. If they were wrong, all they lost was time. They didn't embarrass someone close to the administration. The staffer had been with the president's National Security Advisor for many years and their entrepreneur was an important donor and advisor to the president's campaign on technology and business. *Here we go again*, Colt thought.

Meanwhile, the Chinese spy got closer to uncovering YELLOWCARD's identity with each passing day. But the danger wasn't just the threat of Nadia's identity leaking to the Chinese. It was her getting burned and her identity leaking to Hawkinson.

If that happened, she was as good as dead.

And the threat became more imminent each day that passed.

The NSC's newly formed Directorate of Technological Defense's inaugural action was to run an after-action review of STONEBRIDGE with the thoroughness and rigor of a colonoscopy. The acting director—the NSC expected to appoint a senior military officer to run it permanently within days—wanted to evaluate the operation as a case study. They'd already requested troves of documents from NTCU, which Thorpe was doing his best to resist, but they fully expected the CIA director to support the requests in the interest of "transparency." Thorpe, at least, got a seat at the Directorate's table, so he could explain why this was a bad time to pick STONEBRIDGE apart.

Thorpe called Colt and Ford back to the unit at the end of that first frosty week. Thorpe didn't say why, just that he had new information that he needed to share immediately.

As they walked, Ford said, "I've seen two things come out of the NSC: press leaks and textbook chapters. Neither of which are accurate or insightful."

"I just got a phone call from a friend on the Bureau's foreign counterintelligence team," Thorpe said. These were the FBI's spy hunters. Though the Agency's rivalry with the Bureau went back to its formation and the two forged a grudging respect in post-9/11 cooperation, the relationship would always be strained when jurisdictions overlapped. However, one thing nearly every spook agreed on was that the FBI's spy hunters were the best in the world. "They've got two video-confirmed meetings between Jeff Kim and an unidentified Chinese man. One meeting was here in D.C., the other was outside Palo Alto yesterday." Thorpe led them into the conference room where Gretchen Harlowe, his second-in-command, waited for them. Upon seeing them enter, she queued up the video footage their Bureau colleagues sent over.

Colt and Ford watched the drone footage and accompanying audio. Colt did his best to keep his jaw attached to the rest of his mouth. Jeff Kim clearly asked the Chinese government to take retributive action against Guy Hawkinson. The unidentified man stated the Chinese government could "sanction Hawkinson into poverty."

"Kim is selling his tech to the Chinese in exchange for them taking out Guy Hawkinson?"

"It appears so," Thorpe said.

"We need to get that guy's image into CERBERUS." Ford jabbed a thick finger at the screen. "How good is the facial rec stuff, Colt?"

"Not bad. Are you thinking we expand the search to include public spaces?"

"Customs and Border Protection databases. If he's MSS or PLA, he'll have entered on a doctored passport and bogus name, but at least we'll know where to refine our search."

"CERBERUS can do that?" Thorpe asked.

"Hooks into government databases, state and municipal police systems and scans their traffic cameras, mug books, evidence records, basically anything we take pictures of."

Thorpe gave a mirthless laugh. "Privacy nuts are going to love that."

"Then don't be spies," Ford quipped.

"Gents, we have two CI cases coming together. The Chinese have turned Jeff Kim; Jeff Kim is targeting Guy Hawkinson. Revenge for IP theft is my guess, and we have a covert operation inside Hawkinson's company."

Ford whistled. "That's one menage-a-shitshow. This has to be connected. Those are too many coincidences lining up for my liking."

"I'm not so sure," Thorpe said.

"I don't know," Colt said. "I don't think the Chinese could have known we had someone inside Hawk Tech. I *do* think they would try to capitalize on it if they found out, though."

"Okay," Thorpe said. "How?"

"Fred has already made the point about political leverage. The Chinese are savvy enough to recognize the potential," Colt said.

"Do we think the Chinese would use Nadia's identity to get next to Guy?" Ford asked.

"Why would they want to do that?" Thorpe asked.

"Well, we know they're getting Jeff Kim's tech, right? From the recording, it sounds like virtual reality and some kind of supply chain AI. Maybe that's not all they're getting. Both things seem like they could help the Chinese make some significant advances. Guy Hawkinson already stole a bunch of Kim's tech." Colt shrugged. "What if they're trying to make it a double play?"

Everyone was quiet, considering the implications. Then Ford said, "Can you imagine the trouble this world is in if the Chinese ever got their hands on Hawkinson's xeno-bio-whatever it is?"

"Xenobots," Colt said, and Ford pointed at him.

"That's scary. Political dissidents just start dropping from heart attacks. I mean, they're ethnic cleansing *now*. Imagine what they can do with a weapon that leaves no trace?"

"I want to brace Kim," Thorpe said. "Colt, you know him, so I'd like you to come with me."

"Think it'll work?"

"He either cooperates or we arrest him for espionage," Thorpe said. "Besides, he owes us one."

Last year, Colt's plan to insert Nadia into Hawkinson's company was to use intel they had on tech firms he was looking to purchase and use the Agency's connections to get her hired into one. Then they would manipulate the playing field so that Hawkinson moved quickly with his acquisition, bringing Nadia in with the other accessions. The company they chose was the VR firm EverPresence. They had intel suggesting it was on the short list of companies Hawkinson intended to buy. They just needed a nudge. Colt knew that if Jeff Kim asked about the company, that would whet Hawkinson's appetite and force his hand. Colt flew out to Palo Alto with an offer. If Kim played along, the Justice Department would reduce many of the fines levied against him and allow him to do business with the federal government again. Kim agreed.

Then he bought EverPresence to spite Hawkinson.

That forced NTCU to find a last-minute way to insert Nadia into Hawk Tech undercover.

"Jeff Kim plays more sides than a Rubik's Cube," Colt said. His attention went to Ford, who was squinting through the conference room blinds at the televisions in the other room.

"Can we get that in here?" Ford asked.

"Yeah, one sec," Harlowe said. She activated the large screen in the conference room and tapped a few buttons on the console in front of her, bringing up the CNN feed.

Beneath the bright red "BREAKING NEWS" banner, the anchor said, "US Army Lieutenant General Darius Rubio has withdrawn from consideration from the National Security Council's Directorate of Technological Defense amid allegations of unlawful contact and a potential bribe with a leading defense contractor, Apex Systems. The allegations stem from a report that CNN has obtained showing General Rubio gave favorable consideration to Apex Systems for a 350-million-dollar contract for 'classified technology solutions' in exchange for a fifty-thousand-dollar payment. With General Rubio stepping down, Navy Admiral Glen Denney will assume the role. Admiral Denney currently serves as the Director of Operations for the Joint Staff. General Rubio denies the allegations and says he intends to fight..."

"We need to get that guy into CERBERUS right away," Ford said. "Vet the shit out of him."

"Can you handle it?" Thorpe asked.

"Yeah. I got it," Ford said.

"Okay. Colt, we need to get to California."

## 25

---

*Washington, D.C.*

The newly minted Vice Admiral Denney sat at the head of the long, dark table. A Navy steward brought him a cup of coffee from the mess on a small silver tray, the cup proudly displaying an image of the building in which he now sat above the words "West Wing - The White House." The steward asked him if he'd need anything else. Glen told him he was fine and thanked him. The steward turned and padded across the thick, dark blue carpet and left. Glen took a sip. It was good to have proper Navy coffee again. He had to admit that things moved incredibly fast, but even with presidential horsepower behind it, he hadn't expected it to go this quickly.

Only a month had passed since he'd given General Rubio's name to Liu.

The leak happened shortly after, with "information" coming to light that the general took bribes from an ARCYBER contractor. The investigation was currently underway by the Army's Criminal Investigative Division and the FBI, but Rubio was told he would need to step down from his NSC appointment. Denney got the call.

He didn't know Rubio personally, but he had a reputation for being a dedicated Army officer, family man, and patriot. Denney didn't know if the allegations had even a shred of merit, but something in the speed of the revelations told him otherwise. As the commanding general, Rubio wouldn't be able to award a contract. The contacting officers would do that. In fact, unless it was a major acquisition critical to US Army Cyber Command's mission, it seemed unlikely the general would know the procurement was happening, let alone be able to influence it. The implications were unmistakable.

Liu ruined a man to put Denney here.

Glen did not want it this way. He didn't want this. He wanted to command the Naval Air Force of the Pacific Fleet, the role they had groomed him for, the role he'd *earned*. General Rubio was eminently qualified for this job. Glen wasn't a cyber or information operations officer. He had no background in technology. He was a pilot; his job was in the cockpit. Glen thought about turning it down—*It's an honor to be considered, but I can best serve the Navy and my country elsewhere*—but quickly thought better of it. If Liu went to these lengths just to make Denney a more valuable asset, imagine what he'd do if Glen turned that down. Glen tried to talk with the CNO about his future after this tour wrapped but the CNO wouldn't meet with him, just a terse conversation in the Pentagon's E Ring. The CNO assumed Glen went behind his back, angled for this job, was playing for political favor with the administration. He did his best to convince the Admiral otherwise, but the CNO didn't believe him. Glen said he didn't think it wise to turn down the president's offer. The CNO only said, "Presidents come and go. The Navy endures. Fair winds, Admiral."

From there, political inertia took over. This working group was a key initiative for the president, who promised to get tougher on countries that tried to steal America's technology, undermine its edge in the world. An edge that had come from being a free society. The usual patriotic bumper sticker bullshit. Denney had a perfunctory meeting with the National Security Advisor and was notified later that day that the job was his. His confirmation was fast-tracked through the Senate, and he'd had a quiet ceremony with only his family in attendance.

People filed into the conference room, principles taking their designated seats at the table behind the cardstock displaying their name, rank, and the department they represented. Denney scanned the cards—CIA, NSA, DIA, Office of the Secretary of Defense's Science and Technology Division, Joint Staff Directorate of Communications (J6), US Cyber Command, Homeland

Security, Department of Commerce. The one he was really interested in was the National Technology Counterintelligence Unit. In true government fashion, their charter was almost identical to his. The only difference was that NTCU, based out of CIA headquarters, was an operational unit. He understood the FBI ran it, but they drew most of their support from CIA and NSA.

Glen learned from the reams of briefing packets he'd received that NTCU was behind the STONEBRIDGE operation. The National Security Advisor told him that Senator Preston Hawkinson had his "undies in a bunch over that one. Didn't like us poking around in his nephew's business." The advisor informed Denney in somber tones that he'd already directed the Technology Defense Directorate to do a ground-up review of STONEBRIDGE. They needed to be absolutely certain this operation could not blow back on the president. Senator Hawkinson was a vociferous and especially prolific voice in the opposition party. His history with the president was long and irrevocably divided. "Now, if this thing has legs," the National Security Advisor calmly said, "we'll back it. If not, I want it folded up fast. We don't need to give this prick any ammunition." Glen assured the advisor that he would get the Directorate's best and fastest work.

Glen kicked off the meeting, thanked everyone for attending, then turned it over to his chief of staff, an NSC staffer loyal to the advisor. He reminded everyone that the meeting was TS/SCI and contained code word intelligence. No one was to speak outside of this forum or distribute information to parties not code word cleared. The director's intel cryptonym was PINBALL, which Glen felt was ironically appropriate. It was how he felt most days. The chief of staff brought the agenda up on the screen. Since it was Denney's first session, he started with introductions from the various agency representatives.

"Sir," the NSA man began. He wore a dark suit, crisply pressed shirt, and a power tie, the visible antithesis of his agency's reputation. "The top INFOSEC threats against the US remain Russia, China, Iran, and North Korea, in that order. Though, it's fair to point out that everyone from Venezuela to Israel to Bulgaria has tried to hack us. The Russians are currently inside much of our critical infrastructure and have been for years. They're in power plants, hydroelectric dams, utility companies. They've hacked thousands of municipal governments across the country."

"What are we doing to stop them?" Glen asked.

"I think that's why we're all here," the NSA man told him. Then he added in a sardonic tone, "At a policy level." *Shots fired*, Glen thought. The NSA man clearly thought Glen's question suggested no one was doing anything yet. "Utilities are government-regulated, but they're private companies. Congress tried passing a law requiring them to patch their operating systems, most of which are old and riddled with vulnerabilities. Then the trade associations lobbied to get the restrictions removed or watered down. Said it was government overreach and an affront to capitalism. The net result is that we can *only* play offense. It's like watching a soccer match that is 500 to 499. We can't force private companies or citizens to make their networks harder targets by improving their own security; hell, most government agencies only use cursory antivirus protection and those are often years out of date. So we play offense. We try to attack them before they attack us. Frankly, the Russians could shut the lights off across a lot of this country, and break a lot of dams."

"If they can, why haven't they already?"

"Two things. One, a cyber weapon is not like a missile. Once you use it, the code is out there in the open and people can figure out how you did it. Then they patch holes and take other weapons off the table. The other reason is the Russians know we could put them back in the dark ages. It's a lot like the sixties and mutually assured destruction, but with bigger sticks."

NSA spent the next ten minutes discussing each of the major information threats and what his agency was doing about them, then they moved on to the next organization. His chief of staff worked their way around the table to the NTCU rep. "What can you tell me about STONEBRIDGE?" Glen asked. His question clearly took the unit rep, an FBI agent by the name of Gretchen Harlowe, by surprise. This was not what she'd been told to brief. "The National Security Advisor wants to know progress, and I'd like to get up to speed quickly."

"Yes, sir. Well, STONEBRDIGE was an operation to gather intel on a foreign intel threat in an American commercial company. We believed that they illegally appropriated trade secrets from another company and then sold them to the Russian foreign intelligence service." Her eyes made a furtive circuit around the table. "That's all I can say in this forum."

Glen sat up straight in his chair. "Ms. Harlowe, the National Security

Advisor wants me to be fully briefed on this matter so that he can update the president. I think I'm cleared to know."

"Sir, the president authorized the operation. I think he's up to speed."

"Would you like to speak with him? I can arrange it."

Harlowe's eyes narrowed, and she wisely held her tongue for several seconds. "If you like, I could arrange a detailed briefing in a more suitable location."

"This will do," Glen said firmly, losing his patience.

"We have a source in place now, codenamed YELLOWCARD, but we're extracting her shortly. There isn't much more to pursue and we are closing the operation soon."

"How soon is 'soon?'"

"Admiral, I'm not discussing operational details in this forum."

Glen waved a dismissive hand and nodded for his chief of staff to continue. He didn't think Harlowe realized her mistake. A quick scan across the room showed that no one else appeared to either. In her fluster, driven by his calculated escalation, Harlow revealed the operative's gender. This would narrow the field considerably, especially considering the ratio of men to women in technology companies.

This better satisfy Liu considering the price he'd paid to get it.

When the meeting broke, Glen pulled his chief of staff into his office. "Listen, I need you to cover me for about an hour. I've got a meeting with a Senate Intel Committee staffer in about twenty minutes. I'm trying to find out just how exposed we are with this STONEBRIDGE thing."

The chief nodded in knowing appreciation of the skullduggery that made this town work. Glen knew the man's next call would be to the National Security Advisor. He changed into civilian athletic gear with a ballcap to hide his military haircut and slid on a pair of gold mirror Oakleys, then left the West Wing. As soon as he was through security, Glen started jogging. He stopped about a mile from the White House, caught his breath, and pulled out his phone, selecting the covert messaging app.

He finally had his way out.

# 26

*Palo Alto, California*

Colt and Thorpe had a chilly flight to San Francisco and said less on the short drive to Palo Alto. Thorpe might have been a cop at heart, but he appreciated the complexities of intelligence work more than Colt gave him credit for. Colt also admitted that his temper got the better of him, clouded his judgment. If he'd been honest with Thorpe about Ava when she contacted him, Thorpe would've (rightly) blasted him for maintaining the relationship, but he also would have understood the underlying pragmatism of it.

Instead, Colt kept it to himself, compounding the lie with more lies and undermining both his credibility and his source's. Thorpe would now wonder what else Colt might be holding back. The feeling of guilt was as awful as it was inescapable.

"Kim is one of the smartest guys on the planet," Colt said. "His biggest problem is that he knows it. I got fairly close to him on my undercover assignment. He's also a utopian."

"What does that mean, exactly?" Thorpe asked in an interrogation-room tone.

"He thinks his technology is going to usher in a better era for mankind. He also doesn't believe in government."

"What is he, an anarchist or something?"

"No, nothing like that. He just thinks that the government is cumbersome and ineffective. That technology, particularly AI, can solve most of those problems we rely on government for but better, faster, and more effectively. He told me once about a vision he had for replacing the air traffic control system with AI. Dynamically rerouting aircraft along optimal routes based on weather and traffic, all updated in real time and minimizing the amount of jet fuel used."

"Puts a lot of trust in a computer."

"Never call it a 'computer' around him. He thinks it's insulting and reductive. Jeff would tell you an AI doesn't get a hangover, or oversleep. It doesn't get sick, doesn't have a bad day."

"A person can't get hacked," Thorpe said, though the intelligence officer in Colt knew that wasn't exactly true.

"Anyway, try not to come off as a big government-authority type. Jeff will just shut down on you."

"Good to know," Thorpe said. The conversation dried up after that. Colt drove, having been to Kim's house before. Kim hired a security service to man the front gate with an armed guard, something he put in place after his experience with the Russian SVR, though Colt believed Kim had that AI of his, Saturn, monitor every inch of ground inside the compound.

When they arrived, Colt gave his and Thorpe's names to the guard in the shack, who verified they were on the list and then signaled for the twelve-foot-high iron gate to open. Thorpe wanted to arrive unannounced for the shock value, put Kim off balance. Colt advised against that, saying Jeff hated surprises (they were a thing he couldn't control) and it would just be harder to get him to cooperate. Surprisingly, Thorpe agreed. Colt pulled through the gate and headed up the short driveway flanked by eucalyptus and cypress trees to the sprawling, ultra-modern home.

Jeff greeted them at the door.

"Mr. McShane's employer is still listed as the Department of Commerce," a detached, omnipresent voice announced as they crossed the threshold into the home. "He is unarmed. Special Agent Will Thorpe of the Federal Bureau of Investigation is carrying a Glock 19M in a shoulder holster. The weapon is legally registered."

"Will, meet Saturn," Colt said. Thorpe's eyebrow lifted several degrees, but he said nothing. Colt thought identifying the weapon was an interesting touch. Last time, the system just informed Kim that Colt was unarmed. Could be an educated guess, Colt reasoned. It was an FBI-issued pistol.

Kim wore navy pants and a loose-fitting, long-sleeve white shirt.

"Good morning, gentlemen. May I offer you something to drink?"

"I'll take a coffee," Colt said.

"Nothing for me," Thorpe said.

"Follow me, please." Kim led them to the patio.

"Mr. McShane's coffee is ready," Saturn said from all around them. Colt wondered where the speakers were. Kim departed and returned with a white cup and saucer. He retrieved two bottles of water from an outdoor refrigerator and handed one to Thorpe.

Kim regarded them in silence for a few moments and then said, "How can I help the federal government today?"

"Mr. Kim," Thorpe said. "I run the National Technical Counterintelligence Unit. We—"

"I know what you do," Kim said. "I knew your predecessor."

Colt watched Thorpe bristle. A wave of tension and suppressed anger washed over him. Special Agent Rinaldi had been turned by the Russian SVR. He sold out Jeff Kim, and his actions ultimately allowed the Hawk Security Group men to storm Kim's company. Rinaldi also murdered one of Colt's friends, a CIA officer he'd gone through the Farm with.

Rinaldi and Thorpe had history, though exactly what the latter never said.

Colt hoped the man was sitting under a warming lamp in hell.

"Yes, well, on behalf of the FBI, please accept my apology. We should have caught him."

"Yes, you should have," Kim said. "Now, why are you here?"

Thorpe unzipped his ballistic nylon briefcase and pulled out a tablet. He activated the device, pulled up an image, and turned the screen to show Kim. Colt saw it was actually a collage of pictures showing Kim meeting with the unidentified Chinese man in Washington, D.C. and here in California.

"Can you tell me who he is?"

"He's the President of the Americas Division of XZE Corp."

"What does XZE Corp do?"

"Advanced robotics, primarily, but technology companies in China tend not to specialize as they do here. I'm discussing a potential partnership with them to pair their robotics technology with my smart port system. May I ask why you are photographing my meeting with him? This seems like a tremendous violation of my rights. I assume that there is an accompanying warrant for surveillance?"

"Mr. Kim, we believe this man is an intelligence officer with the Chinese Ministry of State Security."

"That's impossible," Kim said.

"You should know that it's anything but impossible, Mr. Kim," Thorpe said. "Both the State and Commerce Departments have to clear any prospective partnerships first and they have no record of this. But they wouldn't, would they? We have compelling information suggesting this man is with Chinese intelligence. No, I'm not going into how we know that."

"I know. Just trust you," Kim said dryly.

"Jeff." Colt broke into the conversation. "This is serious business. We're trying to protect you."

"I haven't found the government to be very effective at that."

"I came here last summer," Colt said, "and offered you a deal. In exchange for lifting Justice Department sanctions against your company, you were to help us with an operation. Instead of feigning interest in EverPresence to get Guy Hawkinson's attention, you bought them."

"Maybe I didn't like the idea of the government meddling with a promising private company just so you could do whatever the hell you intended to do."

"I don't give a shit about your rationale, Jeff. We had an agreement. And we still upheld our part of the agreement. You're free to do business with the government and abroad. You never would have made that acquisition if it wasn't for us."

Kim stayed silent.

Thorpe said, "But we will reinstate each of those sanctions. You're going to find it hard to ink a deal without an export license. Assuming this is all legitimate, of course."

"You can't threaten me, Agent Thorpe. And you sure as hell can't intimidate me."

"Oh, Jeff—may I call you Jeff? Jeff, I forgot to mention that besides these photographs, we have audio. Would you like to hear it? It's pretty interesting. Because on that audio, it's clear that you're asking someone to take out a business rival in exchange for handing over some of your tech."

"Special Agent Thorpe, if I'd recorded everything you said from the time you arrived, I could have Saturn create a soundbite of you reciting the Gettysburg Address. It would be so convincingly rendered you couldn't tell the difference. The point is, I don't trust any supposed recording you have, especially if it's intended as a point of coercion. Now, if you're asking me whether I met with a private company to discuss a potential business arrangement?" Jeff Kim spread his hands, as if he'd just revealed a magician's trick. "And if that company has some political leverage with a country that's interested in holding Hawkinson accountable in the appropriate international body, then yes, I would likely listen to what they had to say. Off the record, of course."

"That's a dubious argument."

"Jeff," Colt said in an even voice, "Special Agent Thorpe tells me you've got a fifty-fifty shot at federal prison. Your lawyers might beat that, but Pax AI doesn't survive. The Justice Department will tear that company apart and prevent you from ever doing business again. That's if you're right that this man works for a Chinese tech company and you're just buying influence. Now, if you're lying to us, the FBI will arrest you and charge you with espionage. You will go to jail." Colt let that sink in. "I know how badly you want to get back at Hawkinson, but there's a right way and a wrong way. Believe me, I want to get him just as much as you, probably more."

"I doubt that very much."

"Jeff, he stole some shit from you. I was on that island of his minutes before the Russians flattened it. This is so much more than personal for me," Colt said. "Now, here's your option. We make a deal, and this time, Jeff, you damned well better honor it."

"What do I have to do?"

"You've agreed to give some of your tech to this man. You're going to let us have it first."

"Out of the question," Kim said.

Thorpe reached into his jacket and drew out a folded piece of paper. "Mr. Kim, I have a warrant for your arrest. I will execute this warrant if you do not cooperate with us."

"What are you going to do with my code?"

"We're going to install some digital tracers on it. It's like dye. We just want to see where it goes," Colt said. That wasn't even remotely the extent of it, but he would not tell Kim that. Their inject would act as a digital tracer, covertly reporting back to NTCU whatever systems and networks the Chinese deployed it on. Essentially, whatever computers they used to look at or reverse-engineer or build on Jeff's source code. NTCU expected it would land within Chinese intelligence, the PLA, and other government entities, and then be distributed to research institutes and state-run tech companies. This would be the most comprehensive tracing of Chinese intellectual property theft ever.

The exploit would self-replicate and seek other systems, metastasizing across any network it touched. There, it would lie dormant until called, lurking behind the digital walls. This would give NTCU the back door they desperately needed into the Chinese intelligence community. When the time came, the unit could wreak havoc, or simply watch and wait, continuing to collect vital information on Chinese information operation capabilities.

"That won't work," Kim said dismissively. "I've already agreed to manage my transfers digitally. It's faster, more secure."

"Then come up with a reason not to," Thorpe said.

Kim breathed out his frustration with a hiss. "I told him he would need a download code to access my files and that I would provide that separately. I suppose that could work."

"Would they trust a thumb drive?"

"I should hope not," Kim said snidely. "It would be better if it were a laptop or something. I agreed to sell him an additional capability. If I provide you with a laptop, you could add your code to that."

Thorpe looked over to Colt for confirmation. Colt nodded and said that would work.

"I'll want to inspect this before I hand it over. Make sure it's undetectable."

"Jeff, you don't want to play hardball right now. First, I doubt you'd find it.

Our people are pretty good at this sort of thing. Second, even if you could find it, what would you do about it? You would do nothing. Why? Because if this doesn't go exactly as planned, all of those nasty things Special Agent Thorpe talked about will happen. Immediately."

Jeff Kim opened his mouth to speak, thought better of it, and closed it. Instead, he simply stared a vitriolic but otherwise useless dagger across the table. Kim was boxed in. He would know that a government prosecutor would use the events at the Pax AI headquarters to establish a pattern of skirting the law, possibly even collusion with foreign actors. They'd play up the argument that Kim was just another rich asshole who thought he was above the law. It would play hell with a jury, especially now with the anti-tech fervor. All that was before the government showed they gave Jeff a chance to cooperate last year and he, instead, used that information to buy a company. He'd used inside information to complete Pax AI's rebound and given them nothing in exchange.

"Is this why you didn't come after me last year? When I bought EverP-resence?"

Colt smiled, shrugged, and said nothing.

"Fine," Kim finally said.

"When is this transfer supposed to happen?" Colt asked.

"We don't have an exact time set, but within the next few weeks."

"What did you say this man's name was?" Thorpe asked. "The 'President of the Americas Division?'"

"I didn't," Kim said. Thorpe's expression dropped, and his face could've passed for a side of granite. "Liu Che," Kim said. "Are we done?"

"We'll take that laptop now," Thorpe said.

---

Jeff watched them leave.

He told them it would take a day or two to prepare the files. He promised he would overnight it to any location they chose. Colt said that he would stay in California until the laptop was ready and he'd personally carry it back. Jeff hoped he hadn't given them too much resistance, but if he'd simply agreed to their demands he feared they'd see right through him. Deception didn't come naturally to Jeff, though, given his recent experiences, perhaps this was a skill he needed to hone. The government offered him salvation. Liu would take out Hawkinson, make him pay for what he'd done, and the Central Intelligence Agency would take care of his Chinese problem. He would be sure to be sufficiently contrite when he met Colt tomorrow to hand over the laptop and grudgingly thank him for the second chance.

# 27

Nadia couldn't get anywhere near Guy Hawkinson.

Hawkinson traveled extensively. Rumor was he was scouting locations for a new data center, but no one knew for certain. Nadia even asked his secretary when he'd be back so that she could book time for a "mentoring session."

She'd barely seen him lately, let alone been able to get close enough to use the LONGBOW. There were no instructions from Langley about the USB hidden in the pen. That was some real James Bond shit. It also seemed a hell of a lot easier to pull off than lasering Hawkinson's phone, but Colt was clear that Langley's priority was the LONGBOW. When Ava did the handoff, she made it seem like the pen was a backup, but no one gave Nadia any instructions on when the backup was to be used. The stakes were far too high for a mistake, and she genuinely didn't know what to do next. It was a lonely feeling, knowing you were out of your depth.

She also didn't want to ask for clarification, given what Colt said about keeping their comms off the books for the time being. Nadia suspected that if this business about a Chinese spy on the National Security Council was true, Colt was being doubly cautious about what they said in official cables.

During her training, he'd told her that leaks happened once other agencies got involved. Ford said once, "If you want to make sure something gets printed in *The Washington Post*, tell the State Department." She and Colt had precious few moments for their briefing, and he hadn't had time to cover her backup communications plan. Nadia had to assume Chuck Harmon would share that when they met next.

There were half a hundred ways to secretly communicate on the internet. Hackers did it every day.

Well, she couldn't just shelve her assignment because there weren't instructions from headquarters. They expected her to act on her own, right? If she couldn't get onto Hawkinson's phone yet, Nadia had another way.

That other way was Tyler Gales.

Gales was the MIT research fellow Hawkinson hired out from under them to head his genetic engineering project. She'd been courting Gales for a few weeks now, playing the part of a semi-shy computer scientist enamored with the tech. Gales was a good-looking guy, so it didn't seem out of place for her to flirt with him, though he was so caught up in his work he didn't seem to notice. Still, Gales enjoyed her company, and they met outside of work often. Today, however, he was taking her inside.

This was a risky move. Nadia did not possess clearance for the lab, so Gales would have to let her in and vouch for her. She'd be recorded. Nadia first confirmed with Hawkinson's executive assistant that he was going to be out of the office that day by politely pestering the woman for an appointment. His executive assistant was an ex-Army communications officer who worked for one of Guy's people on active duty and followed him to Hawk Tech after she separated. Nadia worked her way into the woman's graces. As comm officers attached to special operations units, they had similar backgrounds. Nadia hoped to cultivate her as a source. The exec confirmed Guy was in Buenos Aires and would be for the week, as was his number two, Matt Kirby. In fact, many of the company's senior staff were out of the office this week, either at business development trips out of the country or coordinating with their new research partners at Cambridge.

The only one she was actually concerned about was that strange, lurking harpy, Samantha Klein. She wasn't a Hawk Tech employee, but she had almost unhindered access to most of the building. The woman gave her an eerie feeling. Colt talked about that a lot. He said there was a kind of vibe on the street that you pick up when you'd done this enough, that you can almost feel when someone was watching you. It hadn't helped her with that creepy blond guy, but she sure had it whenever Klein was around.

Nadia brought a pair of coffees with her and met Tyler Gales in the common area.

"Good morning," she said, and handed him a cup.

"Oh, we're not allowed to have drinks in the lab. Just water," he said.

"Well, drink up now, because this is good stuff." She flashed him a conspiratorial wink that she suspected he probably missed. Nadia took a drink of her own coffee. It burned on the way down. Her cover story for why she was in a restricted lab was to see if her efforts on the open source data aggregator could help the bio-science team. Nadia would play the scientist card, a fellow nerd geeking out over the possibility of developing some truly next-gen tech, and if she wasn't totally oblivious to the security procedures, at least casually ambivalent.

Gales led her into the lab by badging in and then placing his hand on a vertical plate next to the door. A bright green line that reminded her of a document scanner took several passes of his hand before flashing his name and employee number on the display above it. He then entered a separate code to show he was taking a guest (Gales previously explained that there were motion detectors on the door to alert security to people attempting to bypass the control). Meanwhile, the hand sensor told them it was completing its sanitization sequence. At Gales' direction, Nadia tapped her badge on the plate and then touched her hand to the sensor, logging her presence. Gales led her in.

The lab had dimmable windows that allowed for full transparency, complete opacity, or anything in between. They were currently a dark blue, which showed only the ghostly outlines of people on the other side. Gales showed Nadia to his station. Much like her own, it was a computer with multiple wide-screen monitors, each with a different data feed. "We do most of our work on computers. In fact, it was the AI that led us in the discovery that xenobots could be programmed. This is going to blow open a whole new field of bioengineering." Gales logged in and then opened up a password storage application on his machine, which he used to get him into the other work systems he needed. That done, Gales turned to show her the genetic sequencing equipment in the room beyond. Though they could enter (if properly sanitized and suited), robots did most of the work.

"I want to show you something really cool," he said. "But I need to check and make sure I'm not messing up someone else's test. Can you hold on a minute?"

"Sure thing."

"Cool. I'll be right back. Uh, don't go anywhere." Gales walked off with a quick stride, disappearing behind an opaque door.

Nadia didn't know how long she had. She sat down, grabbed the mouse, and made a quick scan of the file directory. Shooting a glance at the door he'd left through but seeing no activity, she turned back to the screen and scanned the files, opening anything that looked promising and quickly closing it. There would be a digital trail of any files she accessed, but she doubted Gales would think to look or know how to do it. She continued scanning. Still nothing but project data. *Wait,* she thought, and clicked on a file labeled "Source Material." This opened up a large subdirectory that would take much more time to go through than she had.

Nadia looked over at the door. Still nothing.

As her eyes tracked down the long list of sub-folders, she realized she hadn't thought to look for cameras. If anyone caught her accessing Gales' machine, there would be no explaining her way out of it.

A folder named "Client Repo" grabbed her attention.

Nadia clicked on it, but the file was locked. A dialogue box popped up, asking for a password.

Eyes to the door, Nadia opened Gales' password app, which had not yet self-locked. She scrolled down and grabbed one called "ProjectDB," then copied and pasted it into the dialogue box.

The password box flashed an angry red and shook like it was in a quake. She made another fast scan at the passwords, landing on "ResearchDB," then grabbed it and pasted it into the dialogue box.

She was in.

There was a single document file inside the locked folder. Nadia clicked on it.

Ten names were listed, and Nadia recognized two of them.

Wesley Muir ran an artificial intelligence lab at Carnegie Mellon. His program was like *Top Gun* for computer geeks. She'd applied twice and didn't get in, having to "settle" for Cornell. The other was Natalie Ikeda, who ran a company that looked to blend AI with advanced robotics in order to reframe the manufacturing industry. Ikeda also ran a nonprofit putting tech resources in underprivileged school districts with a focus on teaching children from low-income families to code. Nadia recognized many of the names on the list, though she couldn't immediately place why she knew them.

Using a technique they taught her at the Farm, Nadia committed each of the ten names to memory and closed the file. She'd been on the system for approximately two minutes. Another dialogue box popped up, this one a chat window. When she read the sender, Nadia's blood shot cold.

**S. Klein [EXTERNAL] - Dr. Gales, may I speak with you?**

She heard the door open.

Nadia flexed her fingers into the CTR+ALT+DEL command, locking the screen, and rotated the chair to the door, meeting Tyler's quizzical expression.

"I was locking this for you. You shouldn't leave it open."

"Right, cool. Thanks. I forget I'm at a real company with processes and shit sometimes," Gales said, smiling.

*He looks distracted,* Nadia told herself. *Is he nervous? And why is Klein IMing him?*

"Hey," she said, "I just remembered that I need to give a demo of our open source troller for a potential client. I'm so bad about remembering stuff like that. Can we raincheck this?"

"Yeah. Elizabeth needs me to help her on a test, anyway." Gales motioned to the door.

"Cool, maybe a beer tomorrow?"

"I'd like that," Gales said, but his mind was clearly on other things.

Nadia left the lab and came face to face with Samantha Klein, who had her arms folded and was wearing a bullshit red pantsuit like she was in *The Devil Wears Prada.*

"May I ask what you were doing in that lab, Ms. Blackmon?" Samantha said in a slippery voice. "*I* don't have access to that room, so I know *you* don't."

"You just answered your own question then, didn't you? If you don't have access, then you don't get to ask me why I do." As Nadia brushed past her, pulse racing, Klein grabbed her arm.

"Just a minute."

Nadia shook off her grip with a hard jerk of her elbow.

"You don't work at this company. I don't need to tell you anything," she snapped. She lengthened her stride, ignoring Klein calling after her to stop. Nadia didn't look back and reached the hallway, guessing Klein was fast on her heels. Maybe she'd bought a second or two blowing past her, but Nadia believed Klein was not used to people ignoring her commands. Nadia pressed the "up" elevator button and then dashed for the stairwell, bounding down it two steps at a time.

What did that list mean?

Nadia repeated the names in her mind like a mantra.

No way were those people Hawkinson's clients. Clients of what? Hawk Tech didn't offer any products to individuals. Certainly not in the bio division.

Colt's words echoed in her mind.

Archon killed Sir Archibald Chalcroft with xenobots. They used stolen DNA to target them.

This wasn't a "client list."

It was a target list.

---

Nadia hit the ground floor and shouldered the door, blasting it open and using the momentum to carry her into the lobby. She immediately went to the phone lockers, found hers, then turned and headed out the door. Nadia thumbed through her apps as she walked—she had to get a message to Chuck Harmon immediately, then figure out how to stay hidden for two hours until he could get here.

"Stop her," Klein shouted. Looked like the elevator trick hadn't worked.

The rent-a-cop at the door looked confused. This woman who wasn't an employee was shouting at him to stop the woman who was. Nadia snapped him a don't-mess-with-me look that she'd perfected on insubordinate airmen and man-child fighter jocks. "Don't listen to her. She's just a consultant."

Nadia hit the street.

And there he was.

The blond guy from Vienna, black jacket open and a hand reaching in while he made long strides down the sidewalk. The Hawk Tech office was on a manmade quay in the middle of the river. The Archon agent was between her and the bridge that connected with the city on either side. She could run in the other direction, but it would just be the long way around to a spot her opponent could get to faster. She couldn't go back into the building and make a run for the garage. Klein was there and would stop her. Then she remembered a small footbridge connected this quay with the next one.

Nadia turned on her heel and took off at a run, following the sidewalk as it curved around the quay's western edge. She heard a shout and footfalls behind her and knew he was close. Nadia extended her stride. She saw the bridge and hit it at full speed, not even bothering trying to juke him. The path was narrow, just wide enough for one person at a time, with a waist-high metal barrier on either side and, beyond that, the Rhône.

Nadia could hear the Archon agent gaining on her as she ran, and she wondered what the Agency people would think of if she yelled for help. There was a large concrete building on the next quay, some kind of museum. Nadia was just a stride or two from the end of the bridge when a hand with a vise grip dropped onto her shoulder.

# 28

*Queenstown, Maryland*

Jason Wilcox, Former Director of the National Clandestine Service, and Mary, his wife of twenty-two years, were given a one-acre plot of land overlooking the Wye River on Maryland's Eastern Shore as a wedding gift from Mary's parents. The property had been in their family for generations. They saved a lot of money with Jason's many overseas tours and lived frugally when in D.C. Eventually, they built their weekend getaway, a two-story contemporary with cathedral ceilings and amazing views from any room of their waterfront along the river. They'd come here any weekend they could get away, especially after their children left for college. Certainly, they would have liked a few more years at the Senior Intelligence Service pay rate, but they were a pragmatic couple and grateful to get out of D.C., however it happened.

Wilcox greeted Colt warmly on the sunny afternoon in early May. He wore golf shorts, a white and gray striped polo, flip-flops, and a burgeoning beard. Colt wore faded red chinos and a navy short-sleeve button-down and boat shoes. This area was near Annapolis, where he'd attended the Naval Academy and remembered it fondly. Colt flew back from San Francisco two days ago, turned the laptop over to the tech team, and told Thorpe he had a personal errand to run that Friday.

For the first time in his Agency career, Colt felt utterly lost and needed advice.

Wilcox led Colt through the spacious house on a quick tour of the ground floor. The view was amazing. This place seemed like they built it out of windows. They walked out to the patio where Wilcox had a built-in gas grill, smoker, and prep area that would make some downtown restaurants envious. He retrieved a pair of beers from the patio fridge and handed one to Colt, saying, "Let's take a walk."

Wilcox led Colt down a curved concrete path to the shoreline, popping his beer as he went. Colt followed suit. Wilcox filled the first few strides with small talk, asking about Agency scuttlebutt. Colt noted he didn't ask what things were like under Hoskins' tenure. "So, what'd you want to see me about?"

"I'm not even sure how to explain this, boss," Colt said, shaking his head. "But it's bad. The Chinese have an asset in the NSC. Worse, we believe Nadia is about to be compromised." Intelligence officers had highly specialized expertise and experience, and they didn't just forget it when they left the service. In fact, it was common for many senior officers to consult occasionally on issues they'd been experts on during their Agency careers. But Colt was in dangerous territory. This visit was not official, not cleared, and an unauthorized disclosure if discovered.

But he didn't know what else to do.

"Is that because of Senator Hawkinson's witch hunt?" Wilcox said. He knew the rules Colt was breaking, but if he was going to let that stop him from helping his former protégé, Wilcox didn't let on.

Colt nodded. "For what it's worth, I think you bought us some critical time." Then he shared with Wilcox what they'd learned about Hawkinson and his potential bio-weapon.

"I knew Archie Chalcroft," Wilcox said. "Well. Damn it." He took a long pull on his beer.

"I met with someone claiming to represent Trinity. They confirmed that the Chinese have a spy in the US government but don't know who, or didn't trust me enough to say. They also told us Archon murdered Chalcroft. Still..."

"You don't know if you can trust them." Wilcox finished Colt's unspoken thought. "It's tough. Relies on trust. It's impossible to prove whether they are who they say they are, or if it's an Archon trap. What do Ford and Thorpe think?"

"Ford is pissed that I didn't tell him I was still in contact with Ava Klein. Thorpe lit me up over hiding the contact and then meeting with them."

"He's not wrong, Colt." Wilcox turned to face him. "When I took over NCS, I hand-picked that team. You, Thorpe, and Ford are all there by design and you can trust those two absolutely." Wilcox took a sip of his beer as he looked over the water. "They may be the only two you *can* trust. After our meeting with Katz last year, I went to see the director. Despite pretending to be surprised at the meeting, I'd actually known about Trinity long before then. I knew enough to know that they weren't some weird, computer-worshipping cult. I played dumb in the meeting because I wanted to see what he was willing to say. Make sure he was telling the truth. I shared what I knew with the director. You know what he said?"

"What?"

"He called it 'deep state nonsense.' That is a direct quote."

"Jesus," Colt said.

"I think Archon is among the most serious threats to our country and to the world. They don't recognize borders, they don't recognize laws, none of the existing systems we have for dealing with problems work against them. Hell, even terrorism is a solved problem. I mean, we know how to fight them and we've adjusted our laws accordingly. We worked out the jurisdictional issues. Archon transcends all that. Their members are citizens of friendly nations. Of our own. Who even goes after it? Are they terrorists, are they organized crime, are they something else? I wanted the director to be aware so that we could try to shift the IC's thinking, but he discounted it entirely."

"There's something else," Colt said. "This Trinity agent, I don't even know what to call her, gave me an exploit. She wanted me to have Nadia inject it into Hawkinson's secure network. She said they were just looking for a window, but I think they mean to do something else with it."

Wilcox drained his beer, took Colt's empty one, and said he'd be right back. A few moments later, he reappeared with a pair of fresh cans.

"You're in a tough spot, kid," Wilcox said, handing the beer over. "On the one hand, you broke some rules keeping contact with Ava. Not telling Thorpe and Ford about that meeting was wrong."

A shock of shame went through Colt's body and his heart sank. Getting chastised by Wilcox was a terrible feeling. Especially since he knew his mentor was right.

"The exploit, that's a tough call. Illegal, without question. To paraphrase a DCI I once worked under, if we're doing things we're afraid to tell Congress, then maybe those are things we ought not to be doing. But how do we fight an enemy that has no walls? 9/11 happened because it was everyone's job to figure it out first and it was nobody's job to figure it out first. I view Archon in much the same light."

"What would you do in my shoes?"

"Tough to say," Wilcox said honestly, shrugging. "For what it's worth, I didn't agree with them giving you that hack we designed. I thought the pen thing was too risky."

"What did you say?"

But Wilcox just gave him a wry smile. "Why don't you go replace that and we'll have a real chat?"

They sat in a pair of whitewashed Adirondack chairs facing the river and listened to it gently lapping against the rocks. "Ann is her real name, and everything she told you is on the level. She asked for my approval to contact you and I gave it to her. I urged against the exploit, however, for all the reasons I've already said. I told Ann that if one of our officers gets arrested trying to do an unauthorized hack of a civilian target, not only does NTCU get folded up but the only real operatives we have in the field probably go to jail." Wilcox shook his head. "They overruled me."

Colt's head swam. This was too incredible to believe.

"How long?"

"Have I known about Trinity? Since Vancouver, but before that shit went down with Kim, Hawkinson, and the Soviets."

"I think they prefer to be called 'Russians' now, boss."

"When they stop acting like the Soviet Union, I'll start calling them

Russians. Anyway, Trinity approached me a few years ago. They gave me compelling information and an opportunity to help. It was Ann who recruited me. She's GCHQ, or was. She's retired now. I met her many years ago. I was Deputy Chief of Station in Bucharest and she ran a listening post there. Anyway, she convinced me of Trinity's mission long before we thought Archon was a threat. Trinity isn't totally unknown, Colt. We have a sympathetic ear with some world leaders, some tech giants."

"Like who?"

Wilcox just smiled. "Let's just say that not everyone is as crazy as they seem in public. Now, as for what to do about your particular situation, Colt, that's up to you. I recruited you into this job because you're resourceful, you're trustworthy, and mostly because I can count on you to make the right decision when it counts. My job, as it has always been, is to put you in the best position to succeed. I'll share this with you, though. Samantha Klein is not to be trusted. She's playing for the other side."

"Are you saying she's with Archon?"

Wilcox nodded.

That revelation hit Colt with the same force as running straight into a brick wall.

"How is that possible?"

Wilcox shrugged. "An overdeveloped loyalty to her homeland and an honest, if misguided, desire to prevent calamity from happening again. Ann *knows* but chooses not to *believe*, if that makes sense. I suspect that's why she said nothing to you and Ava. Ann and Samantha were close once. Ann genuinely believes she can turn Klein around. I have no such illusions. Klein is a true believer. Be careful what you tell Ava, though."

"Thorpe ordered me not to talk to her until further notice."

"Follow the order this time," Wilcox said. "I'm not looped into whatever Ann has cooked up her sleeve. They're keeping me out of it, just on the off-chance that I might get called into another hearing."

"The Senate?"

Wilcox nodded. "As sure as you're born. There's a kind of gentlemen's agreement that you don't call people to testify after they've retired." He drained his second beer. "But Preston Hawkinson is not a gentleman. So, we agreed the less I know, the better."

They finished their conversation, and Colt left shortly after. He had a lot to consider. Wilcox assured him that whatever Colt decided, he would back him up in whatever way he could.

Colt made the long drive back to his home in Falls Church, arriving shortly after dinner. He lit his grill, opened another beer, and put a burger to the flame. When he'd finished eating, Colt grabbed his beer and found his personal laptop. Without a moment's hesitation, he took out the card that accompanied the pen in that Vienna hotel room and typed in the IP address on it. A blank page materialized on his browser, just a void of white space on the net. Moments later, a simple chat window appeared. Colt knew this was a Trinity-developed anonymized browser, similar to the open source version created by the privacy advocates, TOR. The signal would bounce across thousands of individual relays, obfuscating his location, and do the same for the user at the other end. As long as Colt's computer was secure, his message would be too.

He typed into the chat window, **I've decided to help**

Moments later, **Good man. I was worried you'd forgotten about us. You came highly recommended.**

**I see,** came the reply. **What are you prepared to do?**

**Whatever it takes.**

Ann didn't reply for another five minutes. Then, **Our man on NSC says Y/C gender disclosed in meeting. You don't have long.**

**What? What meeting?**

**Directorate of Technology Defense. We are certain this is where the leak is.**

Colt's mind raced. YELLOWCARD's gender disclosed... Thorpe was the NTCU rep to that working group, but he'd missed the first meeting because they were in California. Harlowe went in his place. She must have said "she" by mistake.

Colt typed, **Will be in touch.** Then he shut the browser, cleared his cache, and powered down the laptop before grabbing his keys and driving to Langley as quickly as he could. He needed to get a cable out to Bern Station immediately.

## 29

*Geneva, Switzerland*

The Archon agent yanked her shoulder.

Nadia turned herself into a fulcrum to use her attacker's momentum against him. She grabbed his arm with both hands, propelling him into the wall behind her. He crashed into it with a wet smack and showered her with hot curses. Nadia kicked him in the crotch and bolted for the corner of the building.

The agent lunged and doubled over, sweeping his arm out to tangle her legs. He missed one but got the other, throwing her off balance.

Nadia stumbled, grabbing for the metal safety barrier to break her fall. She faced her attacker and saw him moving already. Regaining her footing, Nadia sprinted the length of the walkway, heavy footfalls close behind her. She hit the front of the museum, angled north, and ran as fast as she could. Pedestrian bridges connected the quay and the museum to the mainland. Nadia hoped she could hit the streets on the north side and lose her pursuer in traffic.

Her mind raced as she tried to remember the map of the city. *The train station was, what, a half mile?*

Nadia ran. Fifty yards to the other side.

It was midday, and there was a lot of pedestrian traffic on the bridge. People got out of the way. Nobody helped her. No one tried to stop the Archon agent chasing her.

Then she heard something that shot pure terror through her body.

The Archon agent shouted, "Polezai!" He sounded breathless, but still forced the words out. That was why no one was helping her. They thought he was a cop.

Jesus, what if he was?

Nadia hit the end of the bridge, where a metal railing separated the sidewalk from the street. She hit the railing and vaulted over the bar but crashed onto the asphalt and rolled several times, mistiming her landing. Car horns erupted all around her. Nadia hadn't even thought to clear traffic.

"Stop! Polezai!"

Nadia rolled to a crouch as the Archon agent leaped over the rail, landing a few feet away. She was in the street. There was nothing she could use as a weapon. As the agent reached into his jacket, Nadia thrust herself up and turned to run, crashing into the hood of a honking sedan. She pushed off the hood and hit the sidewalk, yelling, "He's not a cop!"

Nadia hit the sidewalk and sped up, pushing people who wouldn't move. Someone shouted at her, someone else cursed, someone screamed. Nadia guessed the Archon agent had his weapon out now. He'd never risk firing into a crowd if he was with the Swiss government or police. Nadia knew she had to keep the sight lines broken. She zigzagged between people as she ran up the sidewalk, weaving like a high-speed drunk. She spotted a break in the canyon-like buildings up ahead. Behind her, the Archon op shouted commands. Nadia understood enough German to guess what he was saying. Get out of the way. Now.

She took a hard left after hitting the corner. Grime and exhaust residue climbed up the cream-colored building. Nadia had to hold her arms out to brace for impact. She was running so fast that such a hard turn risked breaking an ankle. Nadia used her arms to absorb the shock and then push herself off, using the momentum to change her direction. She rolled off the wall and sped down the alley, lungs burning. She couldn't keep this up much longer.

And there was nowhere to hide.

The narrow side street could fit a single vehicle and a couple inches of curb. A delivery truck blocked the way.

Nadia heard the high-pitched crack of a pistol shot and dove to the dirty ground on pure instinct. If his aim had been on, Nadia would be dead. She picked herself off the street and ran to the left, aiming for the gap between the delivery truck and the wall. The operative managed another shot, but it hit the wall just behind her. Nadia squeezed between the truck and the wall, chest heaving, but grateful to not be running for just a second.

When she emerged on the other side, breathing heavily, she confronted a confused pair of delivery men, their expressions asking whether they'd just heard gunshots. She took off again, cutting across the thin, T-shaped intersection with another side street, and hit the far sidewalk, using parked cars for cover until she barreled into someone coming out of a bodega. The woman shouted in surprise and shock as they both tumbled to the ground. Nadia picked herself up into a runner's stance and leapt into movement, not even bothering to apologize. Not that she had the wind for it, anyway.

Nadia sped up, aiming for the small park at the end of the street. She sprinted toward it, about to jump over a bench, when a hand struck her from behind. A violent push and Nadia pitched forward, out of control. She stumbled and crashed onto the bench before slamming into the ground with a sharp cry of pain. The agent walked around the bench holding a pistol. His shoulders jerked violently with the struggle to get air into his lungs. He staggered forward on unsteady legs, raising the pistol.

There would be no apprehension, no questioning.

Nadia heard a voice behind her. She didn't understand exactly what he said, but the tone was clear. Maybe someone was finally asking why an armed man was chasing her through the streets of Geneva.

As the Archon agent's eyes went to the speaker, Nadia pushed herself up with her left arm and kicked out with as much force as she could manage, striking the agent's inside right wrist. The force of it crushed the tendons, and he released his grip on the gun. Her kick sent the weapon flying. The agent snapped his head to her, fury in his eyes, and Nadia kicked again, this time a hard downward mule kick to his kneecap. The agent cried out in pain and collapsed to the ground. Then Nadia was on her feet, kicking him once in the jaw before taking off.

She turned right out of the park, aiming for the major streets, then ducked behind a building and put her hands on her knees, barely steady on her feet as she sucked air into her lungs. She cut across the street, ignoring traffic, then hit the sidewalk on the far side and turned to look behind but didn't see her pursuer. Nadia took long strides, but kept it at a walk, her hands shaking. She needed to make it to the train station. Nyon would be safe. The village was located on the western shore of the lake, less than forty-five minutes by rail. Commuter trains ran regularly. She could hide out there, or she could ride a ferry across the lake. Yeah, that was good. She'd check into a hotel and wait for Chuck Harmon to arrive from Bern.

Nadia rounded the corner onto one of the city's major arteries. A light rail rolled past on her right, followed by cars. She continued her route toward the city center and the train station, her breathing and pulse both descending to manageable levels, but her hands and legs still shaking. As she walked, Nadia refreshed the list of names she'd memorized, speaking the mantra to herself, relieved beyond measure she hadn't forgotten it in her flight from the office.

Samantha Klein was Archon.

There could be no doubt of that. She'd been on Nadia since the island, pulled her in for bullshit questioning sessions any time she was in town. Now this? Klein and Hawkinson were tight. Nadia had to assume she was burned. She hadn't gotten to use LONGBOW, and she hadn't gotten to use the pen. She'd gotten out with what she believed was Archon's target list. Still, Nadia couldn't help feeling like she'd failed. She hadn't completed her mission. Now, they'd have no choice but to pull her out.

She reached the end of the block and an intersection of five different streets. A light rail was about to cross in front of her at an angle. The car traffic stopped for it, and Nadia judged she had enough time to make it. As she crossed over the light rail track, she heard a voice growl out in accented English, "I've got you, you little bitch."

She turned to find the Archon agent standing just off the sidewalk, pistol raised.

The light rail's horn blared, and she was totally disoriented. Nadia had no sense of space.

A gunshot silenced everything else.

# 30

---

*Geneva, Switzerland*

The light rail whizzed by Nadia close enough that she felt the rush of air on her skin, smelled the ozone jumping off the overhead cables, inhaled the acrid odor of engine oil. She took several steps back from the train, still in the middle of the intersection. Then she patted her body, checking for injury. Nothing *felt* wrong, but she supposed it could be shock.

The train passed by and Nadia saw the Archon agent on his knees, then slumping to the street. Chuck Harmon, her Bern Station case officer, stood about fifteen feet behind him, pistol in hand.

Nadia was dimly aware of a car pulling up behind her.

"Get in." Nadia turned and saw Chuck's wife, Emily, behind the wheel, wearing dark glasses and a baseball cap. Nadia dove into the car and Emily hit the gas.

"What about Chuck?" Nadia asked.

"We got a plan," was all Emily said. Her voice was stretched tight.

Emily ripped through the intersection laid out like a five-pointed star, angry horns screaming after them. She turned a hard left, narrowly missing a delivery truck. Expletives showered out of her mouth. "Sorry," Emily said once they'd cleared the intersection. "Chuck went to the combat driving class, not me." She made an immediate right and then a left, then another right, winding through the streets.

"What's going to happen to him...the man Chuck shot?"

"Not my circus, not my monkeys." Emily was white-knuckling the steering wheel, and Nadia could see the veins in her arms standing out with the strain. She kept quiet.

They drove across several train tracks, and Nadia could see the station to her right. Emily turned left again and doubled back. She circled the block several times, moving between Rue Jean Gutenberg and Rue Voltaire, driving clockwise with the flow of one-way cross streets. On their third pass, her phone buzzed and Chuck emerged from the park on Rue Voltaire.

Emily stopped in the road to the vitriolic protestations of the motorists behind her. She hopped out and jumped in the back while Chuck got in the driver's seat, moving before he'd even closed the door.

"Are you hurt?" Chuck asked, pulling on his seatbelt.

Nadia patted herself down. "I don't think so," she said. "He hit me once, but that's about it."

The car was silent and Chuck concentrated on the route. He angled them south, driving as fast as he could without drawing attention to them. Chuck took the long way out of Geneva, avoiding the routes that would have brought them closer to Hawk Tech's offices on the Rhône or old town. They arced through the industrial sections of Lancy and Carouge, then headed east into the more distant suburbs.

There wasn't time for a full evasion run, but when they were outside the city, Chuck pulled off the road in a secluded spot and changed license plates. The car was a blue BMW 3 Series, a ubiquitous model in Switzerland. Chuck said he was worried less about them getting picked up by the Swiss police and more about the people that guy worked for. Chuck and Emily both changed clothes when they switched the plates, and Emily had a set of new clothes for Nadia.

Thirty minutes later they were at a small, quiet restaurant in a village outside Geneva with a round of beers. No one touched their drinks.

They had a table in the walled-in back garden. There were no other patrons.

"So, Langley thinks your cover may be compromised," Chuck said in a bone-dry voice.

"No shit," Nadia said, just as dryly. "I can't thank you both enough for being there." Emily put her hand on top of Nadia's in a comforting gesture.

"Colt's cable gave little details," Chuck said, "just that he had credible intel you were in imminent danger. I sent a couple of pings through our secure messenger, but I didn't hear back. Didn't know if your phone was locked in the Faraday cage or if they got to you, so we got in the car and broke some traffic laws."

"Is that guy gonna be a problem?"

"We're generally not supposed to shoot people in broad daylight in the middle of the street, if that's what you're asking. But we'll monitor the situation. If it looks like the US is being implicated, we'll reach out and smooth things over. I don't expect any problems, especially if he's a Swiss citizen. It was pretty clear he was trying to kill you and many people saw it." Chuck finally lifted his beer stein. "Any idea who he was?"

"I don't know his identity but I absolutely know who he was with. Get your pen out. I need you to copy some names down and get these to Colt immediately."

"Slow your roll, kid. I just shot a man and I want to know what it's about. You don't know his name, so let's start with why he was after you. What group is he with and are more of them coming?"

"I'm not sure how much I can actually tell you," Nadia said, and flipped a glance at Chuck's wife.

"I can take a lap," Emily said.

Chuck shook his head. "It's fine. If we're in danger, she might as well hear it, too. Tell me what's going on, Nadia."

"They're called Archon. Colt is the real authority on them. They're like... they're like a terrorist group, but businessmen and politicians, elites. People with money, like turning-the-world's-gears kind of money."

"That sounds less scary than the terrorists I'm used to."

"Hawkinson is one, and so is his sister Sheryl. We think his uncle, the senator, might be as well. They also have this psycho ex-Mossad officer named Samantha Klein. She's a security consultant for Hawk Tech, and she's been on me since we left the island. That guy back there, I think he reported to her. These people manipulate economies, whole industries. They influence society in the direction they want it to go."

"What's their end game?"

"AI," Nadia said. "Artificial General Intelligence, a machine that can think like we do. It can reason, apply common sense, multitask. All the things people take for granted."

"Is that even possible?" Emily asked. "A computer that can think like us?"

Nadia shrugged. "No one knows, actually. There's some missing link between what machines can do now and AGI that no one has figured out yet. But Archon believes that not only should they be the first, they should also use AGI to eliminate what traditional government does today."

"Why?" Chuck asked.

"So people will decide that they don't need government anymore. Meanwhile, Archon is in control. Look, I know it sounds crazy. Jesus, it *is* crazy, but this shit is all real." Nadia paused. She reached for her beer and then retracted her hand. "I'm probably not supposed to tell you this, but I need you to believe me. Archie Chalcroft, the British Member of Parliament?"

"He was about to become head of MI6."

"They killed him."

"No, they didn't," Chuck scoffed. "He died of a heart attack."

"That's what I'm trying to tell you, Chuck. Hawkinson has been developing a bio-weapon. They use these things called 'xenobots,' they're like microscopic, bioengineered robots, and they're targeted with a person's DNA. That's why Hawkinson has been hacking these genetics companies. They used this weapon to kill Chalcroft because he was one of their enemies. Only the DNA targeting isn't dialed in yet, so it also affected his kids."

"So that's why his wife survived?"

"That's why his wife survived," Nadia agreed.

"I really wish I'd taken that lap," Emily said.

"Now, I got a list of names. You need to send Colt a cable today with this list. I think they might be targets. I got it from the bioengineering lab at Hawk Tech. I used a source to get inside the room, and when he was away, I used his credentials to get onto his machine and snoop around. These names were in a locked file called 'Client List.' I think that's a code so that the engineers working on it won't know what they're actually doing. I need you to believe me, Chuck. This is as real as it gets. The guy who attacked me was one of their operatives. I don't know who he was, but he tailed me to my meet with Colt in Vienna. He's got to have police or intelligence training. That's what makes these guys so dangerous. They can come from anywhere."

Chuck pulled out a pocket notebook and pen. Nadia recited the names from memory, and he copied them down.

When he was finished, he showed the list to Nadia for verification, then said, "Okay, let's talk about getting you out of here. We're taking you back to Bern. You'll get a new passport made up, just in case Hawkinson has traction with the Swiss authorities and tries to flag your real one."

Nadia shook her head. "I'm not leaving."

"What are you talking about? Of course you are."

"Nadia, be smart about this," Emily said calmly. "You did a great job, but you need to be careful. It's time to go."

"No, I've got it worked out. I can wedge between Klein and Hawkinson."

"You can't go back in."

"I'm not giving you a choice, Chuck." Nadia pushed back her chair and stood. "I'm not leaving now. There's too much at stake." She pointed at the notebook on the table. "Make sure that gets sent *today*. Tell Colt I'm staying. He'll understand. I need to do something."

"You don't have a cover anymore," Chuck said.

"The mission isn't done, Chuck."

Nadia left the restaurant with long strides. Chuck caught her in the parking lot.

"I can't let you do this. Your cover is *burned*, Nadia. Do you understand what that means? Colt told me about your training, how they rushed you through it. You're not prepared for this. And the people who sent that guy?" Chuck pointed toward Geneva. "They've already told Hawkinson they failed. If you step foot in Geneva, you are as good as dead."

"I don't see it that way and you need to hear me out."

"No, I need to get you on an airplane."

"Chuck, damn it, listen to me. Colt gave me an exploit that will let us get onto Hawkinson's phone. We'll see all of their comms. I can't leave until that's done. Now, Hawkinson didn't order me hit, which means it was Samantha Klein. All I have to do is paint her with the crazy brush. I just need Guy to come back here so I can hit his phone. Then, I promise, I will leave. He trusts me. If he thought I was a spy, he'd have killed me already."

"Nadia, Langley gave me an order to put you on a plane. I realize that you don't work for me, but you do work for them."

"Chuck, damn it, you're not listening. None of you are! I have information that they don't. They can't pull me out now."

Chuck studied her. Nadia knew this feeling well—he was sizing her up.

"Let's call Colt and see what he says," he finally relented. "But if he tells you to leave, you have to leave. Deal?"

"Deal. How are we going to call him?"

"Your phone. He briefed me on LONGBOW. You can have secure calls on that. It won't stop someone from listening in if they were out here, but I think we're probably safe as long as we keep it short. This is the kind of thing they'd kick my ass over, but I suppose a sketchy phone call is the least of my sins today."

Nadia dialed NTCU's emergency line that immediately connected her with the ops center. They patched her over to Colt's direct line.

"Nadia, what's going on?"

She filled him in on everything that happened that day.

"Well, Chuck is following protocol. Drive back to Bern with him and fly home."

"Colt, I can't." Nadia dropped her voice to a whisper, suddenly remembering they were outside and not in a vault. "I haven't been able to get close enough to our guy to use the thing. Given what we know about this bioweapon, we can't pull me out now."

"Nadia, you have no cover anymore."

"I can convince Hawkinson to let me stay. He trusts me."

"Out of the question."

"You have to let me try, Colt. You can't yank me out of the game while we're still down a point."

"Klein is a member of Archon. She obviously suspects you and sent her lap dog to take you out. Why do you think Hawkinson is going to trust you over her?"

"I can convince him that she's off her rocker, paranoid and jumping at shadows. She's had it in for me ever since the island when I beat that stupid lie detector."

"For the record, you *failed* the lie detector," Colt said. "You just convinced Hawkinson that the machine didn't work."

"Same difference."

"This is what I'll allow," Colt said. "I need some time to come up with something you can use. This only works if we can discredit Samantha Klein. You stay hidden until you hear from me, understand? I will do everything I can, but if I can't find any decent dirt, you're out. Got it?"

"I got it. How long do I have?"

Colt didn't answer immediately. "Two days."

"Okay," Nadia said, and hung up.

"What'd he say?" Chuck asked.

"He wants two days to come up with something that I can use to throw shade on Samantha Klein. If he doesn't come up with an angle to drive a wedge between her and Hawkinson, you get to dump me on a plane."

Chuck looked down at his watch.

"Well, I guess you're going to get a first-class tour of Bern. Let's go. Em and I know a great Italian place by the river."

# 31

"What the actual f—"

"Ford," Colt said loudly. "Not helping."

Information collapsed in on them over the past few hours at a dizzying rate, coalescing almost too quickly to process.

CERBERUS matched Kim's "businessman" with an immigration photo and fingerprint record from Customs and Border Protection belonging to a Chinese diplomat. He lived with his wife and two teenage children in a house in Northwest D.C., close to the embassy. The FBI foreign surveillance team was on him now. A special agent was carrying a wiretap warrant to a Foreign Intelligence Surveillance Court magistrate now. The drone surveillance matched the passport and CPB photos, but the name did not, clearly showing that either Jeff Kim or the man's passport was incorrect. Either way, he was not the "President of the Americas Division" of XZE Corporation. And a middle-grade consular affairs functionary would have no reason to meet with the CEO of an American tech company.

Colt believed he was a Chinese intelligence officer. Ford gave the name "Liu Che" to his contact in the Asia Division to see if their source in the PLA

Intelligence Directorate could confirm it. Likely he could not, as those were two insular, untrusting, and competing organizations, but it was worth a try.

Nadia's revelations were equally explosive.

He hoped that would outweigh the shitstorm over her attempted murder and sketchy justification to stay in place.

Colt got the cable about eight that morning. It contained a list of names and a comprehensive report on exactly what went down in Geneva. He copied down the names and told Ford he'd be back. Ford put a hand on Colt's chest and told him no more bullshit.

"I can find out if they are Trinity in ten minutes. That will verify if it's actually a kill list, like Nadia thinks."

"You never goddamn learn," Ford said.

"I talked to Wilcox," Colt said, his voice just above a hiss. "I went to see him Friday. He told me he's a member of Trinity. Has been for some time. He said that's why you and I ended up here. He also said Ann recruited him. Everything she told me was true."

Ford was quiet as he thought through the options. Colt knew what he was thinking because he had the same questions.

"Okay. Let's check it out." They went over to Colt's desk and fired up the unclassified terminal that could access the public internet. Colt navigated to the Trinity TOR web address and when the chat box popped up, he typed, **NEED TO TALK NOW. ARE YOU THERE?**

After about five minutes, Ford said, "So how long are you intending to wait before the Agency's internet police fast rope in here and arrest us?"

"We're fine," Colt said. "I had one of the NSA tech guys configure the browser for me. I told him I was contacting a source on the dark web and I needed to make sure it didn't trip any alarms."

"Good God, you might be learning."

Ann replied, **Hello. Do tell, dear boy.**

"Dear boy?"

"She's English, Ford," Colt said. "Also, shut up."

**My op found a list of names. We think they might be the next targets, like Arch.**

No form of communication was truly secure. Colt knew *everything* could be compromised given sufficient time, technology, or access. The routing protocol anonymized the message and sent it through thousands of virtual routers across the world, but Colt was still careful about how much detail he put in each message. He realized "Arch," short for "Archie," could easily be mistaken for "Archon," but hoped Ann knew what he was talking about.

**Pls provide names.**

Colt entered the list and sent it.

**Four of them are ours. The others have strategic value. Are threats to our shared enemy.**

"Believe me now?" Colt said.

"Don't get ahead of yourself, junior."

Ann sent, **Have you used the pen?**

"What's the pen?" Ford asked, leaning over to get a closer look at the screen.

"It's a thumb drive hidden inside a pen. She gave us an exploit in Vienna to inject in Hawkinson's secure network, said it would open up an undetectable port for them to access. She wouldn't tell me anything else. I didn't trust her and she reciprocated."

"Seems fair. Who has it now?"

"Nadia. I wanted to bring it back here, have our guys analyze it, but"—Colt lowered his voice to a mumble—"something happened."

"What happened?" Ford said, pronouncing each word like it was its own sentence.

There was no way to hide this.

"Ava lifted the pen out of my pocket and gave it to Nadia, told her it was from me. I didn't realize it until after I'd met with Nadia. I used Ava to run interference in Vienna. She was getting Nadia safely out of the train station while I was tussling with the guy on the platform."

"Oh, Jesus Christ and all the angels." Ford buried his head in his meaty paw of a hand. "Your libido is the biggest threat to national security since President Clinton."

"Damn it, Fred. Can we please focus? I screwed up. I got it. You lecturing me doesn't help Nadia in the field."

Colt typed, **What does the pen do?**

Ann wrote back immediately. **Writes beautifully.** Then, **Sorry, couldn't help it.**

"She's like that," Colt said.

Ann wrote, **Undetectable remote access to his network. Can launch attacks at time of our choosing. Burn the whole thing down.**

"This is the sort of thing," Fred said, just above a whisper, "that it's better Thorpe not know we can do. Plausible deniability. It's the difference between our company and his."

"You're actually protecting him?"

"I still think he's an asshole, but he's gone out on a limb for me and that earns some grace."

Colt typed, **Op has pen. Will try to use if cover still intact. There was a situation. Oppo involved.**

Ann replied, **Understood. Be careful.**

"You're going to tell Nadia to use that thing?"

"We don't know Nadia's current status," Colt said. "If Hawkinson lets her back in, I think we leave it up to her. I need to warn Ava about her aunt."

"You need to absolutely *not* do that." Ford spun Colt's chair around with force, so the two men faced off in the cramped cubicle. "Let this burn in good, lover boy. You do not do that. I will back Thorpe up to the moon on this. I understand why you want to warn her, but if you do this outside of official comms, Thorpe will burn you, and I will hold the lighter."

"So, I just don't tell her?"

"Are you willing to put it in a cable?"

"No."

"Okay, then. We can contact Katz. Meet him somewhere in town and tell him. We log the meetings like the good little soldiers we are. It's a follow-up to the confab we had last year. But when we do our writeup, we just forget to write down *every little detail*. Then, we've done our part."

Now that Nadia was using the LONGBOW-enabled phone, Colt was comfortable using their covert messaging app. Its design was like the Trinity platform, encrypting traffic and bouncing it across thousands of randomized servers. The encryption was the strongest NSA could devise for a mobile device, but Colt didn't know how long it would hold up against Hawkinson's AI. However, since Nadia couldn't connect her phone to their network, hopefully that meant it would stay isolated from Hawk Tech.

This may be his only chance to communicate. That wasn't even the only threat. Chuck Harmon shot Samantha Klein's bloodhound. He survived and was now in Swiss police custody under guard. Klein would tell Hawkinson what happened. According to Harmon's contacts in the Swiss Federal Police, the Archon agent's name was Bastian Stager, and he was Swiss intelligence. Harmon said they were working on a story with the local Swiss police that an undercover Swiss Federal Police officer shot Stager. Harmon was working very hard to find a convincing reason Stager not only knew about a CIA officer but also tried to kill her.

The cleanup was going to be a bitch.

Apparently, it cost the Bern Chief of Station all the favors he had with his Swiss counterparts.

Colt fed Bastian Stager's name and photo to CERBERUS, cross-referencing it with Hawk Tech. He got hits almost immediately. Once the system started making connections, the speed with which it multiplied them was mind-blowing. The municipal police in Geneva had fifteen reports from seven Hawk Tech employees in the last six months of someone following them, hanging around their apartments. Two of the females called him a stalker. The police description matched Stager exactly. He was a trained intelligence officer who knew how to watch someone and remain unseen. He wanted them to know they were being followed so he could watch their reaction. The one who rabbited would be the spy.

Colt checked those names against the list of people Nadia gave in an earlier report, finding that each of them had multiple aggressive "security interviews" with Samantha Klein since Hawk Tech set up shop in Bern.

Colt sent Nadia another coded message and said they needed to talk. Now.

"If we're wrong," Ford said, "it's that girl's life."

--------

They were just closing down the chat window when Thorpe rounded the corner and appeared at Colt's cube.

"I've been looking for you two," he said. "I just heard from the surveillance team on Liu. He just left the consulate and is driving all over D.C. Looks a lot like a surveillance detection route."

"They got drones up?"

"Can't fly drones over the District, but there are six cars on him and helos orbiting in Maryland and Virginia. CI has high confidence that this guy is the NSC spy's handler."

"How so?" Colt asked.

"CERBERUS," Thorpe said. "I had the analysts run Admiral Denney through the system on Ford's suggestion the other day. Looking at the data traffic on his phone, every time we had a leak over the last six months, a data surge came off his personal cell phone. So then I had them look at Lieutenant General Rubio. He was the Army officer originally named the NSC's Tech Defense Director."

"Let me guess," Ford said. "CERBERUS is having a really hard time proving that he committed contract fraud."

Thorpe nodded. "I asked for a tail on Denney and they shot it down." He held up his hands against the inevitable backlash. "They said we did not have sufficient evidence to run surveillance on a Naval flag officer and—"

"NSC staff member," Ford growled out.

"That too," Thorpe said. "That too. So instead, I used NTCU's direct line with the FISA court and requested the surveillance myself. I brought the CERBERUS findings with me. Judge signed off on it, but he made it quite clear that it's my ass if this goes south. The Bureau is *furious* that I went around them. If the admiral is there, we'll arrest him too."

"Congratulations, Will," Ford said sardonically.

"For what?" Thorpe asked, countering Ford's intonation.

"You're one of us now," Ford said. "Welcome to the Island of Misfit Toys."

# 32

*Arlington, Virginia*

Whatever else he may have been, Glen Denney was an operator, and he knew full well the value of a plan. For the first time in what seemed like an eternity, Glen felt hope. He sensed liberation, freedom. He would speak with the CNO in the coming days and explain Mia's sickness, telling the Admiral that the reason he'd angled for this NSC job was because his wife was in treatment and had a doctor they believed could help her. It was a small lie, but measured against the larger deceptions of his life, an inconsequential one. He would ask the CNO to reconsider him for the AIRPAC command and hoped he would understand the choices Glen made. The CNO was a good man. Glen had known him for a long time. Returning to San Diego would be good for them. The family had been happiest there, and Mia had the fewest relapses into gambling.

If not, Glen would retire at the end of this and probably make mid-six figures as a defense consultant as far from Washington, D.C. as he could get. He would also be of no further value to Liu.

Though that would simply be additional insurance.

Glen's plan would absolve him of those... responsibilities... soon enough.

He arrived at home in the early evening, having skipped out on his late-day commitments, including a "working dinner" in the West Wing with some White House staff looking for tech policy recommendations for some upcoming budget hearings. He'd pawned this one off on his chief of staff, but the group was already taking notice of his absences, his premature departures. The West Wing was not the Pentagon. That place was so filled with senior officers, even a three-star admiral could fade into the background for a time. Glen "confided" in his chief of staff that his wife was ill and undergoing treatment, which was what kept him in D.C. instead of returning to the fleet. He kept the details sparse, knowing that the chief of staff would trade it for other information by week's end. That was how the place worked.

All the kids were attending after-school activities or sports and wouldn't be home until much later. Mia was in the kitchen. Glen walked in, setting his cover on the counter, and kissed his wife gently on the cheek.

"I'm sorry about the other day. I overreacted," he said, his voice solemn. "I need to be more mindful. I know you can't always help it."

Tears welled in Mia's eyes, and she looked away, traces of shame on her face. "I'm trying. I'm really trying."

Glen put his arms around her. "I know you are. Don't worry about the money. We'll figure it out."

He went to the bedroom to change out of his uniform, pulling on a pair of jeans and T-shirt, and he was reaching for his Navy windbreaker before admonishing himself to be less conspicuous. He grabbed a light jacket and ballcap instead, then went to his office. Glen tapped out the code and opened the metal door, removing the contents and closing the door behind him. He placed the item in his pocket and returned to the kitchen.

"Are you going somewhere?"

"I've got something I need to do."

"Glen," Mia said in a halting voice. "Why don't you stay in tonight? Whatever it is, it can wait. The kids are gone. Why don't we have a nice dinner and just talk?"

"I'd love to, but this is... this is something I have to do. But it'll be my last night out for a while. Promise."

"I thought you wouldn't have to deal with congressional testimony in this new job."

A nervous feeling washed over him, and Glen realized he didn't have an excuse for sneaking out to meet with Liu anymore. For a moment, he felt like a cornered animal. "At this level, it's always there, I'm afraid. This time, I just need some air, love. This new job is really taxing. Working at the White House, they're kind of up in your business all the time. And the thing I was preparing testimony for—that situation about the Russian attack on the Hawkinson company—that's sort of in my portfolio now. I just need to clear my head."

"I'll go with you," Mia said cheerfully.

Glen walked over and took her in his arms, bending low to kiss her forehead. "Next time. I really need an hour or two to myself."

"Glen, whatever it is, let's talk about it. I don't want you to go out tonight."

What if he stayed? Something was on Mia's mind, and she clearly needed to be with him. What if he just used his covert messaging app and told Liu what he knew? Then Glen shifted and felt the weight in his pocket and knew that he needed to go. Time to end this, time to wake up from the nightmare for good.

"Tomorrow night, I'll make sure I'm home early. We'll have a nice dinner out on the deck and too much wine. I promise."

"Glen..."

"It's going to be all right, Mia."

Glen kissed her again and left the house through the garage. Once in the car, he removed the Beretta M9 from his pocket and set it next to him on the seat.

Glen would deliver his final intelligence and then inform Liu their relationship was over.

One way or another.

# 33

*Washington, D.C.*

"He's going to Whole Foods? This is the most jacked-up SDR I've ever seen," Ford said mockingly.

The FBI's spy hunters followed the suspected Chinese intelligence officer, Liu Che, from his home in D.C.'s Van Ness neighborhood up Connecticut Avenue into Chevy Chase, Maryland. There, Liu looped around the Chevy Chase Country Club and actually pulled into the club parking lot, where he waited for several minutes, as if to check if he was being followed. Then he drove a convoluted route through the adjacent neighborhoods until linking back up with Wisconsin Avenue and driving south back into the District. Liu pulled into a parking garage in Tenleytown with the FBI chase vehicles orbiting like black flies on a carcass. Thorpe, Ford, and Colt were in a black Suburban about a block behind the rotating chase vehicles. They'd caught up by the time Liu entered the parking garage.

The area was crowded. The parking garage was connected to a Whole Foods Market and sat above a convenience store. A row of restaurants and small shops in front of it faced Wisconsin Avenue and a high school.

"We've got the sedan exiting the parking garage from the rear entrance," the special agent in charge of the surveillance detail said. The agent narrated the car's path as it took a right out of the garage onto a side street and then a left on Albemarle Street. "Looks like he's heading back home."

"There's no way," Colt said. "Why go into the parking garage just to drive through it?"

"Grocery pickup?" Thorpe offered.

"All units, stand by," the lead agent said. "We've got an Asian male matching the subject's description exiting the parking facility on foot."

"Looks like they were dropping off, not picking up," Ford said, leaning forward to clap Thorpe hard on the shoulder.

This was a move similar to the one Colt used to shake Liu's service in Hong Kong.

The lead agent dispatched a car to follow the sedan, even though it meant losing one of their chase vehicles. Running surveillance in the District was already difficult because the airspace restrictions prevented the use of drones, and air support requests had to be coordinated and cleared by numerous agencies. There was a process for it, but not enough time.

Thorpe directed the driver to circle the block.

"Bet he's going to the Metro," Colt said, spotting a Metro station on the corner. No sooner did the words leave Colt's mouth than the lead agent ordered two cars to empty and follow the man down the escalator to the underground station.

Once Liu (Colt knew it had to be him) had dropped out of sight from the street, one team of FBI shadows popped out of their car as it slowed just enough for them to exit. One went to the escalator, one to the elevator, and another team across the street performed a similar maneuver, ensuring they covered all the exits.

Their radios wouldn't work underground, and the shadows updated the ground team by text. Liu took a Red Line Metro south into the District. FBI chase vehicles raced down surface streets, lights flashing in the sludgy crawl of evening traffic. The Suburban carrying Colt, Ford, and Thorpe got bottled up in the perpetual jam of DuPont Circle, though two agents jumped out of their vehicle to cover that Metro station's exits. Colt saw the logic now. Liu's cursory SDR through suburban Maryland was just to light himself up since he likely assumed *someone* was following him. Then his loop back to the Metro drew the coverage out. Without real-time comms between the shadows and the surface pursuit team, the FBI had to cover each of the Metro stops, which thinned their ranks.

"He's trying to spread out the coverage," Colt said. "Think about how many Metro stops there are in the District. Plus, once he hits Metro Center, it links up with three other lines. He'll know how bad traffic is this time of day."

"We'll have a dozen pursuit vehicles massed around Metro stations and he's on his way to Virginia or Maryland," Thorpe said.

"Liu won't double back on the Red Line and head back to Maryland that way. It'd be too easy to spot him. Green Line goes through D.C.'s east side, but Denney lives in Virginia. He's not making that trip this time of day," Colt said. "My guess is it's Blue Line to Virginia."

Thorpe called the special agent running the surveillance detail, and apparently he'd just reached the same conclusion. Thorpe gave the driver instructions to break off and head for Foggy Bottom. From there they could get on the I-66 Westbound bridge and cross the river into Virginia in hopefully less than thirty minutes.

------

Liu saw no one follow him, but he also wasn't about to leave anything to chance. He thought he'd spotted a tail while driving from D.C. to Maryland, but that wasn't a concern. The American FBI agents frequently picked up embassy staff and tailed them just for practice. Liu didn't believe they knew his true identity yet, but one never really knew. He jumped off the train just as the doors closed and made fast steps to the escalator, checking to make sure he was indeed the last person off. On the surface, he walked two blocks south to Farragut West, cutting through some buildings to shield him from any street-level surveillance. Once at the Farragut West Metro, Liu took a Blue Line train bound for Virginia.

He rode the packed train through Rosslyn and its ascent to the surface, watching the brownish track of the Potomac on its long crawl south. Liu left the train at the Arlington Cemetery Station and walked along the sidewalk a short distance to the long concrete parking garage, where one of his colleagues had left a car for him. Liu checked his surroundings for any remaining minders and then entered the garage. The car was on the lower level, a red Kia sedan. It wasn't locked, and they hid the keys underneath the seat. Liu popped the trunk, removed the light windbreaker, and put it on, along with a pair of glasses with clear plastic lenses. Then he left the parking garage, driving south on VA 110 and pulling off at the first exit before looping backward on Washington Boulevard, headed toward the river, the sprawling Pentagon complex on his right. Liu looped back yet again onto the George Washington Memorial Parkway for a short run before exiting into the access way for the LBJ Memorial Grove and the Pentagon Lagoon Yacht Basin.

*Of course the Pentagon would have a parking lot for yachts,* Liu noted sourly. What a glaring example of capitalist excess that America's military leaders could not only afford boats, but apparently had them in sufficient quantity that they needed their own marina.

Liu parked and walked to his meeting spot with Denney.

# 34

---

*Arlington, Virginia*

Glen watched Liu emerge from the indigo pools cast by the thick coniferous trees that formed the LBJ Memorial Grove. There was a granite marker in the grove's center carved in the shape of an extended index finger, and a direct line of sight to the Washington Monument on the far side of the river. The grove, and its companion park named for Johnson's wife Lady Bird, was on a small swath of land between a brackish channel that abutted the Pentagon grounds and the Potomac.

The Beretta was heavy on his hip.

Glen had a concealed carry holster, but was still nervous that Liu would spot the weapon. He'd bought the gun ten years ago when Mia relapsed after several wonderful years of freedom. Glen worried that someone might follow her home to collect on a debt. It was the same model as the armed forces' standard-issue pistol, a weapon Glen used for decades.

He adjusted his jacket, once again ensuring that the bottom hem covered the pistol.

The sky looked like a dying fire, and the trees cast long shadows. In the background he could hear the low din of omnipresent traffic.

"What do you have for me, Glen?" Liu's words dripped with irritation and annoyance.

"I'm sorry this is an inconvenience for you," Glen said.

"Speak."

"In a minute. I have information about the CIA spy in the Hawkinson organization, like you asked. But before I give it to you, I'm telling you we're done."

Liu chuckled. It was a brittle, hollow sound, like glass breaking in a hallway. "I think you misunderstand the nature of this relationship, Glen."

"No, I don't. I'm changing it. We're done."

"You and I have worked together for a long time. I've always been there for you. Together, we helped Mia avoid a terrible fate in Macao. Through the years, our collaboration has relieved some of the pressures of her...illness. I daresay we've also helped keep our two countries from going to war with each other. I think these goals far outweigh the stress you may be feeling now."

"All that talk about a golden retirement? You promised me a way *out*. I've done what you asked and now I'm telling you I'm done."

"After the lengths I've gone through to get you where you are? It isn't just this one maneuver to put you on the National Security Council. My hand has guided your entire career. You are finally in the place I need you to be. I'm not letting you just walk away now."

Glen pulled the pistol out of the holster.

"No, that's exactly what you're going to do."

---

"Where in the hell are they?" Thorpe barked into his phone. It was on speaker so Colt and Ford could hear the conversation, with Thorpe awkwardly holding it up in the speeding SUV.

"Your guy ditched the train and went to the streets," the surveillance team lead said. "We lost him. Our assets are all tied up in the District. I've radioed for backup cars to mobilize in Virginia, but this guy will be long gone by the time we get there."

"Jesus Christ on a three-legged crutch," Ford said. Thorpe sliced the air between them with his glare and Ford said nothing else.

"Where is Denney?" Thorpe asked.

"The admiral left his residence in Arlington about a half hour ago. We tracked him to the LBJ Memorial on Columbia Island. We have a car holding station now."

"Get all of your men there now. Air support if you can get it."

"I don't know, Will," the surveillance team lead said, hedging. "This guy's a three-star admiral, and he's on the National Security Council. I am really uncomfortable with this."

"I don't have time to explain. Just get people there, now!" Thorpe hung up his phone. They'd finally cleared the I-66 bridge and were taking the VA-50 offramp. Thorpe told the driver to turn. "Pull off up here. Do you know where the LBJ Memorial is?"

"Yeah," the special agent at the wheel said. "I can get us there in five minutes, tops." He accelerated, blasting past cars that pulled aside to let them through.

"Thank God we didn't get the B-team," Ford said.

---

"Glen, put the gun down before you do something we both regret." Liu had scoured the earlier edge in his voice. The pistol launched them into a dangerous new universe of trouble, made worse by Glen's unpredictable state of mind.

Liu knew his asset well. Glen Denney was possessed of that singular quality of conceit and arrogance that skirted the pathological. Everyone was a subordinate unless he deemed them a peer.

"I'm not going to do anything *I'll* regret," Glen said. "I just want out."

"Okay, okay," Liu said, hands gently patting the air in front of him. "You want out. I can make that happen."

"Liu, this isn't one of those 'say whatever I want to hear because I have a gun' situations. I know you'll just double-cross me later. I saw what you did to Darius Rubio and you're not pulling that shit with me. You'll be arrested and you'll sit in jail until your government offers mine something valuable in return. Given the state of things, that's probably a long time."

"But you'll be exposed as a spy," Liu said evenly.

"Who's to say? Maybe you made all of this up? Maybe you fabricated whatever 'evidence' you have to frame me. Blackmailed me into spying for you the way you ruined Darius Rubio. Which one of us will they trust?"

Liu regarded his asset with newfound respect. Certainly, Liu had enough information to ruin Glen Denney several times over, but the admiral had thought this through and devised a plausible enough explanation for whatever Liu might offer in his defense.

Liu seethed at Denney's temerity, but he'd played this game long enough to know the pathology. Spies rarely understood the depths of the bargains they made. Oh, Liu managed a few agents who did, but those were the rare individuals who spied for the betterment of China. Denney may have started this to save his wife, but he knew full well what he was doing, even if he tried to deny it now.

Liu could ruin Denney completely and irrevocably. The Service had thorough records of Denney's "collaboration" going back twenty-five years. Liu would be exposed as a spymaster but Denney would be destroyed. This was a foolish and wasteful end to such a strong partnership, one that had benefited them both.

Liu had three options.

One, he could free his asset. Not immediately, but he could offer the admiral an eventual way out. Continue their work for the length of his term on the security council. That would give Liu time to soften the blow with his superiors. That was personally risky for Liu. The Ministry wouldn't understand why he was cutting so valuable an asset loose. He could argue that the admiral would soon retire and his usefulness was at an end. They could always reactivate him later. This was risky also, in that Denney might not agree, given his current state of mind.

Two, he could agree to Denney's demands and take this final report. Gaining access to Hawkinson might mollify his superiors, though Liu would still need to craft a convincing fiction explaining why Denney was no longer an asset. Hawkinson was a long gamble. Liu hadn't approached him yet. He didn't know if Hawkinson would be receptive, but if he was, the Ministry would soon forgive letting Glen Denney go.

The third option was to mollify Denney, then speak to him when cooler heads prevailed and attempt to reset the relationship. The Ministry would expect that.

"Glen, I think there is a way out of this where we can both get what we want. But first, I have to understand what brought you to this." Liu laughed and tried to make it sound genuine. "I actually thought we'd become friends over these many years. And I've certainly helped you out, have I not? With Mia, if not your career."

"You went too far. I worked for thirty years to be selected for the Naval Air Forces command. Thirty years and you just took it away." Denney waved his free hand in a wide, violent arc. The suddenness of the motion made Liu jump. "All because you wanted information. You didn't think to ask what *I* wanted. You didn't think to ask if I was comfortable with the risks involved. Or if I can even do what you're asking. I'm a pilot, not a spy. And I'm not a goddamn chess piece for you to move on some board."

*You're* very much *a spy, my friend,* Liu said to himself. *One of the most prolific I've ever met.*

"I see now that I overreached. I should have spoken to you first." Liu pressed his hands together in a gesture of solemn placation. "I believe our work has avoided an unnecessary conflict between our countries. This partnership will be even more important in the future. The People's Republic will reunify Taiwan soon, and you are now in a position to help influence your country's reaction. You can help them see Taiwan can no more secede from China than your so-called Confederacy could secede from the United States. You can help your leaders see we are simply reconciling with a wayward child."

Denney shook his head slowly. "I just want out, Liu."

"I understand." Liu made a show of sighing and then spread his hands wide. "I see. Perhaps tell me what you've discovered and we will work on a path to unravel your, ah, current situation."

"The CIA spy in Hawkinson's organization is codenamed YELLOW-CARD. She's a woman."

"Excellent. What's her name?"

"I don't know."

"You don't *what*?" Fury roiled up inside Liu. Denney subjected him to this... this bad theater and didn't even have a damned name?

"You're really going to stand there and pretend you don't understand how this works?" Denney thrust the gun forward, then closed the distance between them with a few aggressive strides. Liu judged they were about fifteen feet apart now. "The CIA will not give up the name of their agent. We have laws prohibiting exactly that, which *you* should know."

"I don't think I'm concerned much with your laws, Glen."

Denney ignored the barb. "Their operative is a woman. Hawk Tech is a small company, smaller still after the Russians tried to swat them. It shouldn't be hard to figure out who it is. I can guess why you've been so hot to figure this out. You want to trade that to get close to Hawkinson." Denney shrugged. "I don't care what you do with it. I just want out. Now, are we through, or do I have to kill you too?"

"Glen, I'd like you to put down the gun. We can talk about this. I think the information you've provided has great value. Let's just be calm."

Before Denney could reply, the night erupted into bright light and violent sound. Two vehicles, red and blue lights flashing, raced across the lawn between the parkway and the memorial, bouncing over the ground. The son of a bitch set him up. That was Denney's plan. He'd turned himself in and offered Liu up for his freedom.

"Federal agents, hands in the air!" someone bellowed.

"You stupid bastard," Liu spat.

# 35

The fool was followed.

For all his bullshit talk, his superiority, his damned arrogance, Liu was followed.

Denney fired at Liu, but his aim was off, courtesy of that blinding spotlight. He could barely make out where Liu was standing, but it wasn't where the bullet had gone. Denney fought to get control of his environment, but the sensory overload of the spotlights, police lights, and federal agents shouting was all too much.

Glen's operational training took over. Crises, he knew. Run the cross-check, prioritize actions.

He raised the pistol about forty-five degrees and fired several rounds. He needed a distraction to buy some time, and he wasn't about to kill a cop. Glen dove backward and sprinted for the trees just steps behind him. Under the cover of the thick evergreens, he plunged into comforting darkness. He'd parked on the Pentagon side of the lagoon and accessed the island via a wooden footbridge. Crossing it would be too obvious now, but he could go under it.

Glen ran toward the shoreline and dove into the dark lagoon, praying the sirens and shouting masked his splashing. He was grateful for the high tide. Glen jogged by here often, and knew that at low tide he could walk from one side to the other and barely get his ankles wet. As he ran, the water quickly rose to his knees, then his thighs. Glen holstered the gun. He'd need to get rid of it, but not here.

He dove into the murky water, swimming beneath the surface with long, powerful strokes. His feet dragged on the bottom of the lagoon. Even at high tide, it wasn't deep. He stayed under as long as his lungs would hold and made a controlled break to minimize the sound. Judging his distance correctly, he came up underneath the footbridge and crouched low, keeping his chin just above the water.

***

"You two need to stay back," Thorpe shouted above the din of the rotors.

Ford shouted that he understood, and Colt was thankful that the background noise drowned out most of the expletives he amplified that message with. Colt and Ford were intelligence officers, not cops. They had no legal authorization to act and were here but for the grace of Will Thorpe. When he agreed to let them ride along, Thorpe hadn't expected they'd end up in the field. Then Liu surprised them all and Thorpe found himself as a responding officer and not just a support asset.

Most of the FBI's chase team was stuck in D.C. traffic, so they deployed four additional teams in Virginia and Maryland to cover the Metro lines entering those states once they saw Liu shift to the train. They'd also sent an APB to Metro Transit Authority Police, D.C. Metro PD, Park Police, and the municipal police departments for every neighboring community around the District. But it was still one of the Bureau's foreign surveillance team's officers that picked Liu up exiting a Blue Line train at Arlington Cemetery and radioed it in. Their two other cars posted at the Pentagon and Crystal City Metro Station converged, along with a Park Police unit and four cars from Arlington County Police. The surveillance team lead said over the radio that they had an air support bird inbound from the Park Police.

They pulled off the GW Parkway with lights off and raced halfway up the grassy field before hitting lights and sirens. The Suburban met up with the units posted at the Pentagon and Crystal City Metros before moving in. The chase car that picked Liu up at Arlington Cemetery was already on station in the parking lot.

Things hit the fan when the gunfire started.

Several more shots followed, and Colt heard the FBI surveillance team leader yell for his people to hold their fire. It was just the Bureau guys up here. They had the Arlington cops and Park Police guarding the perimeter and blocking off the GW Parkway.

Watching Ford's expression, Colt wondered if he was going to have to grab his partner's collar to hold him back from diving into the fray.

Colt watched the FEEBs fan out and push into the grove, flashlights waving like bloodhound tails. The helicopter ascended and started a circular search pattern. Except for a footbridge, which was now covered, there were only two ways off Columbia Island: by car or by boat. Colt was close enough to Thorpe to hear the radio chatter from the US Park Police air support bird that there were no boats moving out of the boundary channel, so they were focusing on the channel itself to make sure that Liu didn't try taking to the water.

Thorpe joined the hunt with his fellow FEEBs, leaving Colt and Ford on their honor to not get involved and mess things up. A significant leap of faith, given Colt's recent history and Ford's more distant one.

The helicopter roared overhead and made a low loop of the park.

"What a shitshow," Ford grumbled, leaning against the FBI's Suburban.

Colt looked around.

Something felt wrong.

The feds knew what they were doing. These spy hunters were the best there were, but something about this was off. Colt couldn't identify exactly what, but it was the same instinct he had on the street, that sense that an op wasn't going the way he planned. It was that crawling, dirty feeling one got when they learned a second too late that someone else was watching.

"Thorpe!" Colt shouted. Thorpe was just at the edge of the tree line. He'd be gone in a second. When the agent didn't turn, Colt took off at a run, Ford yelling after him. Colt shouted Thorpe's name again, and this time, got his attention.

Thorpe turned, and Colt ran up to him. "What?"

"Something's up."

"Okay, what?" Thorpe said, angry at the interruption. He had transformed fully into his cop persona at the prospect of chasing down a suspect and didn't want to waste any time.

Colt shook his head. "I don't know, but we're focusing all of our search down there." He pointed south. "What about the bridge?"

"Pentagon Police have that side covered." Thorpe looked at the wagging flashlights in the grove. "Colt, I have to go."

"Will, you have half a dozen agents over there and local cops all along the parkway. Humor me."

"Let us do our job," Thorpe said. "Wait by the truck and don't make me think bringing you here was a mistake."

"You have to think like them. This is where the escape and evasion training kicks in. Denney is a pilot. He's had extensive training in hiding from people with flashlights looking for him. They both know you're going to cover every square inch south of here. The only real way out is across the water."

Whatever calculations Will Thorpe ran down in his mind were lightning fast. "Let's go," he said.

---

Glen bobbed in the water, clutching a wooden pylon that was coated with slime. He could hear footfalls on the bridge above him, could see the flashlight through the cracks in the wood.

They would catch Liu, of that there could be no doubt. There was nowhere left to run.

Better if Glen had killed him. Liu would trade their relationship in a bid for his freedom. That wouldn't work, of course, but it would mean the FBI learned Glen's identity by sunrise. He had a solution for that, though it required getting the hell out of here first. The picture he'd painted for Liu was essentially what he'd told the FBI. A Chinese intelligence officer attempted to blackmail him into spying for them. All this "evidence" Liu would present was merely fabrications and threats, the penalties of Glen not complying with them. He would need an excuse for being here tonight and for running. Soon, the Bureau would have access to Glen's cellphone location courtesy of his phone company. They'd find him soon, unless he ditched it.

*I confronted him. He told me what he did to General Rubio to prove he was serious and I would not let him do that to me*, Glen would say. A thin defense, but it might work.

With his back to the far shore, Glen kicked softly in the water, judging this to be the quietest way he could move. He kept his arms below the surface, moving them in soft strokes. By the time he reached the next pair of pylons, it wasn't deep enough even to glide, so Glen crouched low and crab-walked.

---

Colt, Thorpe, and Ford reached the wooden footbridge that connected the island with the parking lot on the far side. The bridge arched slightly in the middle before descending toward a large observation platform overlooking the water. The platform and the parking lot were both well lit. Colt stepped onto the bridge and Thorpe pulled him back, taking the lead. The lagoon wrapped around the land just above their position like a snake's tail, and other than the parking lot, there was no light. Conceivably, someone could stay in the water and remain totally hidden.

Thorpe radioed the lead agent. "I think one of them might have taken to the water. Does that Park Police bird have FLIR?"

"Checking," came the reply.

A forward-looking infrared sensor was common on surveillance aircraft.

"That's a roger."

"Have them sweep the northern end of the lagoon. Someone could make it clear to Rosslyn without leaving the water and it'd be impossible to see them from land at night."

"On it."

"Let's cover the other side," Colt said.

They started off across the bridge.

Denney rose out of the water, clothes heavy and sodden, water flowing out of him. Hard footfalls on the bridge above told him they were almost on top of him. If he didn't get to his car, none of his backup plans would matter.

Glen drew the Beretta. He believed he had nine rounds remaining. The weapon wasn't underwater that long and remained holstered. It should still work.

He raised the pistol, sighted, and fired three times.

Liu was still alive, mostly due to luck.

Distracted by the crush of light and sound, Denney missed his shot. Then, inexplicably, he fired several more times. Perhaps this was a signal, Liu reasoned, though he couldn't fathom what for. Why would the FBI let Denney carry a weapon? Perhaps the Americans were much looser than his own people would be. *Everyone has a gun here.*

Liu was only a few feet from the tree line. As he ducked beneath the thick evergreen boughs for cover, he could hear the shouts of the FBI agents behind him. But Denney's signal to them backfired because that gave Liu critical seconds to get into the murky shadows beneath the trees. He made the shoreline and ran at full speed. There was just enough light to make out the inky blobs of roots, rocks, and other things beneath the lush tree canopy.

He heard a helicopter fly overhead, just above the treetops. Its noise was deafening and Liu felt the rush of air shake the trees. As the airship banked and flew to the northern end of the park, Liu heard voices above the thundering chop of rotors and dropped to the ground. He wasn't far from the parking lot where he'd left his car, not that it mattered now. Liu watched as two FBI agents with flashlights ran through the parking lot, heading for the grove. They fanned out in a V and headed for the asphalt paths through the park. From his position, he could see police vehicles blocking the road out of the park and the marina next to it.

Liu stayed along the shore, the trees more widely spaced as he approached the marina. He crouched low to reduce his silhouette and inched forward. He needed better cover before that helicopter made another pass. Then he heard gunfire.

---

Three rounds exploded through the dock and Thorpe leaped back, crashing into Colt. They fell into a pile. Colt felt heavy hands loop through his shoulders as Ford dragged him backward out of the tangle of limbs almost as quickly as he'd fallen.

Thorpe crouched and fired down at the dock toward the shots. He half rose into a squat stance and walked backward, keeping his pistol aimed at the bridge.

"How deep is this lagoon?" Ford asked.

"I don't know," Colt said hurriedly.

"We're never going to hit anything shooting through the deck. Don't shoot me, Thorpe," Ford shouted, and vaulted over the side of the bridge. Half a second later, there was a thunderous splash and Fred Ford cannon-balled all two hundred and twenty pounds into the lagoon.

"What the hell is he doing?" Thorpe shouted. Then he radioed, "Shots fired" to the other agents.

---

Glen saw a dark streak next to him and heard something crashing into the water. Had he hit someone? The surface erupted in a white geyser against the purple sky, followed by loud and vivid cursing. The jumper roared like a deranged, waterlogged bear. He was coming straight for Glen.

Glen backed up the bank, water coming off him in sheets, and leveled his pistol. He would not shoot a cop. Shoot *at* one, yes. He'd done that, but only to get away. He would not hurt one of his own, another American.

Except this freakish hulk was surging forward, now only waist deep and gaining speed. And he was roaring in rage, pain, shock, excitement, or some combination of all four. Glen lowered his pistol to fire.

---

Ford reached the tall geek on the bank. He saw the gun even in this inky darkness. The guy hadn't fired, though. He'd had a clear shot for three, four seconds and hesitated. This was not a trained killer or a man who'd been in combat. This was the spy, probably Denney, but Ford couldn't fully make out his features. Denney squeezed off one round, and it blew a hole in the water next to him. That was a warning shot, but something in Ford's mind said it was more a warning for the shooter than for him.

Ford closed the distance and swung his right arm around in a wild haymaker. His punch landed on the side of the shooter's head, and Ford knew he was seeing a galaxy. The shooter stumbled back.

Ford heard a crack like a board splitting and felt a red-hot explosion of pain. His footing was gone and he fell backward, water closing in over his face.

Glen hadn't wanted to shoot the man, but they gave him no choice.

He scrambled up the bank as another person jumped from the bridge and crashed into the water. A third man still on the bridge was shouting into a radio. Glen ran under the observation platform, moving as fast as he could over the uneven muck and broken ground. He emerged on the northern end and pulled himself up the almost vertical, tree-covered bank. Looking up, he saw the low wooden fence framing the parking lot through the trees, backlit by the tall streetlights.

Glen climbed up the bank and kept in a low crouch along the fence, stopping every few seconds to listen for pursuers. His car was on the other side of the fence. Risking exposure, Glen rose to a crouch, holstering his pistol and tucking that beneath his jacket. He could almost touch his car. Glen put both hands on the fence and pushed up, vaulting over it, then made a quick scan of the parking lot. It was a small strip with a handful of spots separated from the main Pentagon campus by Boundary Channel Drive.

A Pentagon Police car was stationed at either end of the parking strip, but he could see the officers running from their cars to the bridge, responding to the sound of Glen's shots. He unlocked his car, pulled out of the space, and jumped the curb to pass the empty squad car. Though following Boundary

Channel Drive along the trees would keep his car hidden, VA-110 would get him home faster, and then he could start figuring out what in the hell he was going to do next.

Glen put the throttle down and was streaking away from the Pentagon within seconds.

# 36

---

*Arlington, Virginia*

Liu bobbed in the water, holding onto the stern of a boat in the marina. He dove and swam under the dock when he'd heard the gunshots, then emerged on the other side, lungs exploding for air. The marina was well lit beneath a purple sky. He would need to stay low.

Liu dove under the dock, swimming the estimated length, and then slowly came up for air so as not to make a loud sound as he broke the surface. Treading water and holding onto the boat for support, Liu moved beneath the dock, staying in between the moored boats.

Except for a few quick helicopter passes, the agents hadn't started seriously searching the marina, so Liu repeated his maneuver, swimming between the docks, stopping to catch his breath at this third one. It extended twice as far into the lagoon than the previous two, shielding him from the shore and the helicopter passing overhead. By the time he reached the end of the dock, Liu's arms and legs burned. With every aching movement, he cursed that treacherous, duplicitous, unappreciative bastard, Denney.

Liu did, however, get what he needed from the relationship. He'd meant what he told the man in their standoff in the grove. Denney was one of China's most prolific spies in the United States. Their understanding of

American naval capabilities was unrivaled, as well as how they integrated with the other services in the Pacific theater. Liu also had America's war plans for defending Taiwan. And so much more.

Liu reached the end of the dock and maneuvered himself around the last boat. Guessing the distance accurately in the dark was hard, but the looming glow of the Pentagon above the far shore added some depth. He figured it to be a hundred feet. He looked up, attempting to sight the helicopter, but could only hear it as it hovered over the park's eastern side. After taking in a lungful of air, he kicked off the dock pylon and glided below the surface of the water, which was getting shallow now. Liu righted himself and kept his head just above the surface, moving to a crab-walk. Even if someone saw him from the docks, at that distance he'd look like a rock or a log. He pushed toward the shore, now in the shadows of the trees along the bank, then turned once to check his rear for pursuit. Seeing none, he scrambled up the bank, then slinked into the trees and disappeared.

---

Glen hit ninety before he'd fully merged onto 110, survival instinct overriding logic. Traffic wasn't that heavy, and he weaved easily between cars as he raced north. It wasn't long before he realized he was going way too fast and decelerated, activating the self-drive so he could think. He needed to tell Mia something. The question was how much. His instinct was to tell her the same story he'd give to the FBI and NCIS: that a Chinese intelligence officer blackmailed him to betray his country. If he told Mia the truth, that he'd done all of this for her, her guilt would be overwhelming. It would crush her, and Glen couldn't bear to have her hurt like that.

He looked down at the speedometer. He was still doing eighty-five.

*The car's not slowing down.*

The manufacturer pushed a software update to the vehicle about a month ago and the damned thing had been buggy ever since.

"Disengage autopilot," he said, gripping the wheel. The car ignored him like an obstinate toddler, like it *heard* him and just didn't care. "Disengage autopilot," Glen said louder, working in some "command voice," but it kept its current speed and the yoke tilted slightly to follow the road's curvature.

Glen pressed down on the brake, and nothing happened. "Disengage autopilot, goddamn it!" He stood on the brake, but the car refused to slow, the yoke unresponsive to his input. Panic overtook his mind, and he couldn't think. The road was about to split. The left fork branched to Wilson Boulevard heading into Rosslyn and the right took a fading turn linking up with I-66. *I-66!* Jesus, that road was a parking lot at any time of day. Glen slammed down on the brakes and pressed the vehicle's starter button. Nothing! He was completely frozen out.

The car raced under the Arlington Boulevard overpass, moving into a slight turn, and Glen saw a wall of red brake lights.

He stood on the brake, yanked the car's wheel left and right, and screamed at the computer to obey his commands. The Tesla slammed into the back of the semi doing ninety. The front end buckled, pancaking with the impact. The windows blew out and the back end lifted into the air like it had been kicked by a particularly irate giant.

Broken glass fell to the ground like shooting stars. The Tesla's rear end hit the streets and bounced as the force of impact transferred. The vehicle was about half its original length now, looking like a discarded, crushed aluminum can.

---

FBI Special Agent Jason Whitfield had just enough time to shout, "Federal officer, search warrant!" before the SWAT door kicker battered the door down with his ram. The SWAT team flowed into the house, looking like a slow-motion video of a kitchen fire. Within the blink of an eye, they'd covered everything. Whitfield followed them. SWAT was overkill, and everyone knew it. They also didn't care. A Chinese spy lived here, and the agents were going to make damned sure *he* knew the FBI *was* on him.

Liu Che evaded them earlier that evening, slipped right through the foreign surveillance team's dragnet with some clever tradecraft, impeccable timing, and luck. Liu set his departure for the height of D.C.'s rush hour, ensuring that most of the surface streets would be complete parking lots. He ran a lazy SDR, ensuring coverage had him, and then surreptitiously got on the Metro, where another team picked him up. Liu hopped stations, and they lost him until, thankfully, one team sighted him in Virginia. They trailed him to the meeting site, but the Bureau couldn't get enough of their own units or support from other law enforcement in time to close off the area.

One SWAT officer brought two teenage kids downstairs, and a second had the wife at gunpoint. That might be a little much, but Whitfield said nothing. He was as angry as they were.

"Ma'am, I'm Special Agent Jason Whitfield with the Federal Bureau of Investigation. I have a warrant to search the premises. I also have an arrest warrant for your husband. Do you know his current whereabouts?"

The woman cursed him in Mandarin.

He and his partner guided the Liu family into the dining room to sit while other FBI agents descended upon the residence like locusts and dismantled it with surgical precision. They started with Liu's office, bedroom, and basement. Statistically, that was where most intelligence officers hid their communication gear. They'd have to wait until morning to dig up the yard. Liu's personal computer and modem were already on their way out of the van.

---

No one would argue that Fred Ford was too obstinate to die.

Colt vaulted over the side when he'd heard the shot and crashed into a shallow lagoon, landing hard on one leg and sending violent shocks of pain from his ankle to his spine. He was underwater when he heard the gunshot. Colt surfaced, oblivious to his own safety, and pushed through the water, getting to Ford just as he slipped under the surface. Colt chose to save his friend instead of pursuing the shooter. Between Thorpe up top and the Pentagon Police on the street, they'd have him wrapped up.

Colt dragged his friend to the surface.

Ford's mouth spouted profanity and water in equal amounts when he'd gotten it above the surface. The gunman had hit Ford in the right shoulder. He was in pain and bleeding, but the wound didn't appear life-threatening. Together, they waded back to the far side of the lagoon, Ford leaning heavily on Colt for support. Colt helped his partner up the bank, the right arm useless.

Once out of the lagoon, they trudged back to the memorial grove, leaking water and, in Ford's case, blood. Thorpe joined them a moment later. Colt field-dressed the wound with a first aid kit from the Suburban while they waited on paramedics. Once Ford was stable, Thorpe pulled Colt aside.

"I didn't want to tell you this while you were working on Fred, but it looks like the shooter got away."

"He's going to take that well," Colt said dryly.

"Arlington County Police are reporting an accident a couple of miles north of here. It's pretty bad. Tesla hit a parked semi doing about eighty."

"Think it's him?"

"Speed and distance sound about right for a high-speed evasion. Not sure how he slipped past the Pentagon cops, though. They've run the plates, but won't tell us who it belongs to until they've notified next of kin."

"He survive?"

"Nope. Died on impact and not pleasantly."

"What about Liu?" Colt asked.

Thorpe shook his head. "Chopper is making constant passes of the lagoon, but nothing's coming up on FLIR or night vision. We're getting a K-9 unit from Arlington and they've got patrol cars hitting every surface street in the immediate area."

"Jesus, good luck with that. There is an interstate right over there and how many city streets? Plus a Metro a mile in either direction."

"You got boats coming in?"

"Yeah. D.C. Metro Police are en route. River is their jurisdiction."

"I love this town sometimes," Colt said.

## 37

*Langley, Virginia*

"You're lucky the FBI was responsible for this shit circus or you'd all be fired!"

"That's still better than being fired *at*," Ford said in a flat voice. He'd left the hospital against medical advice as soon as they removed the bullet and patched him up. Ford went home, showered, dressed, and headed to Langley to keep working, dry popping codeine and chasing it with coffee.

Colt pressed his eyes together and braced for the inevitable "you had one job to do" barrage from Hoskins. There would be a time to point out that they did indeed have one job to do, and they'd done it. They identified Liu Che as the Chinese Ministry of State security officer running a vice admiral as an asset. They also believed Liu orchestrated Denney's posting to the National Security Council by discrediting the White House's original nominee. With an asset so highly placed, the amount of damage Liu could have done to the United States couldn't even be calculated. Yet all Hoskins could focus on was they hadn't caught Liu.

Arlington County confirmed Admiral Denney was the man involved in the high-speed collision who died on impact.

So they lost their spy and his handler.

Liu might be on the run, but he was still burned. The Chinese government had two choices now. Either give Liu sanctuary at the Chinese Embassy where the Americans couldn't touch him, which created a fresh new set of problems for them, or try to exfiltrate Liu. Colt didn't know how the Chinese handled these situations, but he didn't think they would put nearly as much effort into saving their officers as CIA did. There was another option, Colt supposed. They could just make Liu go away.

Hoskins continued pouring thunder down in the conference room. They'd been called up to his office shortly after seven that morning. It was a quick trip. None of them had gone home. They stayed in the NTCU ops center all night, hoping for word of Liu's arrest. None came.

"I'm waiting," Hoskins said, and Colt decided he could start following the conversation again. Apparently, they'd gotten to the audience participation portion.

"Do you have half a clue what goes on inside this building?" Thorpe asked.

"Excuse me?" Hoskins said, as though his mind hadn't caught up with the possibility of Thorpe challenging him.

"Those two"—Thorpe pointed at Colt and Ford—"identified the spy in record time. Like world-record time. The fastest counterintelligence investigations take months, usually *years*, Dwight," he said, dropping a heavy emphasis on the DNCS's name. "NSA picked up encrypted internet traffic from a server they were on in China, between a building believed to be MSS and an IP address accessed from Liu's home and his phone. If we hadn't already been on that server, we'd never have found it because of how many virtual servers they bounced traffic to. Colt and Ford took that information and traced communications to Admiral Denney. They used some pretty good tradecraft to do it, too. They were the ones who figured out that the Chinese planted falsified information in Lieutenant General Rubio's home computer and phone, then tipped FBI fraud investigators to it through an anonymous tip line. If it wasn't for them, the Chinese would have a spy on the National Security Council and we wouldn't know dick about it."

Colt watched Hoskins' face redden.

"That's fine, but he still escaped."

"Law enforcement is *our* job," Thorpe said. "Not yours. Yes, he slipped through the coverage and that's on the Bureau. Turns out, Liu is pretty good at *his* job. Heads will roll in the Bureau."

"I will see to it."

"Oh, for Christ's sake, come off it. What are you even blathering about? Your men did their job."

"I think I've heard enough out of you, Agent Thorpe. You can hand in your badge on your way out the door. I'm going to speak to the FBI director about having you replaced. I hope you like Fargo."

"This is actually the best possible outcome, sir," Ford said in an uncharacteristically restrained voice.

Hoskins' withering gaze swung over to Ford like a baleful lighthouse lamp.

"So, we identified the MSS officer." Ford held up a finger. Colt breathed a sigh of relief to see that it was the index. "We identified and exposed his agent." Another finger went up. "And we still have the blue dye."

"The blue dye?" Hoskins said slowly, clearly confused.

"It was Thorpe's idea. The Bureau got surveillance footage of Liu meeting with Jeff Kim. He's a—"

"I know who Kim is."

"Thorpe and young McShane here flew out to brace Kim and made him a deal. Kim was selling his IP to the Chinese in exchange for them doing nasty things to Guy Hawkinson. Thorpe had the idea of planting an exploit into the code Kim agreed to give the Chinese. Colt can explain the technical stuff better than me, but basically this is going to give us a trail of digital breadcrumbs to see exactly where the Chinese are going to analyze this code. It's also going to give us a back door into each of those systems. We're going to have a set of eyeballs on Chinese intelligence that we haven't had ever. And it was all thanks to Will. You want to fire him, I guess that's your prerogative, but I suspect what he's going to tell his bosses is what I just told you." Ford set both of his hands on the table and shrugged. "Let the chips fall."

Colt's eyes jumped between Ford and Thorpe. He'd seen the two men almost come to blows just because they were in the same room together.

"What's the next step?" Hoskins said through teeth that weren't quite clenched.

"Well, sir," Colt said, "our people have put the blue dye, if you will, on a laptop Kim provided to us. The program is called LUMBERJACK. We also copied the software so we can analyze it for ourselves and see if it has anything we can use. A courier flew it out to Kim yesterday."

"When are they making the handoff?"

"The next day or so," Colt said, hedging. He didn't actually know for certain but was sure that Liu would be preoccupied for a while. "My guess is Kim will meet with a different MSS officer to make the exchange."

"What's stopping him from removing the code, double-crossing us?"

"We'd know," Colt said resolutely. "We configured the program to beacon out if it's tampered with. It would send a kind of distress signal using the machine's onboard Wi-Fi, even if the antenna is deactivated. We can send a signal the user wouldn't know about, but it's buried in the source code and would be very hard to find. Besides, Jeff knows that if this doesn't work, we're going to arrest the shit out of him."

# 38

---

*Toronto, Canada*

After leaving the lagoon, Liu Che eventually made his way to an MSS safe house in Arlington's Seven Corners neighborhood, once he was dry enough for a cab. He hid out there for two days while the station created a new passport for him using blanks they'd stolen from the Canadian Embassy in Beijing. Canada had one of the better passports to travel under, in Liu's estimation. They were rarely questioned. Once he had his new identification, clothes, and phone, Liu took a service-provided car with clean plates to Philadelphia, where he boarded a flight to Toronto. A minor amount of disguise was applied, but as he'd suspected, the American bureaucracy was too inefficient to catch up with him. Liu breezed past the Customs and Border Protection agents without so much as a wish for him to have a pleasant trip.

He had an overnight in Toronto before his next flight.

The FBI arrested Liu's wife for espionage and was holding her in an undisclosed location. They deported his children and they were on their way back to Beijing.

Liu burned at the thought of his wife in custody. They would use her as a disposable piece in their game of nations. The Americans would offer her freedom if the Chinese gave him up. His government would never consider that, and it would only drag her incarceration out. Liu prayed that she could be strong, prayed that whatever energy comprised the universe could carry that message, along with some of his own strength to her. She would need it.

Liu made his call when he got to his hotel using the phone they'd given him at the safe house. The Service designed an encrypted communication protocol using blockchain. The technology let a phone's user know if the blockchain ledger had been compromised, meaning the device had been hacked. The phone also had one of the most secure encryption protocols devised. When the call began, it created a unique peer-to-peer network for that call and deleted it as soon as the call was done, erasing all traces of the connection. They were susceptible only to surveillance at the end point, like if someone was electronically listening in on Liu's side of the conversation from a bug in the room.

"Hello," a woman answered on the other end.

"Hello, Mia." Liu paused to consider his words. What came next would be difficult and must be handled with the utmost delicacy, though he could draw upon a store of empathy from his own situation. Liu didn't know if he'd ever see his wife again. If he did, it would likely be years. "I am sorry for your loss," he said. "It was a tragic accident." Liu said nothing of his suspicion that her husband was collaborating with the FBI. That would only confuse matters.

"Yes," she said in a small voice.

"I hadn't wanted to contact you so soon after... after what happened, but there are some things that I must make you aware of." Liu paused. "I had to leave the country unexpectedly. One of our local officers will give you direct support, but we will continue to collaborate from afar. My commitment to you is as it has always been."

"Thank you." Mia was quiet for a time. "I will not need to keep gambling, will I?"

"No. We will settle any outstanding debts you have."

"Good. I hate casinos. Do you know when the new officer is going to make contact?"

"Why, is something pressing?"

"Well, I'm receiving the Joint Chiefs and their wives later so they can pay their respects."

"And you have the software?"

"Yes. I took the liberty of changing the approach. I created a memorial page for Glen, accessible by a QR code. Doing so automatically downloads the executable file and injects it onto the phone. I might be able to collect the whole set," she quipped in dry tones.

Mia's ability to compartmentalize was extraordinary, unlike anything he'd ever seen. Liu had known her since she'd graduated from State School 577 and became one of the Service's first female covert intelligence officers. He knew Mia loved her husband and that their marriage was a genuine one, though her pragmatism enabled her to acknowledge and rationalize the duality of it, to compartmentalize those two realities in her mind.

"I have a stop to make on my return trip to Beijing, but I look forward to reading your next report. Again, please accept my condolences for your loss."

Liu hung up and moved on to the next task.

He had to check in with the officer he'd assigned to get Jeff's laptop. Liu was furious that Jeff refused to just transfer the files digitally as he had with the previous ones. He had offered some overly complicated excuse about how this code could not be broken down to its constituents and then re-compiled, a requirement for transmission. Liu hadn't the time to listen to the excuse. Jeff knew how to execute a brush pass, so Liu felt confident the exchange would go fine, but he would make clear to his asset the nature of their relationship.

Liu shook his head.

What was with this country?

Only in America would an asset feel so arrogant as to believe they could dictate terms.

His officer assured him all was ready. They would make the exchange tomorrow.

Excellent.

Now all that remained was boarding his flight from Toronto.

# 39

*Bellagio, Italy*

Guy Hawkinson took his jet to a private airfield in Lugano, Switzerland, deep in the alpine lake country shared with Italy where a Range Rover with his advance team met him. They drove him through the lush, tree-covered mountains along Lake Lugano, crossing into Italy and Lake Como. They took a ferry across at Griante into Bellagio.

Bellagio occupied the apex of the Larian Triangle, the spur of land that split Lake Como in two. It was home to some of the most concentrated, quiet wealth on earth. Samantha Klein's villa on the eastern side of the city was a three-story building of yellow stucco and red-orange Mediterranean tiled roof. Ivy covered much of the lake-facing walls. The Range Rover drove through the gate, which opened for them as expected, then up a short, curved driveway to the carport. Palms and cypress dotted the lawn. All of Archon's primary members had generational wealth. They each had shares of several patents and ownership stakes in the companies born out of those patents. The villa on Lake Como seemed at once over the top and completely on point to Guy.

Guy stepped out of the Rover, leaving his jacket unbuttoned. Matthew Kirby and one of his security detail fell into step behind him. A servant led

them through the villa to the wide marble and flagstone patio that overlooked the lake. Samantha stood with her back to them. It was a warm
summer evening. She wore a black dress, and a wine glass was set on the
stone balustrade in front of her. The sun had already dipped below the
mountains and the sky was quickly fading from blazing orange to purple,
illuminated from below by the city.

Samantha turned her head. Black hair like a ribbon of poured night sky
swept across her back, following the motion of her head.

"There are glasses on the table," she said, her voice emotionless.

Guy walked over and inspected the bottle, a local Nebbiolo. He poured a
glass, swirled, sipped, and then joined Samantha at the balustrade. He said
nothing, letting her make the first move.

The muscles in Samantha's jaw tightened.

Guy knew she was in her mid-fifties, but she looked at least ten years
younger. Like most Israelis, Klein was deeply tanned, but her features looked
at once European and Levantine. If he hadn't known her, Guy would guess
she was Spanish, Italian, Lebanese, or Iranian. A trait she no doubt put to
great effect as a Mossad officer.

"So you're just letting her go?" Samantha shook her head. The black hair
waved like a lazy snake. "You know what she is."

Guy smiled and took another sip of the wine. "I do. And that's exactly
why I'm doing nothing." He held up the glass again and then added, "For
now."

Samantha turned to face him.

Guy chose his words with exacting care. While he didn't exactly fear her,
Samantha could cause him a great deal of trouble. She was part of Archon's
inner circle and he was not. Yet. And Klein was dangerous in her own right.
This was a woman who'd spent a career in the inscrutably gray world of
Israeli intelligence. She would take whatever actions she deemed necessary
to accomplish what was, in her mind, the greater good. Eliminating Nadia
Blackmon solved a problem for Samantha Klein and Archon; the fact that it
would have created enormous consequences for Guy was almost irrelevant.
He was a useful tool to Archon, yes, but since he was not yet a full member of
the organization, he was a dispensable one. Klein would cauterize him if she
had to.

"What's the latest on your man?" Guy asked.

"Stager was hospitalized and is under guard by the Swiss Federal Police. He overpowered the police officer and escaped the hospital wearing the man's uniform. He's recovering in a safe location now."

"Do you trust him?"

"Without question," Samantha said. Guy let it drop. He could have Stager taken care of if he became a problem, though not in ways that wouldn't arouse suspicion in Klein.

"We have to treat Ms. Blackmon carefully."

"I was closing a liability, Guy. One that *you* introduced."

"If Stager had succeeded, the FBI would've gotten involved. They investigate crimes involving Americans overseas. They will quickly learn Stager was following several people, trying to flush someone out. Flush them out why?"

"You don't think I can make some police records disappear in Geneva?" The withering skepticism in her voice was hot enough to singe eyebrows.

"Well, if she is who you say she is, they will have other resources at their disposal."

"You're being paranoid."

"Samantha, you've spent six months accusing me of not being paranoid enough. It can't be both ways."

She set her wine glass down hard on the balustrade and Guy was surprised it didn't break. "What's your solution, then?"

"Oh, I've got something special in mind for Ms. Blackmon."

# 40

---

*Geneva, Switzerland*

"Where are you now," Hawkinson asked over the phone.

"I'm somewhere safe," Nadia said. She didn't need to act much to sound scared. Colt had come through. He didn't get into much detail, just told her that they had a new AI that could aggregate massively distributed nodes of information and do the kind of pattern matching it would take an army of human analysts years to accomplish. "He was waiting for me right outside the office, Guy. When I spotted him, he tried to grab me. This is after Klein chased me out of the office."

"I don't know what to say."

"Well whatever you say better be pretty fucking good, Guy, because I'm on the next plane to the States and I'm getting a lawyer. Did you know my sister-in-law writes for *The New York Times*? I'm talking to her next."

"Whoa, let's not do things that can't be walked back."

"Guy—he chased me like ten blocks and fucking tried to kill me!"

"I understand that you're upset. But I'm certain there's a solution to this that doesn't involve attorneys or the *Times*."

"Then why are you siccing thugs on me? And you know what? I'm not the only one. The police told me they had fifteen complaints on that asshole."

"Wait, you talked to the police?"

Nadia could hear genuine worry in Hawkinson's voice now. It was great to finally hear that asshole on defense.

"Of course I did! He tried to kill me. If it wasn't for an off-duty cop, he probably would have. Once I heard about the other complaints, I started calling some of my friends, and you know what I found out?"

"What?" Guy's voice sounded thick and hoarse.

"Everyone who reported that asshole following them was one of the ones that Klein pulled into her bullshit 'interviews.' We were all her little list of suspects. This is going to be a class-action suit, man."

Guy was silent for a long time.

"Nadia, you know that I think you're an invaluable member of the team. Your work on the open source project has been inspired and is critical to our growth in that area. Samantha was completely out of line."

"You think?"

"Please hear me out. We had to take certain precautions after what happened on the island. I am very concerned for all of our safety. The work we're doing...well, it's upsetting some powerful people. Those kinds of people don't always react well. But I will allow that Klein took it too far. I'll terminate her consultancy immediately and we will cooperate fully with the Swiss police. You've got a bright future here and I don't want to lose you over this. I certainly understand if you want to leave—I suppose I can't blame you —but I hope you give me a chance to prove to you that Samantha Klein is not who *we* are."

Nadia told Hawkinson she wouldn't do anything rash, but didn't commit to anything right away. The next day he called her again to say that he'd spoken with Swiss police and terminated Samantha Klein's contract.

Nadia returned to Geneva and to work.

Guy had an all-hands where he explained that they'd had a security contractor take things too far. He was concerned for all of their safety given how the Russians reacted to their work on the island, but he acknowledged that he traded security for safety and that was wrong. Guy took personal responsibility, apologized to his employees, and made stress counselors available to anyone who needed it.

The Hawk Tech personnel who filed out of that room would've run through a wall of fire for Hawkinson then.

Nadia hadn't heard from Colt in several days, but he'd sent a covert message telling her they caught the spy. Langley believed her cover was still viable and that the Chinese could not pass her identity to Hawkinson.

Chuck and the Bern Station team cleaned up the mess with Archon's agent, Bastian Stager. It seemed the Swiss government was happy to oblige. He was still in the hospital, recovering from Chuck's gunshot. The Swiss FIS quietly terminated him, declared him a domestic terrorist, and would move him quickly to trial as soon as he got out of the hospital.

Nadia hadn't seen or heard from Samantha Klein since. Her intuition was Klein fled Switzerland when the Swiss arrested Stager. Nadia was too nervous to appreciate the irony of someone escaping *from* Switzerland. Klein remained a problem. Hawkinson believed Nadia's story. Nadia assumed Klein's rapid flight from Geneva was as much to cover up Archon's involvement as it was to sever any extant link with Bastian Stager. This highlighted the criticality of the LONGBOW shot on Hawkinson's phone. She *had* to find out what Klein was saying to him now.

Nadia also had the concealed thumb drive Ava gave her in Vienna. Whatever that did. She'd received no further instructions from Colt on what to do with it.

Nadia understood a lot of this job was "go here, do this thing we can't really tell you about for reasons we can't tell you either," but this was a hell of a risk. She'd kept that pen in her bag ever since she got back from Vienna. Nadia could tell it was an exploit, but she didn't know what kind. Code could be a peeping tom, a nuke, or anything in between. She was wary of launching this thing without knowing what it could do.

Still, if it was important enough to risk giving it to a Mossad officer because Colt wasn't sure he'd make the handoff, it must be important enough to risk her cover over.

That was the calculus Nadia ran in her mind continually over the last week.

"Screw it," she muttered under her breath.

"What's that?" The voice came from an engineer on the other side of her pod, who spoke without looking up. He was the only one without head-phones on.

"Nothing," she said. "Just having a problem with a code string I'm working on."

"Want me to look at it?"

"No," Nadia said, forcing nonchalance into her voice. That was the last thing she wanted. Nadia didn't know how long she had. She didn't know how long her cover would hold. Colt wouldn't have given this thing to her if he didn't want her to use it. She pulled her notebook out of her bag with the "CIA Hacking Pen" and scribbled a few gibberish notes, then made a casual glance around to verify her surroundings before pulling the pen apart to expose the thumb drive port. Nadia inserted that into her machine and set the notebook on top of it.

Security discipline was good here. In fact, it amazed her that the trick worked in the lab. It wouldn't fly with any of the devs. There was no outside access to the public internet unless the InfoSec team specifically authorized it, and they actively monitored all traffic when they did. So the only way that exploit was going to work was if she launched it from her own machine. Hawk Tech's information security capability rivaled anything Nadia had seen in her career. Algorithms continually trolled their systems, seeking any line of code that was out of place. It was the same tool they used to find vulnerabilities in other systems. Nadia didn't see how any code that she injected could remain undetected longer than a few seconds.

It occurred to her, as she did it, that she might have to get out of here in a hurry and had no plans to do it. Yes, there was an exfil procedure, but that required her to get in touch with Chuck first, and she couldn't do that from here.

Shit.

Nadia leaned back in her chair and scanned the windows that walled off her section of the hallway. No alarms, no private security fast roping in from the ceiling, no black helicopters at the windows.

So far.

Ava told her this was a fire-and-forget kind of thing, just load it and go. It wouldn't require any input from her, and there wouldn't be a feedback loop to tell her it was done. It'd been about a minute, so if this thing worked, it had to be done by now. Nadia pulled the drive out, reassembled her pen, and dropped it in her bag, then made another fast pass of her surroundings. Nothing seemed different.

Nadia checked out her machine but couldn't tell if the program had run, and if it had, where it had gone.

Damn.

Whoever made this was *good*. There was no trace of it at all.

Unless she'd completely botched it and the program failed to even load.

Nadia grabbed her things, locked her machine, and slid out of her workstation. "Grabbing an early lunch," she said to no one in particular, and left.

"Nadia," said a voice behind her.

There's a certain feeling one gets when they are caught doing something they shouldn't be doing. It's a terrible cocktail of embarrassment, despair, guilt, self-pity, and anger, shaken up and poured out on the floor. It was hard to describe, but Nadia felt it as she turned around and saw Guy Hawkinson. He wore a dark blue suit, light pink shirt, and a razor blade's worth of pocket silk showing.

"I'm glad I caught you," he said in a voice that was like oil spilled on glass.

Colt's voice in her mind said, *Look for the exits*. There was a stairwell ten feet away. Nadia was in shape, but Guy had been a Ranger and looked like he could still qualify. No way could she outrun him. She was unarmed and had nothing to improvise for a weapon.

Shit.

"Oh yeah," she said. "I was just heading out for lunch."

"Great, then I'm not interrupting. Could I steal you for a moment? There's something important I want to talk to you about." Before Nadia could say no, Guy pressed the elevator button and the door opened immediately.

After guiding her into the elevator with a firm hand on her back, he thumbed the top-floor button.

"So, what's up?" she asked.

Guy held his response for the time it took the elevator to ring a new floor. After what felt like forever, he said, "I wanted to apologize, in person."

"It's fine," Nadia said. "I mean, it's *not* fine, but it's over. Whatever."

"I have something new in mind for you, wanted to see if you're interested."

*Interested? Interested in what?*

Two floors to go.

The light sparked in her mind. *He's trying to buy me off. Here's a big fat promotion so you don't sue the shit out of me.*

"I have a new project starting and I think you'd be a good fit for it."

*Okay, he's still said nothing of substance. Unless...the security AI already figured out she slipped a hack into their system. Oh shit.*

The elevator dinged. They'd arrived at the top floor. This was where the Hawk Security Group SWAT team would be.

The doors opened to an empty hallway in the executive suite.

"Please," Hawkinson said, extending his arm for her to get out. "We'll be in here." He motioned toward the executive conference room in the center of the floor. "I have a potential new investor. They are bringing new tech and some money to the table. I'd like your eyes on their code to help me evaluate it."

"Of course," Nadia said, her voice hesitant. They'd get her in the conference room. Controlled and soundproofed. They could easily and quietly control her exit from the building.

Which she hoped would be on two legs.

"What's the project?"

Guy reached the door and pulled it open. Several people were seated around the table, a few of the executive team and their head of security. No surprise there.

"Good morning all. Nadia, I think you know most of the people here, but I'd like to introduce you to a representative from the Chinese Ministry of Technical Cooperation, Mr. Liu Che."

# 41

---

*Great Falls, Virginia*

Whatever Colt pictured Fred Ford's house to be, this wasn't it. Part of him wanted to believe that the obstinate and profane old war horse lived in a Quonset hut out in the woods with junked cars he turned into some kind of tactical course, which he would spend his spare time running through. Instead, it was a five-bedroom, two-story brick home on a lot of land. The house was tucked back among the trees, almost to the river, and gave the illusion one was alone in the wilderness. That part, at least, seemed to fit.

In their year together, Ford never mentioned his personal life.

Once he'd seen the house, Colt assumed there was a wife to go with it. The Ford he knew couldn't possibly be capable of this. As with the home, he had something in mind, and the woman who answered the door shattered that. Hillary Ford was a tall, lithe blonde. She was beautiful in the classic sense, but had a presence or a bearing that often came with people whose lineages stretched out a couple hundred years. She seemed to be a force of nature, a powerful current beneath a calm sea. Colt imagined she held up to her larger-than-life husband well.

"You must be Colt," Hillary said when he arrived. She was in Vineyard Vines, shorts, and a light sweater. "Fred is out back. I'll show you."

"Thank you," Colt stammered, a little red-faced for not having brought a hostess gift, not having known there was a hostess. Not having known Fred Ford was married. He said nothing about Ford not telling him in advance. He didn't want to give the bastard the satisfaction.

Colt got the joke. It was exactly the kind of long con that Ford would cook up for just this kind of payoff. A year's worth of ground laying just for Colt to have an awkward walk through his house, embarrassed at not bringing flowers because Ford knew that was how his partner was wired.

"Thank you for saving my husband's life," she said.

"Oh, I didn't," Colt said, still stammering. "I mean, it wasn't that bad."

"Fred told me he can't ever talk about it, but you saved him. He said I'm not even supposed to know *that* much, but you know how he is."

"I do." Colt cracked a smile. "I do indeed."

Colt learned on the route through the house that Fred and Hillary met in their junior year at UVA and had been together ever since. It was the three teenage kids that shocked the hell out of him. Their ages ranged from seventeen to thirteen, all girls, and apparently there was one more at college in Florida.

Hillary showed Colt to the deck and informed her husband that their guest had arrived.

"Hey, super spy," Ford said. "Honey, this is Colt. He works for the Department of Commerce." He winked at her, and she shook her head, smiled, and went back inside. "Beer is over there." Ford pointed at an ice bucket. Colt grabbed a can, popped it, and walked over to Ford.

Colt nudged his head at the house. "They yours or you just rent them for my benefit."

Ford belly-laughed.

"I hope you like steak, because that's about the extent of what I can cook with this sling on. I mean, we'd probably have steak anyway, but still."

"How's the arm?"

"Hurts, but I'm okay. Beer helps. Thanks, man." Ford held up his beer.

And that was that. Whatever may have passed between them before, whatever sins Colt committed, he was now absolved.

"Is the DoD going to posthumously investigate Denney?"

"Thorpe tells me that is 'highly unlikely.'"

"You have to be shitting me."

"Basically, the Navy doesn't want to admit that a flag officer could have been a Chinese spy for his entire career and they never caught it. They said that without a human investigation, they refuse to do anything since all we have is computer-generated evidence, which they consider 'speculative.' Where are we on getting the car from Arlington PD?"

Denney dying in a car crash just after his narrow escape from capture seemed too convenient to Colt. He shared that suspicion with Thorpe, who thought the same. The unit wanted to get their hands on whatever was left of the vehicle's computer to see if anyone tampered with it. Their tech team could rebuild the hard drive and get the operating system running with very little left of it. A long shot, but one they needed to take.

"Working on it," Colt said. "There's a bunch of jurisdictional bullshit right now. They aren't sure whose authority they need to hand it over to us."

"Figures," Ford said.

Colt shook his head. "And without Liu in custody, we lose our smoking gun."

"That's why Thorpe and I are heading to brief the head of US Indo-Pacific Command next week. The Navy brass might not take this seriously, but the war-fighting command needs to know that the Chinese probably have most of our theater plans, or at least the CONOPS."

"You and Thorpe on a road trip, huh?"

Ford shrugged. "He backed us up when it counted. That means a lot. We still got our beef, sure, but we can fight it out when the world is safe. We get anything from the laptop yet?"

"Nope. Handoff went as planned. If the Chinese operate like we do, they'll put the computer in a completely isolated environment and test it, try to identify if it has anything suspect on it."

"Like a CIA-designed super virus?"

"Like a CIA-designed super virus," Colt said, matching Ford's bone-dry delivery.

"See, I get this tech shit." Ford tilted his head back, finished his beer, and set down the empty can. "Get me another brain grenade?" Colt walked over to the ice bucket and reloaded his partner.

"We should start getting pings on it in the next few weeks at the most," Colt said. "So, what's next?"

"Well, our girl is still out there in the wild. For how long is another matter."

"Word from Bern is that it's handled. For now, at least," Colt said. "The problem is Samantha Klein isn't handled, and that's what worries me."

"That is what we call a 'ticking time bomb.' In more ways than one." Ford turned and considered his partner. "We're going to have to do something about Klein, and soon, if Nadia is going to stay in place. Hawkinson may buy her story for now, but I don't think he's going to side with our girl if Klein makes an issue of it with Archon. And there's that other complication. Time is going to come, my boy, and you're going to be inclined to share that little bit of information. There's a choice there and I don't think you're going to like it."

Colt hid his expression behind the beer can, because he knew Ford was right. Learning Samantha Klein was a member of Archon was a terrible revelation on its own. She'd been a celebrated Mossad officer and had, in part, sacrificed her career to help save Colt's life. Now, he wondered how much of that was even remotely true. Colt felt obligated to tell Ava about her aunt, but he didn't know how. But should he? Of course he *shouldn't*. He knew that, but it didn't make Colt's decision any easier.

"So, what are your thoughts on the report?" Colt said. Nadia sent an encrypted message to him last night saying a man named Liu Che from the Chinese Ministry of Cooperation was in Hawkinson's office offering some kind of collaboration.

This was precisely the doomsday scenario they'd envisioned.

But as far as they knew, Denney never learned Nadia's true name, just her gender.

The implications of their collaboration were just as severe. The Chinese already had much of Jeff Kim's intellectual property, as did Guy Hawkinson. If those two teamed up, the Chinese could quantum leap their AI development. The Chinese government already had the world's most sophisticated techno-surveillance state, and Colt saw firsthand how they'd applied AI to give them even greater control. With the advances they stood to make with Jeff Kim's tech, they would become truly scary. A partnership with Guy Hawkinson would be the stuff of nightmares.

Imagine the resources and computing power of the Chinese state behind Guy's open source intelligence crawler. It wasn't hard to envision a world where no network, no data was safe from potential exploitation. Not with how poorly most nations, corporations, and private citizens protected themselves. The unit believed that thanks to the quantum computing technology he already had, Hawkinson was within a few years of making current encryption standards irrelevant, but the Chinese would speed up that development by orders of magnitude and the West might never recover.

All of their secrets laid bare.

No technological development, no military communication, no private chat would be safe from the Chinese.

And that was to say nothing of Hawkinson's bio-weapon research.

"Do you think there is a play between Archon and the Chinese?" Colt asked. "Or is this Hawkinson going rogue?"

Ford shook his head and took a deep drink. "The guy plays by his own rules for sure. Somehow, I don't see a connection between Archon and China. Archon has this whole übermensch thing going. I can't imagine the Chinese would sign on to that, though I bet Archon doesn't put that part in the pamphlet. Archon could be looking for a partner that they know neither the US nor the Russians are going to screw with."

"What are the odds Hawkinson is striking out on his own?"

"Like I said, cat seems to play by his own rules, but it seems unlikely he'd go rogue. We also don't know where he fits in the Archon leadership structure. So we don't really know if he's being directed to do this or if he's acting on his own. Either way is scary." Ford shook his head again. "Could be Archon is forming a super-group with the world's preeminent totalitarian state, or there is an internal power struggle. Neither of those outcomes seem pleasant for freedom-loving gentlemen such as ourselves."

"You know what this means," Colt said dourly.

"I do, but I don't want you to say it."

They couldn't pull Nadia out. Not now. They had to understand what this China link was.

Both men drank their beers in silence for a time.

"I don't know, man," Colt said. "Seems like a hell of a price tag for two hacks. A three-star admiral is dead. Another general's career and reputation ruined. He's cleared of any wrongdoing, but they still didn't give him the NSC job. Even though we *proved* the Chinese set him up."

"Which the Navy still denies," Ford added.

"They could have killed Nadia in Geneva. Archon *knows* she's one of us."

"No, Archon *suspects*. There's a difference, Colt. And, for now at least, only one of them. But, look, intelligence is just like football. Game of inches. We break a lot of bones to move the ball a couple of inches. Maybe we get ourselves killed to put the kicking team in field goal range." Ford shrugged and drank deep. "It's a mixed metaphor, I know, but you get what I mean."

"I know, but like I said, that's a high price to pay for two hacks."

"This coming from you? You beat me over the head with this cyber crap every chance you get." Ford smiled, but there was no humor behind it. "Both ops are about putting us in a better position to score. We don't always get the immediate payoff."

The sliding door opened and Hillary stepped halfway out with a plate of steaks in one hand. She turned to reach back into the house for her glass of wine and joined them on the deck. She set the plate next to the grill and kissed her husband on the cheek. "Solving the world's problems?"

"Nope," Ford said. "I think we're just figuring out there were more than we thought."

Hillary gave a short laugh. "Well, I can add one more to that list. Looks like the presidential campaigns are starting early this cycle."

"Ugh. That's all we need," Ford said. "Who announced?"

"Oh, that loudmouth senator from Wyoming. The snake-oil salesman. He rails about Big Tech and corporate money, but he inherited a boatload of family money doing just that," she said. "He's the one who ripped up Wilcox on TV. Preston Hawkinson."

Tournament of Shadows
Book 4 of The Firewall Spies

**When a series of dangerous cyberattacks is traced back to Russia, a team of elite CIA operatives must uncover the true aggressor—before the kindling tension between two nuclear powers ignites World War III.**

The first strike destroys the Folsom Dam, bringing catastrophic flooding to the Sacramento area.

The second threatens thousands of innocent lives across the Eastern Seaboard; exposing the vulnerability of America's infrastructure.

The Firewall Spies are called into action to identify the source of the attacks before the entire country is thrown into chaos. The incursion is traced back to the Russian Federation, and a reciprocation from the US government risks escalating the conflict into a full-blown world war.

As tensions climb higher, CIA Case Officer Colt McShane begins to suspect that someone else is behind the attacks—someone who wants to see America and Russia at war. Colt leads his team in a series of bold covert actions to uncover the truth, but time is quickly running out.

**Get your copy today at
severnriverbooks.com**

# ABOUT ANDREW WATTS

Andrew Watts graduated from the US Naval Academy in 2003 and served as a naval officer and helicopter pilot until 2013. During that time, he flew counter-narcotic missions in the Eastern Pacific and counter-piracy missions off the Horn of Africa. He was a flight instructor in Pensacola, FL, and helped to run ship and flight operations while embarked on a nuclear aircraft carrier deployed in the Middle East. Today, he lives with his family in Virginia.

Sign up for the reader list at
severnriverbooks.com

# ABOUT DALE M. NELSON

Dale M. Nelson grew up outside of Tampa, Florida. He graduated from the University of Florida's College of Journalism and Communications and went on to serve as an officer in the United States Air Force. Following his military service, Dale worked in the defense, technology and telecommunications sectors before starting his writing career. He currently lives in Washington D.C. with his wife and daughters.

Sign up for the reader list at
severnriverbooks.com

Printed in the United States
by Baker & Taylor Publisher Services